HELLBOTTOM

by Eric Corder

PUBLISHED BY POCKET BOOKS NEW YORK

HELLBOTTOM

POCKET BOOK edition published June, 1972
in cooperation with Parallax Publishing Company, Inc.

This original POCKET BOOK edition is printed from
brand-new plates made from newly set, clear, easy-to-read type.
POCKET BOOK editions are published by POCKET BOOKS, a division of
Simon & Schuster, Inc., 630 Fifth Avenue, New York, N.Y. 10020.
Trademarks registered in the United States and other countries.

Standard Book Number: 671-78198-7.
Copyright, ©, 1972, by Eric Corder. All rights reserved.
Published by POCKET BOOKS, New York, in cooperation with Parallax
Publishing Company, Inc., and on the same day in Canada by Simon &
Schuster of Canada, Ltd., Richmond Hill, Ontario.

Printed in the U.S.A.

For Tom Disch
and a decade of deep friendship

I am counted with them that
Go down into the pit: I am as a
Man that hath no strength:
Free among the dead, like
The slain that lie in the grave . . . .

Psalm 88:4—5

HELLBOTTOM

Book One

1

The train slid to a halt, iron wheels locked and screeching against the rails, steam chuffing up around the windows. The sign on the station house read:

WOODBORO
Population 7,321
God-Fearing White Christians

A white conductor pushed open the door at the rear of the car and fastened it with a hook. "Woodboro! Ever' body off for Woodboro."

Vulture swung his feet from the cold coal stove. It was mild for February, and he was glad. The stove was filthy with years of caked soot. The door hung askew on one hinge. No coal had been provided. The car was old, pre-war, and still bore signs of damage from the holocaust years. It was the colored car.

And the baggage car.

And the livestock car.

Lee had handed his sword to Grant at Appomattox eleven years ago. Most of the South's railroads had been rebuilt since then. With Northern capital and black labor . . . so the niggers could ride with the baggage and the animals.

Vulture stood up, an endless process which brought the top of his head within inches of the ceiling. A dark skinny little boy wearing only a man's shirt cut off at his knees yanked at his mother's skirt. "Looky, maw! Looky the gian'!"

She cuffed him. "Min' yo manners." Then she turned back to the infant sucking at her breast. The boy gaped at Vulture. Vulture smiled. The child went suddenly shy and ran around his mother's side. He peeped over her shoulder.

"Grrahhh!" Vulture roared.

The child ducked away. The mother looked up fearfully. The handful of other blacks in the car shifted uneasily on the benches. Vulture was depressed. He had meant to play with the boy. Nothing worked right these days. He sighed, picked up his grip, and went to the back of the car. His trunk was there. It was large and made of lacquered black wood trimmed with brass. It was meant to be carried by two men. Vulture lifted it easily with one hand.

Outside, between the train and a loading platform, a black man was trying to drag a recalcitrant billy goat to the train. A band of amused whites in coveralls, plaid shirts, and dirty work boots lounged nearby. They carried shotguns, pistols, Bowie knives, and one an old muzzle-loading squirrel rifle. The abundance of weapons struck Vulture as odd, even in the South where most white males considered some kind of weapon *de rigueur*. The goat charged and butted the man in the thigh. The man cursed and lashed out with his foot, then he and the animal went spinning round and round at opposite ends of the rope. The whites guffawed and bent over and slapped their thighs; one fell to the ground, threw back his head, and drummed his heels.

Vulture stepped down from the car.

The whites stopped laughing.

What they saw was a freak. A towering pitch-black monster who stood fully seven feet tall, shoulders as wide as an oxen's yoke, slab-bodied, simian-armed. His tightly coiled hair was sprinkled with gray; a livid purple scar cut across his forehead from temple to temple. The cup of his left ear was missing. His jaw was long and ledgelike, jutting. The whites instinctively tightened ranks. Fingers sought triggers and rested in light readiness, hands edged toward the hilts of knives. A man with a double-barreled shotgun came forward. "Hey, boy, whut business you got in this town?"

Vulture looked down, but said nothing.

The man stepped back and raised his shotgun slightly. The nigger was dressed in a linen shirt and a string tie, dark broadcloth coat, gray breeches and knee-high boots, clothes of a quality to which the white could never hope to aspire. That was reason enough to splatter black brains, but a nigger dressed in such a fashion meant something. Not flash and dickty like a coon merchant, more quiet-like. Government. Yuh. And government, Union at least, was still something to reckon with. Like a cottonmouth that wasn't quite dead yet. Could kill you if you made a mistake.

"Can you tell me where I can rent a rig or a horse?" Vulture asked.

The white man blinked. Damn nigger talkin' like a planter. But no sweetnin' in it. Flat. North. "Ain't no nigger don' rent nothin' here, not whilst white folks gots t' put the traces on they own backs t' turn the dirt when the mule dies."

Vulture looked around. The broad river was to the north. Barges were moored at the wharf, and a small paddlewheeler. Black work gangs were shunting lumber, bales of cotton, and sacks of rice into low gray sheds. The two blacks who had gotten off the train with him were heading south, niggertown. East then, to find a livery stable. He started off.

The white man followed and his friends fell in with him. "You in fo' the trial, boy, you best git yo black ass back the way you come."

Vulture walked without hurry, but his steps were huge and ground-devouring. The white man did a kind of hop to keep pace. "You heah me, nigger? You heah?"

Vulture passed small whitewashed houses, some with picket fences, all with gardens, more vegetables than flowers. There were open lots between them.

"*You heah?*" the white shrilled.

What made Vulture stop and begin to turn slowly was not the voice, but the dull metallic clack of a gun being cocked. Needling a redneck wasn't worth being shot in the back. The white was standing half a dozen paces away, the shotgun to his shoulder, his face florid. There were tight, nervous smiles on the lips of his friends. "I hear you," Vulture said.

"Sir!"

The flesh beneath Vulture's eye ticked. He had addressed people, and nearly all of them white, as *sir* nearly by reflex during the last several years. But that had merely been one of the trappings of civilization, of polite society. And those men had reciprocated.

"Sir!"

"Ah heahs yuh, suh," Vulture said, and with that drawl he mocked himself more than anyone else.

The white lowered his gun. "That's good. Good you got ears what can hear. An' big feet what can walk . . . an' run too. Cause, nigger, mayhap real soon yo ears goin' t' tell you it time t' leave, an' then yo big feet best start bouncin' you jus' like an ol' rabbit. Ol' rabbit with birdshot burnin' in his ass, cause if you set too long, why that nex' load jus' goin' nacherly find yo head."

Vulture turned and resumed walking. The whites followed. They felt victorious and festive now, and they were joking. Houses appeared more closely together, with only a few vacant lots, then became an unbroken line. Some were red brick, a few two stories tall. Vulture passed a school, from which white children were boisterously disgorging. "Harry, Harry, c'mere an' look at the nigger. Hurry up!" Boys joined the white men from the station. One danced before Vulture and mimicked the big man's loose-jointed stride. Then he stiffened his legs, stretched out his arms, and walked with a rolling gait: "Fee, fie, fo, fum! Ah smells the blood of a nigger-man!"

There were giggles and deeper laughter. Cobblestones replaced hardpacked earth beneath Vulture's feet; his bootheels clicked. He did not step up to the wooden sidewalk. There was something wrong in this town. He was accustomed to gawks and sometimes harassment, but this was deeper. Even the eyes of passing whites who scorned the buffoons following him raked across him, lingered angrily. Trial, the man at the station had said. Obviously there was a black involved. Bad town to be in now. He avoided the sidewalk because he did not want to be forced to step aside or even down into the street again if he encountered a belligerent white. Mood like this, the gang behind him would kill him if he insisted on his rights. Lightness giddied through him and for an instant he almost did take to the sidewalk, to force the issue and resolve it all in a few final, savage, glorious moments. Oblivion would be relief. He saw Labe, his brother, arms stretched out, face raised to the sky, turning slowly as the bullets thudded into his body. . . . Maybe Labe had been right. Of all of them, maybe Labe alone had truly found his manhood, and his freedom. Vulture shook his head. God, what it came to! These white men were like rats, worse, for after they'd gnawed a man down to bones they even sucked those clean of marrow.

He passed a millinery shop, two gunsmiths' establishments, a dry-goods store, and then finally a feed and grain store. He stopped, but there was no stable behind the store, so he went on. The street opened onto a good-sized square with a well-manicured greensward in the center, which was dry and winter-brown now. There were walkways winding among hedges and empty flowerbeds and beneath luxurious willows and magnolia trees. The houses around the square were large and boasted spacious and attractive lawns, testaments to uncountable hours of backbreaking gardening, large carriage houses, blocks at curbside from which to step up into surreys, and gay figurines of widely smiling Negroes extending arms whose hands grasped rings for tethering horses. There were also a few churches, and across the square he saw several larger buildings, one with a domed top. There was some sort of commotion around it. He crossed the street and entered the park. A black man in faded gray pants and shirt, barefoot, was on his hands and knees putting bulbs in a raked flowerbed beside the gravel walk. "Afternoon," Vulture said. "Can you tell me where I can rent a horse, friend?"

The man looked up, started at Vulture's size, then saw the following whites and bent his head back down to his work. "Through heah," he whispered, "down Barley Street two blocks an' turn right."

Vulture walked on without thanking him, but the whites had heard anyway and one kicked the black in the side and said, "Nigger, you jus' tend t' yo work." Vulture clenched his jaw. There was a flagpole in the center of the park, disproportionately tall and sturdy in comparison to the small Stars and Stripes snapping in the wind at its top, as if it bore the Union emblem by embarrassing accident. A large memorial stone sat at the base of the flagpole. A bronze plaque was bolted to it. The legend said: *In Honor and in Loving Memory of Woodboro's Brave Sons Who Gallantly Gave Their Lives in Defense of Their Homeland during the War between the States.* A large Confederate flag was flanked on both sides by crossed rifles. Beneath these, the roll of the dead went well over one hundred.

Vulture emerged from the park and saw that the domed building was the city hall and the courthouse. Down a few doors was the sheriff's office and jail, a two-story building of rust-colored brick. The windows of the second floor were all barred. A loose mob of whites was strung along the street: men, women, and children, the elegantly dressed as well as the shabby. A handful of country folk and idlers, the same kind who had followed him from the train, were calling up to a jail window: "You set tight there, Jeb. Ain't no harm goan come t' yuh." "Doan you fret none, boy. We see ever'thin' come out right." "Them nigger lovers treatin' you all right, boy?"

A white man grinned down from one of the windows. "Ah's jus' fine," he shouted. "Got me a downy pillow, jellies, jams, an' a mess o' fried chicken. All sorts o' stuff. Ladies Missionary Society brung it ovuh." He thrust an arm through the bars and something in his hand caught the sun. "An' looky here, even a gen-u-wine crystal drinkin' glass. Livin' better 'n some kind o' foreign king. Ah jus' goan 'joy mahself till they figgers out was plain Christian charity t' shoot thet ol' nigger 'stead o' haulin' him t' a tree limb an' settin' him t' fire."

His friends laughed, and one called, "Thet's the truth, Jeb, thet's the Gospel."

The rest of the whites were hooting and jeering or simply staring angrily at a militia unit drilling in the street. The militia was black. Most Southern states had rid themselves of such abominations by '72 or '73. It was a small squad, twenty men. Their uniforms were patched, their rifles old wartime single-shot Enfields. They were commanded by a black lieutenant, which pleased Vulture. He had been a corporal during the war. He had heard of colored sergeants in some of the other black regiments, but he'd never seen one. Negroes had been considered fit to fight then, but not to lead. Not even their own kind. His foot tapped to the cadence. "One-two-three-four. One-twwwooo-three-*four!* Left-right-left-right. Left-rrrright-your-*right!*" The whites behind Vulture drifted away to heckle the militia. On command, the blacks came to foot-stamping halt, then went through a dazzling manual of arms with their Enfields, finishing with twenty rifle butts snapping down to the cobblestones as one.

"Goddamn trained monkeys," someone yelled. "We wanted to take Jeb out o' jail we shove them popguns up yo asses an' walk right ovuh yuh!"

Two white deputies with shotguns sat in rocking chairs on either side of the jailhouse door. They looked mildly uneasy.

The militia resumed its drill and Vulture walked off. Few of the whites in the mob had noticed him, none paid him any real attention. But the man who had first accosted him followed, and two others. Vulture went down Barley Street thinking with a little nostalgia of his own days as a soldier. Freedom, he'd once thought, had to be taken with force. Once in hand it could be guaranteed, and equality achieved, by intelligent men of good will. This might indeed be true, but it was impossible to prove: these last few years in Washington had taught him that most men were stupid and brutish. Perhaps the gun and the knife were the only factors of real significance.

A sign on a blacksmith's shop advertised rigs and horses for hire. Vulture stepped inside. It was hot. A black boy working bellows at a coal forge was sheened with sweat. The white smith was hammering at the glowing end of a leaf spring. Slick wet channels sliced through the grime that covered his skin. He was naked from the waist up, chest protected from sparks and tiny pieces of hot metal by a heavy leather apron. Each time he struck with the ten-pound hand sledge, his heavy jowls quivered and drops of water were flung from his jerking head. The three white men crowded in behind Vulture. He ignored them. The smith raised the spring, turned it over, grunted approvingly, and then dipped the glowing end into a nearby bucket of water. Steam hissed. When the smith finished Vulture said, "I'd like to rent a horse from you, sir."

The smith regarded him with amusement. "They all gone lame, boy. Tell you what, though. Big as you are, whyn't we fit you up with a saddle an' rent you out to some nice gentleman? We'll split the price fifty-fifty. How's that sound?"

Vulture breathed deeply, held the breath a moment, then exhaled slowly. He felt loose and relaxed. It was what he had done, and how he had felt, during the war before combat, and a few times in the Capitol. "Not too fucking funny."

The smith kept on smiling, his sense of the proper order of things prohibiting comprehension; his brain replayed Vulture's words, trying to bend them into something acceptable. It failed. His mouth pulled tight and he hefted the sledge. The whites behind Vulture closed in. The black child abandoned the bellows and ran into the street. Vulture edged toward a work bench along a wall where there were wheel spokes and tools and piled horseshoes. A white snatched up a piece of lumber and leaped to block him. Vulture was quicker. He reached the heavy table, grabbed it with both hands, and hunched his shoulders. Wood creaked, then crackled and split, and Vulture wrenched the great slab from its moorings, jagged pieces of siding breaking loose with the bolts, and heaved it away. The whites scrambled aside. The bench knocked over tables and tool racks, crashed into the forge, and sent sparks spiraling up to the ceiling. Vulture picked up a spoke in each hand and backed to the wall. The whites formed a semicircle around him. Vulture bellowed and clubbed the empty air with a spoke. The man with the shotgun cocked both hammers and centered the weapon on Vulture's chest. "Ah cover 'im," he said. "You boys go ahead."

"Ain't nobody goan t' do nothin'," said a voice from the front of the shop. "Got my own scattergun dead on yo back, friend, so you just set that down nice and easy. Gentle-like, you know?" It was a deputy sheriff. The boy who had fled was standing at his side, frightened.

"Now hold on, Walt," the smith said. "This nigger—"

"Drop the sledge, Harley! Ever' one of you, empty hands! This town goan stay quiet if we have t' blow t' hell half the people in it."

The whites lay down their weapons. Vulture dropped the spokes. The deputy relaxed some, but still kept his gun at the ready. "Now what's this about?"

"That there nigger freak come in on the four 'clock train," the white from the station said sullenly. "Clothes an' all like that, you kin bet on the honor of Jess Davis hisself he fresh from some robbery. Come t' raise a nigger mob t' lynch ol' Jeb Merril."

"Who're you?" the deputy asked.

"Me? Whut call you got questionin' me? Whut Ah done?"

"Doan know yo face. Sheriff wants us t' keep an eye on strangers—God knows there's enough in town—partic'ly ones what get into trouble."

"Ain't no trouble. Me an' mah frens, we jus' ride in t' see justice done."

"Well maybe you just best ride back out."

"That ain't no way fo' one white man t' talk t' another."

"Doan know 'bout that, just know I got a job t' do."

"Whut about the nigger?"

"I'll see t' him."

"He got a gun," the man said with sudden inspiration. "Big Navy Colt revolver stuck in his waistban'."

"Open yo coat," the deputy said to Vulture.

Vulture did, slipped out of it, raised his arms to shoulder level, and turned around.

"Ain't no gun there," the deputy said.

The white man chewed on his lip. It had seemed a good thing to say at the moment. "Probly hid it in his grip," he said lamely.

The deputy was losing interest in the white man—he wasn't strong enough to be real trouble—and becoming curious about and somewhat suspicious of the giant Negro. "What's yo name, boy?"

"Gideon," Vulture said. "James Gideon."

"You got proof?"

Vulture took a wallet from his jacket pocket. "My floor pass to the House of Representatives, United States Congress."

"Shee-it!" said the man from the station. "Goddamn nigger cong'essman."

The pass looked official and impressive to the deputy, but he raised his gun. "Ain't no nigger congressmen from this state no more."

"That's right. This is from Congressman Philip Jackson's office. He's a representative from South Carolina. I'm on his staff. You'd most likely have noticed that if you'd read farther." The last was to save the deputy's pride; it was obvious from the way he'd looked at the pass that he couldn't read.

The deputy flushed, looked again, and nodded. "Right. There it is all right."

"Jackson," said one of the whites. "He a nigger, ain't he?"

"Yeah," the smith said. "One of them that wanted t' cut up the plantations and give the land free t' the slaves."

"Shee-it!" said the man from the station.

"What you come to Woodboro fo'?" the deputy asked.

"Personal reasons."

"What kind of personal?"

"To see an old friend."

"Who?"

"Emory Woodson."

"Huh! You open that grip and that trunk then, boy."

"Why?"

"You just do like I say!"

The other whites crowded around the deputy, emboldened by his anger. "And fast!" one of them said. The deputy glared at him, and he drew back.

Vulture opened the grip. The deputy pawed through it while the other whites looked over his shoulder—two fresh shirts, a change of socks and underwear, a thick book, toilet articles. The trunk was closed with a padlock, which Vulture had to open. There were more clothes, two greatcoats, another pair of boots, a pair of shoes, three or four books, and half a dozen autographed photographs in oval frames. The deputy's probing hand came up with a double-barreled .44 derringer.

"I tol' yuh!" said the man with the shotgun.

The deputy put it back in the trunk. "He ain't doin' nothin' with it. Got a right. Okay, boy. You look clean. But let me give you some advice. Woodboro ain't a bad town most times, fo' black or white. We treat our nigras better'n others, that's a fact. But this ain't most times, which I guess you didn't know if you come here innocent. Lot o' bad feelin'. So what I'm tellin' you is, you conclude up your business here real fast and leave. Or else you stay out at Emory Woodson's till this is over. Trial's next Friday. Things should settle down few days after that. Wouldn't do fo' you to ride in here with Woodson. Lot o' people doan like him. Just might give some of 'em fits t' see him an' a great big foreign buck like you together these days. You unnerstan'?"

"Yes. Thank you. Maybe you can tell me where I can rent a horse to get out to Woodson's."

"No such thing. Used to be a nigger with a stable 'bout a year back, but his place caught fire one night, burnt him up with ever'thin' else. Charlie Dobbs, now he rents a horse t' a good nigger now and then, but doan reckon he'd want t' chance anythin' like that now. You goan have t' walk."

Vulture nodded and asked directions. The deputy told him.

When the deputy returned to the sheriff's office he poured a cup of coffee, sat down, removed his boots, stretched his legs, and contemplated his wiggling sock-cased toes. There were holes in the socks, and a painful blister on the little toe of his left foot. He wrinkled his forehead and sniffed. Uh-huh. He needed a bath, or at least his feet did.

Sheriff Gibney's revolver lay disassembled on his desk. He was cleaning it again. The deputy shook his head. Gibney was a stocky, balding man, a livid blusterer who'd bellow at you half a day, then shake your hand. Occasionally someone would interpret all that fury as the bluff of a weak man. Bad mistake, that. If a tongue lashing couldn't get the job done, then Gibney would just as willingly administer a pistol whipping. And if necessary he'd fire a ball through a man's head without a moment's unease. He'd ridden with Mosby's Rangers during the war, and rumor had it that a neglected pistol had malfunctioned then and almost cost him his life. The deputy didn't know if there was any truth to that, but he *did* know that Gibney broke down and cleaned his weapons at least once and often two or three times each day. And he raised truly terrible hell, even docked pay, when he found any of his deputies' guns dirty.

Gibney spat tobacco juice into a cuspidor. "Ennythin' to what the boy said, Walt?"

"Yeah. A bit. Harley an' some trash was ready to get on

top the bigges' godawful nigger I ever seen. I mean, it would o' took a two-man saw t' bring the boogie down."

"Who was he?"

"Educated nigger. Down from Washington, works for the gov'mint."

"Come to see about the trial?"

"Naw. Doan think he even knowed about it. Came to see Woodson. Old friend. Got me goin' a spell, thought maybe Woodson really was puttin' together some kind o' nigger squad like the boys are sayin'."

"What boys?"

Walt shrugged. "You know. You hear it on the street a lot."

"I don't want none of our boys chewin' that crap."

"They ain't, least not that I know."

"Well, you hear ennyone else sayin' that, you tell 'em to shut up fast. Use your gun butt if you have to."

"Right."

"What'd you do with the trash?"

"Run 'em out o' town. Doan know that it'll do much good, nothin' to stop 'em from comin' right back in."

"Too many around." Gibney ran an oilcloth through the barrel of his revolver. He looked tired and disturbed. "And too many local people talkin' blood. Can't cotton how a man can lose his head so easy."

"They just doan like niggers."

"Nobody likes niggers. But the law's the law."

The black militia marched past the windows and the jeering grew louder.

"Stupid, them showin' off like that," Walt said. "Liable to blow the town up in our face."

Gibney held the barrel to a kerosene lamp, squinted down its length, and grunted with satisfaction. He set it aside, rested his chin on his palm, and looked out the window. "Hard to tell. You look at 'em, you just know they for real. Wouldn't o' minded few o' them boys alongside me during the war—if they was white, o' course. Might strike a spark like you say, or might make somebody think twice before tryin' somethin'. Wisht I knew for certain, Could maybe get 'em t' stop if I was sure they was makin' trouble 'stead keepin it down. Don' like this not knowin', don' like it atall. Well . . . reckon you should get back out an' walk around, move your badge."

"I guess." Walt drained the last of his coffee. "Sure feel better if we had more men. Would o' been blood at Harley's if I hadn't showed up. An' we got t' go all the way t' Friday. Powerfully doubt the fifteen of us is enough."

"I know, but iffen I put badges on some more, I'm afraid I'd be tellin' 'em: 'Boys, you just go do whatever you want, you the law now. Ain't no more I can trust that far."

Walt was flattered and proud. There was nothing he wouldn't do for Gibney. The sheriff had been responsible for everything good in Walt's life. Twelve years ago, when Walt was nine, his father had come home from the war without any legs. A man who'd worked the land all his life wasn't much good anymore when you took away his legs. He died three months later. Walt's mother followed him to the grave the next winter, dead of lung fever and, the boy knew, of the loss of her husband. Neighbors sent the boy to Woodboro, where his only surviving relative lived, a half-senile great-aunt. Most of the time she couldn't remember his name. He hated town life, yearned for the open country; he hated his aunt, grieved for his dead parents. When he was sixteen, Sheriff Jules Gibney routed him and two other boys from a warehouse near the river. They had slashed open sacks of flour, chopped into barrels of kerosene and molasses and spilled them onto the flour, were passing new repeating rifles from a crate through a kicked-out window when Gibney came through the front door. The sheriff didn't bother with Walt's friends—he knew who they were and could talk to their fathers, who would come down hard on them. But Walt was different. Gibney dragged him to the street, flung him down, and made him scuttle to jail on all fours, cursing him and planting a boot in his buttocks each time he tried to stand. Gibney kept him locked up three days, arranged to assume responsibility for him with his great-aunt, brought him home to Mrs. Gibney, and told him if he tried to run off he'd see the boy went to prison. Walt slept in their house, ate with them, played games of cribbage and checkers with the sheriff at night, and went to church with Gibney and his wife on Sunday. Gibney worked the boy janitoring around the jailhouse, running messages, and sitting in court until a bailiff whispered that the sheriff's testimony would be required next. He also hired Walt out to farmers around planting and harvesting time, and to merchants when their clerks were sick. He gave the boy a small salary himself, and allowed him to keep what he was paid by people for whom he worked. Now and then Gibney would say "my boy" when speaking of Walt to friends. When Walt turned eighteen, Gibney hired him as a deputy. A year later the sheriff stood up for the groom when Walt married Gibney's niece, Lucinda. Two months ago Lucinda had borne a little girl. She was christened Julia. So far as Jules Gibney and Walt were concerned, she was Gibney's granddaughter.

Walt poked the blister on his little toe. It was going to burst soon. He should probably get some sulfa for it. He pulled on his boots. He sighed, shifted his holstered revolver to a more comfortable lay, and picked up his shotgun. Gibney stopped him at the door.

"Walt?"

"Yeah?"

"I think you should soak your feet tonight."

"What kind o' soak's good fo' a blister?"

"Don' know 'bout that. I meant the water and soap kind."

"Oh. Okay. All right if I swing by the house to check up?"

"Sure, long as you don' set too long. Kiss 'em both for me."

Walt touched his hat with his finger and left the office.

Jimmy Hildenbrandt rode up on his big sorrel and they were all here now, the Hearth was complete. Wallace Swett looked enviously in the moonlight at Hildenbrandt's sorrel while Hildenbrandt took his gear from a saddlebag and put it on. Swett's mount was an old and spavined clay-bank mare. Didn't seem right somehow for a Torch to have to ride a horse like his while an Ember, and a fairly new member of the order on top of it, sat on such a fine gelding.

"Y'all ready?" Swett asked. The nine Embers indicated

they were. Swett raised his arm and chopped it down: "Then . . . *ride!*"

They put their heels to their mounts and galloped out of the grove and across a hundred feet of meadow, then swung north onto the road. It was a perfect night for it, a nearly full moon beyond the thinnest layer of clouds. Swett loved such nights for riding, the unreal and ghostly quality of the light. He imagined the niggers and what they saw: trembling black hands pulling back the corners of dirty flour-sack curtains, terrified eyes popping as the phantasmic Knights thundered by with their horses' hooves striking sparks from stones on the road, the twin horns of each man's hood thrust forward as if seeking something to gore, long red capes flapping back like trailing flames in the wind. Niggers had died of fright just looking at the Knights, Swett knew that for a fact. He hunched over the mare's neck and urged her on. He was a young man and powerful, but he felt even greater strength flowing into him now, the indomitable might of righteousness and a just hunger for vengeance. He was exhilarated. "Room, gimme room!" he shouted. The nearest riders pulled off a little to the sides. Swett grabbed the long bullwhip coiled around the pommel of his saddle, played it out, and began cracking it around his head. He leaned back in the saddle, staring almost directly up at the moon, and screamed: "AI-YA-YA-YAAAAAA!"

Their first stop was a shack set back from the road near a small spring. They ringed the front door, spread far apart and keeping back a good distance. Swett didn't expect any trouble until later, but he wasn't the kind to make a dumb mistake. The Hearth's last Torch had gotten himself killed that way. They'd gone to discipline an uppity nigger. Nothing serious, just a little snaking with a bullwhip. But the damn black fool blasted off a round from a Sharp's buffalo gun and the big slug caught Torch Leslie Allen square in the throat, blew his head right off his neck. Godamighty, Swett had never seen anything like that before! They must've put a hundred shots into the cabin, but it had thick log walls and the nigger kept shooting back. So finally they set fire to it. Some of the Embers felt a little sorry about the woman and the two children who burned with the darky.

Swett cupped his hands to his mouth: "Skillet. Skillet Jones. We wants you!"

There were several moments of silence, then a muffled reply. "Who wants me!"

'You knows that, Jones. I, the Beatified Torch, and the Knights of the Canescent Dominion wants you."

"Whuffo?" There was fear in the voice.

"'T' talk. Ain't goan come hard on yuh iffen yuh walks out now. Ah gives mah word as a White Christian genneman. But yuh goan fert'lize the groun'. wif yo blood iffen yuh makes trouble."

The Knights heard Jones and his woman arguing in the shack. The woman's voice hovered on hysteria. "Get shut!" Jones roared. "Got no choice." There was the sound of a slap. The woman began to sob. The door opened and Jones came out. He had pulled on trousers over his red flannel longjohns, but the suspenders hung down at his thighs and he was holding his pants up by hand. The Knights dismounted. Two took him by the arms and hurried him over to a tree where a third bound him with rope. His pants dropped to his ankles. He twisted his head and breathed in gasps and kept asking why, how come they wanted him, what had he done? And he begged please don't kill him, he was a good respectful nigger, he never done nothin' wrong. His wife was shrieking in the shack.

One of the Knights slapped Jones and told him to be quiet. Swett walked back and forth before the black man flicking the whip against the ground. "Yuh broke yo work contrac' wif Mr. Peterson, Skillet. Him needin' han's like he do, thass bad, real bad."

"No suh, Masta. Please. I dint do wrong. Masta Peterson say Ah cut a peach saplin' when Ah cleanin' weeds, say Ah stole a shoat, say Ah sneak off early near ever' day. He say he ain't gon' pay me but half mah year's wages come Chris'mas an' Ah gots t' make mah mark on a new contrac' for nex' year."

"We hears tell yuh file a paper wif the court agin him."

"Only fo' what rightfully mine, suh. I dint do none o' them things."

Swett lashed the whip across Jones's chest. The Negro screamed. "Now, Skillet, yuh knows Mr. Peterson a god-fearin' man whut woul'nt lie. Ah confess, Ah is perplexed. Yuh was allus a good nigger t' now." He nodded to a hooded man near Jones. The man drew a knife, grabbed the crotch of the black's longjohns, and cut away a piece, exposing the genitals. Jones writhed against his bonds and whimpered, his scrotum tight with fear. The white man took the black genitals roughly in hand and laid the flat of his knife across the penis.

"No," Jones whimpered. "No. No. No. Oh, please. God, no. No!"

"Skillet? You gwine be a good nigger?"

"Yas, Masta, yas! Ah swears it!"

"You gwine take thet paper outta court?"

"Ennythin'!"

"Gwine go back t' work fo' Mr. Peterson fust thing come dawn? An' sign that new contrac'?"

"Yassuh! Yassuh! Ah be the bestes' nigger in the county. Please, suh!"

"Well . . . all right, then. We give you one more chance."

"Thank you, Mastas. Thank you suhs!"

"But nex' time you troublesome, we cut fo' sure."

The Knights left Jones still tied to the tree and weeping uncontrollably. They rode to a cluster of five cabins on the edge of a small plantation. These were owned by the white planter and rented from him by the Negroes who worked the land as sharecroppers. Lamps glimmered through the windows of two cabins as the Knights turned their horses. The lights quickly vanished. Swett liked that. The planter had hired out the woman's husband to a friend, so he was gone; the other four bucks didn't have one pair of balls between them.

They called Josephine Green. They waited on their horses; it was always better for the nigger to have to look up. The door opened and Josephine stepped out. There was a quickening in Swett's groin and he scrunched forward in the saddle, pressed himself against the pommel. Josephine Green was a light brown woman, tall, with widely rounded hips, melon-heavy breasts, and full globes for buttocks. She stood before them in a gray shift that was molded and tautened by the swollen contours of her body. Her eyes were cast down at her bare feet, her arms hung limp at her sides. She knows, Swett thought with pleasure. She knows she done wrong an' gots t' pay fo' it.

He said somberly: "Josephine Green, you has ignored the warnin' o' the Knights of the Canescent Dominion. You is still spreadin' yo legs fo' thet poor deluded white man Charley Stoffle. Does you confirm the troof o' whut Ah say?"

The woman didn't respond. A rider edged his mount up alongside her and kicked her in the head. "Answer when the Torch talk t' you, nigger!" She reeled and went to one knee, then pushed herself up, holding the side of her face.

"No more o' thet!" Swett said to the man. He wanted her untouched, for a while at least. He tried to make his voice stern, but benevolent. "Ah wants t' hear why yuh failed the heed o' our comman', Josephine."

Her shoulders slumped, her arms pulled in against herself. Her head bent so far that her chin touched her chest. "Ah showed it t' him, but he say not to pay it no mind." Her words were barely audible, but her voice was thick and smooth, like syrup, and it caused a painful sweet throb between Swett's legs. "He say he fix it up all right," Josephine whispered.

"Now how yuh reckon he gwine do thet, huh? The Knights o' the Canescent Dominion got nothin' t' hold agin nigger bitches fo'nicatin', adulteratin', or whorin' fo' white men. Thet all part o' the nachul order o' things. But when it make trouble in a good Christian family, why then the Knights jus' gots t' step in an' rectify it."

"Yassuh. Ah tol' him, suh, Ah truly did."

"Ain't enuff. Po' Miz Stoffle wif them three li'l young uns, an' the middle un not right in the head an' all. She gwine plumb t' a desperate frazzle wif ol' Charley ovuh heah most ever' night. She beg an' plead an' cry her po' heart out, but Charley, all he think about be yo musky nigger body. He don't listen t' his brother, he don' even listen t' his pappy. So we warn yuh nice an' politelike, but yuh keeps whorin' fo' him. Why yuh do thet, woman, why yuh whore fo' that po' white man?"

"Please, suh. Ah tol' him, God's troof."

"They othu ways t' make money, 'stead o' destroyin' a good white fam'ly."

"Suh, I never took no money in mah whole life from no man."

"Then whut you do it fo' . . . love?"

The Knights laughed.

"Well?" Swett demanded.

"Ah guess so . . . fo' Charley."

"Fuckin' nigger cat," a Knight snarled.

Swett got off his horse. "Well," he said softly, "Ah reckon we gots t' teach you some things." The other Knights dismounted too. One asked if they should take her inside. Swett was breathing fast. He said no, the other niggers would all be peeking from their cabins now, and he wanted them to see. He had two of his men move the horses back and then he ordered Josephine to come forward, out of the shadow of the cabin and to a spot where the moonlight spilled down full upon them. She complied silently. Her pendulous breasts quivered with her steps. Swett's organ strained against his pants. "Lay down," he said.

She did. Her wide-lipped mouth was open a little. She stared blankly up past the ring of hooded figures into the star-filled sky. "Move her around theah," Swett said. He fumbled with his belt buckle. "Couple o' you hold her arms an' legs. Rest step back thet way. Don' wan' the othu niggers to miss enny o' this."

Swett hooked his thumbs in his pants and his drawers and pushed them down. He dropped to his knees between Josephine's legs. His penis was bucking, his pelvis twitched under its own direction. His hands were slick. He tugged the woman's shift up around her waist. Her belly caught the moonlight. There was a rich triangle of dense black hair above the juncture of her thighs. Swett groaned. He dipped his head, laved that hair with his tongue. He seized his penis with his hand and squeezed it. He caught the bristly hair with his teeth. She winced. "You gwine git yo fill o' white men," he said. "You gwine git a life full, woman." He flung himself atop her. The fingers of one hand dug into her great breast, the toes of his boots scored the earth, his other hand hammered his penis against her thighs, then found the cleft, thrust it in against her dryness even though it hurt him a little. Both his hands were on her breasts now, crushing. Unbidden, her body began to moisten itself. He lurched atop her, rapidly losing control

of his movements. "Shit," he rasped. "Oh, shit! Sonabitch!" He pumped wildly, but Josephine lay still as table
meat, and Swett began to lose his edge. "Make her move,"
he grunted. "Hurry up!" One of the Knights jabbed the
sole of her foot with a knife point. She cried out and
jerked. "Thass it, keep at it," Swett said. The Knight used
his knife until the woman began to roll her hips of her own
volition. It wasn't much, and it was only to escape further
pain that she moved, but Swett was satisfied and stiffened
anew. He thrust his fingers into Josephine's hair and
forced her head back and bent her neck, which caused her
soft body to arch involuntarily toward him. He blew
against the fabric of his hood, which hung down over his
face, and twisted until his mouth was free, and he pressed
his mouth down on hers. When he got one with really
thick lips it was almost more than he could bear. He took
the upper fleshy ridge between his teeth, ground it and
sucked on it, sucked on it ever more frantically as a swelling heat rushed through his loins, burgeoned, oh, so large,
so large it would split, then felt it burst gloriously and
spurt, spurt, oh God yes flood into her!

He collapsed on her with a groan. After several moments he sighed and pushed himself up. He stood off to
the side and adjusted his hood. The damned things got
pushed all the hell around when you had to be active. He
pulled the chinstrap snug.

The second Knight splattered himself over the girl's leg
before he had even entered her. "Aw goddamn t' hell!" he
said. He punched her in the stomach, went to his feet, and
kicked viciously at a stone. The Knights laughed. Swett
fished in his shirt pocket for a paper and the makings. He
rolled a cigarette, twisted the ends closed, and struck a
match to it. He wasn't much interested in what was going
on now. He felt good, content. He would have liked to
pull off his boots and lay out on a bed. He stretched.
There was still work to do.

Johnny Murphy was sixteen years old, the youngest
member of the Hearth, and he had never had a woman.
He'd tried twice before in his life, but he'd remained tight
and shrunken between his legs, like a frightened possum
curled in upon itself. He watched the others in an agony of
apprehension, his hand dug deep into his pocket, working

himself, trying to prepare. But nothing happened, *goddamn it, nothing happened!* When his turn came he was sick to his stomach, and his bowels threatened to void themselves. He went to his knees without opening his pants, then did so quickly and threw himself down on Josephine, terrified that one of the others had seen his flaccid state. He reached as he had seen the others do and pretended to insert himself. He made what he hoped sounded like a grunt of pleasure. The woman was moaning, still staring without expression up into the night. Johnny pounded his hips. His dead organ banged against her ineffectually. Tears spilled from his eyes and he cried without sound. He took her head in his hands. If she said one word—*one stinking word*—he'd jam his thumbs into her eyes and crush them to jelly. He couldn't sustain the pretense any longer. Soon someone behind him would see that things were not right, and then they would all know about him. "Oh," he said. "Oh. Yeah. Ooooohhhh!" He grinned at the two Knights holding her arms to show them how much he liked it, forgetting that his hood prevented them from seeing his face. He stood up and began to say, Now that was really fine. He got as far as, "Now that—" and then his voice broke. "Kill her!" he screamed. "Kill the rotten nigger bitch!" He kicked her.

Swett pulled him away. "Easy, Johnny boy. You save thet for later. Git holt o' yo'self."

Swett led him to the horses and left him there. Johnny sat down cross-legged on the ground. He was morose. He wondered with sudden hope if any of the others had had to pretend like him. He looked at them craftily and tried to remember each of them topping the woman. And as he went over them one by one, his hopes crumbled bitterly.

When the last Knight finished Swett went to the side of the cabin and kicked over a rain barrel. Most of the water sloshed out, but a little was still trapped, and it dribbled and left a spotty trail as Swett rolled the barrel to Josephine with his foot. He knelt down beside her. "Well," he said. "You had enuff white prick t' fill yo kettle a spell?" She made no answer. Swett didn't like the way she just stared like that, didn't like it at all. It unnerved him.

Under Swett's direction, the Knights draped her on her stomach over the barrel. They tied her wrists, ran the rope beneath the barrel, and tied the other end to her knees. On the one side her bound wrists touched the ground, on the other her knees. Facing the Knights, after one of them pulled up her shift, were her full round buttocks. They were stunning in the moonlight, firm, unblemished, a creamy chocolate, smooth, taut. Swett flicked the bullwhip to its full length, then brought it hissing back on itself. It sliced directly across the woman's buttocks with a sharp *cr-rrack!* She spasmed and screamed. Swett pulled back for another lash. He hesitated, staring at the dark welt that bisected the declivity between her cheeks.

He tossed the whip down and walked up behind the girl. She was whimpering in anticipation of the next stroke. Her buttocks quivered. Swett placed a hand lightly on each one. There was an exciting resiliency to them. Her skin was a little cool in the night air, and perfect to the touch, like the marble egg his mother kept on her night-stand. He ran his fingers along the welt, which had its own warmth and which was swelling even as he stood there. His tongue wetted his lips. He kneaded her buttocks, spread them. He'd never done it himself, but he'd heard from others. . . . And some did it to animals that way, cows and mares, and sheep, yeah, a lot did it to sheep. . . . Suddenly he had the buttons of his fly open, and he was spreading the girl's cheeks, and pushing, but it wasn't easy —"No! Oh God, yuh kill me!" she cried. "Yuh rip me!" . . . and that got her, all right; he dipped his head and spat on her, then once in his hand and slicked himself down, and pushed again, and he was doing it, and she was screaming and bucking, and he was opening and closing her around himself, and *Christ Fucking Jesus . . . !*

A little later he held the whip out and said, "Someun finish up theah." Johnny Murphy grabbed it and laid into her like a real mule driver and soon little was left of her buttocks but bloody meat. Swett took the whip back even though Johnny protested and said he wanted to take her down to the bone. "Ain't necessary," Swett said. "We done whut we set out t' do."

They left her tied over the barrel for her neighbors to cut free. They sat loosely in their saddles letting their horses walk for nearly half a mile, subdued partly by their disciplining of Josephine Green, but more by contemplation

of their next, and last, stop of the evening. There was one
little detail to attend to first. Swett said, "Johnny, you
write out a note t' Charley Stoffle. Tell him no mo' warnin's. He try t' see thet black whore agin, we snake him
like t' kill him. You put it up on his door afore you git
home t'night."

"Ah'll do thet, Wallace."

"Know you will, Johnny." Swett, even though only
three years Johnny's elder, had a kind of fatherly affection
for the boy. Johnny'd go far in the Knights, make a good
Torch of this Hearth when he, Wallace, moved up to a
higher office. Just a mite excitable, that was his only fault.
But he'd straighten out, Swett was sure, as he grew further
into manhood.

"Le's have a weapons check," Swett said. He liked the
sound of that. Precise. Military. "Full loads, but hammers
on safety. Ah wan's t' heah it." The Knights assured him
in turn that their guns were indeed fully loaded, and hammers on safety. "Right." Swett was all seriousness now.
The first two actions had been funnin' in a way—no one
said that a soldier in the cause of God's White Race
couldn't enjoy himself now and then—but this was different, and, as the Beatified Torch, he was responsible for
the success of their final mission and the performance of
his Embers. "We saved Huggins t' las' so t' be sure
ever'thin' be quiet and late an' he be asleep," he explained. "Now whut we do is, we come up at full gallop,
jump down, bust right through thet door—thass me, Lem,
and Fred—grab him, throw him outside, an' finish it up.
Dick an' Johnny, jus' t' go ovuh it agin, is the ones whut
handle his woman. Now ever'body got it? Good. 'Member,
it's the fast whut do it. Slow people is dead people. Le's
go!"

Tom Huggins was a wiry sour-faced black activist who
worked ceaselessly to enroll Negroes in the Radical Republican faction, who had managed to get out more than
200 Negro votes in the last election. He had leveled a
shotgun and driven off his land a trio of whites who had
come to convince him that these activities were neither to
his benefit nor to the benefit of his race, and he'd been
preaching to local blacks that they should buy arms in
order to defend themselves. He would have been taken

care of earlier, but there had been too many federal troops in the area until last week. Now the troops had moved, and it was time for Huggins to pay the piper.

It went exactly according to plan, and Swett was pleased with himself. In the lead, he jerked the mare's head savagely to the side before Huggins' door. Even as she came to a foot-stamping halt he was leaping from her back. Lem and Fred were right behind him and they struck the door together, tearing the simple bolt lock from the frame and stumbling into the dark interior. Jimmy followed with a candle, which he shielded from the mild breeze with his hand. The cabin was only a single room. Huggins was asleep with his wife on a straw mattress in the corner. He lurched up as Swett and the others burst in and he grabbed for a shotgun hanging on pegs over the mattress. Lem's revolver roared, deafening in the confined space, and Huggins went down clawing at his knee. Two children on a pallet in the opposite corner screamed. They stood up, an old blanket falling about their feet, and clutched each other. Huggins' woman screeched, seized a stool, and flung herself at Lem. The stool bounced off his shoulder. Fred swung his rifle and its butt caught her across the mouth with a crunching sound. She fell to the floor. Huggins was trying to pull himself up the log wall to his gun. Someone kicked him between the shoulders and he collapsed again.

"Git 'im out!" Swett ordered.

Two Knights grabbed his arms and dragged him through the door. They dropped him a dozen paces from the cabin. "You bastards!" he shouted. "You white sonabitchin' bastards! Rot in hell, you white devils!"

Swett shot him in the stomach. The black doubled himself and his legs kicked.

Huggins' woman appeared in the doorway, a hand on each side of the frame, weaving, her mouth pulped. She made an unintelligible sound.

"You tell 'em," Swett said to her. "Ain't no nigger ack like no white man. They's black and they's white, an' it allus gwine be like thet." He kicked her in the stomach and she fell back into the cabin. "Kill 'im," Swett ordered.

The Knights opened fire. Pistol and rifle slugs tore into Huggins with loud smacks and booming shotgun fire knocked the body about on the dirt. Each man reloaded as his weapon emptied, and fired again, and all the while Jimmy Hildenbrandt, who carried one of the new Winchester repeating rifles, worked the lever of his gun and sent round after round into the corpse with an even measured cadence.

Huggins was literally torn to pieces.

Swett raised his hand. "Thet's it. Let up. We done."

The shots tailed off. There were faint echoes from the nearby hills, which remained for several moments.

"Okay," said Swett. "Mount up an' le's git."

They swung onto their horses, sliding pistols back into holsters, rifles into scabbards, and resting emptied shotguns over pommels. Swett glanced around to make sure all were ready. "Split up an' head fo' yo homes when we reach the crossroads," he said. "Now ride!"

Nearly an hour later, the night was beginning to lighten as he reined his horse toward the barn. He yawned. He wouldn't get any sleep at all. Chores were chores, and they just didn't wait on the Dominion.

Two huge columns of stone marked the entrance to Elysium. Creeper vines and wild ivy had all but overgrown them. Vulture turned off the main road onto a wheel-rutted private way. The sun was down; only a shrinking aureole of dark scarlet remained on the western horizon; the moon was almost full. Huge oak trees bordered the road, massive and stern in the hazy gray light. Not far ahead a pair of dogs began to bark furiously.

Vulture paused a hundred yards in from the columns and shifted the large trunk from one shoulder to the other. There was a soundless and slight movement, and suddenly a young black man with a repeating rifle was barring Vulture's path. "Evenin'," the youth said amiably. "You got business here?"

"Evening, friend. I've come to see Emory Woodson."

"Cap'n dint say we was expectin' visitors."

"He's not expecting me. He doesn't even know I'm in the state."

"Yuh? What's yo name?"

"Got a legal name, but the one I was born with is Vulture. I served under Captain Woodson in the war."

"Yuh did, uh? Well, let's go up an' say hello to 'im." He stepped aside and gestured for Vulture to precede him.

The road passed through dogwoods, willows, and elms. Scrub brush grew in profuse entanglement. Vulture saw scattered pinpoints of cabin lights. They came upon a rolling grassy area with evidences of old and abandoned flower gardens. There were walkways between thick shrubs that had once been carefully sculpted but had reverted to wildness many years ago. A stone fountain stood pitted and cracked and dry in the center of a broad fishpond, one wall of which had caved in. It had been, Vulture recognized, rather elegant before the war. The Great House itself was of modest size, not more than twelve rooms, but it was handsome and in excellent repair. Eight tall pillars rose from the veranda to support a sundeck on the second floor, then continued to the roof lintel. There was a trio of peaked dormers with French windows. Sweeping willows flanked the house on either side. The youth with the rifle brought Vulture to the edge of the veranda and motioned him to wait while he went up to the door and knocked on it. When the door opened, light spilled out around a white man. "Yes, Henry?"

"Cap'n, this here fella says he—"

Woodson turned as Henry pointed. "Vulture!"

"Hey, Emory."

They met and hugged each other strongly. "Why didn't you let me know you were coming, you old sonofabitch?"

"Didn't know myself until a couple of days ago," Vulture said.

"Ah reckon it's all right, Cap'n," Henry said.

"Hell yes. Henry, this is Vulture, one of the best soldiers I ever served with. Vulture, this is Henry. He carries that rifle loosely, but he can put a slug through the head of a running rabbit at a hundred yards."

Henry smiled. "How do. Sorry if Ah 'peared unfriendly-like."

Vulture shook the boy's hand. "No offense."

Henry said he'd be getting back then. "Guards?" Vulture asked Woodson.

"Yes. It's been quiet a while, but there's a trial in town that's stirring up a lot of anger."

"I ran into some of it. Not serious. It could have been if

a deputy hadn't showed up. Not too bad a peace officer, considering the context."

Woodson nodded. "One of Sheriff Gibney's boys. We put Gibney in office two years ago. He doesn't like me, or Republicans, or Negroes. But he takes the law seriously, and if the law says the rights of *all* men are to be protected, then by God Gibney will see that they are. Come on inside. Let me give you a hand with that trunk. Christ, it's heavy enough. You have a friend in it?"

They entered a foyer with dark hardwood floors. A broad stairway curved up toward the second floor. They left the trunk there and Woodson led Vulture into a high-ceilinged drawing room. Hundreds of books stood in glass-doored cases that were recessed into the walls. "You've grown to reading in your old age?" Vulture asked.

"They were here when I bought the place."

The room was illuminated by candles in a chandelier and in waist-high flambeaux. Logs crackled in a wide fireplace of fluted marble. An ormolu clock on the mantel chimed the half hour. Vulture looked around with pursed lips. In one corner stood a massive piano with densely carved volutes and arches, classical palmettes and small bosses. There was a table with broad pawed feet, done with gilded leaf brackets and topped with green marble. On this stood a glittering service of cut glass in deep diamond patterns. Across the room, on a second table, was an etched silver service. There were stools of ebony, an intricate sofa of mahogany and plush, broad-seated rosewood armchairs with trumpet legs and tufted armrests. "It's not the way you used to live, Emory," Vulture said quietly.

"It was all here, came with the land. Sit down, Vulture. What can I get you? Whiskey? Brandy?"

"Brandy would be good."

Woodson poured from a decanter. Vulture saw him limp when he brought the snifters. That was new; not pronounced, but noticeable. Woodson sat down and raised his drink. "To seeing you. You could have written more often."

"That's true on both sides. To seeing you."

They studied each other in silence a few moments.

Woodson was a man of medium height with sharp aggressive features, cold, pale blue eyes, and fine brown hair which he wore to his shoulders. He had put on weight since Vulture had last seen him, which softened the ascetic and somewhat predatory look that used to mark his face, and filled out his body some, but he still looked in good condition. His hair had thinned and moved back his forehead a little and his mouth had a more relaxed and pleasant cast.

"Well," Vulture said. "The years have told on us."

"They do that," Woodson said. "It's been—what?—seven years?"

"Eight."

"What happened? They run you out of the Capitol? You just have an urge to come down home again?"

"No. I'll tell you about it. For what it's worth. Right now I just want to get slowly drunk and listen to what you've been doing." He sniffed the brandy, sipped, closed his eyes, rolled it around in his mouth, and swallowed.

Vulture's speech rang strangely on Woodson's ears. He remembered the black man from the First Southern Volunteers, fourteen years ago, in 1863: a huge, tar-black, and buffoonish fugitive slave whose physical strength surprised no one, but who was, startlingly, possessed of a great native intelligence, a quick and thoroughly logical mind. He had been desperate to learn—it had seemed almost a physical need—and he'd sought out the better-educated white officers who were willing to talk to him, and Geoffrey Williams, a schooled freeman from Massachusetts. His slurred, nearly incomprehensible speech patterns gave way reluctantly, and he became enraged with himself whenever he lapsed back into them.

"Not too much to tell," Woodson said. "I was with the occupation army and later the Freedman's Bureau. I served a term in the legislature, then I settled here in Elysium."

"Didn't know legislators were paid enough to buy places like this."

Woodson tasted his brandy. "It went for back taxes, a fifteenth of what it was worth before the war."

"I saw some cabin lights. You working it with sharecroppers?"

"What are you getting at, Vulture?"

"You wrote me you bought some land. You didn't tell me you were running a plantation with niggers."

"Everybody has a piece here. There are twenty-five families, thirty able-bodied men. The men give me whatever they can after the crops are in. I put it toward what it cost me for the land they're working. Three own their own parcels already, six more should take title next fall. Just when the hell was it you became such a jackass?"

Vulture didn't say anything for a while. Then he stood and walked to a photograph over the fireplace. "Mary?"

"Yes."

"Pretty woman. I'm sorry for what happened."

"Time goes by. You don't forget, but you move further away from it and it gets a little easier."

Vulture saw himself for a moment in a cold and wet fog, gray in the early dawn, seated numbly with Labe's body in his arms. A burial detail was moving closer. He heard the squeak of the wagon's swollen axles. Pitch torches were jammed in sockets on its sides. They made dull coronas of light in the fog. The soldiers talked to him gently until he let them take the body. They swung it atop the other corpses piled on the wagon. Then they moved off into the night. Vulture shook his head sharply, cleared his mind. "Still politickin'?"

"Uh-huh." Woodson regarded the black man with a frown.

"Have a woman?"

"One in town I see now and then."

"White?"

"What does it matter?"

"I want to know."

"She's black."

"Your whore?"

"No."

Vulture finished his brandy and poured another. "I had two black mistresses in Washington. And in the five years I was there I had thirteen different white women."

"You counted?"

"Yes, I did! And I'm not talking about prostitutes. Three were senators' wives and one was a cabinet member's daughter. With two exceptions every one of

those bitches came to me first. You know what I thought
sometimes when I was humping up and down between
those white thighs? I thought: *I'm cutting your balls off,
white man!* What do you think of that, Woodson, huh?"

"I think it's pathetic."

"Don't patronize me, you bastard."

"You know, don't you, your brother might have said
the same things."

"My brother sucked vengeance like other people sucked
their mother's tit. He fed on blood, and it was sweeter
than any milk."

"It killed him."

"Not before he got what he wanted."

Woodson took a cigar from his pocket, clipped the end
with a penknife, lit it, and puffed until it was burning
evenly. "I don't give a shit what you or anyone else does
with his life. Not really. But what happened? Once we
were friends. Now it looks like you've come all the way
from Washington just to tell me you hate white men."

"I don't know why I came. I just had to leave there."
Vulture dropped back down into an armchair, which
creaked under his bulk. He stared at the wall several moments. "You were my first white friend, Emory. Fact,
you're the only white man I've ever met who *truly* never
seemed to care what color a man's skin was.

"I fought for my freedom, Emory. You know that. I
bled for it, I damn near died for it. When I was a slave I
hated the man who owned me, and the overseer who cut
my back with a whip. There were other men too. But always *men,* not color. I didn't hate white. Because white
trained me and gave me a uniform and a gun and white
bled and died alongside me. I didn't hate white because
white built and staffed the school I went to after the war. I
didn't hate white because I met whites like Charles
Sumner and Ben Butler who fought in Congress to guarantee the freedom we'd won.

"But I learned, Emory. I got to prefer the ones who
came right out and said that the nigger was an inferior
simple-minded human who had to be watched over, cared
for, and disciplined for his own good, or even that he was
some kind of high species of ape. I preferred those men
because they were honest at least, and you always knew

where you stood with them. With the others, the old-time abolitionists, the Radical Republicans, the transcendentalists, and all the rest, you go along for years thinking you're all men together, but then one day you make some kind of social presumption, or you disagree with them, and they let you know damn fast that beneath everything they're white and you're a nigger and that's the way it's always going to be."

"None of us have been at it very long."

"Ain't gwine change in a jillion skillion years, Masta."

"Save that crap for a minstrel show. Maybe it won't change, but maybe it will. We've built the machinery, we've made a start; it won't be easy to stop it."

"Easier than melting butter in a pan. A year from now, Emory, your life won't be worth any more than mine, and mine won't be worth more than a bucket of pig slops. We've been sold out. The war ended this week, in 1877, not in 1865. And the South won."

"How?"

"Which way do you think the electoral count is going to go. For Hayes or Tilden?"

The Presidential election had been in bitter dispute since November and was still unresolved. Samuel J. Tilden was the candidate of the renascent Democratic Party, the party of the South. The Republican's choice was Rutherford B. Hayes. The electoral votes of South Carolina, Louisiana, and Florida had been contested, and neither man could win until the question had been settled.

Woodson said, "Tilden, probably. But he won't be able to do much damage. Not with a strong Republican Senate to control him."

"Hayes is going to win," Vulture said flatly.

"I don't see how, but all the better. He's been allied with the Radicals since the end of the war."

"Most of us, Emory, we begin naive and innocent, and the years harden us. You're odd; it works just the opposite with you. When I met you, you were the most practical realist I'd ever seen. Now you dream just like a little child."

Woodson smiled. "Second childhood, it gets us all sooner or later."

Vulture looked at him with hatred. "Hayes is no different from any other white man. I said they turn away from you whenever the moment suits them. Well, the moment suits Hayes, and he's not only turning away, he's taking the shackles out of storage and dusting them off. He's made us slaves again in everything but the name."

"That's a big accomplishment for one man."

"But not for one race. Hayes has made a deal. If the South delivers its votes to him, he'll give the South what it wants—federal appointments filled with Southerners, Southerners in his cabinet . . . and a return of 'home rule,' guaranteed by the withdrawal of all federal troops south of the Mason-Dixon line. From here on in the South can do anything it wants; the federal government will look the other way."

Woodson examined the ash of his cigar. "Very sound," he said at last. "There were good minds behind that strategy." He nodded, appeared to commune with himself, then looked up at Vulture. "You're right, they have won. It was an . . . *interesting* war."

"Fuck you, white man."

"So it draws to a close now," Woodson said softly. "All of it." He stubbed out his cigar with slow deliberate motions. "I wonder if it would have been any different if Mary had lived."

"What?"

"Nothing. You're welcome to stay. If it's too white, I'll find some place where you'll be more comfortable."

Vulture stared at the floor, the muscles of his jaw working.

Woodson said, "I'd like you to stay, if that means anything."

Vulture hurled his glass against the wall, shattering it. "Goddamn it to hell!" He went to his feet, stalked to the door, hesitated, then turned. "Yes, it does mean something, you white sonofabitch!" He closed his eyes, curled his hands into great fists, and pressed th m to his temples. He breathed deeply. His body loosened. "I'll stay, Emory. But there's something inside, something that keeps telling me that you're still white."

"I always have been," Woodson said.

Vulture took a bottle up to his room. Woodson got blankets and fresh linen from a standing closet in the hall for him and said goodnight. Downstairs he extinguished the lights in the drawing room and stood a few moments in front of the embers glowing in the fireplace. Then he went and hung a greatcoat over his shoulders and stepped outside onto the veranda. His breath misted delicately in the air. He moved onto the dry grass with no particular destination in mind. A hound began to bark, and a second, not much farther away, followed it. "Hush that, Tanner!" Woodson called. "It's me." The dog recognized the voice and fell silent, as did the other after a few additional unsure barks. Woodson realized he was making for the mud pond a little into the woods; but this did not cause him to quicken his pace. He reached it, shunned the stone bench, and sat on the ground. He tipped a cigar and lit it.

Woodson had been raised on an Illinois farm, but had never felt the rapport between man and earth that was integral to working the land successfully, of loving and caring for it and watching it bring forth bounty even as a loved woman brought forth children to a man, the fruit of their bond. He never understood his father's ties to the earth; his father couldn't comprehend the boy's lack of them; they quarreled constantly and bitterly. He left home in 1843 to join John Frémont's new expedition and he spent the next three years exploring and mapping the western reaches with the great Pathfinder. His spirit flowered and his body hardened under the adversity. Frémont engineered a rebellion against Mexico among emigrant Americans in California. The attempt to establish the independent "Bear Paw Republic" failed, but Woodson experienced combat for the first time there, and he was exhilarated by it. When the war with Mexico began Woodson enlisted in the army. He was with Winfield Scott when Scott took Vera Cruz and he fought in the bloody march to Mexico City. After the war he returned to the Rocky Mountains, which he had explored with Frémont, and for a while he lived with an Indian woman and ran a trap line, enjoying the solitude. But he grew bored, left the mountains, and joined a small private army of Americans under the command of a freebooter named William Walker. Walker and his men toppled the Nicaraguan government and were immediately recognized by the United States, which sought mercantile advantages, as the official regime of that country. Walker's army was driven out two years later. It fought in Central America, gaining and holding power, then losing it to rival armies of freebooters and to indigenous forces. Woodson quit when Walker began to challenge powers that were, to Woodson's judgment, vastly superior. A year later Walker's force was crushed between the huge grindstones of Great Britain and the United States, both vying for influence in South America. Most of Walker's men were killed. He himself was captured by the British Navy and turned over to the government of Honduras, which executed him.

Woodson idled in Mexico. There had been good plunder with Walker, and he lived well, even sumptuously, with four servants and an olive, fiery, and petulant whore who was plump to a point just short of fatness. In the newspapers, he watched the United States declare war against itself. Most people thought the war would be brief. But by early 1862 it was clear that the conflict was going to be long and brutal. Woodson followed it closely, intrigued with the way it was developing. Also, he felt himself sagging, becoming flaccid and blunted. So, after a week of toying with the idea, he left Mexico by ship, debarked in New York, and enlisted in the Union Army. A year later he held a captain's rank and was soon to be promoted to major. He was drinking one night in a Maryland saloon with other officers who were deploring Lincoln's decision to begin organizing Negro regiments. To Woodson, the philosophic and moral questions of slavery were irrelevant. He didn't care much one way or the other. His father had been deeply religious and of abolitionist sympathies, and, as a lingering heritage, Woodson was mildly opposed to slavery, but the issue caused him no real gut reaction. What did influence him was his own experience. There had been two black men with Frémont, and Woodson hadn't seen any difference between them and the whites in the expedition. He had known and been friendly with black and black-Indian mountain men in the Rockies. Black men had fought alongside him under Walker's command. He saw the idea of the cowardly nigger as nothing more than one big steaming pile of bullshit. And he said so. And, drunk, he offered to prove this when challenged by volunteering to serve in one of the black regiments with no upgrade in rank, even though the government was offering higher pay and easy promotions to such officers and he could have been jumped to full colonel with no difficulty.

The First Southern Volunteers was a regiment of ex-slaves. Some had been liberated by the Union Army, but most, like Vulture, were fugitives. There was also a sprinkling of freemen from both the North and the South. They were neither more cowardly nor any braver than other men Woodson had fought with. They were soldiers, and they learned as all soldiers do, through experience. By the end of the war Woodson would have led them against any troops he had ever seen. He also sensed, but didn't especially understand, a kind of fondness for the black soldiers, a kinship with them. No matter how free or potent the Negroes felt, they were never allowed to forget that their lives were not without circumscription, that this was still a white man's world. They were aliens; so they tended to give themselves more completely to each other and to their soldiering; and Woodson understood this because *he* had never had any real place in the world of other men either. Woodson also respected and admired them for the unique courage they needed in even deciding to become soldiers. Though many hated the white men who had trafficked in their flesh, they had had to prostrate and grovel all their lives before the feet of masters who quite literally held the power of life and death over them; it was not easy to cast aside such deep fear and subservience. At least half their white officers either openly hated them or considered them worthless. The Confederate government refused to recognize them as legitimate soldiers. It proclaimed them insurrectionists and the best a black man captured in battle could hope for was to be sold into slavery; more probable and more frequent in fact was his summary execution. The Negroes had to face all this atop the dangers of war shared in common by all men, and Woodson was impressed.

Woodson remained in the South after the war ended and joined the Freedman's Bureau. The bureau was a federal agency created to help find jobs for the ex-slaves, to locate and assist them in buying land, and to protect them from the abuses and depredations of the Southern hierarchy, which fought viciously to regain control and force the newly freed Negro back into his old position. In 1867 Woodson participated in the state's constitutional convention and was then elected to the state legislature. Whites in the South, and in much of the rest of the country, waited confidently for these Southern congresses of niggers, carpetbaggers, and scalawags to collapse under the weight of their own incompetence. They did not. Instead, they passed acts of universal manhood suffrage, granted sweeping rights to women, abolished debtors prisons, began the restoration of their shattered society, and, above all else, established the South's first system of public education. It interested Woodson for a while, but the novelty soon waned and he resisted the attempts to persuade him to stand for office a second time.

But politics still appealed to him. Not the closed form of the legislature, where, although there were small internecine skirmishes, everyone was more or less in agreement, but the hot and fierce contest between the Radical Republicans—the "Justice, Equality, and Freedom" party—and the old power structure, which had regrouped and was growing stronger by the month.

Emory Woodson fed on strife. It was his meat and drink. It was the pulse of his heart. Without it, his body and his mind grew sluggish and eventually he slipped into a spiritual torpor, only to be reawakened by the slow thrumming tensions, the deepening vibrancy of conflict— as a hibernating bear senses the imminence of spring, new life, and begins to rouse itself. Victory or defeat had little significance; only the contest mattered. Of course the point of any contest was supposed to be the winning, and it added a certain piquancy to the game, so Woodson did labor with maximum energies to win. But still the final outcome was not particularly meaningful to him.

A large insect fell to the surface of the pond and struggled there, sending tiny ripples away in widening concentric circles. Woodson watched meditatively, puffing on his cigar. Within moments the placid surface geysered as a bass crashed through it, seizing the insect, then plunged back down to leave the reflection of the moon shattered and twisting, the sparkling fragments rushing toward each other, recoiling, then slowly joining again until the moon was serene and whole once more. Mary had loved this pond and he had sat with her on this same spot for endless hours. She wouldn't let him fish it, was endlessly fascinated with the variety and the inevitable predaciousness of its inhabitants.

Mary Wells-Barrett was the daughter of a Presbyterian minister. Woodson had met Mr. Wells-Barrett once. The man was a frenzied old-time abolitionist who had rejoiced at the coming of the Civil War, saw the Deity manifest in it. "There can be no remission of sin without the shedding of blood," he had told Woodson. Clearly the man was unbalanced. Mary was not, but she had inherited her father's staunchness and zeal, a hard intractability. Woodson had helped her found a school in town. Later he attended a meeting at which Luther Stringfellow, editor of the *Woodboro Recorder,* told the audience that 432 white teachers had given birth to mulatto babies in the South the previous year and that another 214 had been raped or otherwise molested by niggers. Mary stormed to the platform, cupped her hands to her mouth, and shouted: "That's just plain hogwash and drivel!" Stringfellow was too startled to do anything but stand and stare at her. "I've taught colored men and women and children all over the South for the last six years. And I can tell you I have never seen one, not a single white teacher bear a Negro child in that time. [Subsequently she told Woodson she'd encountered half a dozen such cases, but was damned if she'd admit that to the likes of Stringfellow.] What's more, neither I nor any other teacher I know have ever suffered abuse at the hands of a colored man. The only time the sanctity of my petticoats and pantaloons was endangered was by a drunken 'white gentleman'!" Woodson wasn't sure if her denial of Stringfellow's charges or the casual public reference to her underthings inflamed the audience more; whichever, there were sudden cries of "Bitch," "Whore," "Nigger-lover," "Slut," and other insults. Half a dozen men rushed the platform, and Sheriff Gibney fired his shotgun into the ceiling. Woodson managed to get Mary out of the hall and away . . . to Elysium, which he assured her was the safest place for her at the moment.

They were married one week later.

It was a wild love. Woodson's most vivid memory was of her on horseback, eyes absolutely blazing, long black hair whipping behind her, shouting into the wind as she spurred her mount on, racing him to the orchard.

A year and a half later she was dead, along with the baby who had been eight months forming within her. She and Woodson had campaigned for Lawrence Reid, the Republican gubenatorial candidate, and were returning home after a night rally. It was sudden and efficient, a perfectly admirable little ambush, and completely unexpected since federal troops had been patrolling regularly and the Knights had curtailed their activities. Four of them. They opened up with shotguns and rifles from both sides of the road as the surrey rounded a bend. Woodson's hip was torn apart. He was hit once in the leg, once more in the arm, and another bullet furrowed his temple and pitched him unconscious to the dirt even as his revolver was half drawn from its holster.

An owl was hooting when he woke. The surrey was gone. He dragged himself to Mary. Blood. God, so much blood. He'd seen it all his life, but not with her, Jesus Fucking God, not with her! He screamed, and the owl took flight from a nearby tree. He clawed his revolver the rest of the way from its holster and fired all six rounds into the empty night, shrieking, and then he threw the empty weapon, as if to fell someone, and fainted across her.

Henry and a dozen other black men armed themselves and rode out when the horses returned the empty surrey to Elysium. They found Woodson atop Mary. The doctor was a miracle worker; Woodson now walked with only a slight limp and, though the change of seasons frequently caused him pain in the liver and in one kidney, it was not intolerable. Mary had taken a shotgun blast directly in her swollen belly and her growing baby, and another between her breasts. A rifle slug had entered the precise center of her right ear and exited just a little to the side of her left ear.

Woodson pushed himself erect; his knees were stiff. Old, growing old. He walked up to a knoll from which there was a commanding view of what used to be the formal gardens of Elysium. The chirping of the pond's frogs grew fainter, and was lost. He came to Mary's grave. It had been several months since he had been up here last.

There were weeds and thistles, and the grass was tall, nearly obscuring the stone.

Casualties were just that, nothing more. A year after she was dead Woodson had begun to neglect the grave. Mary and the unborn baby were casualties; the war went on. He did not visit the grave often.

He looked at the thin tombstone in the moonlight, but did not read it. If what Vulture had said was true, then the war was indeed over. This war. He had spent too many years in the South. It was his home now, he was bound to it. And he was too old. There were no more wars for him. This was the last.

And so he would die. He saw his death, a wraithlike beast padding from its lair after a long sleep. A beast still slow, a beast somewhat distant yet, but a beast of sensitive nose, snuffing the wind now and turning toward him.

"It would not have been any different, Mary," he said to the grave. Then he turned toward the house and his bed.

2

Colonel Thurlow MaCullum sat behind a massive mahogany desk, a man as finely carved and richly appointed as the furniture in his office. He was dyspeptic. He always grew nervous at crucial moments, and this afternoon's meeting was certainly of vital importance. His nervousness chronically manifested itself in severe gaseousness which embarrassed and angered him, it being, he considered, a rather low and vulgar condition. "Constantine."

"Suh?" A liveried, aging black man who was unobtrusively arranging bottles and glasses at the bar looked up.

"Bring me some of the mint."

Constantine spooned mint leaves—for the juleps—onto a pressed-glass dish and carried it to him. MaCullum chewed the leaves, hoping they would placate his stomach. He was reasonably confident, but still one could never be entirely sure, and much depended upon this meeting. The men who would be here soon represented the Democratic power of the state's three largest counties. If he controlled them, he could control the rest.

He straightened yesterday's copy of the *Recorder* so that it squared with the lines of his desk. Since the end of the war the paper had carried beneath its title the banner: *Superiority of the White Race Is a Natural Law.* The entire front page of this issue was given to a single article. MaCullum read it again.

THE COMING BLOODBATH

A guiltless White man languishes today in the Woodboro jail. The confinement of this hard-working tiller of the soil, this gallant and honorable man who served our people and our cause so well in the War between the States, is the loathsome result of the perfidious testimony of two of the most notorious, lying, drunken, degenerate niggers known to man.

Jeb Merril is the unfortunate victim of whom I speak.

Readers of the *Recorder* have already been apprised of the odious facts concerning this case. *They are also perfectly aware of the identities of those alleged "White" men who have plotted in collusion with the would-be nigger assassins!* This publication is confident that justice will be done and that Jeb Merril will be exonerated. To all who have been involved in his persecution, we say only: There will be a day of reckoning.

More urgent, and quite ominous, are the reports recently brought to our attention by citizens of unquestionable reliability and moral rectitude. These indicate that certain black fiends are sowing *seeds of insurrection* among local and outlying niggers, the aim being to form a GREAT NIGGER MOB TO DRAG JEB MERRIL FROM JAIL AND LYNCH HIM, THIS HORRIFIC ACT TO BE THE SIGNAL FOR A MURDERING RAMPAGE OF BLACK MONSTERS THROUGHOUT THE STATE. Their ultimate goal is the slaughter of every able-bodied White man and the establishment of a nigger kingdom!

We tell you frankly and simply that this will never happen, even if White men must ride saddle-deep in the blood of every black buck, woman, and pickaninny in the state to prevent it.

This may well be the moment in which the North finally realizes the depths of depravity contained in the Curse of Emancipation. When Sambo was taken from Africa, he was little more than an animal, rife with slaughterous jungle passions, a practicer of unspeakable acts, a heathenish and obscene idolater, a savage murderer of his own kind, and an eater of human flesh. We have seen thousands of misguided female teachers and missionaries attempt to educate the black beast. For their pains they have been violated in the foulest fashions, unfit to describe on the printed page. And what has this "education" accomplished? It has taught the three P's to a gibbering, apelike multitude of burly, black buffoons—Pulpit and Politics, which lead to Penitentiary.

Can any sane man believe the negro capable of comprehending the Ten Commandments, let alone the miraculous Conception and Resurrection of our Saviour? Every effort to inculcate the great Truths of Christianity but tends to bestialize the negro's nature, and by obfuscating his tiny brain unfits him for the duties assigned him, yea, even such simple tasks as the hewing of wood and the drawing of water.

We have been forced to look upon dark-faced hordes frolicking in the offices and legislative bodies of our great State, mocking and defiling the accomplishments of our revered forefathers, performing hideous jungle dances upon what they believe is the corpse of our fair Southland. Their center of power is the grogshop. Better whiskey and more of it is their rallying cry. They multiply like the locusts of Egypt.

We have, in the past eleven years, seen incidents more numerous than grains of sand upon a beach of hulking black brutes committing crimes of Murder, Assault, Burglary, Robbery, Arson, Well Poisoning,

Livestock Theft, Conjuring, Conspiracy, Kidnapping, and Willful Introduction of Disease.

And Rape. ENDLESS RAPE! Ceaseless and savage violation of terrified, defenseless White women at the brutal hands of black animals. The twisted "pleasures" of this gross crime appeal more to the negro's lustful imagination than do the facts of the punishment raise his fears and cause him to stay his attack. He sets aside all fear of death in any form when the opportunity is found to gratify his bestial desires!

Gentlemen of the South! The time has come to say: "Enough! Enough of these foul and hideous outrages! White men will no longer be preyed upon by this monstrous black beast!"

Oil your long and true rifles.

Swab your thundering shotguns.

Grease the actions of your wrath-dealing revolvers.

Press the edges of your long knives to grindstones.

The black hordes are making ready in all their wretchedness, their gorilla ferocity, and their demoniacal cruelty.

Be ye no less prepared!

We will render this a White Man's land, and the black man's grave!

It was powerful stuff, and it worried MaCullum. Within hours after the paper had come off the presses half a dozen Negroes had been beaten in various parts of the town, and another one slashed so badly he was not expected to live. A gang of white trash had invaded niggertown and gone on a shooting spree. Fortunately none of the blacks had returned fire, and deputies had driven the whites out with only one casualty, a gang member shot in the leg.

Luther Stringfellow, editor of the *Recorder* and author of the editorial, was MaCullum's only serious competition. The article was an accurate statement of Stringfellow's sentiments, but MaCullum knew that today's conference had influenced the timing of its publication. This did not help his stomach any.

The first to arrive was Naylor from Delacroix County. MaCullum came out from behind his desk, told him how good it was to see him, and then belched. "Excuse me, suh, excuse me. Some rancid butter, I believe. Seems no one keeps it properly iced these days."

"All the niggers gone to hell," Naylor replied. "You find one that knows how to keep things going, he's worth his weight in gold."

"That's the truth."

Half an hour later the room was full and beginning to haze with cigar and pipe smoke. There were a dozen men in all. Constantine moved quietly and gracefully among them, almost unnoticed, cleaning ashtrays, shifting spittoons, removing emptied glasses, and bringing fresh drinks. MaCullum occupied a large chair in a commanding position, having decided against remaining behind his desk, which might give the impression of his being too distant, aloof. He told them he was convinced they had at least an even chance, and perhaps somewhat better, of recapturing the governorship from the Republicans in the coming election.

"The tenor of the times is more favorable than it has ever been since the war," he said. "I feel we might even swing a portion of the colored vote away from those damned Loyal Leagues to the Democratic party. However, with or without them, I believe that the right candidate running an intelligent campaign can beat Lawrence Reid. The Republicans are no longer impregnable." He paused several beats, then announced, "And gentlemen, I'm not going to indulge in specious modesty, or time-wasting ploys. I think I am the candidate best suited to carry our party's standard. You know my war record. It is factual rather than immodest to say that I am held in general esteem throughout this state. You know that my business places me in frequent and close contact with members of Congress and private citizens, both North and South, of considerable influence and resources. As your candidate I can pledge an extremely well organized and well financed campaign, and when I'm elected I promise you full cooperation in whatever areas *you* feel merit attention.

"Gentlemen, forgive my bluntness, but I did not feel

this was a time for skirmishes or reticence. I have been candid with you. Please be so with me."

A man named Benjamin Oberst said, "By God, Thurlow, you jus' made me happier 'n a bear with a grub tree. I been studyin' on how to ask you this very exact thing, an' you saved me all the trouble. With you runnin', boy, ain't no race to speak of. We *got* the state."

MaCullum was appreciative and slightly humble in calculated proportions. He had been in contact with Oberst and a few more of these men for weeks. Three were unequivocally his. Two were probables. Three, including Stringfellow, were dead against him. Four could go either way. He needed eight. That would give him the three largest counties in the state and enough leverage to swing the others he needed.

"I'm interested," Richard Kirby said.

Excellent. Kirby was one of the unknowns.

Stringfellow said, "You're no—"

Judge Durfee, who had already privately pledged MaCullum his support, cut in smoothly: "I think that this is a most fortuitous announcement. I have in my pocket a letter that arrived just this morning, and with your permission, gentlemen, I'd like to read a paragraph to you." Without waiting, he drew a letter from his breast pocket, ran his hand through his silver hair, and cleared his throat. " 'As regards your question concerning the coming election in your state, I must admit to some vexation. There are two or three good men for the job, differing with some severity in their political stances, but all with attributes to recommend them. After much consideration, it is my opinion that Colonel Thurlow MaCullum is the man who offers you the best chance of regaining control of your own lives and destinies. I hope you will agree with me.' "

"The signature, gentlemen, is that of the Honorable Jefferson T. Davis, former President of the Confederate States of America. And I do indeed agree with him."

Actually, Durfee had had the letter more than a week. He and MaCullum had decided to withhold it until this meeting, when Stringfellow would surely object to MaCullum's candidacy, and use it as a trump against him.

MaCullum took in the faces around him without seeming to glance directly at any particular man. The letter had the desired effect, he saw, and he was elated. He had been a good officer, not one defeat marked against him, and he had carried his wartime training back into civilian life. Strategy was everything, and he had planned this meeting as carefully as any battle. The quick declaration of his candidacy was to catch off-balance those who had expected nothing more than feelers. This attack was to be followed by immediate support from Oberst and a frontal assault by Durfee. Stringfellow would be hurled back and would be hit by interruptions from MaCullum, Oberst, or Durfee every time he attempted to regroup and mount a counterattack. MaCullum had further weakened the man by forcing him to fight on MaCullum's territory and by arranging the seating so that, with each man given a chance to speak in turn, Stringfellow would be the last. By then, MaCullum felt, Stringfellow would be able to offer only token resistance.

"Thank you, Judge," MaCullum said. "I'm truly flattered by your and Mr. Davis's support. Its significance is great." He turned to the man next to Durfee. "How do you feel about it, Harry?"

It went very much the way MaCullum had hoped. A few men, such as Gordon and Richardson, were perfectly aware that they were being manipulated. MaCullum had anticipated this but had decided to go ahead anyway, reasoning that they would understand that he actually *was* the best candidate and *did* have best chance of beating Reid. Further, they were the kind of men more likely to appreciate the dexterity with which the desk had been stacked than to object to its stacking. MaCullum also counted on some of them jumping onto the bandwagon once it seemed to be rolling.

They came at last to Stringfellow.

Luther Stringfellow was a tall man, thin, almost gaunt. He had the face of a desert prophet. Topped by wild black hair, its planes were severe; they looked nearly sharp enough to cut. His eyes were small and jet black. His mouth was tight and thin, ridged with pale lips. He dressed habitually in dark trousers and a frock coat that fit his body tightly, like a shroud. His wrists and hands, dangling from his sleeves, were bony. He'd retained his composure through the meeting. Even when his own two partisans, Michaels and Bell, had knuckled somewhat under MaCullum's pressure, he had reacted with nothing more visible than flaring nostrils and, once, a hand clenched into a fist on the arm of his chair.

MaCullum had hoped the man would lose his temper and thus appear something of a fool; he would have to goad the editor some. "Luther?"

Stringfellow looked into each man's face before answering. "Frankly, I am disgusted with these proceedings."

"I appreciate your honesty," MaCullum said, pleased. "Would you tell me why?"

"Mainly because there are two kinds of Republicans—niggerlovers and opportunists. And I don't know which one you are MaCullum. Maybe both."

"I'll take those words as metaphor," MaCullum said.

'No, you take them literally. That's how they were meant. Now I agree with Mr. Davis that there's only two or three men worth considering for the nomination. There's Colonel Thurlow MaCullum, maybe Mayor Rawson up in Ellenville, and there's Luther Stringfellow. I like Rawson, I admire him, but he's not our man. So that just leaves the two of us. I don't know what got into ol' Jeff, writin' a letter like that. Used to be a real firebrand. Maybe old age is doin' something funny to his head."

"Perhaps it's just your frustrated ambition."

"You're a whore, MaCullum."

"I sympathize with the limitations of your reference frames."

Stringfellow looked at the others. "I don't understand you. Don't you realize how he's playing you?"

"The question," Floyd Tindal, who was one of the uncommitted, said, "is why you think you'd make a better candidate."

"Because somebody's got to stop the niggers. Because somebody's got to whip them back into line. We're entitled to govern ourselves, and in our own way. This is *our* land, not the North's or the niggers'. I'll do it. MaCullum won't. It's that goddamn simple."

Tindal said, "I tend to agree that you'd make a better governor—at least your social philosophy is more harmonious with my own—but we're concerned not with who would serve more effectively but with who has the best chance of being elected."

"Well, Jesus Christ! What are you people, blind? The white men in this state want one thing, and one thing only, and that's to crush the goddamn nigger back down where he belongs. They know I'm the one who'll do that, and they'll vote for me."

"You're living in the past, Luther," Judge Durfee said. "We tried it your way once, and the armies of the North tore us to shreds. It's a new age. It requires new tactics. We need subtlety, Luther, not blood."

"You doddering old codger, you've lost your guts is all. You don't know your people anymore if that's what you think. I tell you that they've been in agony for twelve years. They want an end to it now. They want revenge. They want things set right again, the way they used to be."

"MaCullum can give us a good campaign," John Hammond said.

"How? He says he's held in general esteem. Any more than I am? He talks about Northerners that will help. Haven't we had enough of the North?"

Someone murmured, "The interests of Northern capitalists and Southern politicians do not necessarily exclude each other."

"He tells us he'll give us a well-organized and well-financed campaign. *Any* candidate we nominate will have the mental and monetary resources of the party behind him. He feels we can capture some of the nigger votes. I tell you that the minute anyone tries to butter up those black bastards, he's going to have fifty thousand white men staying away from the polls in disgust."

"I agree," Michaels said.

"I don't," MaCullum said. He went to his desk, picked up a copy of the *Recorder,* and came back to his seat. "Luther, I want to talk to you about this."

"What about it?" Stringfellow snapped.

"You've got to stop this kind of writing. Or at the least declare a moratorium until after the election." He slapped the newspaper into his hand. "This is a revolver looking for someone to fire it, a sword begging to be picked up. We've got a tense situation in this town. You keep this up and all you're going to do is give some hotheads an excuse. And once it starts, we're going to have a lot of dead bodies."

"The niggers start anything, we'll finish it. That's right, by God."

"You damn fool! It'd be a massacre the way things stand now. We'd be flooded with federal troops. Congress would come down on us in a hundred ways. We'd be lucky if we could put so much as a justice of the peace in office."

"We're not going to see a white man go to jail on a couple o' niggers' word. And you talk about a massacre, I tell you you never saw one like what'll happen if the niggers try an' take Jeb Merril out of jail to lynch!"

"Don't be stupid with me. No niggers ever lynched a white man and no niggers ever will. That nigger mob and uprising of yours are sheer fantasy—useful in swaying the rabble sometimes, but dangerous to us now."

Stringfellow sprang to his feet. "Did you hear him?" he demanded. "He doesn't believe the niggers would cut our throats if we gave them half a chance. He loves 'em. You heard him! Come the age for his daughter, he'll pick out some big buck for her. Or maybe the Republicans bought him. Yeah, maybe that's it. They've paid him to sabotage us. You want to know about the nigger conspiracy? You come talk to my informants and listen to how they're arming, how they're drilling in secret, how they're practicing at night on sneaking up behind a white man and sticking a knife in his back. How they're teaching each other how to murder a white man's family."

"I've seen your informants," MaCullum said. "I saw the same kind during the war too, the kind that crawled out of the swamps and the backwoods and the hill country. They *had* nothing and they *were* nothing. Scum, the dregs of humanity. The war gave them boots and clothes and food and an opportunity to drown all their hate and sickness in blood. I saw that kind, the human animals, the gore eaters and the killers, the kind that served under Quantrill and rode with Bryerson's Butchers."

"Listen to him," Stringfellow shrilled. "He's turning his back on his own race. He'll hand us all over to the niggers if you let him. We'll stop him! *I'll* stop him!" He spun, knocking over his chair, banged open the door, and stomped out of the room.

Beautiful, MaCullum thought, absolutely superb.

Constantine quietly righted the chair and closed the door. There were several moments of silence. MaCullum sighed. "I suppose an apology is in order. I. . . ."

"Not at all," Judge Durfee said. "I found the scene quite valuable. Clearly we cannot bestow candidacy on a man so mercurial and excessive. He would disturb people."

"Possibly not," Gordon said. "He may, as he says, be representative."

"His tactics are crude," Oberst said. "They can accomplish only short-term results. For real and lasting victory we need the kind of subtlety MaCullum offers."

"Stringfellow would be a liability in office," Durfee said. "We would never know when he might explode and do us damage."

"He could be controlled," Gordon said.

MaCullum saw that he could not count Gordon in his camp. They lingered in discussion for another half an hour. When the last of them had left MaCullum stretched, patted his stomach, which was now quiet, and said, "Clean up in here, Constantine. I'm going for a walk. I'll be back in an hour or so."

He left the office and went down the flight of stairs on the outside of the building. The first floor was occupied by a bank, in which MaCullum owned a quarter interest. It was a bright clear day. He felt good. He had six of them for sure. Stringfellow had three. MaCullum needed the remaining two, Hammond and Carswell. He was fairly confident he could get them.

He started down the sidewalk with a sprightly gait, whistling. It really was a fine day.

Wilda, Wilda, sweet potata-girl
Wilda, Wilda, gots mah head a-twirl.

She sat with her back against the wall. Her hands were in her lap. She smiled at her fingers, which climbed one atop the other, one atop the other, one atop the other. . . . Orange light played with her. It leapt about. It sat on her. It danced away. She laughed softly with it. It lived in the lamp, she knew, the one high up on the wall behind the wire screening. She was glad of the screening. It stopped some of the others in the big room from stealing the friendly orange light and keeping it for themselves, or from breaking the lamp and making the orange light leave to find another place to live.

"Likealite, lickylite, litylite, littylike," she sang. She made a church steeple with her fingers.

In the corner an old black lady screeched and threw herself about on the floor. The chain attached to her wrist manacles clattered. She tore at the ringbolt in the wall until her fingers were bloody, and then she collapsed. Long lines of spit hung from her toothless mouth. The orange light shimmered in her eyes. She screamed. Wilda smiled at her. In another part of the room someone began to moan. A mama crawled over to the old lady and hit her until she was quiet.

A shadow fell on Wilda. She looked up. The old one had come for her tonight, the gran'pappy white. She didn't know whether to go with him right away or not, but he told her by reaching down and tugging her shift up around her waist. She was naked beneath the shift. Her belly was brown, and a little round, soft, loose. It and her hips were crisscrossed with white scars, and some of the scars had little dark tracks in them, almost the color of the rest of her skin. She'd got the scars after they'd begun taking her to that other place at night, where the men were. Her belly had grown hard and started to swell, and when the scars first cut across her the men here at home had become angry and kicked and punched her in the stomach. She got very sick. All sorts of goo and blood came out from between her legs. She thought she was going to die.

Oh doan *you hear mah true lub song?*
Oh doan *you hear me sigh?*
Way down there in Sunbury
Ah'm bound to live an' die!

Dying was something you did when there was a lot of blood, but sometimes without it. And other times there was a lot of blood and you didn't die. It was very unclear. Where was Sunbury? Dying was when you went away or they took you away and you didn't come back anymore.

Did you know you were gone? Dying was wonderful and scary all at once. When the first mama died there was lots of blood and everybody was sad, but then they were happy.

What a happy time, chil'n,
What a happy time, chil'n,
What a happy time, chil'n,
Bright angels biddy me home!

She, Wilda, Wilda, the sweet-potata girl, didn't die, and the men were satisfied once she bled, and they left her alone. Until the next time, when it happened all over again. She didn't want her belly to swell anymore.

The gran'pappy white stood over her and took his big thing out of his pants and squeezed it and pulled it. Once, after she had gone to the other house at night a few times, she had taken hold of it herself. But she hadn't understood; he wanted to do it himself and he hit her a couple of times in the face until she let go. It was turning red under his moving hand. He crouched over her and now he started to bounce up and down. He was making a funny slushy sound in his throat, and her hands, trying to clasp and hold each other, wouldn't work right for her and got all tangled up in themselves, and she whimpered.

The gran'pappy white went, "Ghhaaaa!"

A line of warm and sticky wetness slapped across her cheek. Sometimes he fell on top of her at the end. He didn't tonight, just went to his knees and braced himself with one hand against the wall. His eyes were closed and his tongue hung out and his breath was rattly. Wilda tapped the pads of her thumbs together. After a little while he took her by the arm and pulled her to her feet. He brought her downstairs. Two more whites were there and some of the other black girls.

Where is you, chile?
Where is you, chile?

Hidin' in the dark, 'neath the ol' willer tree,
Hidin' in the dark, where no one can see.

Where is you, chile?
Where is you, chile?

Jus' wants t' set
An' talk a while.

She could see them, but they couldn't see her. Not one little teeny bit. She could reach out and touch them if she wanted and they wouldn't know who had done it. No one could see her, no one at all, and she smiled.

Alworth, who was in the charge of the institution at night, watched Benson bring the girl down the stairs. "What took yuh?" he said irritably. "They late, an' we losin' money."

Benson muttered something that was as usual unintelligible. When the girl came closer to the lantern light, Alworth saw the glistening slickness on her cheek and in her hair. "Benson, you sonofabitch! I tol' yuh, you dirty 'em up, then by God you *clean* 'em up. Cain't bring 'em out all scummy like this!" He lashed out at the old man with a supple switch. The switch, which was never out of his hand, was usually enough to control most of the inmates; a shot-weighted billy hung from his belt for those who were violent or hysterical. Benson ducked away grinning a mouthful of yellow, stumpy teeth. Alworth rushed him, swinging the switch. The old man spun and went scuttling down the hall cackling laughter. Alworth pursued him only a few steps, then returned and told the other man to fetch a rag and pail of water. Roughly and with disgust, he scrubbed the girl clean. She never stopped smiling. He had a daughter about her age. Whenever he happened to think of Wilda and his own daughter, which was not very frequently, he was a little glad that the black girl was an idiot.

He and the other man tied one wrist of each of the black girls to a length of rope, then Alworth secured the end to his own wrist. "You find Benson," he said to the man. "Probably hidin' in the cellar. Jus' listen for his giggle. Crazy old coot should be locked up here 'stead o' workin'. Get 'im started on the slop pails. Ain't been emptied for days. I be back in half a hour."

He led the girls out into the night. The building was old, more than half a century. Alworth was always afraid it was going to collapse around his head some night. Originally it had been an orphanage for white children. That was before Alworth had even been born. Then it became a warehouse, and later, as the town grew and encircled it with the arms of its commercial district, a pen for slaves waiting to be auctioned on the block. After the war the Reconstruction legislature designated it a temporary orphanage for black children. Funds were appropriated for the construction of a new orphanage, but Colonel MaCullum and the other big men in town had somehow managed to divert those monies in part to the white orphanage, which was already quite adequate, and in part to the pockets of various private citizens. Alworth admired clever men like that.

So the ramshackle old slave pen was still the black orphanage; it had also become during the last half dozen years an asylum for lunatic Negroes from the town and the surrounding countryside. Alworth had worked there nights for five years. They had nearly fifty inmates now—about a dozen orphans, the rest all moon-crazy niggers. Alworth, father of five hungry children, husband of a weary wife who now received him in her bed only with reluctance, man of enterprise and imagination, had discovered the institution to be a veritable bounty from heaven. He, like every other attendant, gratified his desires with the patients at will, thus saving his wife from further tribulation, and quadrupled his modest salary by leasing girls to Henderson's bordello.

Henderson ran a lucrative operation near the levee, the wharves, and catered exclusively to the Woodboro men who worked with their hands and their backs, and to the gawky farm boys, and to the barge and riverboat men. All his girls were black—more than a third of them supplied by Alworth—and he charged thirty cents for half an hour in a tiny sweat-smelling room.

Alworth's dream was to open his own house, but he didn't have enough saved yet, and he didn't think he had as many girls as he'd need. He'd discovered that the customers only wanted girls who were, say, between thirteen and twenty years old, and, though you could slip them some borderline cases, they wouldn't accept girls who weren't at least *halfway* decent looking. There was even the bigger problem of finding girls who were manageable. Out of the fifty niggers in the asylum, he was only able to use five, and he'd had to work damn hard to get that many. Some were just plain wild, like spitting cats, and he couldn't break them no matter how much he beat them. Others curled up into tight little balls, hard as rocks, and it took the strength of four or five men to straighten them out and hold them that way so they could be useful. Just not practical.

It was a problem all right.

He came to Henderson's through the alley and banged on the door. He had to jerk Wilda, the first in line, up the stairs. She seemed as lively as a gutted catfish tonight. She was like that. Just plain strange. Some nights, Henderson told him, she'd lie there like a giant turnip, and the only way you could tell she was human was that she looked human, and maybe she'd laugh or babble some. Other nights she'd damn near rape the customer, grab him, lick him, smother him, make him finish before he'd got his pants half off. Strange one, she was.

He remembered when the federal troops brought her in, five years ago. She was maybe eight years old. Been living alone in the woods. Naked. Like an animal. Couldn't talk. Been eating frogs, berries, bugs. Never saw anything like it before. They'd waited for almost three years because she was so skinny, and didn't look anything like a girl till then. When they'd busted her, three of them, two turns each, she'd clawed and shrieked and fought like some kind of devil from the Bible stories. Fists and boots weren't enough, had to use the billy on her. A lot. It splintered her arm—which still turned at a funny angle below the elbow —broke her nose. She looked a little weird now, to Alworth anyway. Nobody else seemed to mind much.

Henderson opened the door. His chin was lost in a roll of fat. Alworth was tempted to laugh whenever Henderson talked—mouth looked like a moving hole in his throat—but he never did; he got half of each thirty cents paid for the girls. "Where the hell you been?" Henderson said. "Ah got twen'y evil and restless men in the parlor. This trial, ah tell you, we should have one ever' week. Must be, Jesus God, must be more'n five hunnert strangers in town."

"Well, we here now." Alworth untied the rope from his wrist and handed it to Henderson.

He smacked Wilda on the buttocks as he went down the stairs. She was a favorite at Henderson's. Who would of thought that, considering the beginning? Oh, he liked her all right. Topped her two or three times a week himself. But he sure wouldn't pay thirty cents for her. Then again, he never paid nothin' for none of 'em.

But who could figure a nigger? No one, 'specially not a nigger that was crazy besides. He laughed in the alley. "Them niggers, goddamn, they surely are somethin'."

After supper Swett put more wood into the stove, stoked up the fire again, and then did the same in the fireplace. He filled the big black iron kettle and the larger pots with water, put the pots on the stove, and hung the kettle in the fireplace.

His two younger brothers danced around him. One sang, "Wallace goin' courtin', Wallace goin' courtin'."

Swett made to cuff the boy, but was too slow. "G'way," he muttered, embarrassed. "Git."

The boys faced each other. One bowed to the other. "How do, Mista Smalls. Come to call on yo daughter Arrybell."

"How do, yo'sef, Mista Swett. Reckon you 'bout the uglies' thang I evuh seed. Cain't cotton how Arrybell gon' look on you wifout faintin' daid away. Best git on back home."

They burst into laughter, fell into each other's arms, and pounded each other on the back.

"Make 'em git, Ma," Swett said angrily. "Make 'em git, or Ah swear Ah breaks they haids." He didn't like his brothers and never had. He didn't like *any* little kids. They were all pesty and stupid.

Mrs. Swett was clearing the table. She stopped, looked from Wallace to her other sons, then back to Wallace. Her lower lip trembled. "Thet ain't nice t' talk thet way, Wallace." Her eyes moistened.

Mr. Swett was sitting on the households' only soft chair, whose cushion Mrs. Swett had once repaired by stuffing it with straw. He was moodily picking his teeth with a sliver of wood. He stood up. "C'mon, boys. Gots some hay that wants pitchin'." The boys followed him from the house.

Wallace knew that his father liked him pretty much, and was proud of his being a Torch of the Knights. But his father didn't like him courting Arabella Smalls. The Swetts owned ninety acres, worked fifty-five of them, and leased the remainder to Henry Smalls on a sharecropper basis. Swett's father thought the boy would be marrying way beneath his station. But otherwise he was proud of Wallace, and Swett was, after all, nineteen years old, a man and entitled to make his own decisions. Besides, Swett had seen the hot, sidelong glances his father sneaked at Arabella whenever she was around; even if he'd never get to taste it, the meat was just too tender to object to with any real force.

Swett went outside to the shed and brought in the big tub, which he set in the corner of the kitchen. He poured steaming water, tested, added a little cold water, then stripped and climbed in. His knees stuck up almost to his chin. He splashed and soaped himself vigorously while his mother picked up the flat iron from the stove, spat on it, nodded when it sizzled, then began pressing Wallace's linen shirt. His father's shirt, actually, the only truly fine shirt in the house—worn at Christmas, Easter, weddings, and funerals—but Wallace's to use for the duration of his courtship.

Freshly shaved, a little pomade on his hair, Wallace kissed his mother goodbye and left, taking the old clay-bank mare even though it would almost have been easier to walk, the Smalls's house being just the other side of a stand of hardwood that was only half a field away. He put his heels to the mare the last few hundred yards and galloped up to the house, scattering wing-beating chickens and two goats, rousing an ancient hound dog who rushed a little way after the horse snapping toothless gums and then stumbled in the dust and lay there several moments before he picked himself up and walked away in weariness and shame. "Ai-ya-ya-yaaaaa!" Swett yelled, because he loved the sound, and because he knew it impressed Arabella. He reined the mare up, swung off, and tossed the reins to one of Henry Smalls's filthy children. "Heah boy, tie 'er up."

Smalls had thirteen children, and three more had died in infancy. Arabella, at seventeen, was the oldest. Swett hated them all, except for Arabella, whom he loved, of

course. They were a terrible pack. They clamored ceaselessly for food, they were sore-ridden, one had a clubfoot,
another a blind blue walleye, another—who was almost as
large as Swett—ran about naked and giggling, which embarrassed and enraged Swett, and his thumb was always in
his mouth.

Henry Smalls was on his porch, one end of which had
collapsed years ago and was overgrown with weeds and
vines; thick green moss was advancing up the doorjamb.
Smalls was puffing a corncob pipe. Swett spat tobacco
juice as he left his mare. He didn't like the taste of the
stuff, but he enjoyed working his jaw around it and arcing
the thick brown liquid through his pursed lips. It made
him feel good, particularly in the company of older people. "Hey thea, Smalls," he said. He mounted the porch
and started to push open the front door. Smalls's hand
come down on his shoulder and spun him around. The little man's face was tight, eyes squeezed narrow.

Swett blinked at him. "Yuh?"

"Nuff yo," Smalls said. "Nuff yo come hur walk inna
house li'e yourn, take a gurl an' ack li'e us yo Daddy's
li'estock. Usen ain' an'muls! Mah house! Yo be man,
b God, ast mah pe'mission, tre t wif 're pec'. Yuh lissen,
b'God boy. Yuh unnerstan?" He had Swett by the front of
the boy's fresh-ironed linen shirt, his grimy hands soiling
the fabric.

"Leggo, yuh crazy ol' coot." Swett pushed him.

Smalls grabbed the boy and tried to shake him. "Ah
tells yuh ain' goan be no co'tin' whu' wiffout mah say! Yo
git quit o' mah lan' lessen yo ack propuh now! Ah says, ah
says!"

Swett shoved him again and the smaller man went ped-
aling backward, arms windmilling, then tripped over a
stool. He sprang up, charged Swett, and pounded him
about the head and shoulders. One of his fists caught
Swett on the nose. The boy bellowed, took Smalls by the
throat with one big hand, then began slapping him with
the other. He pressed the little man up against the rotting
boards of the house and continued to strike him.

"Don' evuh do thet agin, yuh dumb bastard! Now you
listen t' me, an' you listen good! This be mah Daddy's
land, not yours, an' Ah comes an' goes as Ah pleases. You

doan mean no more t' me than yo houn' dog. Ah nevuh gone out o' mah way t' do yuh no good, but Ah dint nevuh do yuh no harm neither. Ah treats yo daughter with all the respec' a good Christian girl's entitle' to. Yuh gots no miseries from me, no call t' make complaint. So you jus' stay out o' mah way! Heah?" He had been rocking Smalls's head from side to side all this while with heavy openhanded blows. The little man's cheeks were crimson. Swett sent him crashing to the corner of the porch. A rusty old single-barreled percussion-cap shotgun leaned against the wall there, its broken stock bound with wire. Smalls looked at it.

"You go on ahead an' try thet," Swett said. "Ah bend yuh ovuh the porch rail an' bust yo back." Smalls didn't move. Swett walked to the door. He said, "You kin shoot me when I walk out o' heah. Kin shoot me in the back near any time yuh want. Ah cain't stop yuh. But you jus' keep in mind thet mah Daddy, an' the Knights o' the Canescent Dominion, they won't take kindly t' thet at all. They pro'ly jus' tie yuh down in a pen full o' starvin' hogs."

He went inside the house. It was only a single room and it was littered with rags and dirty tin dishes, cluttered with a rough plank table and benches, some crude three-legged stools, an old wagon seat, and half a dozen filthy straw pallets pushed up against one side; it smelled of sour milk, fatback, vomit, and urine. Only a little light penetrated the greased brown paper that served as windows. Arabella stood next to her mother in the dimness. She wore a shapeless dress of rough gray cloth cinched at the waist with a red cord. Her hair was tied into two braids with red ribbons. She was a round-faced, big-boned, and fleshy girl.

"How do, Ar'bella," Swett said.

" 'Ou gots blood onna nose," she answered.

Swett wrinkled his upper lip and felt it. "Ain't nothin'." He drew his sleeve across his lip before he realized what he was doing. He stared at the red streak on the fine white linen. "Go'damn, damn, damn!" He kicked over a chair. Three children ran madly about the room screeching.

Mrs. Smalls hugged herself and babbled something. She was a string-haired, haggard woman. She wore a dirty flour sack with head and arm holes. Her belly was pendulous and slack. Her long breasts drooped down almost to her waist. "Eeeeehhhhh," she keened.

Swett took Arabella by the hand and brought her out of the house. They went past her father, who turned his back on them, through a squall of children, and out to a grove a little ways off, which grew around a spring gurgling from a rock fissure. Two of the Smalls boys tried to follow, snickering. Swett threw stones at them until they turned away. He dropped down with a sigh in the privacy of the grove, stretched out, and cupped his hands under his head. "Ah swear, Ar'bella, sometimes Ah like t' scream fo' want of a barrel stave t' beat the Smalls ovuh they haids wif. Cep'in' you, o' course."

" 'Ou gots sicha temper."

"*You* gots," he said. "Wif a 'Y.' *Yeh*-ou."

She was the smartest in the family, and had a little schooling too. But she still didn't talk a whole lot better than the rest of the Smalls, and he was trying to teach her.

She sat down next to him and ran her hand through his hair, over his forehead.

He closed his eyes. "Thet feels right good," he said. "Mah Daddy, he comin' round jus' like Ah said he would. Still fussin' an' high-leapin' some, but my Maw says he already talk to Banker Wilkens 'bout a li'l passel o' land, fo'ty acres, jus' down the road by Johnson's Holler. Goan give it us fo' a weddin' present."

" 'A's good, Ah's liken t' it. Wan's," she said lazily, "wan's t' brood sucklers fo' 'uh—*yuh*," she corrected herself.

Swett thought about that. Kids runnin' around all over the place. It wasn't a nice thought. But . . . well, maybe it was different when they were your own kids. Could try it with one. One couldn't hurt too much.

Her hand drifted over his closed eyes, his cheeks. Her warm palm fell upon his lips. He kissed it and felt desire spring into his loins. She pressed down tighter, he licked her skin. And then her hand was gone and her lips were on his. He kissed her softly at first, but gradually, under her insistence, with more strength, with hunger. She broke away and braced above him. She dipped a little, and her dress bowed down from her throat and shoulders, and he could see, naked, a great portion of her heavy pearlike breasts. She looked at him in a strange, sly way and ran her tongue over her lips. She took his callused hands and placed them on herself. Even with fingers spread and reaching his hands could not contain her fruits. She closed her own hands over his and forced him to grasp her tightly. She shut her eyes and raised her head slowly and a low barely audible sound escaped her throat. Swett kneaded her several moments. "Oh, Jesus Christ!" he moaned.

Then he jerked his hands back and sat up. "Ah'm sorry, Ar'bella. Ah truly am. Ah'm shamed fo' mahse'f." He was in torment, struggling against the bucking insistence between his legs.

Her fingers dug into his shoulders. "Wan's 'ou!"

He pried her hands loose. "No, no, you doan have t' say thet. It all right. You doan gots t' go provin' nuffin' t' me. Ah kin wait til we's married."

The girl threw herself down. Swett rubbed her shoulders lovingly. She began to sob. "Ah unnerstan'," he said. "Deed Ah does, an' Ah loves yuh fo' it." He did, too, vastly—overwhelmed by the depths of her love, as indicated by her willingness to sacrifice her chastity for his pleasure. Poor, sweet little girl! Ready to endure his embrace to show him how much she loved him. Tears moistened Swett's eyes. "Ah unnerstan'," he repeated again and again. But still, it took a long time before Arabella was consoled.

Sylvester Jackson hooked his finger in the neck ring, swung the jug up on his arm, and swigged deeply. The twelve-day-old corn ravaged his throat. Once, for a brief but sweet time, he would have scorned anything but good Kentucky bourbon, and would have drunk it from nothing less than cut glass. He had risen only to fall, and was bitter. He was a reddish brown man with large sky-blue eyes. He was Steven Rydstrom's son. The law didn't say so, but the blood did. Bill Rydstrom was Steven's son too. Only once Steven had squirted his seed into a black womb, and that was Sylvester, and once he had squirted it into a white womb, and that was Bill. They had grown up together on the Rydstrom plantation and they were brothers, even if Sylvester lived in the slave quarters and Bill in the Great House. Bill inherited the plantation early in the war when his father was killed. Needing money, he sold off a dozen slaves, including Sylvester. Sold his own brother. Like a cow. Like a hog. Later, when Sylvester won and then lost his seat in the legislature, it had been the same thing again, even worse, for with it vanished all the station and luxury he had so newly acquired. Sylvester was drunk at the moment. Such moments had been occurring with increasing frequency over the last few years.

"I tell you, this Loyal League business, this work-with-the-white-man stuff, it ain't gonna get us nothin'," he said. "Vote, tote, shoat, 's all the same. Deception and duplicity, the tongue of the realm."

Spanner and the half dozen other black men in the small general store on the edge of Hellbottom Swamp smiled indulgently. If you could understand half of what Sylvester Jackson said you were doing well. And even that half was mostly nonsense. But they could appreciate Jackson's antagonism toward the white man and, since Jackson had never given anyone reason to distrust him, he was liked well enough and tolerated in his angrier moods, and in his incomprehensible speech.

"Ain't true," said a man who was whittling a doll for his child. "Sylvester, outside mah fambly, mah vote be the most valuablest thing I own. It one thing I wou'ln't sell fo' all the money you could beg or steal the rest o' yo life."

"As unreal as a soul, that's what a vote is," Jackson said. "What can you do with it? Sell it to a white man for fifty cents? That's what they pay. Eat it? Shoe your mule with it? Trade it for seed? Ain't worth the paper it ain't written on."

"Ah won't make o' meal o' that," the whittler said stubbornly. "It make me stan' jus' as tall as any white man when it come t' electionin'. We gots some godamighty fine gennemen settin' in office. An' sure as hell weren't no ol' massas and white trash that put 'em there."

"Amen," said another man.

"Illusion," Jackson said. He drank again from the jug and wiped the back of his hand across his mouth. "You ever see old folks a-dyin' over a few months? Just before the end—just before the death rattle starts way down deep —they perks up, they feels better, they even gets out of bed sometimes and dances around—glory, glory, Hallelujah, things has come to good and the bad times is gone forever. An' then they die."

"Whut you sayin'?" a man asked. "Seems like ever' time someun tries t' talk wif you, you start t' jabber an' gibber so thet not even the 'postles wif they knowledge of the tongues could reckon you."

Jackson sighed and took another drink.

"Tell yuh," said an old man with patches of dark scalp showing through his gray hair. "Tell yuh, young un, yuh nevuh worked yo good life 'way 'neath the lash, yuh nevuh looked on three o' yo famblies bred an' raised an' sold away from yuh. Yuh nevuh——"

"I know, I know, granddaddy. We were all slaves once."

"Not from birthin' through t' sniffin' yo grave dirt, yuh weren't. Gots freedom now, gots the God's troof Day o' Jubilo. Got's mo' 'an enny nigger dast t' dream in mah day. Ain't t' say we gots it all, ain't t' say they not a mighty road t' walk yet. But li'l by li'l, it gwine come. An' some day, some day them chilliun we be great-great-great-granddaddys to, why they gwine walk side t' side wif white men, an' ain't nobody t' say they enny difference."

"And that's the day you'll see flaming water," Jackson said.

"Well whut you propose?" a man said irritably. "You wants us t' put the white man in chains an' make him *our* slave?" There was laughter.

"I propose that the government give us this state, or Alabama, or Louisiana, or Mississippi. It doesn't matter which one. But one whole state just for Negroes alone to live in. Let us work out our own destiny."

"Sylvester," the whittler said. "Ah knows it fo' sure now; you is one hunnert percent genu-wine moonstruck crazy. The white men ain't even goan stomp yo head, they jus goan fall down an' split they bellies with hilarity."

"Then let 'em send us to Haiti, or even back to Africa! They say we're such a problem, well that's an easy way to be rid of the problem."

"Whut I want wif Haiti or Africa?" a man asked.

"You can be with your own kind."

"I wif mah own kind right now."

"Africa's your home."

"Shee-it! Right heah's mah home, ain't nevuh had no other. Not a nigger in the whole country whut even knows fo' sure they is such a place as Africa."

"You people," Jackson said angrily. "Hellbottom Swamp ain't like no other place. You ain't been bothered here, you been able to do what you please because its too damn hard for the whites to get you here. But the Confederacy is going to rise again, the old masters will be back. And once they are, they'll come. They have to, sooner or later, because they can't allow you to exist."

"They come befo'," Spanner said with an edge of threat in his voice. "We lived in the swamp then, an' they died tryin' t' get us out. We kin live there agin."

"It'll be different this time," Jackson said.

And as soon as he had spoken the door opened and two white men walked into the store. Jackson saw them as summoned by his words, the instruments of his destruction, and he dropped the jug. It shattered and whiskey sloshed over his shoes and pants.

"We lookin' fo' a nigger name of Sylvester Jackson," one of the whites said.

Jackson mewled.

Spanner lifted an axe handle and turned it over in his hands. The whittler set down his doll. He picked his fingernails with the point of the long blade, eyes unwavering on the whites.

"Lem, thet one, he look like whut Jackson's s'pose t', don' he?"

"A-yuh. You Sylvester Jackson, boy?"

Jackson, terrified, could only nod.

"Got a horse or a mule?"

Jackson nodded again.

"Then come along."

Jackson inched back in his chair. "What do you want?"

"Nigger, I tol' yuh once. Now move!"

The whittler said, "Man ast whut you wants, white man. Seems how he deservin' of a answer."

The white men looked at each other. Both were armed. The Negroes' faces were casual, but all of them were watching the whites intently. The one called Lem worked his tongue around in his cheek. Then he said, "Okay, step ovuh in the corner wif me." Jackson did, and the white man bent his head close to Jackson's ear and whispered to him. "We wait outside," Lem said when he finished. He and the other white man left.

The old man had been holding a heavy harness rig while the men were present. Now he set it down and said gently, "Whut they wan's wif you, young un?"

"What's a white man ever want with a nigger?" Jackson said miserably. "Nothing for the nigger's good, that's certain. I've got to go with them. I'll be away a couple of days."

"You doan have t' go with nobody iffen you doan want," Spanner said. "We take care o' them boys fo' yuh."

Jackson shook his head. "No, it's not that simple. But thanks."

They could see by his face that he loved them, and they were a little embarrassed. They stood up when he left, and went to watch him climb up on his mule between the white men, who were already mounted. The mounts were turned, heels were put to flanks, and the three riders swung left at the fork, heading south.

Swett didn't know what to do with his hands. He put them in his pockets. He clasped them behind his back. He let them hang at his sides. Finally he crossed his arms and placed one in each armpit. Summoned by Clayton Lowery, which stunned Swett no less than if he'd been summoned by God, he and Johnny Murphy had made the several-hour ride to Lowery's plantation, had their horses taken by a black man who looked and acted just like an old-time slave, and then were told, not asked, to wait in the formal parlor by a Negro in light blue livery who was openly contemptuous of their rough dress. Swett was driven thoughtless by the opulence. Thirty-five thousand acres, that's how big they said Lowery's plantation was. There must have been half a mile of lawn and gardens alone, and he was sure the Great House was larger than the one the President of the United States lived in.

Standing under the soaring ceiling of the parlor, surrounded by lush furniture of deep-hued blue and red cushioning and polished and gilded dark wood, Swett could only respond with panic. Johnny, however, seemed to be enjoying himself and lounged easily in a chair. "How kin yuh loll like thet?" Swett whispered hoarsely. "Doan this make yo stomick scroonch all up?"

"The man gots t' squat t' shit, jus' like you an' me, don' he?"

Swett was shocked and repulsed. Johnny courted sacrilege. Lowery was one of the founders of the Knights of the Canescent Dominion, the original Purified Holocaust. He'd resigned in '68, but his name was still held in deep reverence, and when he chose to enter the affairs of the Knights, which was not frequently, his wishes were honored as if they were those of the present Holocaust.

"Why you think he sent fo' us?" Swett asked. Johnny shrugged. Swett's forehead creased. His eyes narrowed and his jaw tightened. He hunched over a little and his belly muscles tensed. His attempts at thought were similar to his attempts while sitting in a privy; each required of him heavy concentration, each was usually an abortive endeavor, and when he was successful the fruits of both labors were of about equal value. Swett grunted.

"What's the matter?" Johnny asked.

There was something there, Swett sensed it. He waved Johnny down. He closed his eyes. That was it, that was it. A little more now . . . Ah! There it was. Of course. He should have known it all along. Lowery had called him here to promote him to Wildfire, the man to whom the Torches of each Hearth in a given area reported. It had to be. That explained Johnny too. The boy, whom Swett had praised to his own Wildfire, was going to be elevated to Torch as Swett's replacement.

Swett opened his eyes and sighed. He was content, and even relaxed enough to sit down. They waited another half hour, but Swett hardly noticed. He was lazily adrift in vague plans for the Knights, simple blurred images of action, and in warm contemplation of the respect and admiration that would be his.

It took him a few moments to refocus his mind when Lowery entered, but when he did he sprang up smartly and stood as close to attention as he could manage. "Good afte'noon, Mista Lowery suh."

"How do," Johnny said.

Lowery nodded curtly and sat down without inviting them to do so. His hair was snow white, sparse on his high forehead. His face was long and thin, but his cheeks were going jowly and there was a dewlap of wrinkled flesh at his throat. His skin was burnished by sun and wind. He wore a tan hunting jacket with black velvet lapels. His high field boots were glossy. He placed his elbows on the arms of his chair, folded his hands, and rested his chin atop them. He rubbed his upper lip abstractedly against a single large diamond set in a silver band on one of his fingers.

"Which one of you is Wallace Swett?"

"Ah is, suh." Swett took a half step forward.

"You are an ill-mannered and arrogant pig."

Swett hadn't heard correctly. "Suh?"

"You've abused a certain Mr. Henry Smalls, physically beaten him, mocked his hospitality, and humiliated him in his own home."

"Ah nevuh! All Ah—"

Lowery slapped a hand against the chair arm. "Silence! You're not here to defend yourself. Henry Smalls is poor and clearly he appears elderly and ineffectual to you. But while you were stumbling around tugging your mother's skirts and wetting your pants, he was facing Yankee cannonades, rifle fire, and bayonets. He served in six campaigns, two under my own command, and was four times decorated for bravery and heroism.

"This is the man you choose to mistreat and degrade. Swett, you're a vicious little child whose only worth to date has been the demonstration of a rather crude talent for knocking niggers on the head. You will desist from offending your betters in any manner whatsoever, and from this day on you will address Mr. Smalls as 'sir' and you will ask permission of him to set foot on the land he farms and to enter his house. If he grants it, you will be grateful. You will behave in a respectful and humble manner to him at all times and you will follow his wishes to the letter. I won't speak to you again. I do not correct failure, I punish it." He turned to Johnny. "Are you Jonathan Murphy?"

"Yessuh!" Johnny was terrified.

"From what I'm told, you have a fine future ahead of you in the Knights. I want two things from you. First, be this barbarian's conscience, help him to remember what he's been told. Second, if he doesn't carry through, I want to be informed. Can you do that for me?"

"Ah . . . yes, suh. Ah s'pose Ah can."

"Thank you, boy." Lowery rose and started to leave the room.

"An' thet's it?" Swett's face was scarlet. "Thet's whut you called us heah fo'?"

Lowery paused, turned his head slightly, and said, "Yes." Then he went through the door.

The butler appeared and took them out. Their horses were brought. Swett rode pale and trembling, eyes burning into the general emptiness of the day. Johnny, confused, tried twice to open a conversation. Swett didn't respond. Lowery's plantation was two miles behind them when Swett jerked his mare savagely to a halt. Johnny rode on another hundred yards before he realized Swett wasn't with him. He turned and came back.

"You snakeshit li'l bastard!" Swett roared. "Ah sponsor yo membership, Ah teach yuh ever'thin', Ah treat yuh jus' like a—a—" His eyes teared with rage. *"An yuh do this t' me!"* He lunged and aimed a powerful roundhouse blow at the boy. Johnny ducked away, and the sudden movement spooked his horse. It reared, whinnying, and pawed the air. He fought to control it. While he did, Swett went galloping off.

Johnny had been just as surprised as Swett. Smalls, sick with frustration and anger and shame, had finally been driven to appeal to his old commanding officer. Lowery had no recollection of Smalls at all, but directed a secretary to look into the matter. Attendance to such things was one of those obligations incumbent upon men of Lowery's stature in the South. Lowery had thought that a rebuke administered in Murphy's presence would carry a sharper sting (and certainly Swett was deserving of one). But his primary reason for having Murphy there was because he reasoned that the boy, toward whom Swett felt some kind of big-brotherly affection, according to the report, would spark in Swett a sense of moral responsibility, a need to serve as *exemplar,* which of course would be a much deeper motivation to treat Henry Smalls properly than was Lowery's threat. Clayton Lowery was quite possibly the finest planter in the entire South; he knew land and crops as if they were extensions of himself. But he knew next to nothing of human beings.

Swett pushed his mare brutally, maintaining close to half a mile between himself and Johnny. He was making low, guttural sounds in his throat, and there were images in his mind of Johnny taking a shotgun blast flush in the chest, of him writhing beneath a slashing bullwhip, of him. . . .

Rutherford B. Hayes publicly swore the Presidential oath of office on Monday, March 5. The South fell into a sinkhole of depression; four more years of this intolerable oppression; my God, would it never end?

Scattered reprisals were taken against black men throughout Dixie. In Woodboro, Hayes's ascendancy was of less immediate impact than the impending trial, but it did serve as an excuse for another assault against the town's Negroes. One was stabbed to death, several were beaten and whipped, and a Loyal League meeting hall was burned down. Sheriff Gibney and his deputies drove wandering blacks back into niggertown, where, out of sight, they would not catalyze trouble, and used pistol barrels and shotgun butts and occasionally a round or two fired in the air to turn white gangs away from niggertown.

But even as the South bewailed Hayes's election, and black men suffered for white men's bitterness, a small cadre of wealthy, influential, and political Southerners who had been the architects of Hayes's victory were already meeting in offices and parlors and in the plush chambers of private clubs to hammer out the specifics of their return to power.

A mourning dove lamented in a honey locust tree above a sluggish river. Vulture lay on his back chewing needles from a longleaf pine and savoring their pungency. Two woodpeckers were telegraphing insanely to each other in the woods behind him, racheting indecipherable messages in frantic bursts. A squirrel chittered at something in annoyance. Vulture watched fat white clouds drift through the pale sky above.

He could have gone to Canada, South America, Europe even; he had enough money saved and these were all sensible options. But blind impulse had driven him South, and he was only now beginning to understand why. The despairing edge was leaving him, he felt a loosening through the whole of his massive body, brief moments of peace stole up on him. The harsh winters, the strange accents, the stiffness and angularities, all the subtle alienness of the North which had oppressed him without his even realizing it were behind him. He was back home, where things were gentle and known, walking the dark soil from which his roots had never really been wrenched, coatless in sunny late-winter days, happy—as with old friends— amid the sweet gums, the sycamores and willows, the rosebuds, creepers, and wild azaleas, the flushed deer crashing through the forest, the raucous mockingbirds. In bitterness, confusion, and fright he had turned home, to the South, which was his mother and which swept him up in strong comforting arms and soothed and solaced him.

It was so good to be back.

He was lying on the bank of a river that wound through Elysium. A man named Hector sat beside him watching for the first sign of tightening in the lines that depended from two long cane poles into the river. Butts wedged into the dirt, the poles rested on forked sticks. The fishhooks were imbedded in frogs which Hector and Vulture had caught and killed, then belly-slit to prevent them from floating. The frogs now lay on the muddy river bottom, swaying a little in the lazy current.

Vulture had baited Woodson the first few days, but the white man ignored the challenges, once even laughed. Vulture met Elysium's blacks. They weren't, as he'd first thought, Woodson's field hands, his slaves. Elysium was a community of hard and aggressive men who had a wary respect of each other and had banded together simply because it was advantageous to do so. Jealous of their independence, but willing to cooperate, they forced high crop yields from the fertile soil. And they had secured the old plantation as a kind of military camp. Sentries were posted at night, hounds were chained at various places to warn of intruders, there was an impressive stock of weapons—with which most men were proficient—and some of the buildings were equipped with bullet-stopping planks, rifle ports, and barrels of water and buckets of sand to fight fires with.

These were the kind of autonomous and determined black men who especially rankled the lower and more dangerous types of whites in the South, and thus the blacks most likely to be attacked and murdered. In fact, many of them had been menaced in the earlier days of the Reconstruction, and even at Elysium one had been shot down as he plowed his fields and two more had been wounded on separate occasions.

Hector nudged Vulture, who had closed his eyes and was almost asleep. "Yuh?" Vulture said. "Interest?" Hector was one of the handful of blacks who lived in the Great House with Woodson. He was a lean and silent man. Vulture sat up. The tip of his pole was quivering and the line angled sharply off to the side. "That looks good." He stood and went quickly to the pole, eased it out of the ground and off the stick. He was careful not to put tension on the line and disturb the fish, which was turning the frog over, positioning it for swallowing.

Vulture grew excited. He felt the most delicate of tugs . . . once . . . twice . . . three times down the length of the pole. Then, after an agony of poised waiting, the tip of the pole arced and the line pulled upriver. Vulture jerked hard and set the hook. The pole bowed. The upriver pull stopped. At the end of the line was an immovable weight and solidity. "Jesus," Vulture said. "He's on, and he looks like the one we want."

Hector got up and removed the other pole, laid it on the bank so it would be out of Vulture's way, then squatted down with his haunches on his heels to watch.

Vulture pulled back on the stout pole with gradually increasing pressure. It nearly doubled, but the fish didn't move. Vulture gripped the pole in one hand and gently struck the butt with the palm of his other hand. The vibration traveled up the pole and down the strong braided line. He struck again, and this time the fish made a slow, wide loop. Vulture followed the movement with the tip of the pole, keeping tension in the line. It was clearly a big and strong fish and would require some time to wear down, some skill to keep the line from snapping. The fish eased downriver. Vulture tried futilely to turn it back up against the current, which would help to tire it. But he couldn't and so he had to walk down the bank after it. Hector stood up and followed a few paces behind with his hands in his pockets. Vulture maintained constant pressure on the fish, directing it in toward the bank, reluctantly allowing it to move back out when it resisted him too forcefully.

At one point the fish was determined to drive its way across to the opposite bank. The pole, the line, and his long arms combined to give Vulture nearly forty feet of leeway, but the river was much broader than that at this place and the fish could not be stopped. "Got to go in with him," Vulture said to Hector, and stepped into the water. The fish took him in to his shoulders and then deeper, and for a few moments he had to tread water with one arm. Then the fish swung upstream and Vulture returned to the shore, dripping, feet squishing in his boots. He worked the fish back to the point where it had originally taken the bait. The line went deep and stopped. Vulture tried tugging it. He twanged the pole. Nothing. His arms tingled with weariness. "He's dug in to rest," he said. "If I don't take him now he's going to start all over again. What do you think?"

"Get 'im," Hector said.

Vulture braced, then gave the pole a sharp jerk. The fish stirred. Vulture jerked twice more. The fish bucked back and thrust downstream. It shook its head from side to side, sending shock waves through the pole. Vulture tried to force it toward shore. The pole bent into a horseshoe. It made sharp crackling sounds. Vulture yanked a handkerchief from his pocket. The line was tied at the tip of the pole, but did not end there. It continued down to the midpoint, where it was tied again, and thence to the butt, where it terminated in a third tie. The cane began to splinter. The fish fought wildly. Then the pole broke and left Vulture with only a short length in his hands. He grabbed the larger, dangling portion and worked up it until he reached the free line at the tip. He wound this line twice around his hand, which was protected by the handkerchief. He locked the fingers of his other hand around that wrist and began backing away from the river. The fish came grudgingly, but its best efforts had already been expended. It thrashed in the shallows, then was out of the water. Vulture hauled it several feet farther before he dropped the line and went with Hector to the fish's side.

It was a huge channel cat. Long whiskers drooped from its jaw, tiny eyes stared stupidly, mouth and gill covers opened and closed slowly. Its scaleless bluish body iridesced in the sunlight, its forked tail turned to the side, then straightened.

"Fo'ty, fo'ty-five poun's," Hector said admiringly. "You played 'im jus' right."

Vulture found a thick branch and hit the catfish hard, twice, on its sloping head. The sleek body stiffened, quivered, and then went slack. Hector gave Vulture the sharp long knife he kept sheathed at the back of his belt. Vulture turned the fish over, opened its belly, pulled the guts free, and cut out the gills. He threw the gills into the river. While he gathered and soaked grass and then packed it in the fish's intestinal cavity to drain off the body heat, Hector picked up the offal and brought it to Friend, who was chained several yards away.

Friend was a large, deep-chested, red and black hound with a great flat head, fearsome yellow eyes, and long jaws studded with teeth that were half the length of a man's thumb. He was a ferocious brute who was never out of his master's sight, and he permitted no one to approach Hector closer than six or seven feet. He had succeeded his sire, with whom Hector had lived for eight years as a fugitive slave in Hellbottom Swamp. Friend was a nightmare beast who, as his father had done, lunged and raged at the end of his chain in utter silence; there was something Hector had done to the dogs' throats with his knife when they were pups. Man and animal could move as silently through forest or swamp as a cottonmouth, and both were as deadly.

While Friend tore large dripping mouthfuls from the catfish guts and swallowed them greedily, Hector and Vulture sat down beside the fish carcass and lighted pipes.

"We git Melanie t' cut it up t' steaks, cook it in a covered pan wif onions an' bacon an' pepper sauce. Goan be right delicious, it is."

For Hector, speech at such length verged on garrulousness. Vulture liked the man immensely. It was impossible to know him, and his reserve, his self-reliance, his air of completeness in himself fascinated Vulture and made him envious. They smoked until Friend had finished the guts.

Then Vulture forced a forked stick through the catfish's lower jaw and slung the fish over his shoulder, holding it by the stick. Hector loosed Friend's chain from a poplar and wound its end around his wrist. The dog rushed for Vulture. Hector slammed it back. "Git shut! *Shut!*" Reluctantly, Friend allowed himself to be controlled.

They left the river and walked home through the pine woods. Vulture remained a good few yards to the side of Hector and Friend. Occasionally Friend would bare his teeth and Hector would jolt the chain and tell him to stop. The late afternoon sun fell in golden patches through twined branches above them. Jays screeched, chipmunks scampered for cover, twice foxes sprang away from them. They flushed a covey of quail; the birds exploded from the brush and sped away on whirring wings nearly too quick for the eye to follow.

Vulture was almost happy.

It was worse in town than Woodson had feared. Buggies, surreys, and wagons snarled at intersections. Drivers cursed and sometimes slashed at each other with whips; he saw a pair grapple and fall to the cobblestones. The sidewalks were awash with unshaven men in homespun, flannel, and denim. The hotels were sleeping three and four to a bed; stables, storage sheds, any place that offered shelter and room for a man to roll himself up in a blanket was being rented at high prices. Tents were pitched in the outlying districts and in vacant lots. The smell of bacon, fatback, and mush hung about cooking fires. There were waiting lines at most saloons. Dice games drew crowds at alleys and corners. A desultory Indian and a plump slatternly woman in green satin and dark stockings danced on the platform of a patent medicine wagon while a man in a stovepipe hat sold brown pint bottles to the spectators. Planks had been set atop barrels and behind them strident men hawked whiskey and beer from kegs and buckets. There were numerous families. The children were flush-faced and sportive, as if they were at a carnival.

Woodson rode to the Woodboro Guaranty and Trust and mounted the stairs to MaCullum's office. A black servant admitted him.

MaCullum shook his hand warmly. "My dear Captain

Woodson, come in, sit down, make yourself comfortable please."

"Mister," Woodson said. "Not captain. The war's been over a long time."

"So it has, so it has. But I'm told your Negroes still call you Captain. Is that correct?"

"They're not *mine*, MaCullum."

"Quite right. Bourbon?"

"Fine."

MaCullum snapped his fingers and Constantine brought two drinks. The white men seated themselves across a small marble-topped table.

"I was delighted by your note," MaCullum said. "I've always felt that we should get to know each other. It's unnatural for two men of such . . . influence . . . to live in the same town and be virtual strangers. But what is it that brings you here now?"

"We're sitting on top of a riot, MaCullum. I've done what little there is to be done on my side. But my side isn't going to start it. I think you can help defuse your side."

MaCullum swirled his bourbon and stared at it, trying to decide on the right ploy. He stood, went to a window, and opened it. Street sounds filled the office. MaCullum looked down and stared several moments before returning to his chair. "I could tell you that a riot would mean nothing to me personally, and that even if it did I couldn't do anything. But both statements, I'm sure you know, are not true.

"No one man can arbitrate a mob's behavior, but I *have* taken what steps I can. I've arranged for the more impetuous sons of some of our planters, the kind capable of rallying rabble to them, to be kept at home by their fathers until this is over. The most brutish and violent of our local sharecroppers and white trash have been warned to stay away. And the sheriff of Gantry's Landing has sent three deputies, at my request, to help Sheriff Gibney. I grant that's not many, but they're skillful and absolutely trustworthy men. There are also some twenty men in the streets, indistinguishable to the eye from the riffraff, who are in the employ of myself and—other 'friends of the peace.' Most of them would be happy to hang a nigger for fun, but they're being paid to talk against mob action and to warn us of any dangerous plans. Although I personally loath and detest the Knights of the Canescent Dominion, there *are* certain indirect channels of communication available to me. I can assure you that the Knights have been forbidden by their leadership to enter Woodboro before the end of the trial.

"There is a very specific reason why I want to prevent a riot." MaCullum raised his eyebrows and leaned forward slightly, inviting Woodson to ask what that reason was.

"It would favor Stringfellow," Woodson said flatly.

MaCullum sat back, stunned.

Woodson said, "It's been clear for months that you were going to bid for the nomination. And equally clear that Stringfellow is your only strong competition."

MaCullum had Constantine bring them fresh drinks, and in the interim he regained his poise. "You're quite correct, of course. Your perspicacity only convinces me that I was right in thinking we should establish some sort of loose partnership."

"Toward what end?"

"Let me put it this way: Who would you rather see as governor of this state, Thurlow MaCullum or Luther Stringfellow?"

"Lawrence Reid."

MaCullum waved a hand, as if shooing a pesty insect. "The Republicans are not going to win."

"Why not? We've had only minor setbacks since the last election. We'll be able to mobilize again. And Hayes, our new President, is a Republican, as you might remember."

"None of that matters. I guarantee you that things will change radically by the time of the election."

"Because Hayes bought the presidency? Because the price he paid was our betrayal?"

"My God! How did you learn— What *else* do you know?"

Woodson smiled.

"All right," MaCullum said. "Yes, that's what I meant. And if you know that, then you also know there's no chance you can win. We are our own people again! That means *we* are going to rule, and we do it either by Luther Stringfellow's methods, or mine." MaCullum paused. "The niggers will follow you, Woodson, even if they don't understand what you're doing. They *trust* you. With you stumping on my behalf, we could take this state by land-slide!

"Don't look at me like that. Think! You're no one's fool. You can have virtually anything you want. Power, position, money. Lord, man, we can even bring you in as lieutenant-governor during my second term. And I'll give you my word that the Negroes of this state will be dealt with fairly.

"Woodson, credit me: I am not a nigger hater. I *know* Negroes. And obviously you do too. Slavery was unfortu-nate. It's gone now; it won't return. We do indeed have a moral obligation to the Negro. But it is *not* served by granting him total freedom, by trying to delude ourselves that he is equal with the white man, that there are no fun-damental differences between the races. He is backward and childlike, Woodson. You know that. Cast upon his own resources he has no choice but to fall idle, to starve, to become corrupted, which allows the Stringfellows to rise among us and jeopardizes his poor black life. We must preserve and protect the Negro, as a mother cares for her infant. For he *is* an infant. We must return him not to slavery, but to a state that incorporates what was best in slavery: our benevolent guardianship in return for his loy-alty and a little labor.

"The time will come, Woodson, when the Negro will take his place in the ranks of the civilized peoples. But that time is decades, centuries, perhaps even a millennium away. And it is our sacred trust to guide and succor him while he evolves. The South admits to its errors; let the North admit to its own. Help me, Woodson! Help me save what was best in our antebellum world. Help me restore the dignity of the white race and the hope of the black race. *We owe this to the Negro!* You know in your heart that I'm right, that the good future of both races lies in my hands and in the hands of men like me.

"What do you say, Woodson?"

Woodson lifted his glass, drank, and set it down on the table empty. He wiped the back of his hand across his lips and stood up. "I say you're a sonofabitch, MaCullum. I say you're a vicious and incredibly stupid man. You and your kind may win. And not just the election. But win or lose, I'll do everything I can to destroy you. I say: Thanks for the bourbon, and go fuck yourself."

He walked to the door. Constantine was there, opening it and saying, "Your hat, suh."

"I don't indulge in petty angers," MaCullum said from behind Woodson's back. "The offer stands. You think about it. There's one other thing, too. If you don't contact me by tomorrow night, you'll regret it. Go over your past, Woodson, say about six years ago, and see if you think my threat is idle. You're welcome for the bourbon. I've a lot more of it. This time tomorrow would be fine. I'll be waiting for you."

Constantine said, "Goodday, suh," and closed the door.

Walt hated everybody—the goddamn white trash running through his town like a wild fever, that bastard Jeb Merril grinning up in his cell, the sonabitchin' niggers, even Jules Gibney cleaning his rotten stupid guns over and over and driving his men like some mad mule skinner. The deputy had had hardly any sleep during the last three days and was now walking the streets as if in a thickening fog. It wasn't enough that what he saw through his bloodshot eyes frequently blurred, or that sometimes his legs just refused to hold him up any longer, making him stumble toward a wall to lean against, or that he had drunk so much coffee that his stomach was in wild rebellion and threw back most of the food he tried to put in it. No, that wasn't enough by God; two days ago his daughter had to go and rock her high chair over and break her collarbone, and then his wife had to pick yesterday to come down with a throat as red and raw as a piece of fresh-butchered meat. Doc Whately said they'd both be all right, and Mrs. Gibney had moved in to help out a while. But it was all too much, too goddamn much, and this morning, when he'd dragged his exhausted body out of bed an hour before dawn, he'd paused while pulling on his boots, and sitting on the edge of the bed he began to cry. Just rocked and hugged himself, and bawled like a baby.

When this trial was over he was going to tell the sheriff he needed a week off. First he was going to sleep for three straight days, then he was going to build a toybox for Julia and finish that sewing table for Lucinda, leisurely, pleasurably, and end it all up by taking them for a day-long picnic on Sagmill River. And if Gibney wouldn't give him the week off, then he'd quit, by God! But he knew the sheriff would, and he felt better thinking about it.

Walt checked his pocket watch. It was one-fifty, time to start for the courthouse. The militia trooped from its headquarters on Perry Street every day promptly at two o'clock, marched to the town square, and drilled before the courthouse for precisely one hour.

Gibney had brought the commanding officer, Lieutenant Turner Brown, into his office and tried to talk him into stopping.

"No Sheriff," the black man said, "Ah'm sorry, but we cain't do thet. We got a constitutional orduh t' maintain the peace an' law o' this state. We ain't 'tagonizing no one. We doin' our duty. You kin understan' thet."

Gibney grumbled something. He knew Turner Brown a little, and couldn't question the man's sincerity. A pretty damn good nigger, he thought grudgingly. He shared Turner's sense of duty, and he had to admit that, although he had little use for niggers in general, he was relieved to be backed up by the militia's guns. Still, he felt he had to say something more. "If somebody does start somethin', you people are likely to be slaughtered by the time I can reach my front door."

"Thet the shell, not the sweet-nut. Ah was with the Massachusetts Fifty-Fourth at Fort Wagner. We took cannon fire pointblank from both flanks t' reach them parapets. They made bloody paste outten the sand an' whut was left o' our bodies. If they was evuh a time t' turn tail, thet was it. Don' reckon Ah goin' t' do it now."

Gibney had shrugged and looked for a moment almost as if he were going to shake hands with the black man. But he hadn't, and that was the end of the interview.

The militia was drilling by the time Walt reached the square. Lester Stample was already there, walking glum-faced between the blacks and the mob of whites who gathered daily to harass the black soldiers. Another deputy sat in a chair outside the jail. Stample scowled at Walt for being late. The crowd grew more numerous each day. Walt noticed more women and children than he had seen before. The language some of the women used against the militia shocked him.

Today there were almost as many curses directed at him and Lester as at the militia. But being so weary made them easier to ignore; he settled into a slow rhythmic stride and his mind happily began to shut down and fold in upon itself. Though still moving, he was very nearly asleep.

He saw the rock rise out of the mob and drop down against the head of one of the soldiers. He saw the black man drop his shouldered weapon and crumple to the cobblestones. But it was not until the crowd roared that he reacted. He brought his shotgun up, his mind replaying the scene and trying to identify the man who had thrown the rock. The mob was raging now and beginning to edge forward.

Turner Brown called: "Collummmn *halt!*" The militia stamped to a halt. "Lehhhhf *face!*" The soldiers turned to the mob. "Reeaady *arms!*" Nineteen rifles were whipped from shoulders and held diagonally across chests. Fingers rested on trigger guards, thumbs went to hammers. Brown opened the flap of his holster. His hand curled around the butt of his revolver.

The mob wavered. Here and there were men calling for reason and placing hands on the shoulders of other, angrier men; but mostly the mob seemed ready to ignore the weapons they faced, waiting for some signal to rush the militia.

Stample shoved into the whites and seized a bearded man by the shirt. Others pushed and jostled the deputy. "Walt, help me for Christ's sake!"

Walt shook his head. He tried to reach Stample, but met resistance. He forced his way through the first ranks of the crowd, and then there was a man in a slouch hat before him with a Bowie knife. "Back off, depity, or Ah slit yo gizzard." Walt's stomach spasmed with fear. Then he was swept up in quick, savage fury. He swung his shotgun up and down and laid open the knife-wielder's scalp. The man went down. Hands reached from the side. Walt kicked for a groin and another man fell. He bulled and clubbed his way to Stample. Stample was on his knees trying to protect his head from the blows that were falling on it. He still clutched the bearded man's shirt with one hand. Walt bellowed rage and lashed out with the barrel and stock of the shotgun and with his boots. He was punched. His shirt was torn. A knife opened a shallow line across his forearm. A man in front of him ducked a blow, then rushed again. Walt brought the double barrels to bear on the man's face. "Yuh want it?" the deputy shouted. "Yuh want both loads? C'mon, yuh bastard! *C'mon!*" The man backed away. Walt crouched slightly, turning on the balls of his feet and moving the shotgun slowly. *"You* want it? You?" His finger twitched on the first trigger. The circle around him widened. "What's the matter?" Walt yelled. "Where'd all the big bad men go, huh!"

"Walt!" It was Gibney and the deputy from in front of the jail. "Okay, you done good, son. Now rest easy with that scattergun."

"Gonna kill me one, Jules." He was still turning. "Gonna kill me the first shit-suckin' sonabitch what moves."

Gibney moved forward and gently raised the boy's shotgun until it was pointing in the air. Walt jerked back. Gibney tore the gun from him and slapped him across the cheek. *"Walt!"* The deputy trembled and blinked several times. Then he groaned and his shoulders slumped. Gibney patted him on the back and handed his shotgun back to him. "Lester, take yo prisoner in an' lock him up," Gibney said. And then to the mob, "Break up now! There ain't anythin' more for you here. Go on and get out 'fore there's more trouble an' people start gettin' hurt." A corridor opened and they passed out of the crowd, stopped before the militia. The soldiers were facing the whites with expressionless faces, their weapons still at the ready. The soldier who had been felled lay unmoving.

The crowd had begun to loosen and some of its members were drifting away. But many remained. "Break it up," Gibney shouted. "I told you, move on there!"

"Let's go," someone said. He took several persons with him.

A big-shouldered farmer called, "Are we goan be bluffed by nigguhs an' a nigguh-lovin' sheriff?"

Gibney strode to him and slashed him across the face

with his pistol barrel. The farmer screamed and his hands went clawing to his face. Dark red blood spurted from between his fingers. Gibney took him by the shoulder and spun him toward Walt. "I'm goin' t' arrest every man here who don't jump like a frog when I tell him. An' when my jail's full, I'm goin' t' chain 'em in the basement. An' when there ain't no more room I'll start shootin' off kneecaps."

Seeing the big farmer reduced so quickly destroyed what remained of the crowd's belligerence. It broke up and dispersed.

The unconscious soldier was carried into Gibney's office and Doc Whately was summoned to attend to him and to the farmer, whose nose was broken and whose mouth was split. Gibney took Walt to the side. He uncorked a bottle of whiskey and told the boy to drink. "More," he said. "Get a couple o' good swallows in your gut. That's it." He took a slug himself before closing the bottle. "Now I want you to go on home. You take a hot bath, sleep six or seven hours, and have a good meal before I see you again."

The boy opened his mouth to protest, but didn't say anything. He just nodded and mumbled thanks.

After Walt left Gibney, he went to the telegraph office. He took a sheet of paper, addressed the message to Governor Reid, and with the pained effort of semiliteracy wrote the words in block letters. SITUATION WOODBORO TRIAL DESPERT NEED US TROOPS REAL BAD MUST HAVE THEM OR PROBABLY RIOT IN TOWN. He signed his name and gave it to the operator. "Send this right away. And run over the answer as soon as it comes." The man read the message. He whistled softly. "An', Tom," the sheriff said, "anybody hears about this, anybody at all, I'll lock you up for interferin' with the process of the law, bein' an accessory to violence, an' half a dozen other charges."

The reply arrived two hours later. Reid regretfully had to inform the sheriff that recent orders from Washington denied him the power to employ federal troops at his discretion. He had cabled Washington requesting that they authorize a force to Woodboro, but he was not optimistic. He urged the sheriff to do all in his power to preserve order and wished him good luck.

Gibney tore the telegram carefully in half, then into

quarters, then into eighths. He balled up the pieces and threw the wad into a corner. "Shit," he said. He went to the stove to pour another cup of coffee.

3

"Doan care whut they tol' us," Swett said angrily. "This changes evuhthin'."

Johnny Murphy shook his head unhappily. "We *cain't,* Wallace. We got *orders* t' stay away."

Swett glared at him. "Ah'm tellin' you the Knights is all goan be theah. Iffen we the only Hearth thet doan show up, then the fust thin' evuhbody goan say is we dint have the brains t' figure thet it all shinin' in a differen' light now. An' the secon' thin' is, they goan say we had the brains but we was jus' too cowardly t' fight the Great Nigger Horde."

"But the Wildfire would o' told us if the orders was changed."

"There ain't been time, yuh dumb bastard. The paper jus' come t'day. They cain't git the word out thet quick."

Swett had called an emergency meeting of the Hearth in the abandoned barn it used when Jimmy Hildenbrandt, the only member who could read, informed him of the contents of today's *Recorder.* "Give us thet part about the troops agin," Swett said.

Hildenbrandt scanned the editorial. "Heah it is. 'This paper learned last night that Lawrence Reid, infamous nigger-loving Republican governor of our state, has maliciously refused to send United States soldiers to protect the unjustly accused Jeb Merril from the Great Nigger Horde which plans to murder him in Woodboro tomorrow. Twice in the last two years Reid has sent such troops to protect the lives of savage nigger murderers. But now, when a White man's life hangs in the balance, he gleefully says *No!* and sits back to await the slaughter of this honest White victim at the hands of ebony savages.' Those are the exact words, Wallace."

"Y'all heard it," Swett said gravely. "Yuh know what Luther Stringfellow says. The White man look weak t'morrow, the Nigger Horde goan make its move. Once thet happen, it jus' may well be too late fo' all o' us."

Leonard Sikes slammed his fist against the wall. "We cain't let it happen!"

"You damn certain we cain't. An' we ain't!"

"Thass right!" Billy Thompson said. And most of the Knights nodded their heads or slapped gun butts. Only Johnny Murphy and one other looked doubtful.

"We meet here at dawn t'morrow," Swett said. "Iffen we leave wif the fust sun, we be in Woodboro an hour 'fore the trial." He looked at Johnny. "Thet mean ever' man. Y'all know the penalty fo' disobedience t' a direct order."

When the Hearth assembled the next morning, every man was present. The hooves of their mounts were drumming on the road before the first roosters crowed.

It never occurred to Woodson not to attend the trial. But he didn't want any of Elysium's blacks to go. There were several people in Woodboro who would be happy to put a bullet in him if a riot did begin. His skin was white, though, and would protect him in the confusion. The black men had no such advantage, and would be targets.

"Don't tell them what to do," Vulture said irately. "You're not Ol' Massa, or even the company commander anymore."

"It's a simple question of sense. If I were going to step off a cliff unknowingly, I wouldn't think a man who warned me was trying to give me orders." But Woodson felt faintly uneasy, and he wondered if there might be some small part of him that did enjoy the occasional and subtle trappings of bossman.

"Maybe being able to walk off a cliff no matter what people say to you is what being free really means."

"That freedom's all yours," Woodson said.

"I want it, and every other kind there is. I'm going with you."

Three others decided to ride in too—Henry, the sentry who had stopped Vulture the first night, a man named Apical du Genestoux, and Six-Finger Sadler, who had an extra, jointless, and rigid digit rooted just below his little finger.

They circled so as to arrive in the southern end of Woodboro, niggertown. They saw many horsemen, sometimes parties of five and six, and a few family-laden wagons. Most were white, but there was a scattering of black riders, and a few more on foot. Woodson was uneasy about the Negroes. They had enjoyed at least the rudiments of freedom and equality in this state for the last several years and, though they knew the white man was agitated by this trial, they saw no reason to remain away, either believing that the law was capable of giving them the same protection it had more or less done in the recent past, or else feeling that to hesitate would be to betray their hard won rights and to encourage the white man to attempt further encroachment. Woodson understood that and he respected the blacks for it. But still he wished they hadn't come. It could be very bad.

He felt suddenly cold. He shivered, and the sensation passed. He wondered if his body had sensed the Beast, who by this time must have drawn closer. It was a relentless hunter, the most relentless.

They rode through niggertown's dusty streets past shacks with mud and stick chimneys, past naked black children who stared at them, past pigsties in grassless yards, and were followed by a pack of mongrel dogs that worried the horses. Here and there stood white frame houses with tended lawns and flowerbeds, the homes of black merchants and the more successful black tradesmen. Many of these houses flew the Stars and Stripes and several of the flags were larger than the one in the town square. They stopped before a modest dry-goods store with a small shed at the rear in which there were a buckboard and a pair of mules. The shed was large enough to hostel half a dozen more animals. A black man came through the door as Woodson reined up. "Ah's pow'ful sorry, Massa," he said. "But Ah gots mo' white gennemen's ho'ses stabled now 'n I kin rightly handle." Then he saw the four black riders. He looked to Woodson again and tossed his head as if to say it was all beyond him, then said to them, "Plenty o' room fo' yuh, brothus. Jus' bin careful not t' allow no white trash ho'ses heah. Ho'se thet give consent t' carryin' thet kind o' animul ain't worth the powder t' put a bullet in its brain."

"The troof, God's holy troof," du Genestoux said.

"His horse too," Vulture said, indicating Woodson with his thumb.

"Sure. He with you, thet good enuff fo' me."

They put the horses in the shed. "We need a guard," Woodson said. "If it happens, this is our escape. We can't leave it to chance."

Henry slid his Winchester .44 from its scabbard. "Ah didn't come fo' no trial. Reckon y'all can tell me how that went. Got me fifteen rounds in the tube heah an' Ah can reload in less'n half a minute. Don't figger no one else can lay down cover like me. So Ah expect y'all better get over t' the courthouse."

Woodson and the other black men looked at each other. "All right," Woodson said.

Jules Gibney struck a match, lit a kerosene lantern. He trimmed the wick and went down the stairs to the courthouse basement. The lamp illuminated dusty piles of old furniture, wooden filing cabinets, and huge cobwebs. The sheriff went to the far side, to a stout oak door secured by three heavy padlocks. A thin crack of light was visible at the bottom. Gibney knocked three times, then three times more.

"Yeah?" said a muted voice.

"It's Gibney." He slipped a folded piece of paper with his initials under the door. It was a simple and near foolproof code. Then he unlocked each of the padlocks. He heard the heavy bar being removed from the other side. He opened the door.

A deputy was standing there with a shotgun leveled directly at Gibney's chest. The sheriff had given orders that anyone with him be gunned down, even if it meant shooting through him. The deputy peered around Gibney, then lowered his gun and said over his shoulder, "It's all right." There was a second deputy in the small room, and two Negroes. All of them were armed. There were bedrolls on the floor, and bottles of drinking water, tin plates to which traces of a recent meal adhered. The guards were two of the men sent by the sheriff of Gantry's Landing. The Negroes—Leon Clover and Blueberry Poteet—were the witnesses against Jeb Merril. Gibney had held them in protective custody two weeks and had moved them from the jail to the courthouse basement five days ago. They had guts all right. Their families had already been escorted from the county by the militia, and their homes had been burned to the ground a week ago. After the trial, either the militia or Gibney would have to see that they reached their families safely.

"It's time," Gibney said. "Leon and Blueberry, you boys leave yo guns here. Can't have armed witnesses in court. It looks all right so far. Court's full-up o' course, an' the judge got t' do a lot o' bangin' fo' order. But we got eight deputies in court, two more out back. Got a pretty damn nervous mob in the square—white and black—but there's deputies posted there too, and Turner Brown's militia is lined up in front of the courthouse. Think we can handle it, think we're gonna come through."

Gibney led them upstairs. An angry murmur swept the courtroom as the Negroes appeared. The judge banged for silence. A man shouted, "Nigger bastards, we gwine cut yo hearts out!" The judge ordered him ejected. He scuffled briefly with two deputies until one cracked him over the head with a gun barrel.

There were nearly 150 spectators. More could have been squeezed in to stand around the walls, but Gibney would not permit that. About a fourth of them were black. The prosecutor and attorney for the defense made their opening remarks, brief statements in which the former stated he would prove that Jebediah Merril did willfully murder one Eustace Clover, Negro, and that he would ask the death penalty, while the latter told the jury of eleven whites and one black that this case would never have come to trial if their fair state had not been crushed beneath the pernicious iron heel of Radical Republicanism and that he was confident the jury would acquit his client without leaving the box as soon as they had heard the evidence: self-defense was the right, nay the holy obligation of every living creature on the face of God's good green earth, and as sure as God created the waters, the firmament, and the heaven, Jebediah Merril had killed Eustace Clover in self-defense.

Jeb Merril kept turning his head around at the defendant's table and grinning and waving at friends.

The first witness was Leon Clover, brother of the deceased. With slow careful questions the prosecutor drew from him a simple story. Jebediah Merril and Eustace Clover had been neighbors. A good stream ran through both their properties and both depended upon it for the irrigation of their crops. Merril, upriver of Clover, had dammed the stream to create a pond on his farm, and then dug a channel which diverted the water north to the property of Orin Honeywell, his cousin. Clearly, this would have spelled the destruction of Eustace Clover's farm, which he had worked since the war, and the mortgage on which had just been paid off last year. Eustace Clover decided to ask Merril to channel the runoff from his pond back to the stream's natural course. But, never having spoken to Merril and knowing Merril's reputation as a furious nigger hater, Eustace asked his brother Leon and Blueberry Poteet to accompany him. Leon and Blueberry remained by the pigpen, some thirty yards from the cabin, while Eustace went up and knocked on the door.

"Jeb Merril," Leon said to the prosecutor, "he take one look an' see it a colored man theah an' he start wavin' his arms an' screamin', *'Git off mah land, git offen mah land, you black nigguh bastard!'* Eustace back up a step or two an' try t' talk t' him. But Jeb Merril all red in the face an' squealin' like a dyin' pig. He run forward an' knock Eustace down an' kick him. Eustace scramble away, then he git up an' he yell back: 'You cain't treat me like this, white man.' Jeb Merril say, *'You jus wait right heah, nigguh, an' Ah show you whut Ah kin do!'* Then he run into his cabin. Ah called t' Eustace. Ah said, 'Eustace, thet white man crazy, we bes' git us away from heah.' But Eustace doan pay me no heed. An' the very nex' thing, they's a shot from inside the cabin. Bullet come right through the window. Eustace fall on his back. Jeb Merril step through the door agin, say, *'How you like that, nigguh?'* an' he shoot Eustace two, three mo' times.

"Ah doan think he knowed me an' Blueberry was theah till we started t' run. He fire the rest o' his pistol load at us, but he dint hit us. We come straight away heah t' Woodboro an' tell the sheriff."

Blueberry Poteet told essentially the same story. Jeb Merril's attorney declined cross-examination. "It would be more likely," he said, "for blood to flow from a turnip than the truth from the mouths of these two . . . Nigros."

Sheriff Gibney was called to the stand. He testified that he'd ridden out to Jeb Merril's farm after the two Negroes notified him of the shooting. The body of Eustace Clover had been dragged away from the house and dumped atop a manure pile behind the barn. Clover had been shot three times in the chest. The sheriff made a thorough search of the area and was unable to find any kind of weapon which Clover might have dropped. He then went to investigate the stream. It was dammed to create a pond, and the run-off was spilling into the natural bed. However, there was indeed a new channel, which would take the water directly north to Orin Honeywell's property. This channel was wet and muddy and had small pools, as if it had been full quite recently. The sheriff also found a shovel with fresh turned earth clinging to it at the scene.

Gibney was jeered when he stepped down and there were shouts of *nigger-lover*. The judge rapped for order. When it was quiet, Jeb Merril was called to the stand. Several persons whistled and applauded. Merril waved. Deputies threw out two white men before order was restored. Merril claimed that the Clover brothers and Blueberry Poteet were notorious wife beaters and drunkards. They hated him because his crops were always much larger than theirs, the product of his honest and hard labor as opposed to their shiftless laziness. On the day of the shooting he'd been coming in from the fields when he saw the Clover brothers and Poteet skulking around his cabin, where, his wife being at a quilting bee, his three young daughters were alone and helpless. He demanded to know what they were doing. They gibbered at him unintelligibly and made obscene gestures, obviously drunk. Merril ordered them off his land. All three suddenly flourished knives and attacked him. He struggled with them briefly and was fortunate enough not to be cut. Then he managed to break away and run for his cabin. They pursued him. Merril reached his home, slammed the door, and drove home the bolt. The Negroes were trying to break down the door. While his young daughters screamed in terror, Merril rushed to the cabinet in which he kept his revolver, loaded the weapon, and, just as the door was about to splinter, fired once through the window. Eustace Clover fell down, and the other two black men fled. Merril stepped outside to see how badly Eustace Clover was wounded. The Negro gained his feet and attacked him with his knife, and Merril was forced to fire twice again. To protect the sensibilities of his children, he had dragged Clover's body away from the house and left it behind the barn. That, he said, was all there was to tell, and every word of it was God's holy truth.

No other witnesses were called. The prosecution and the defense gave their summations: Jeb Merril was guilty of cold-blooded murder and should hang for his crime; Jeb Merril had heroically defended his own life and the chastity and lives of his three young daughters against the onslaught of three drunken black savages, and he should be acquitted immediately.

But the jury felt that some deliberation was in order, and retired. After fifteen minutes the spectators in the courtroom grew restive. At thirty there was a loud grumbling. At forty-five, the whites were glaring at blacks, and there was much open, angry talk.

The jury returned. When they were seated the judge asked if they had reached a verdict. The foreman rose and said, "We have, Your Honor." The court tightened. "We find the defendant guilty as—"

A white man with a drooping mustache jumped up and roared, "The hell you say!" He pulled a revolver from beneath his shirt and fired at Leon Clover and Blueberry Poteet. Clover fell dead and Poteet hurled himself to the floor.

Sheriff Gibney killed the white man with two shots. Then someone else fired and the sheriff was hit in the chest and driven backward to the wall. Five more slugs from different revolvers struck him. His pistol dropped from his hand. He slid slowly down the wall, leaving a wide red streak, and came to rest in a sitting position. His legs were bent, knees high and spread somewhat. His head drooped forward between his knees, then he leaned slowly and fell to the side, dead.

There were shouts and screams. Deputies and specta-

tors exchanged wild fire. Men pushed, shoved, shot, and
knifed each other, crawled beneath benches to hide or
rushed to reach the weapons at the rear of the courtroom.
Everyone entering the court had been disarmed and the
guns and knives were in the charge of two deputies. But
many men—black and white—had hidden second weapons
in boots, in the crotches of pants, and beneath shirts and
coats. Three Negroes had overwhelmed the deputies
guarding the weapons an instant after Leon Clover had
been shot. They commandeered the guns and fired blindly
into the first wave of whites to surge against them. They
went down beneath the second wave.

Vulture was sitting between Woodson and a fat-lipped,
surly white farmer. When the fighting began the farmer
snaked an old paper-cartridge revolver from his jacket
pocket and cocked and aimed it at Vulture's head. But
Vulture's hands moved as soon as he saw the weapon, and
one grasped the barrel, the other the farmer's wrist, just as
the revolver came to bear. He twisted the gun so that it
turned and pointed at the white man's chin. The farmer
gaped in horror and his eyes crossed as he stared at the
muzzle. Vulture laughed once at him, short and unpleas-
antly, then forced the man's finger back against the trigger.
There was a crash and a blossom of flame and white
smoke, and the farmer's jaw was shattered. A tooth and
fragments of bone went spinning away. Vulture pried the
weapon from the dead man's clutching fingers and tossed
it to du Genestoux, who was the only one of their party
not carrying a firearm.

Du Genestoux cocked the gun and aimed carefully at a
deputy. The deputy was armed with a Winchester and was
hysterical, working the action of his weapon and firing in-
discriminately into the spectators. Du Genestoux considered him more of a threat than anyone else he could see at
the moment. He pulled the trigger meaning to kill the
man, but the deputy dropped his rifle, grabbed his
shoulder, and began to shriek; du Genestoux was a poor
shot, which is why he had not concealed a firearm, but he
was satisfied with the result.

The air filled quickly with the smell of burned powder,
vomit, and urine. Vulture reverted by instinct to a soldier

of the First Southern Volunteers. "Out the back, Cap'n?"
The locked front door was impacted with struggling men.

Woodson looked to the rear. The prosecutor was leaning against the judge's bench holding his side. Blood
seeped between his laced fingers. The judge was not to be
seen. Two whites were beating a Negro before the exit.
"No, we'll run right into their arms that way. Take the
first window." He pointed with his revolver.

A bullet creased du Genestoux's cheek and ripped his
ear in half. He screamed without knowing it and fired
three shots at the first armed white man he saw, missing
each time. Then Woodson's hand came down on his
shoulder and Woodson said, "We're taking the window.
Let's go." Du Genestoux told Six-Finger Sadler, who was
on his other side.

Sadler was armed with a shotgun, stock and barrels cut
short. He'd carried it for years saying, "If a man be so far
from me he got t' use a rifle, then he be far enuff that I can
sneak away. Closer 'n that, ain't no gun better 'n this." He
had only brought two shells in addition to the two already
in the chambers, and now he was unhappy with himself;
he hadn't really expected trouble, carrying the gun on a
loop inside his coat more because of habit than anything
else. Sadler followed du Genestoux toward the window,
eyes and gun swinging from side to side.

A mob of more than a thousand persons had waited
outside the court building, spilling into the square. Maybe
a third of them were black. Of those, half were "good niggers," no lovers of the white man, but customarily careful
not to irritate him. Many had at first mixed with the
whites, rolling their eyes and saying, "Yassuh!"s and expecting that to stand them in as good a stead as ever. But
they had discovered that the whites were mean today, that
appeasement was not possible, so they had withdrawn to
stand with the other black men, the ones who kept away
by their *own* choice, the ones from the Loyal Leagues and
the small farms, the ones who depended upon the white
man for nothing save an occasional mortgage renewal and
periodic supplies.

The white crowd was in a holiday mood—once the
blacks moved away—and men offered each other chaws of

tobacco while the few women admired the homemade clothes and store-bought bonnets of women they'd just met, and the children, fewer still, played tag. Here and there dice games were underway and boys moved about selling box lunches and dipper drinks from foamy buckets of beer. But after the first two hours the crowd grew sullen, and still later an unnatural quiet fell over the square and whites and blacks waited for the verdict in silence.

Lieutenant Turner Brown stood on the top of the courthouse steps with folded arms looking out over the crowd. Except for an occasional shifting of weight from one leg to the other, he hadn't moved since the trial had begun. His men were ranged on the steps beneath him, standing at ease with their weapons. There was little heckling; and several of them found the silence more unnerving than the loud insults they'd been lashed with through the week.

Brown heard two muffled explosions. He turned and looked stupidly at the courtroom doors wondering what the sounds were; accepting them as shots would have been too horrifying. But they were followed almost instantly by two more, and then a quick volley, and he had no choice. His hand went to his holster, opened the flap, and seized the butt of his Navy Colt. Some of the militia were looking at him with frightened faces. Beyond them whites were moving forward. One shouted, "The nigguhs kilt Jeb Merril!" The cry was taken up instantly by dozens more.

"Listen t' me!" Brown yelled. "There's no—"

There was a quick spattering of shots. Bullets chipped the stone steps and went whining away, and three of the militia twisted and fell.

"Open fire!" Brown commanded.

The soldiers threw their weapons to their shoulders and fired almost without aiming into the mob, which was rushing now. A few white men fell. The whites shot back. Four more of the militia dropped. Brown shot a man in the stomach. The whites were atop the militia before the soldiers could reload their old single-shot rifles. They clubbed with the stocks, but went down as grain before a scythe. Brown was hissing in rage through clenched teeth. He shot another man, a boy really, who was in the vanguard, and missed a third. Then a shotgun blast ripped into his chest and he bounced off the doors and pitched forward and went rolling down the steps. Boots ground into his body as the white men surged over him and began battering at the locked doors.

The courthouse windows were set high up the walls. A struggling group of blacks and whites pressed around the one to which Woodson and his party headed. Panic rendered distinctions of race suddenly irrelevant and each man clawed for his own salvation. A white man had pulled himself up and was standing on the sill straining to open the jammed window.

Vulture flung people aside, grabbed the white man by an ankle and the back of his shirt, and lifted him high into the air. Men shrank back in snarling fear. A bullet smacked into Vulture's shoulder with a little gout of blood and he grunted. Woodson found the man who had fired and killed him with a quick shot before he could get off another round. Vulture hurled the white man, who crashed through the window with a shower of glass. Vulture seized Woodson by the jacket, jerked him up with one hand, and sat him on the sill. "Go on," he yelled. "I'll hold 'em."

Six-Finger Sadler was knocked down. He fell between two benches on his back and saw a white man standing over him with a heavy length of wagon spring poised. Sadler jerked up his shotgun and squeezed the first trigger. The gun roared, bucked in his hands. The white man's crotch blossomed red. *Sonofabitch,* Sadler thought, *three shells left. I get outta this, I gonna carry a pistol too.* He gained his feet and followed du Genestoux to the window.

Vulture kicked a Negro in the stomach, which sent him staggering backward, doubled, and kept the window free. "Haul ass!" he shouted to du Genestoux. He menaced the others around him with his derringer. An old black man with gray hair and a furrowed face was stumbling hysterically toward him, pursued by three white men clubbing him with pieces of doweling. The old man turned with a shriek, whipped his arm in a looping arc, and slashed open the throat of the nearest white man with a straight razor. One of the other whites worked behind him and lifted his club high with both hands. Vulture shot the white, surprised that the derringer was accurate at that range. Half a dozen steps and the old Negro collapsed into his arms. Vulture lifted him to the sill. "Jump, Uncle, jump." The old man disappeared.

The barred doors to the courthouse were bulging inward with the strain of the battering they were receiving from the other side. Du Genestoux fired the last two rounds of his pistol into them, then leaped up to the window. He paused on his knees to catch his balance. A gang of white men appeared at the rear entrance. Two or three were armed and they began shooting at the scrambling blacks. One, in wild eagerness, hit two white men before his third bullet found a black. And the black was du Genestoux, and the bullet hit him in the spine. He screamed and pitched headlong through the window and landed flat on the ground as if he'd belly whopped into water.

Vulture fired the second barrel of his derringer, but at that distance the shot was wide by several feet. A frantic white man presented himself before Vulture with a rifle. The muzzle poked into Vulture's throat and the white man screamed, "Move, nigger!" Vulture ducked to the side thinking, Dumb bastard. The rifle fired when Vulture shifted and the muzzle spat searing flame onto his skin, but the bullet passed harmlessly. Vulture kicked the man, shattering his kneecap, and tore the rifle from his grasp.

Sadler hung his shotgun carefully in its coat loop, then sprinted for the window. He vaulted up and through in a single fluid motion.

Vulture turned the rifle on the whites streaming through the rear entrance. He didn't know if he hit anybody, but the sudden fire sent them diving for cover, which was good enough. He threw the empty rifle away. As he turned to escape he was knocked aside by a white man who charged with his head low, butting, and who then scrambled up and through the window. Vulture followed him. The front doors splintered and banged in and whites flooded into the courthouse.

Vulture came down on both feet in a narrow areaway between the courthouse and the brick wall of a private home. Woodson was guarding one direction, and Sadler, having just replaced the spent shell and snapping the breech of his shotgun closed, the other. Du Genestoux lay at their feet groaning. The white man who'd cleared the window before Vulture ran to Woodson's side. He saw in a moment that Woodson was with the Negroes and he backed away in fear and disbelief. "Get out of here," Woodson said. The man turned and ran toward the square. Two more Negroes dropped through the window and fled down the areaway to the rear of the courthouse.

"We're dead if we go either way," Woodson said. He told Six-Finger to smash through a window in the house. Sadler used his gun butt. "Apical," Woodson said to du Genestoux. "Can you move?"

The black man grunted in pain. "Mah back is broke. Finish me, Cap'n. Doan want them trash t' have me."

Woodson hesitated.

"Please, Cap'n!"

Woodson shot him behind the ear. They went through the window into a carpeted dining room. Vulture became entangled in the heavy drapes. He pulled. The cornice ripped from the wall. The door was flung open and a pale young white woman appeared with a shotgun in her hands. She trembled, lower lip caught between her teeth. Sadler swung his own gun to bear, but Woodson pushed it aside. He leveled his revolver at the girl and said quietly, "Drop your gun please, Miss. We don't want to hurt you. We're only trying to escape a mob." The girl's eyes rolled up in her head and she fainted.

"That was stupid," Sadler said. 'She could o' fired at least one load befo' you dropped 'er."

"She hadn't cocked the gun," Woodson said. He stepped over the unconscious figure into the center hall. "Otherwise I'd have let you kill her."

Vulture slipped the derringer back into his pocket and picked up the girl's shotgun. Sadler noticed the blood and asked, "How bad?"

Vulture's shoulder was a dull ache, his right arm responded sluggishly. "I'll do."

They started up the stairs to the second floor. A man's voice called, "Eleanor?" and then with a little alarm, "Eleanor, where are you, dear?" A portly man with white hair and spectacles came around the corner above them. He stopped short and stared. Then he screamed, *"Murderers!"* and ran back. Woodson pounded clumsily up the stairs after him, cursing his game leg. Vulture streaked past him and caught the white man from behind. He slammed the white against the wall. The man's head snapped back and struck with a thud. Vulture released him and he fell. The hall was illuminated by a skylight in its center. Vulture, whose head barely cleared the ceiling, reached up and undid the latch, pushed the skylight open, and hoisted himself up, through, and onto the roof. He helped Sadler and then Woodson up, with his left arm, then reset the skylight.

Below, whites appeared simultaneously at both ends of the areaway between the court and the house. Five men spilled through the courthouse window, three blacks and two whites. The whites at either end of the areaway opened fire hitting all of the men in the center and a few members in the opposite parties. Then they converged. A man stuck his head through the window Sadler had smashed, saw the collapsed girl across the room, and said, "Look like trouble heah."

He climbed in, a balding man in grimy overalls, a sun-burnt man whose hands were callused and large-knuckled and whose few remaining teeth were yellow and cracked. His eyes were fixed on the girl; on her open, white-stock-inged legs which were visible almost to the apex of her thighs amidst a flair of petticoats; on the tender halves of breasts revealed by her low-cut bodice. *So fine, so fine!* He'd never seen anyone that elegant and delicate and ex-citing, and all unconscious and helpless besides. He went to her and dropped on his knees.

"What is it?" someone called from the window.

"Doan know yet," he snapped. One hand moved over the girl's crotch and the other forced itself beneath her bodice, and the fingers of both closed and tightened. He squeezed her hard, and she whimpered. His jaw clenched but his lips remained open and he expelled his breath in high little whistles.

"Hank? Hank? Whut yuh got?"

He jerked as if struck, hearing others climbing through the window. "Nigger raper," he said hoarsely. "Look roun' fo' 'im, goddamnit!" He released the girl, tearing her bodice in his haste to pull his hand from her breast. One round globe with a large pale pink nipple was fully exposed. He sprang up shaking. "Looka here," he rasped. "Looka here whut the black animul done!"

There were curses and cries for blood. Men ran about the dining room and into the parlor, to the kitchen, throwing aside furniture and banging open doors. "We got 'im, we got the sonabitchin' bastard!" someone cried from the hall. A Negro was dragged from a closet and thrown to the floor. Boots kicked at him from all sides and he curled into a ball trying to protect his head and stomach.

"Ah dint do nothin'!" he screamed. "Ah run from the court an' hid t' save mah life. Ah dint touch her. *Please!*" His front teeth were kicked out. His ankle was stomped on and broken.

"Hold up!" Hank shouted. He thrust men away from the black. "We want t' do this propuh an' give the rotten nigguh bastuhd whut he deserve."

"Right!"

"Thet's it!"

"Le's go," Hank said. "Drag 'im outta heah."

Two men seized the dazed Negro by his legs and hauled him to the kitchen and out the back door. Some of the others gave him an occasional kick. His head bumped down the steps as they pulled him into the yard.

The morning had gone well. There hadn't been any real trouble and Walt had begun to believe that everything was going to be all right. He was still dog tired, but he knew the whole business would be over in an hour or so and things would get back to normal then; that boosted him, gave him the strength he needed to get through the remainder of the day.

He and three other deputies had been assigned to random patrol in the area encircling the town square. They were to check taverns and put a stop to talk that might lead to violence. There was a bad mood in town, no denying that, but from what he had seen in the square folks were pretty well under control, and he hadn't discovered much to fret about on his rounds—just a couple of half-drunk sharecroppers who changed their tunes right enough after he roughed them up some. When he'd come within a few blocks of his own small house he had paused and debated with himself. He sorely wanted to check in on

Lucinda and Julia. He rubbed the back of his ear with his finger, worried one boot with the toe of the other. Five minutes, he decided. Just five minutes. Wouldn't hurt anything. He made a turn and hurried down the street.

He entered his house and smelled chicken stew, of which he was inordinately fond. He went to the kitchen and found Lucinda at the stove, Julia on the floor banging a pot with a spoon. "Hey, buttercup," he said to his wife, "what you doin' up an' fussin'?"

She came to him and kissed him and said, "Ain't had no fever fo' hours now. Got no mo' excuse fo' layin' about, an' I know my poor man goin' t' be hungry when he comes home this night. The shame of it all—I ain't cooked a meal fo' you near on five days now."

Walt squeezed her. "Goddamn, I love you!"

"Don't you use that language in front o' the baby," she said, but she gave him another kiss.

Julia threw aside the spoon and held her arms up to her father, the right one ludicrous in it tiff splint and bulky bandages. "Dadadadadadadadadada," she said, and had been saying since he had entered. He swept her up and she giggled. She pulled off his hat and swatted the back of his head. He nuzzled her neck and cheek. She shrieked joyously and squirmed and kicked against him.

"Sit down an' I'll pour you a cup o' coffee," Lucinda said.

"Well. . . ."

"Oh go on. You've earned it. It's all made. You'll be up and out in a fingersnap."

Walt held the cup in one hand and kept the other arm looped around Julia's waist. She hit him on the ear with her splint. He said "Ow!" and she laughed. She'd adjusted well to the splint; it now seemed to her a quite marvelous attachment and they couldn't stop her from whacking things with it.

Walt overstayed himself, mostly because Julia was in such good spirits and responded with delight to everything he said. Lucinda sat on the other side of the table and smiled at them. Finally he said, "I got t' go. I just truly got to." He gave the baby to Lucinda.

She lowered her lids partway and said softly, "You hurry home now when you're done, hear? Cause the stew just a bitty part o' what I got t' show mah man how much I love him."

"Oh, I will," Walt said. "You can just believe I will." He picked his hat from the table and his shotgun from the corner and left, whistling and spring-footed.

A block later he stopped whistling so he could hear the noises better.

Gunshots.

Jesus Christ.

He started to run toward the square.

A Negro burst into view, legs pumping and arms wind-milling, casting anxious glances back over his shoulder. "You! Hey, you!" Walt called. Hoofbeats drummed and nearly a dozen riders appeared, bearing down on the black man. "Stop!" Walt shouted. "Rein up there!" The riders didn't hear him so he fired one barrel into the air. The riders halted and looked at him. The Negro clambered up a tree. Walt held his shotgun ready and jogged toward the horsemen. "What's going on here?" he demanded.

Wallace Swett was whipping his limping old mare, but she was still several hundred yards behind the rest of the Hearth. She'd gone lame shortly after they'd set out this morning. He'd forced her on for another quarter hour, but when the limp worsened he'd got off, found a stone in her shoe, and dug it out with his knife. He'd been sloppy, though, and cut her hoof, and after that the best she'd been able to do was a slow trot. Swett was furious, but there was nothing to be done, and the Hearth hadn't reached Woodboro until well after noon. By then there was no chance of getting near the courthouse, so after glaring at the niggers in the square and on the court steps and seeing that things seemed under control for the moment, he took his men off and they searched until they found a saloon that wasn't too full. Gunfire from the square had brought them rushing into the street an hour and a half later.

Swett heard a gunshot. His men stopped. "Come on, yuh stupid ho'se!" he ranted. He neared and saw a deputy approaching the others. He stopped his horse, slipped his revolver from its holster. He held it in one hand and grasped his wrist with his other. He aimed very carefully, then pulled the trigger.

The slug hit Walt half an inch below his badge, directly in the heart. It passed through his body and erupted from his back with a spout of blood. His face assumed a look of bewilderment. He took three more steps, a gross red stain spreading across his shirt, and then he fell forward to the street, the shotgun spinning from his hand.

"Get thet nigguh!" Swett shouted to his men.

The initial thrust of the white mob had been against the militia on the steps. As soon as the black soldiers were overrun the whites launched a second attack against the few hundred blacks who were banded on the eastern rim of the square, and who had already begun to flee. There was a quick flurry of gunshots which brought down whites and blacks alike, but then, since the bulk of the weapons were long guns, and not the newer repeating types, the shots became sporadic and infrequent and empty weapons were used as clubs. Running Negroes were grabbed from behind, struck, spun backward to other white hands which pummeled and mauled them and then threw them farther back. Passed through the mob in this fashion, some were killed and many more severely injured. When they were finally let loose to fall insensible to the ground they were trampled as the whites rushed over them.

One young black bleeding from half a dozen knife slashes ran screaming into the pa k, pursued by the band who had cut him. The closest white was only a step behind and he lashed out at the boy as he ran, the tip of his Bowie knife cutting open the youth's shirt and slicing into his skin. At the center of the park the boy found the way blocked by more whites. He veered to the side and in desperation leaped up on the stone war memorial at the base of the flagpole. The whites gathered round, jumping and cutting at him. The boy clung to the flagpole and shrieked and kicked. His pants were quickly ribboned and saturated with blood. He flung his head back in agony and when he saw the Stars and Stripes flapping above him he bellowed and hacked at the rope with the blade of his small clasp knife. The rope frayed, then parted, and the flag came fluttering slowly down. "He desecrated the flag!"

someone shouted. Many of these whites had served in the Confederate army and had done their best to destroy that same flag, and still hated it, but suddenly they filled with righteous anger on its behalf and two of them climbed up on the rock, one behind the boy and one before him, and they stabbed him to death. He fell to the ground. The flag slipped down beside him, one corner coming to rest on his thigh and beginning to soak up the bright red blood. More Negroes were running through the park in front of other whites, and the men left the boy's body to join a new chase.

Across the square, in her townhouse, Mrs. Catherine Heermann was holding the drapes back from her living room window. She watched the Negroes being run down in the park. Her thin fingers stroked her throat and little thrills of excitement rippled her stomach. "Oh," she said. "Oh my." A rifle ball fired several hundred yards away punched a neat round hole in the window and crackled the pane in a spiderweb pattern. It also struck Mrs. Heermann high in the center of her forehead, lifted the top of her skull as if it were hinged, and splattered blood and pieces of brain tissue on the white plaster wall behind her.

Most of the blacks were able to escape the square. They fled down streets and through alleys ahead of shouting gangs of whites; they hid in sheds and privies, in crawl spaces beneath houses, and in root cellars. Several, especially those who lived in Woodboro and who had enjoyed if not amicable, then at least equitable relations with the town's whites, burst through fence gates and pounded on front doors begging to be let in. A handful were admitted and hidden by whites; most were not, and a few were shot down on the porches.

Six or seven black men with guns burst into a dry-goods store. One shot the white owner when he reached for a pistol. The others turned and fired a volley into the whites who were sprinting up the street after them. The whites took cover and returned fire. Bullets shattered glass, ripped through the siding and punctured cans, broke crockery on the shelves. One Negro was hit in the hip. The black men dragged bolts of cloth and sacks of salt and flour to the front, and rolled up pickle and molasses barrels. They crouched behind the barricade and settled down to a steady exchange of fire with the whites.

Hortense McClintock sat on her front porch in terror. She was seventy-three years old, an invalid who lived with her son. She'd read the *Woodboro Recorder* avidly all last week and knew that the muffled gunfire she was now hearing meant that the Great Nigger Horde had risen. She could not believe it! She had been confident that a display of determination would cow the niggers, and that later the black ringleaders would be rounded up without loss of white life and hanged. Just as it had happened with Denmark Vessey and his black murderers in New Orleans when she'd been a girl. More than 150 of the savage brutes; she couldn't recall the exact number. She'd been so confident that she'd had her boy put her in the rocking chair in the sun with her blanket and shawl this morning and had told him to run along to the trial and enjoy himself. And fifteen minutes ago, when Marc Antony had come lumbering down the street and asked if she needed any chopping done, she'd said yes and told him to go around the back and set to it right away. Now she looked desperately to the houses on either side and began to yell for help. Her voice was not terribly loud, and neither of her neighbors was home.

Marc Antony was chopping wood in the back yard of the McClintock house. He was an immensely powerful and simple-minded black man who could swing a double-bitted ax from sunrise to sunset, and a few hours past, without feeling much strain. An hour of his services, and a family had enough kindling and split logs to last a couple of weeks. He was a great favorite in Woodboro. A farmer once won a fifteen-dollar bet by hitching his plow traces to Marc Antony in place of his horse, and getting a full acre plowed by noon. The ax was poised in mid-swing above Marc Antony's head when he first heard Mrs. McClintock screaming. He frowned and thought about it for a moment, then he trotted around to the front of the house to see what was happening.

Mrs. McClintock's throat constricted when she saw Marc Antony before her, ax in hand. Her mind chittered to itself, and she heard her voice snap without conscious effort: "Whut you doin', nigguh! *Drop thet ax!*"

"Yassum." Marc Antony complied instantly; obedience was a reflex with him. He stared at the gray-haired old lady in confusion. He'd come out here to help her, he thought.

Too dumb t' 'member he spose t' kill me, Mrs. McClintock thought with sudden craftiness. Or maybe he waitin' on frens t' come. She knew what to do now. "Pick me up, an' carry me inside," she ordered.

Marc Antony was pleased to understand.

Mrs. McClintock gritted her teeth, forced herself not to scream, to remain still, when the black man lifted her from her rocking chair and brought her into the house. "Set me down on the chair 'side mah son's writin' desk," she said. When he did, she wet herself with relief. "Now turn yo' back t' me!" The black man obeyed, and Mrs. McClintock nearly cackled with glee. She forgot, for a moment, there had been such a thing as the Civil War, and she thought: No wonder they's slaves, ain't so much as a mule's brain in they haids. She yanked open a drawer and picked up her son's six-barreled pepperbox pistol. Marc Antony's broad back was two feet away. While he stood patiently awaiting her next order, she cocked the pistol, aimed, and fired a ball directly between his shoulder blades. She cocked, turning the cylinder, fired the next barrel as he fell, cocked. . . .

They were looking at the deputy he had just shot. "Wallace," one said, "that was a law officer."

"One of them white men workin' hand an' prick wif the niggers like Luther Stringfellow wrote," Swett answered. "You saw how he shot at yuh. Lucky yuh ain't dead now."

"That's true," Jimmy Hildenbrandt said.

"Now I tol' yuh: Get thet nigguh. They a whole townful lef' t' fight."

The black man was thirty feet up the tree, keeping the trunk between himself and the Knights. Hildenbrandt and another man moved their horses so that the black was exposed no matter which way he tried to move. They slipped their rifles from the scabbards. Hildenbrandt sighted, fired, and the Negro came crashing down through the branches and struck the street with a thud, raising a small cloud of dust. Hildenbrandt's horse whickered and danced away.

They turned toward the square. A block later Billy Thompson stood up in his stirrups and pointed. "Looka there!" A big, fine, chestnut stallion was galloping toward them with reins whipping free. Its rider was holding the saddle pommel and swaying widely from side to side. As they watched, the rider lost his grip, rolled backward over the animal's rump, hit the street, and cartwheeled twice before coming to a crumpled stop. "Stop 'im Billy!" Swett said. Billy Thompson put his heels to his mount and went after the chestnut. The rest of the Hearth trotted to the fallen man. Swett dismounted, rolled the figure over with his toe, and knelt beside it. "Gut-shot," he said after a moment. "An' broke his neck in the spill."

Thompson joined them, holding the reins of the chestnut. "What I do with him?"

Swett saw there was neither brand nor ear notch on the horse. "Hell, Ah take 'im. This pore boy ain't goan need 'im no mo'." He transferred his personal gear from the crippled old mare to the stallion, but didn't switch saddles; the chestnut's was better. The stallion snorted and stamped its feet when Swett mounted. It flattened its ears, twisted its head around, and tried to bite his leg. Swett jerked the bit hard. The animal went up on its hind legs and whickered. Swett laughed and whipped its ears with the ends of the reins. The horse came down hard, kicked once, then accepted its new master and was calm. Swett was pleased. It was a marvelous animal.

He signaled his men forward again. They rode at an easy walk, guns in hand, looking for niggers. Mostly they saw gangs of whites who were searching possible hiding places. Twice they caught glimpses of black men slipping between houses and they snapped off a few rounds, but they missed. There was occasional gunfire and shouting from various places around them.

A group of whites was beating through the dense bushes in a vacant lot half a block up from the Hearth. They flushed a black and raced after him with shouts. Swett pushed his horse into a gallop. The others followed him. "Outta the way!" he screamed to the whites. "Clear back!" The whites veered to the side in the face of the thundering horses. The Negro ran straight on, head down, arms and legs pumping.

Swett overtook him rapidly and edged the chestnut to the side. The black was struck by the big stallion's shoulder and knocked forward off his feet. He somersaulted, then he was up, shaking his head, and off again. Swett cut the chestnut in front of him. The black wheeled. Johnny Murphy blocked him on the side, then the other members of the Hearth boxed him, and they began to trot around him in a circle to the cheers of the whites standing and watching, knocking him down with their mounts whenever he tried to break free. The Negro turned in confusion, arms outstretched. Billy Thompson dropped a noose around his neck, yanked it tight, played out some fifteen feet of line, then wound the other end around his pommel and kicked his horse. The horse bolted out of the circle, the line tightened, and the black man was thrown down and dragged. He reached up in the billowing dust and grabbed the rope to keep tension off his throat. The rest of the Knights rode after Thompson. They whooped and waved their hats and gave rebel yells. They dragged the black man two blocks, his clothes shredding, his skin tearing off, and then suddenly they were hit by a fusillade of shots. A bullet buried itself in Swett's thigh. Another tore through Thompson's head and flung him from his saddle. A third broke Jimmy Hildenbrandt's wrist.

The fire had come from a broken-windowed and barricaded dry-goods store. On the other side of the street several whites were crouching behind cover. They shot furiously into the store now, and one of them yelled, "Git over here, you damn fools. Hurry! Hurry!"

The Knights clattered up on the wooden sidewalk and through the interstice between two buildings. They dismounted and tied their horses. "Mah God, we rode right into it," one said. Hildenbrandt was screaming. Swett cut open his pants and examined his wound. It hurt like hell and the bullet was still in there, but it had missed the bone and he could still walk. He tore a strip of cloth from his pants and tied it around the wound, stemming the blood flow. He grimaced with pain. "Well, we found the Nigger Horde all right." He was stunned, for he had begun to think that everything was under control and it was all going to be a lark. He checked his rifle to see that it was loaded. "Le's go," he said soberly. "We gots t' help them boys out front."

Three of the two-story brick homes were built side to side, and they crossed the roofs of these, keeping low to avoid being seen from the street. Then a ten-foot gap separated them from the next roof. Only Vulture might have been able to make the leap, so they decided to wait until things quieted, then go down through this house and make their escape. While Sadler kept watch on the roofs Vulture and Woodson crawled forward on their bellies and cautiously looked down to the square. The fighting there was brief and one-sided. Most of the whites broke into groups and followed the fleeing blacks. A few remained in the square. Some bent their heads together and gestured with vehemence. Others walked about numbly. The dead soldiers of the militia were sprawled on the courthouse steps. The streets and the park were dotted with other black bodies, and a few white ones. Dark splotches of blood stained the cobblestones and the dirt. A group of young boys was beating a black corpse with sticks. Not far from them two white men helped a Negro to his feet, draped his arms across their shoulders, and walked him away. Woodson admired their guts.

"Nigguh raper!" Hank called. "We cotched a nigguh raper wif a pore nekid li'l white girl! Come help us!"

They dragged the Negro through the streets by his legs. Men, and a few women, flocked to them. Some spat and kicked at the black man. Others pushed them back. "Doan kill 'im yet."

An agitated man yelled, "This is my house. Do it here, right now. Tear down my fence an' use it for kindlin'!"

He was cheered and slapped on the back and several voices began to chant, "Do it *now!* Do it *now!*" The man tore a plank from his fence, broke it over his knee, and threw the pieces into the center of the street. Several men set to help immediately. A sledge-hammer and an iron stake were brought forward. Hank took the hammer and drove the three-foot stake halfway into the hardpacked earth. Someone handed him a bottle when he was done.

He threw his head back and drained a third of it while his Adam's apple bobbed. He was applauded. The stack of firewood grew as the fence was dismantled and men came running with armloads of dead branches and wood from other sources.

Two men were holding the Negro. He screamed and jerked against them. Someone kicked him in the stomach. "Souvenirs!" a voice demanded. Those nearest closed in around the black man. Two beat his mouth with pistol butts. One reached into the bloody orifice and began pulling out broken teeth and tossing them up in the air. "Heah yuh go, neighbors." Someone flourished a knife. "Dig the bastard's fingernails off."

But a flushed youth arrived with a bucket of coal oil and Hank shouldered his way to the black and shouted, "Y'all kin git whutevuh souvenirs yuh wan's latuh. We gots the oil now, an' we gwine give the animul his jus' desserts." He seized the Negro's bloody shirt and hauled him to the stake. Men pushed wood around to form a bed and, Hank flung the barely conscious black man down upon it. A rope was brought. The Negro's wrists were bound to the stake. The whites piled more wood atop him, then sloshed on the coal oil.

Hank raised his arms. "Quiet! Git shut you people. . . . Thass bettuh." He took the hand of a fat girl in a blue bonnet. "It be fittin', Ah think, fo' a gentle white lady t' strike the match an' avenge the pore girl whut suffered under thet lustful black nigguh." He dug in the pocket of his overalls and produced a kitchen match. He gave it to the girl and picked up a stone for her.

She giggled and looked at her father who was standing nearby. "Paw?"

"Go on, darlin'."

She struck the match and tossed it gingerly on the wood. It went out. "No," Hank said. "Yuh gots t' touch it easy t' where the oil's soaked. Heah, Ah help yuh." He gave her a second match and when this was lit he held her by the wrist and steadied her hand. A tiny blue flame sprang up from the wood, ran in a quick line, leapt to another piece. . . . "Thass it," Hank said. "Stn' aside now."

The pile was aflame in moments. The whites cheered. The oil ignited the wood and it began to crackle. The black man twisted. His eyelids opened. He screamed. The dry wood was blazing now, and snapping and popping and shooting tiny showers of sparks out with explosive bursts. The black man kicked. Pieces of wood spun away from him. The circle of hooting whites pulled back. The Negro shrieked and tried to gain his feet. The stake rope kept him hunched grotesquely over as the flames licked around him. He fell, pushed up again, spasmed, and bucked against the rope.

"That's it, boy, give us a dance!" There was laughter.

The rope was burning and the black man yanked against it. It parted suddenly. The Negro was thrown off balance. He recovered and came staggering out of the pyre, remnants of his clothes blazing, hair gone, skin blistered. The crowd gave a moan of fear and shrank away. A white man with a pole jabbed him in the stomach and forced him back to the flames, where he stumbled and fell to all fours. The fire roared up about him. He stood and lurched to the other side, where he was met by a second white who drove him back with a rake. He collapsed on his back in the flames, and he rolled and thrashed and emitted high inhuman sounds.

A pot-bellied white swallowed several times. "Jesus! Jesus, forgive us," he whispered. He raised his rifle and put a bullet into the black man's head.

The man closest to him whirled: "Whut you do thet for!"

"I . . . I. . . ." The pot-bellied man was afraid. "Kill the nigger!"

Others echoed him. And several bullets were fired into the burning corpse.

The firing between the blacks in the dry-goods store and the whites across the street brought more white men swarming to the scene, and soon there were as many as fifty guns slamming rounds into the store. Its façade was gouged and ripped and splintered, and the Negroes' guns were silenced one by one. During a brief lull Johnny Murphy, who was crouching behind a rain barrel which was leaking through bullet holes, leapt up and yelled, "Let's take 'em! There ain't many left!" He ran across the street, followed by most of the Hearth and a handful of the other whites. Johnny hit the door with his shoulder and reeled in. Another white jumped through an empty window. There were three rapid shots, and then Johnny was in the door waving his rifle: "We got 'em!"

Swett had hobbled after them. He stopped and watched Johnny being praised and congratulated. He sneered. The boy wasn't complaining now, by God. Once they'd put a little whiskey under their belts and things had started to happen he'd become a regular fire eater. Men were heaving the black bodies through the broken windows into the street where others lined them up for display and called on people to come and see the fate waiting all members of the Nigger Horde.

Swett limped up to the Knights. "All right, all right, we done good heah," he said. "But Ah jus' wan's t' refresh yo' minds 'bout who it was whut dint want t' come in t'day, whut thought we should hide like rabbits whilst the niggers went 'bout they killin' an' murderin'." He stared at Johnny.

"Goddamn, Wallace, that wasn't what I meant, I jus'. . . ."

"Yuh jus' *whut?*"

"Aw, nothin'." The boy looked hurt. He kicked at a stone. Then something new came into his face. He raised his eyes to Swett and looked the Torch up and down, slowly, as if taking his measure.

It might have been stopped after the first brief bloodletting had there been anyone to wield authority. The mob was scattered and most of the whites were purged of their wrath. Satisfied, they turned to liquor and to congratulating themselves and friends on their manliness and moral rectitude. A few voices cried that this had only been a skirmish, that even now the Great Nigger Horde was on the verge of a major assault and that the whites had better strike again and break the back of this revolution before it could gather momentum. But this cry was ignored; the niggers wouldn't dare try anything else after the whipping they'd just taken.

So men crowded into saloons to drink and regale each other with tales of their heroism. Henderson's brothel was jammed. It was understaffed too, because Alworth refused

to bring his girls from the asylum fearing they'd run into
trouble on the way. Henderson sweated copiously as he
worked to mollify his impatient customers, and he limited
each man's stay with a girl to seven minutes. It was still
too much time, and the men were growing ill-tempered.
Fistfights broke out. Henderson feared they'd wreck his
place, but even more he feared they'd just start taking his
girls without paying him. That was precisely what was
happening at Molly Flannagan's on the opposite side of
town. Molly's place catered to the wealthy. It was a large
sumptuous home, richly carpeted and mirrored, with sofas
and chairs of velvet, a gilded French piano, a finely
stocked bar, and wide canopied beds. A party of roistering
whites from the streets forced the door when they were refused admittance and stabbed Molly's large Negro bounc-
er. They chased the screaming girls through the house,
flung them down, and took them where they lay—on the
stairs, in the halls; and Molly herself, who had not serv-
iced a man—at least not for money—in the last seven
years, was spread-eagled atop her dining room table.

Men grew drunker and began to complain to each other
about the way they had been forced to live these last few
days: camping in vacant lots, fleeced by gamblers,
snubbed by the local citizenry, overcharged for liquor and
victuals. They became indignant and belligerent. Some saloon keepers were manhandled and thrown out of their establishments. Men leaped behind bars and threw bottles
from the shelves to their comrades, rolled barrels of beer
and kegs of whiskey outside and broke them open with
axes, dipped tin cups, hats, and hands into them. They
kicked into stores and stole weapons and clothes, whatever caught their fancy. A few black girls and women who
worked in white homes and who were trying to sneak back
to niggertown were caught and dragged into alleys and
raped. Their screams only attracted more men who then
stood watching and waiting a turn themselves. Some sodden and bellicose whites went staggering up neat and attractive streets shouting obscenities and demanding to
know why the chicken-hearted residents cowered behind
their locked doors and let *them* take all the risks and do
all the fighting.

It could have been stopped, earlier. But there was no

one left to stop it. Luther Stringfellow had been clubbed just after Leon Clover was shot. Friends took him home, laid him unconscious in his bed, and were now, while Stringfellow's wife wrung her hands at his side, tensely standing guard against nigger assassins. Sheriff Gibney lay dead on the courtroom floor. Six of his deputies were also dead, five more wounded, and the five who remained were not fools; they had sensibly removed their badges and stuffed them in their pockets. Three had gone home to their families, the other two had joined the rioters. Colonel Thurlow MaCullum was sitting in his office with no intention whatever of taking to the streets. He was, on the contrary, getting quietly drunk, watched and attended by the ever faithful Constantine. The damage was already done. A riot was a riot. What difference did it make whether ten niggers or a hundred died? Those of Woodboro's other influential citizens, who for their own reasons—humanitarian and tactical—were distressed by the bloodshed and wished to see order restored, made no attempt to intervene. Do you try to reason with a rabid dog? And the bulk of the white townsmen had suffered long under Reconstruction, had no special love of Negroes, and were in fear of the white mob, which was composed of Woodboro's scum and poor country trash. They locked themselves into their houses and hoped it would all be over soon, sat with loaded guns in their laps prepared to shoot anyone, white or black, who tried to violate the sanctuary of their homes.

Woodson, Vulture, and Sadler weren't able to come down from the roof until sunset. There were too many whites walking or sitting in groups of three and four smoking and talking. Occasionally some entered the courthouse and carried out the body of a friend. No one knew where Jeb Merril was. The assumption was that he had escaped and was in hiding.

The setting sun was infusing dark, low-hanging clouds with fire when the three men decided the time was right. Sadler worked the skylight carefully with his knife. Its lock popped. They waited to see if the sound alerted anyone inside. They heard nothing, so they raised the skylight cautiously and went through it one by one, crouching in the shadowy hallway with weapons ready. Vulture's right arm hung at his side. Woodson and Sadler had put a compress over the wound and fixed it in place with a piece of cloth cut from the big man's shirt. His shoulder ached and there was warmth, not unpleasant, beginning to radiate from the bullet hole. But when he jarred or moved his arm he felt deep, sharp, stabbing pains.

The house was empty. Sadler went out the back door first, and after several moments he whistled softly. Vulture and Woodson bent low and ran to the fence, where Sadler was squatting with his shotgun. "Looks clear to me," he whispered. "What say we head straight up this way one, two blocks, then circle south to niggertown?"

Woodson nodded. "I'll take the left side, you and Vulture stay on the right. Move in relays. The first two men cover, the last comes up to take the lead."

They moved down the alley in that fashion, one leapfrogging while the others peered warily about. They stopped at the street, checked to see that it was empty, then sprinted across and started down the next alley.

The fragmented mob began to coalesce again. The men were surly, bored, belligerent, and drunk. Niggers were reported sniping at whites. It was rumored that a great massing of darkies was taking place in niggertown right now, and as soon as the animals had worked up their courage with liquor they were going to launch another attack.

The whites began to move toward niggertown without any really clear idea of what they were going to do: impress the niggers with a show of strength maybe; punish their leaders; crush a black army. They carried clubs and guns, pine torches, and there were lengths of rope coiled around some shoulders. Many of the younger ones capered and strutted and sang lewd ditties and "Dixie." Some of the older men linked their arms around each other in melancholy, and slurred through the lachrymose words of old wartime favorites—"Lorena," "Aura Lea," and "All Quiet along the Potomac." There had been good moments in those years, some glorious days, some sweet camaraderie. Several men wept openly and fell without knowing it into a marching step as they approached niggertown.

They made to within four blocks of their horses before they ran into trouble. The rich light of the dying day was fading. They were still moving with stealth, but were looser and more confident. They stopped a moment at a stone well next to a horse trough. Sadler bent and drank from a ladle. A rifle cracked and a bullet chipped stone. Sadler screamed and threw his hands to his head. Vulture and Woodson fired at the white gang that had appeared behind them. Vulture seized Sadler's arm. "Run!" Sadler tore loose, stopped long enough to pick up his shotgun, which was leaning against the wall, then set off after Woodson and Vulture.

The whites were a block behind, and sure they had found a traitorous white leader of the nigger rebellion. They snapped shots at the weaving figures, but, running themselves, they had little hope of hitting them.

Henry sat in a chair on the dirt street, his Winchester across his knees. Oscar, the owner of the store, was beside him. Oscar's head was bent and he was snoring. A tall singleshot swing-block 45-70 rested against the arm of his chair. Henry heard gunshots, then saw Vulture, Woodson, and Sadler pound around a corner three blocks away and come running toward him. He punched Oscar. "Heah they come!" He levered a shell into the Winchester's chamber, faded back to the store, and knelt so that he was partly protected by the doorjamb. Oscar came around behind him, broke out a pane, and rested the barrel of his gun on the sill.

"Hold yo fire till our own is clear, lessen you good enough not t' hit one of 'em by mistake," Henry said.

"You jus' fret 'bout yo'se'f, boy," Oscar said.

The whites burst into view. Henry shot the first one, worked the rifle's action and shifted the muzzle a little to the left, paused a fractional moment, then dropped the next man. He was humming softly. He shot four men in as many seconds. Hunting, he always aimed for his quarry's head, and didn't miss often. He'd never fired at human beings before, but he had decided earlier to shoot for the stomachs; if you missed a deer it wouldn't turn and kill you, but a man might. Henry didn't want to be dead at the hands of his own pride. So he picked the stomach, which was a target so large he couldn't possibly miss. The remaining whites broke and ran for cover.

"Goddamn, boy," Oscar said. "You dint even give me time t' draw a bead."

"Doan talk, Uncle. Shoot. They still plenty lef' fo' yuh."

The whites opened fire again. Woodson was knocked from his feet. "Sonabitch!" Henry growled. Oscar's rifle boomed and rolled forth a cloud of white smoke. The heavy low-velocity slug tore through both sides of a wagon and hammered a white man a dozen feet backwards. Oscar chuckled gleefully. Woodson struggled up and came for the store. Henry stood and fired the remaining rounds in his weapon as fast as he could work the action, not bothering to aim, just spraying bullets and driving men back down behind cover. Empty brass casings clinked to the floor around him. Then Vulture was through the door, and so was Sadler, the left side of his face bright with blood. Woodson stumbled after Sadler. "Where you hit?" Henry asked.

"Not," Woodson said. "Tore my boot heel off, that's all."

Bullets splintered through the storefront. One hit Henry's arm, but its force was spent and it dropped at his feet. Oscar flipped open the 45-70's block. An extractor rim seized the spent shell and ejected it. He inserted another huge, finger-length cartridge, locked the block, and cocked the hammer. He aimed. His rifle thundered again. Down the street, water geysered high from a horse trough a man was crouching behind. Vulture was beside Oscar, the butt of the shotgun he'd picked up from the girl caught under his left arm, the muzzle lying on the sill. Henry fed shells into his Winchester. Woodson checked Sadler. "Cain't see, outten it," the black man said. His eyeball was ruptured. It leaked a clear viscous fluid which mixed with the blood from his temple and cheek. "Ah lost it, dint Ah?"

"I think so."

"Well . . . you best go help the others. I'll bring the horses around."

Vulture fired, opened the breech, and emptied the spent shells. "Oscar, you have any ammunition for this?"

"Uh-uh."

"Any other guns?"

"Nope."

Vulture tossed the shotgun aside. "We better get out. Those aren't the only whites in niggertown, and we won't be able to hold off any more."

"Six-Finger's bringing the horses," Woodson said between shots.

"I'll help him." Vulture slipped out the back.

There was no target visible, and Henry took a moment to look at the bodies of the first four men he'd shot. They were sprawled not far from each other. One was feebly trying to crawl. Henry raised his rifle and fired. The man twitched and lay still. Henry felt very little about the dead men, much less than he felt after he had killed a deer, or a rabbit; even though an empty larder had to be filled, he was still a bit sad when he took the life of something beautiful.

"We're all set," Vulture called from the rear.

Woodson fired two more quick shots, then turned away. He reloaded as he went to the horses.

Henry said to Oscar, "C'mon, Uncle. Yo ass be skinned iffen you stay here."

When Oscar didn't reply, Henry touched his shoulder. Oscar fell away from the window and collapsed on his side. The front of his shirt was soaked with blood and he was dead.

"Henry!" Vulture called.

"Comin', comin'." He folded the dead man's hands over his stomach.

It was nearly dark, a half moon high up the horizon, many stars glittering already. Sadler and Vulture were in the lead. They galloped around a corner flush into a wall of torch-carrying men, knocking several aside. Their horses reared and pawed. Flailing hooves felled two men, and then the whites recovered and swarmed shouting toward the horses, grabbing for the reins and trying to pull the riders down. A man seized Sadler's leg and nearly toppled him. Sadler clubbed him with the gun. Another seized his horse's bridle. Sadler fired the shotgun into the white's face. The blast deafened his mount and scorched its hair. The animal screamed and whirled, lashed out with its hind feet, and Sadler put his heels to its loins and was free of the whites. Vulture kicked away the men clawing at him and followed. The horsemen turned off the street, away through the spaces between shanties. The whites pursued them on foot, but were soon outdistanced.

They were in trouble. The whites had moved on nigger-town from the southeast. The streets were too narrow to accommodate the mob as a body, so it had splintered into smaller groups, which struck off in different directions. Woodson's band moved carefully, probing ahead, then drawing away when they glimpsed dancing torchlights or heard shouting or saw the sudden illumination that told them another black home had been set afire. They were shot at a few times from a distance. Once they were in brief contact with the marauders, but they were able to disengage quickly and escape and their only casualty was Henry's horse, which was shot to death. Henry climbed up behind Sadler.

"We're pretty well surrounded," Woodson said. "I don't think there's any more point in trying to find a hole. Let's try for the warehouse district and hope they're not there. If they are, we'll simply have to go through them."

Henderson sent 'em. Oh, thet jellyroll bastuhd! Save his blubbery neck, put 'em on me. Sweet Jesus evuhlastin', State goan have mah balls, goan jail me fo' this an' fo'get wheah Ah is!

Alworth fumbled the key and dropped it. The whites had come from Henderson's. The fat brothel keeper had persuaded his most unruly patrons that there were girls for everyone in the asylum and that Alworth would let them in at no charge, a reward for having put down the nigger rebellion. So about thirty drunks had gone staggering over there. But Alworth had put the wooden shutters up on the ground-floor windows and locked both doors and wouldn't open up no matter how hard the whites banged on the doors asking and then demanding entrance. In a flash of inspiration, two brothers had set fire to the building, and then they'd all settled down to wait for the black females to come running out.

Alworth retrieved the key, was wracked by a coughing fit in the thickening smoke, then finally managed to fit it into the hole and turn the lock. He shoved open the door and shouted: "Run you nigguhs! They fire all around yuh!" It was doubtful his words were heard, but they weren't necessary; the black girls and the few women locked in this room had been choking in the smoke and screaming and beating on the door for several minutes. When the lock opened they broke free and knocked Alworth to the floor in their rush to the stairs.

Fire, fire!

Several minutes passed before Wilda saw an image of flames in her mind and understood what the others were saying. She remembered a fire from a long time ago. A pot had been in it. She'd touched it. It hurt. Terribly.

"Fire, fire!" she screamed, and she joined them clawing at the door.

Then the door opened and Beth, one of the girls who went with her at night to the house where the white men were, took her hand and told her to come and they ran over the white man who had fallen to the floor.

Alworth picked himself up. He glanced into the room. All but three had fled. Two old ones were chained. They shrieked and lunged against their iron bonds. Another had her hands wrapped around the window bars and her feet planted against the wall and was jerking at the bars. "Run!" he shouted at her. He couldn't do anything about the ones who were shackled. Those keys were downstairs. He went to the next door, where the really little girls were kept. "Benson!" he shouted. "Scoggins! Where are yuh, yuh bastuhds? Help me!" He unlocked and pushed open this door, and was thrown backward against the wall by a *whooomphing* ball of fire. The flames had eaten up through the floor, simmered, then blossomed when he'd provided them with fresh oxygen. He didn't think anyone was left alive in there. He put his handkerchief to his mouth and nose and crawled down the hall on his belly, eyes tearing in the smoke. He could see only a foot or two ahead of him. Stairs, he had to reach the stairs.

Beth dragged Wilda down the burning stairs. Wilda pulled and fought against her like an animal berserk in a burning barn. The flaming bannister collapsed as they reached the bottom. There was no door anymore, only a fiery portal. Wilda balked and pulled free of Beth. Beth tried once to capture her and then fled the building.

Ah gwine t' Alabama, Oh,
Fo' t' see mah mama, Ah!

"Girl . . . help me, girl." It was a croaking voice. Benson, the old man, was lying on the floor. A beam pinned his legs. His face was gray, his lips were twisted away in pain from his few stumpy yellow teeth. He held out a thin blue-veined hand to her. "Pull me loose, girl!"

Wilda put her finger to her lips and studied him.

She went from Ol'Virginny, Oh,
An' Ah'm her pickaninny, Ah!

The fire was burning fiercely. Wilda's hair began to crackle. Her skin was taut with heat.

"Please!"

Wilda picked up a jagged length of timber. It was burning at one end.

"Thass it!" Benson said eagerly. "Shove it unduh the beam theah an' pry it up. Ah kin drag mahse'f out then."

Wilda hit him on the head with the timber. His scalp was laid back. He looked at her with bewilderment, then horror, and he raised his hands to protect himself. Wilda hit him again. The timber snapped one of his forearms and struck his head with a heavy *chunk*. She hit him twice more, caving his skull in. Then she dropped the timber and walked out into the street smiling.

She live on the Tombigbee, Oh,
Ah wish Ah had her wif me, Ah!

Alworth reached the stairs and found them unpassable. He panicked for a moment, but then he bit down on his lip and brought himself back under control. The window on the landing. Unlike those in the dormitory rooms, it wasn't barred. He went to his feet, choked and blinded by the smoke, opened the catch, and raised the window. The new draft stoked the flames behind him and they licked higher and more broadly and scorched his back. He climbed through the window, hung by his fingers from the sill, momentarily frightened by the drop, then shut his eyes and let go. He landed badly, felt his ankle give, and had the wind knocked from his lungs. He lay with his mouth working like a fish tossed onto land, suffering agonies of strangulation. Sparks and a few pieces of burning siding fell down on him. When his breath returned he beat out the smoldering patches of his clothes, then crawled away from the house, cursing the pain in his ankle.

He stopped well away from the fire and sat up, holding his already swollen ankle and looking back. Flames were shooting from every window of the second story, including the one from which he had jumped, and had broken through the roof in several places and were darting around the edges of the shutter-sealed windows on the first floor. A section of wall bulged outward, groaned, separated from the rest of the structure, leaned, seemed to hang suspended a moment, then collapsed with a great roar and a high swirling of sparks. Two three-sided rooms were exposed. In one, the upper, a charred figure dangled from chains bolted to the wall. Alworth despaired.

Wilda walked away from the house. Her arms were limp at her sides. Everything looked strange and a little funny in the dancing firelight. She saw Beth down on the ground wrestling with some white man. Her feet hurt, they must have been burned. She didn't mind much.

Three white men approached her. Their arms were spread wide, ready to catch her if she ran. She stood still and waited. "Hell," one of them said, "this un's moonstruck, ain't gwine no place." He took her arm. "C'mon, honeychile, we cain't stay heah lessen we wan's t' git fried like fatback." One of his companions guffawed and then vomited over himself. The first man said, "Purely disgustin' t' see a man whut cain't hold his likker." They took her a good way back from the burning house.

Now Ah'm a good big nigger, Oh.
Doan reckon Ah git no bigger, Ah!

But Ah'd like t' see mah mama, Oh.
Down theah in Alabama, Ah!

The men pulled her shift off. "Well, now thet a damn skinny chicken. Reckon they a meal theah fo' all o' us?"

"Tain't much, thass true. Rib-thin, but it all juicy dark meat, Jake." They howled.

"Looka them little titties," Jake said. "No bigger 'n toad warts." He touched one tiny breast.

Wilda's head flashed down and she bit him on the wrist.

"Oww!" Jake hit her in the mouth. She fell. He pulled her back to her feet. "Now Ah'm gwine t'——"

There was gunfire close at hand. The white men looked up. Hoofbeats drummed . . . then three horses, carrying a white man and three blacks, plunged from the darkness into the firelight and came galloping straight toward them. They let go of Wilda and scrambled out of the way. Wilda stood quietly, watching the lead horse loom upon her.

They'd run into whites at the edge of the warehouse district. Only two were mounted, and Sadler had shot one. The other raced after them, but kept out of range, and screamed and hallooed for help. Woodson had wanted to drive directly through the warehouse district and out of Woodboro. But evidently there were whites moving on niggertown through the district, spin-offs from the handful of cheap saloons bordering the commercial section. The rider had managed to draw some of these in, and they fired as Woodson's band rode by in the moonlight, and then set out on foot, blasting wild rounds on the run. Woodson and Vulture saw a line of whites spread across the street in their path and reined up sharply.

Woodson shouted to Henry and Sadler, who were a little behind doubled up on a horse, to turn north toward the river: "Right into it! Swim it. It's our only chance!"

They cut for the river. Henry held one arm around Sadler's waist, gripped the rifle with his other hand, twisted and fired at the pursuing rider. He missed, trapped the stock between his arm and side, worked the lever, fired again, and this time dropped the man. The whites on foot slowed a little, afraid of a nigger who could shoot them with one hand from horseback.

Woodson rode into a large aureole of light which spread from a burning building. Whites went stumbling to the sides. One figure remained in his way. Woodson would have run it down, but a corner of his mind registered the obstacle as a child, naked and emaciated. He managed to swing his horse to the side, and as he passed he leaned and dipped, almost without thinking, and his arm snaked around the child and snatched it from the ground. The child was frail, but still the shock nearly tore Woodson from his saddle.

He rode past the burning building into the darkness again, and then his horse's shoes were clattering on the wooden pier at the end of the street. There was an instant of abrupt silence, a moment of suspension. His stomach rose. His mount struck the water with a jarring impact that threw him from the saddle and wrenched the child from his grasp. He was underwater, turning. He forced himself limp, felt his body begin to drift, struck out in that direction and broke through the surface. The moon was behind heavy clouds and the river was in darkness. He saw his horse and he swam to it. The child was nowhere visible. "Make for the opposite shore," he called, in case it was still alive. There were two large splashes in rapid succession—Vulture's mount, and the one ridden by Sadler and Henry. His horse was trying to swim back to the pier. He used the reins to turn it around, holding the pommel and trailing his body in the water alongside the animal. He heard thrashing and thin whimpering several feet away but it was too dark to see the child. He swam toward the sound, holding the reins in one hand and coaxing the horse to follow. He was already tired and breathing hard. He didn't think he could cross the broad river under his own power, and was afraid of losing the animal. He found the child. Its efforts were frantic and barely keeping it afloat. It was choking and coughing water. It fought him. He struck it, meaning to knock it unconscious. The blow was only grazing, but the child suddenly calmed. "It's all right now," Woodson said hoarsely. "I've got you. You're safe." Behind, new hoofbeats echoed hollowly on the pier, and moments later running boots. There was shouting. Then gunshots. He heard a few bullets *thwack* into the water around him, but none was close. He pulled the child to the other side of the horse, and he discovered as his hand touched a small breast that it was a girl, and a little older than he'd thought. "Hold tight to the saddle with both hands," he told her. "I'll guide him and he'll get us to shore." She didn't answer.

Vulture couldn't locate his horse. He held his breath, doubled over in the water, untied the laces, and let his heavy boots sink to the bottom. Then he stripped off his shirt and pants. He abandoned his shirt, but tied knots at the bottom of his pantlegs, took the pants by the waist-band and swung them over his head in a loop that trapped air. With the waistband held a few inches below the sur-face the pants made a kind of balloon. It wasn't much, but it would help a little to buoy him up. His right arm still re-sponded, but moving it was painful and he didn't trust it to be useful very long. He set off for the opposite bank with steady, measured kicks. It was going to be difficult. He knew there was a good chance he would drown. He let his mind slip into a deep and exquisitely pleasurable hatred of the white man, a consummate hatred, and it warmed and soothed and loosened him; it was like sleeping lightly on soft grass in the afternoon sun.

A lucky shot hit Henry's and Sadler's horse in the neck. It whickered and roiled the water. Sadler was panicky when he lost his grip. He couldn't swim. He managed to catch the animal's tail, and he gripped it frantically, dis-regarding the bruising his thighs took from the horse's kicking hind feet. Henry wrestled the beast back under a semblance of control. "Bullet cut some kind o' vein," he whispered. "He bleedin' bad. Ah gots it stopped some with mah hand, but he goan give out on us 'fore we make land."

Sadler vomited. The thought of water filling his lungs, of him sinking toward the muddy bottom clawing out and finding nothing solid, nothing to save him, the vision of catfish feeding on his bloated body, terrified him more than anything ever had in his life. He tried to tell Henry that, but all that came from his throat was an incoherent babble.

"Hush," said Henry. He knew Sadler couldn't swim and guessed what was agitating him. "Doan worry none. Ah help yuh when we lose him."

The current was strong in the center of the river, and it carried each of them, as they entered its main flow, an-gling downstream. Woodson and the girl came ashore a quarter of a mile below. Woodson was chilled and shiver-ing violently. He was unspeakably weary. He hurt as if he had been beaten for a long time. The horse shook itself mightily, throwing off a spray of water. Woodson sank to the hard ground, the effort of tying the animal's reins to a bush beyond him. The girl dropped down nearby. She hugged herself and rocked back and forth. Woodson saw that she was trembling with cold. He pushed himself painfully to her side. He put his arms around her. "You're all right," he told her. "We're safe here. We'll rest a while, then I'll take you to my home." The girl said nothing. She still tried to rock in his grip. "There will be friends for you," he said. "No one will hurt you." After a little while she quieted. But Woodson didn't notice; he was asleep.

The horse lasted longer than Henry expected. It took them past the midpoint. Then it began snorting and whistling. Henry could feel its strength failing. Blood from the neck wound eddied around his forearm in warm contrast to the cold water. The animal shuddered. Its head dipped beneath the surface, then rose again, and it whinnied shrilly. "He goin', Six-Finger," Henry said. He swam back to Sadler and looped an arm gently around the man's chest. "Now jus' let go nice an' easy. Lay back slow. Thass it. You doin' fine. Relax, you got t' stay relaxed an' trust me. Jus' let yose'f float like. Thass real good. Heah we go." Henry moved out with a one-handed stroke and an easy scissor kick. The animal foundered, seemed to rise up, struggled feebly, then was gone. Henry didn't fight the current, allowed it to do with him what it wanted, but kept striving for the shore. After several minutes he changed the arm with which he held Sadler. Soon he was doing it at ever shortening intervals and gasping for breath. His eyes blurred and he could not refocus them. A heavy pounding began in his chest. He fought with exhaustion, fought viciously, but finally it overcame him, and he lost consciousness. Some part of him, though, refused to succumb, continued with tyrannical force to spur his weeping body on, and, though Henry was dead to all that was happening, he and Sadler moved raggedly nearer their goal.

Sadler's feet touched bottom. "You done it, Henry!" He tried to stand, but Henry's arm was locked rigid. They both went under. Sadler came up sputtering. "Henry, let loose!" Henry's legs still kicked and his free arm chopped at the water. Sadler struggled and broke Henry's grip, took him by the shoulders and shook him. Henry stood up abruptly, then pitched forward. When he didn't reappear immediately, Sadler sucked in a deep breath, clenched his jaws tightly and closed his eyes against the horror of being submerged, then ducked below the surface and grabbed frantically until he found Henry. He dragged the youth up to the shore where he laid him down on his stomach. Sadler kneaded Henry's knotted shoulders. "You done a mighty job, boy," he said softly. "I owe you." Sadler didn't think Henry could hear him, but he told him to stay there anyway while he went to look for the others. Henry's body twitched and jerked.

Vulture was the last to reach land. It had been a slow and laborious crossing. His right arm had passed from agony into leaden numbness. When he strode dripping from the river up the bank it hung like a piece of dead meat at his side. He sucked in air with heaves of his massive chest. He was tired, yes, but not depleted. He could have gone on longer had it been necessary. He was pleased with himself. He delighted in his strength as he would have in rediscovering an old and loved companion. He undid the knots in his pantlegs with one hand and his teeth, then put the pants on. He looked at his arm. He poked it. He didn't feel anything. He willed his hand closed. There was no sensation, but his fingers did curl slightly. That was good.

The mob terrorized niggertown for several hours. With torches high, men ran down the poor and darkened streets shouting, chanting, and cursing. No lamps were lit in the mean shacks and cabins, where grim black men stood and faced their doors with guns, or with axes or clubs, and black women crouched behind them with frightened children gathered. Mostly these dwellings were left alone, but if a black man were seen around one, or a bright light shown, or faces peeped out from behind burlap curtains, then the mob attacked and broke down the door and dragged people out and beat them. Houses that stood out from the others, that manifested any special care or wealth, were struck with special violence. The whites tore down the fences, trampled the gardens, smashed windows, strewed the pots and pans of the kitchens into the street, and assaulted furniture and then the houses themselves with axes and sledgehammers. A few homes were put to the torch, others were simply left in ruin. Most of the black men were beaten and kicked senseless and left to lie with blood oozing from their mouths and ears. Sometimes the women were manhandled a little, but not many were molested; the mob was too exhilarated and destruction-hungry to dally with females. The children were ignored, and they fled hysterical and screaming into the night.

There were two specific targets on which the mob converged, the homes of Clarence Addison, a merchant, and Samuel Brooks, a speculator in cotton, rice, and sugar. These were the two wealthiest blacks in Woodboro, and their pillared and porticoed, spacious two-story homes shone like beacons in the dull and brackish clapboard sea that surrounded them. Addison was seized when he stepped from his house to try and reason with the whites. Brooks was found hiding with his family in a small larder in his cellar. Both men were hung as leaders of the black conspiracy. The knot failed to break Addison's neck and so he writhed and kicked several moments at the end of the rope before his own weight garroted him. Brooks's wife and daughters clawed at the whites as the noose was placed over Brooks's neck. They were beaten, and the youngest's jaw was broken by a rifle stock. One of Brooks's servants tried to cut down his master's slowly turning body and was shot. Both houses were set afire. An old black woman ran shrieking from Addison's, her flannel nightgown in flames. The whites opened a path for her in their ranks and she ran through them and into the night, her screams trailing after her, little swatches of her garment smoldering on the street.

There was some resistance. A few individuals fired on the whites from the darkness, ran, found new positions from which to snipe, fired, ran again. This drove the mob to fury. The whites killed several innocent black men as well as three or four snipers, and in one place, where an ambush felled two of its members, it burned an entire block of shacks to the ground. But the sniping was brief, and as the night wore on the mob's energies were sapped and its appetites gradually sated. Men began to leave niggertown for their rented rooms, their tents, and open-field pallets, and by three in the morning there were only a few groups left, very drunk, roaring incoherent challenges and clowning and posturing for each other. When dawn came niggertown was again the sole province of the blacks, but few ventured into the day. Those who were abroad crouched dumbly by piles of ashes, or sifted them for possessions that might have come through intact. Some others wandered without direction through the streets as if dazed, and now and then there was a grief-stricken wail as a corpse was recognized.

Woodson's horse had wandered off while he slept. Vulture's had been lost in the river, and Sadler's and Henry's had been killed. So they set off on foot. They approached the first Negro shack they found to borrow blankets, clothes, shoes, something warm to drink; anything; they were exhausted, only Woodson had footwear, their teeth were chattering. But they were driven back by rifle fire, and a frightened voice shouted they'd be killed if they came closer. The man could not be reasoned with. Nor could the one in the next cabin. And the cabin after that was burning.

The night riders had been at work.

Luckily they only ran into one group, about a dozen horsemen, and were able to take cover before they were seen. What remained of the night was an agony of unendurable cold. The blossoming sun stirred a resurgence of spirit, but then they saw the thin columns of smoke rising in the cold morning air in the distance, in the distance where Elysium lay.

They reached the plantation a while after sunrise; that is, reached its wreckage. Woodson stared at the desolation of the Great House. All that remained were the tall brick chimneys at either end—the rest was a great pile of ash and charred timbers, a few bright flames licking here and there. He wondered how much of himself was still standing.

Vulture and the girl were with him. Sadler and Henry had gone to look at their own homes and for their families. Vulture touched Woodson's shoulder. Woodson looked up and saw Hector approaching from a stand of trees. Hector's eyebrows and some of his hair were burnt off. His face was sooty. He carried a rifle in the crook of his arm. Friend was with him, leashed, and snapping his teeth at them in eerie silence. Hector stopped several yards away and told the dog, "Down!" Friend ignored him. Hector placed his foot over the leash close to the dog's collar and forced the animal to its belly. He dropped the leash and said, "Stay!" There were dried crusts of blood on the animal's muzzle. Friend rose and moved forward, hackles up, when Hector stepped from him. Hector turned and shouted. The dog went down again and this time reluctantly held position.

"Cap'n," Hector said as greeting. "The rest dead?"

- "No. Only du Genestoux. Henry and Six-Finger went to look for their families."

"Not likely t' find 'em. Might be better for 'em if they don't."

They looked at the bodies sprawled around the ruins of the Great House. There were more than a dozen and they were all black.

"Tried t' run t' make a stand here," Hector said. "No time."

Woodson looked away, to a field, where the nearest cabin stood, a neat structure of split logs. "The other houses?"

"The same. Ah scouted, dint see 'em all. Dint have to."

Woodson turned his eyes to his feet. He scuffed up dust. He couldn't think. After a moment he said, "What happened?"

"They come a little befo' midnight. Fo'ty, fifty riders." He shrugged. "Ah got Farley Baiter's wife in the woods. Dover Packett's two younguns."

"That's all?" Woodson asked in horror.

"All Ah know. Maybe couple mo' hidin' round. Pretty sure some run off. But not many, not many."

Woodson tried to remember. Had there been sixty in the community, seventy? He was an old man, a beaten man. He was afraid he would collapse. What? There must be something. "How many riders were killed?" There was that.

"Four. Five. Maybe seven. They took 'em away."

"So few?"

"They come fast, Cap'n." It was not an apology.

Cap'n. Woodson clutched at the word. It was a rope thrown to a man hanging from a c'iff, whose fingers were losing purchase. Cap'n. Yes. War. He had warred all his life. War. This was war. Around him was a battlefield. He straightened. "Scavenge," he said. "Go through the rubble, search every building. We need clothes, guns, and ammunition. Food."

"Salt an' sugar," Hector said. "That's whut you miss the most. The food we kin catch. But we gots t' have salt an' sugar. Coffee an' tobacco sets a fine treat too, if we kin scrounge any."

It was an awkward party, but there was nothing to be done about it. There was Woodson, Vulture, Sadler, Henry and his wife and baby, Mrs. Baiter, the two Packett children, the girl Woodson had brought from town, a little boy named Eddie, and Hector and Friend. Henry was still sniffling and wiping tears from his eyes. He could scarcely believe he had found his wife and son alive. Sadler was insular and quiet. He'd turned over the scorched remnants of his home to find the bodies of his family. His face was haggard and empty. His ruined eye frightened the children.

They were dressed and warm. They had eaten. They'd salvaged a great many articles, commonplace things in normal times, treasures to them now. Most were superfluous and had to be discarded, and it was hard to abandon what had been reclaimed from disaster. They tied the essentials into packs made from blankets—some patent medicines, some quinine and alum, gray powders for the stomach, fishhooks and line, canvas for shelter, rope, a few dried vegetables and fruits, some salt pork and jerky, and, perhaps most important, five hundred rounds of ammunition of various calibers. "You know we can't stay here," Woodson told them. "Some of us killed men in town. Since they burned us out, they'll claim Elysium was a domicile for insurrectionaries. We wouldn't even stay alive long enough to stand trial."

He told them where they were going, but the telling wasn't really necessary. The two neighboring states had been wrested from the Reconstructionists more than a year ago; if they were clever enough to stay free until they crossed the border, they would only be arrested, speedily tried, and more speedily executed. The niceties of jurisdiction would be considered later.

There was no choice. Their only chance was to reach Hellbottom Swamp.

They shouldered the packs. Woodson looked to Hector. Hector nodded and set off with Friend toward the hills. The others followed.

Woodson didn't look back, and he thought no further ahead than the next step. The Beast had sprung at him in Woodboro, a little too late, and once more at Elysium, a little too early. It had lost him.

He wondered how long it would take to find him again.

Book Two

1

Heavy rains lashed from dark skies and turned the earth to mud. The rivers, which fed the swamp and which were already swollen with melted snow from the mountains to the north, overran their beds and went swirling across the ground in lazy eddies.

Hellbottom Swamp lay like a great festering chancre in the bottom of a broad valley ringed by hills of jagged rock. Stunted grass and gnarled trees fought for marginal life on this rock and in the soil of the valley itself, which was dry and stony and hostile to vegetation. The swamp was nearly a hundred square miles of treacherous, vicious, labyrinthian gloom that hosted a multiplicity of life, as a piece of rotting meat hosts swarming maggots. It was a place of predators, and life was precarious for all creatures, from the flitting gnats struck off by swooping bats, through the soft ground squirrels crushed between the jaws of grunting boars, to the russet deer dragged beneath the water by massive alligators. The swamp itself was a hunter; not a sinewy quick and toothed thing, but a vast and mindless, infinitely patient organism that triumphed, always, in the end and that had been feasting for aeons upon the remains of those who fell dead within it and upon its own dying parts, endlessly replenishing itself.

In the past, fugitive slaves had fled to it for sanctuary, some with death warrants posted, most simply runaways. Not many survived. None ever mastered the swamp, but a few did cling to their lives long enough to learn the ways in which to compromise with it—essentially a matter of becoming one with the swamp. Periodically the whites organized search parties and went to Hellbottom. Sometimes they managed to trap and kill a fugitive, who wasn't often the man they had come for, but they were unable to penetrate the swamp very deeply and frequently they lost men to quicksand, to a cottonmouth, to one of the hunted who

would silently pick off a straggler, or they caught fevers
which killed them a few weeks later. Usually they emerged
without ever having seen a black man, shaken and vowing
never to return.

The swamp blacks were hard, wary, and singular men
who never fully relaxed. Their eyes caught the most subtle
movements, their ears the softest sounds. They could remain frozen, an unmoving part of the terrain, for an hour
or more, they could vanish into cover in an eyeblink. They
swam, when they had to, with easy fluid movements that
did not disrupt the placid water. They padded soundlessly
over twigs and moved through brush without disturbing it.
The swamp punished even the simplest mistakes with
death, so they were, like all other creatures in Hellbottom,
the finest of their kind. They were lethal, ruthless.

They lived alone. One might visit another's shelter to
see if there was tobacco or salt to trade, or a man would
go to the aid of a sick or injured person and tend him
quietly until he could care for himself, or needed burying.
But beyond that they had nothing to do with each other.
Once a man raided someone else's cache. Supplies, which
were precious, were held sacrosanct by the swamp blacks.
Three others came together briefly to hunt the man down,
and he was dead by nightfall.

News of the war's end, and emancipation, was slow in
reaching the men in Hellbottom; one who had lived deep
within the swamp for eleven years, avoiding the others so
successfully that they were not even aware of his existence, did not emerge until Lee's surrender had slipped
three years into history. Free, some of the wives, brothers,
the older children, and friends of blacks who were known
to have fled to Hellbottom came to the swamp in search of
them. Most did not find their men.

The valley land around Hellbottom was worthless. No
white had ever bothered to claim it, and not even the land-
hungry hordes of newly freed slaves tried to settle it. But
there was a thin ribbon of good loamy soil circling the
swamp proper, and crops would grow well there. The
swamp changed men, stripped them of the desires and
concerns of ordinary humans and made them unfit for the
realm of the commonplace. The little land that could be
worked around Hellbottom suited them fine, offered luxu-

ry in fact when contrasted with their life in the deep swamp. Only a few left. The rest took wives and families from among those who'd come looking for men long dead, and they settled on the edge of the swamp.

Small farms were strung loosely along the periphery. There was no actual town, but in three locations there were some clustered buildings—a couple of shanties, a dry-goods store, a blacksmith's and cooper's shop, storage sheds, and a church—which served as focal points and meeting places. They were Spanner's Store, Elmer's Smithy, and Tit-Bird Crossing. Privacy was fiercely guarded and universally respected in Hellbottom. Enough crops were raised to feed families and stock larders, and a little surplus was grown for sale so that the few goods they could not produce themselves could be purchased. If a man wanted or needed money for a special reason—a new mount, breeding stock, an iron stove for his woman—he left the valley and hired himself out to a construction gang, or, less commonly, as a fieldhand for a few months. But if it were a matter of pure survival, he knew his neighbors would not let him or his family starve. Hellbottom protected its own.

The desperate, the hunted, and the weary were taken in with little question. They were fed and sheltered, but were expected to begin making their own way soon. If they didn't, then they ceased to be recognized and they could die with no one remarking the event more passionately than he would the setting of the sun. Hellbottom Swamp embraced uncounted legions of bones.

The rains tapered off and then finally stopped on Friday night. Vulture, who had been in Hellbottom for a month, did not learn this until Saturday morning. He was sleeping on a table that groaned under his restless shifting.

Comfort Davis nudged him. He made a strangled sound in his throat. She shook his shoulder. The wound had closed well and cleanly; it ached sometimes now, but was no longer painful. He opened his eyes. "Rain's ovuh," Comfort said. "Got work t' do." Vulture grunted and sat up. The table made a sharp splitting noise. He muttered, stretched, flexed the muscles of his back. He was exhausted. He sniffed and said, "Coffee. Oh that smells good!"

"Makin' eggs, an' pork too," Comfort said. "An' hot-bread." She stood barefoot in dark ankle-deep muck. She'd scraped the goo from the fireplace, laid a bed of small stones to keep the wood dry, and built a fire. It was the first fire and the first cooked food since the cabin had flooded three days ago.

She had changed into a bright yellow calico dress and when she bent to the fire the cloth taunted over her buttocks, limned the seam between them. Vulture's groin twitched. She'd worn nothing but gray cotton during the rains, her spirit as dismal as the weather. Two weeks ago he would have been confident of seducing her if given the chance to spend three days in her cabin, but the rains oppressed him too and blunted his appetites: they were two miserable animals waiting for the skies to empty themselves.

Comfort was a well-fleshed, rounded, and strong woman, dark, full-breasted, and swaying-hipped. She'd come to Hellbottom when her husband, overworked and depleted as a slave and never whole during the few years he lived free, died one winter of pneumonia. She asked for nothing, paid some cash she'd earned cooking for whites outside to have her cabin built, and shared her first two crops to reckon out the small balance owing.

Hellbottom men came sniffing around her like rutty dogs, and the women distrusted her for that, but she soon made it clear that she wasn't a bitch in heat. Elmer Hayes didn't believe her and broke into her cabin, a little drunk. She hurled a pot of hot molasses into his face—which was now marked with slick reddish scar tissue. No one ever tried to force her again, though many dreamed about it. She did allow one to come to her, a heavy bullnecked old-time swamper named Attila who lived alone. Attila had a woman and two children in Hellbottom. He worked their few acres for them, but he had left them several years ago.

"Make a lot of that food," Vulture said. "I'm hungry." He felt better with the rain stopped and the smell of cooking, and he smiled at Comfort's bottom.

"Enjoy the look," she said without turning. "That all you get."

He was stung. "Maybe. Maybe not." He pulled off his socks, rolled up his pantlegs, and pushed his longjohns high up his calves. The wet mud was cold. He folded the blankets and went to put them on top the chest of drawers. The mud sucked at his foot, but he'd already started forward, and not being able to lift his foot quickly enough he lost his balance. He jerked free, splatted down in a half-step, was still falling, tried to pull the other foot loose, then pitched headlong into the mud. It nearly enveloped him. He lifted his head, furious, and spat the stuff from his mouth. He tried to wipe it from his closed eyelids, but only caked more on with his hand. Comfort laughed. "Shut up," he said. "Shut up, goddamn it!" He groped and found one of the blankets, fingered out a clean swatch, and wiped the mud from his face.

Comfort was leaning against the fireplace, bent at the waist and pointing at him. Rich laughter rolled from her and filled the cabin. Vulture sat up and glared at her. "You," she gasped. "Oh . . . you . . . nigger in the mud . . . oh you so funny. . . ."

Vulture looked down at himself. It *was* a little funny. He smiled. Comfort clutched her stomach and shook her head. Vulture chuckled. Then he laughed. He dove for Comfort. She shrieked and side-stepped awkwardly. He skidded in the mud and banged his head into the wall. She pointed again and howled. He lunged and caught her around the leg with one hand. "Don' you dare!" she said. "You ruin mah dress!"

"*Two* niggers in the mud," Vulture said. He yanked her down.

She fell in a sitting position, legs straight out. Rage took her face. Vulture very deliberately scooped up two handfuls of mud, raised them as if offerings to the gods, then crowned himself with them. Comfort giggled. Vulture grabbed another handful and threw it at her; it struck between her good breasts. She flung some back at him. They roared with delight and slung mud back and forth until they were both covered with the goo, and their ears were plugged with it, muting the sounds of their hilarity, and their mouths were dank with its taste. And then they began hurling it at the walls of the cabin. It struck in starbursts and slid ever so slowly down the rough wooden planks. They laughed themselves into pain, and finally Comfort threw herself backward into the mud on the floor and cried: "Enuff! Enuff. Ah goin' t' bust open if we keep this up!"

Vulture crawled to her side and grinned at her. Her arms were flung out behind her head, her eyes were closed. Her breasts were flattened a little against her chest, large saucers, and when she giggled they quivered beneath the wet mud on her dress. Vulture lay down atop her. He pushed mud from the hollow of her throat and nuzzled it. "Uh-uh," she said. "I ain't yo woman." He slid up a little, his engorged sex pressing into her thigh, and kissed her on the lips. He gripped her shoulders with his hands. She turned her face away. "I tol' you no," she said evenly. "Now get off me." He was intensely aware of her soft flesh beneath his loins. He remembered Lydia—a giantess of a camp follower, a woman to match him—and the knockdown nose-breaking brawl they'd had, the goatishness, the final rape that wasn't really rape but something much, much better, and the ecstatic delirium of them both. He liked sex best that was hard, that bruised. Comfort looked at him calmly, waiting. There was an air of sureness about her. Vulture rolled to the side and let her go.

She sat up and began stripping muck from her arms. Vulture watched her and wondered why he'd stopped. She glanced at the soiled walls. "We def'nitely made the Devil's own mess in here."

Angry, he said, "You can just damn well thank me that's all that happened."

She stood. "Firs' thing we do is we shovel the floor off. Then we wash down the walls. We save fu'niture til last. You think?"

Vulture rose and went to the door in silence. Mud wedged it tight against the jamb. He seized the edge with both hands and yanked savagely. The door split down the center, top to bottom. "An' aftuh the fu'niture you build me a new door," Comfort said. He threw down the piece that had broken off and went outside. Sun was shining through a dense mist. A rainbow was forming. A frightened deer bounded into the brush. Birds, which had been silent for days, were finding their voices again.

He'd dug drainage ditches earlier in the futile hope of circumventing the flood. Unthinking, he'd left the shovel standing against the wall. It had been knocked down by swirling waters and was gone. Stupid. He cursed. Washington had unsuited him for this kind of life. He went down on all fours and searched in the mud with his hands until he found the shovel. He swung it against the wall, knocking loose most of the mud, then made his way to the shed. The shed was small and low-roofed. A person of average height had to stoop to enter. Bending was too uncomfortable for a man his size; he crawled. His pallet of straw-stuffed cloth had burst. What remained was half buried in the mud against the far wall. Wet straw was mixed here and there with the mud in the rest of the shed. Comfort Davis had agreed to feed Vulture and put him up in her shed until he'd built his own shack. In exchange he was to work around her property and help her when it came time to put seed into the ground and, later, to harvest. Comfort's cabin was on higher ground than most, and they'd hoped they would escape the rising waters. But they didn't, and four nights ago Vulture had awakened when the shed flooded. He knocked on her door and she told him he could sleep on the table. Before he rolled himself into the blanket he put stones and chunks of firewood under the feet of her simple rope-spring bed and raised it off the floor.

The second shovel was where it was supposed to be, resting on pegs among other tools. He took both shovels back to the cabin.

They began with the farthest wall, opposite the door, and shoveled mud from there into a long mound, which they then shoveled—along with the mud from the rest of the floor—into a huge pile next to the door. It took them until well past noon. Comfort stopped to make lunch, but before she went to the fireplace she stepped up to Vulture, who had torn down the rest of the door and was shoveling the mud out through the empty jamb, and she touched him.

"Yah?" he said.

She slipped her arms around his sides, pressed in, hugged him. She rested her head against his chest a few moments, then released him and walked away. Vulture looked after her. What in hell did that mean?

Seventy or eighty people had come. Woodson was surprised, since many cabins had been flooded, some even destroyed, and livestock had drowned and larders in root cellars had been destroyed; there was much work to be done. But there had already been a full day yesterday to attend to the most urgent repairs, and the Hellbottom blacks were not easily demoralized. Most important, though: Sunday was a strong legacy from slavery times—church day, meeting day, gossip and visiting day. Its observance would give way to little less than holocaust.

They were in a cleared area behind Spanner's Store. A few uneven rows of split-log benches were ranked before a large stone, half the height of a man. Obadiah Isley was mounting that stone now. Isley was a brown man with a high round forehead, a huge nose, and, though slimly built, fat cheeks. He wore a plum frock coat with long tails. The sleeves were too short and they exposed several inches of white shirtcuff.

Isley raised his arms and called: "It's the Lord's Day, it's the Seventh Day, it's the Day of Rest, it's the *Sabbath!* Brothers and sisters—hear the Word of the Lord!" His voice was thin and high, nearly falsetto.

"He's the preacher," Woodson said to the girl. He still didn't know her name. In the beginning he'd thought she was mute. She wasn't, but might have been for all the use she put her tongue to. Her singed scalp had healed and was now covered with prickly hair only recently grown long enough to begin to coil. Her eyebrows and lashes were also returning. "Do you like prayer meetings?" he asked her. "I'll bet you used to go to them once, didn't you?" She watched Obadiah without expression.

Conversation subsided slowly, people moved toward benches, children were collared and forced to sit. Obadiah stood with his arms crossed over his chest, looking a little piqued at having to wait. Woodson led Wilda by the hand to a bench at the rear. She went docilely.

Obadiah cleared his throat. "Brothers and sisters. The dirt under yo feet is sodden still, but God's golden light is shinin' down on you today, an' that dirt gonna warm soon, gonna dry soon, gonna nourish the tender roots o' seedlin' plants soon. I know it. You know it. Cause that's the way that Jesus planned it. Now some o' us been hurt this last week, an' *all* o' us suffered miseries and sore afflictions.

But the rains is gone an' that golden glory-light is floodin' down in its place, and it's spring now, brothers and sisters, *Hallelujah IT IS SPRING!*

"We been delivered now, we been delivered befo'. You all know it. You *know* that the soft an' lovin' hand o' Jesus done stayed yo ol' masta an' kept the lash from yo' back mo' times than it fell, done guided you through the dark nights on yo flight t' freedom, done found you water when you was thirsty, food when you was hungry, an' a safe place to rest when you was weary, Oh God A'mighty *so weary!*" Obadiah swept his arms out and paused with his face turned heavenward. There was sweat on his face.

He looked suddenly back. "Have you suffered?" he shouted. "Have you known the Fiend's own agonies? Has your flesh been torn? Have yo women been taken by the mastas? Have yo men been worked t' death in the hot dry fields? Have yo chillun been removed from you?"

"Yes," a woman said with a sob. "Yes, they has." There were a few other low murmurs.

"I said, Have you *suffered?*" Obadiah screamed.

"Ah has, Lord, oh Ah has!" someone answered.

"Have you known pain?"

Several voices responded.

Obadiah raised his fisted hands. "Have you been *tormented?*"

—Yas!

—All mah pore life, God.

—Oh, rock me in yo arms, sweet Jesus!

"Have you known pain?"

—Too much, Lord!

—Ah cain't stand it no more!

—In mah soul, mah soul!

"Have you known agony?"

There were wails. Several persons were standing and waving their arms. A few clutched them e!ve and stumbled about. Two or three had fallen to the ground and were writhing there. Some of the quieter men ground their teeth.

"Brothers and sisters: HAVE YOU SUFFERED?"

There were loud cries of assent.

Obadiah's arms dropped to his sides, his shoulders slumped, and his head hung down. His listeners sustained their tumult several minutes. Finally he looked up, raised his hands, and quieted them.

"You have known nothing!" he shrilled. *"Nothing!* Who among you has seen Gethsemane? Who among you has sweated blood, been crowned with thorns? Who has had iron nails driven through his hands and feet, has felt the fatal lance pierce his side and tear apart his fragile, fluttering heart? Not one of you, that's who! I tell you you have *not* suffered. I tell you you have been as chilliun in a garden of delights. I tell you you do not *know* what it is to suffer!"

"Lord fo'give me," a man screamed.

"He does! He does! And yo chilliun, and yo chilliun's chilliun. Yea, until the last son born to man and the final reckoning of His righteous wrath. But who was it who rose from the dead? Brothers and sisters, who was it who rose from the cold tomb and rolled back the great stone to step into the light of day again?"

"It was Jesus!" came a voice.

"Yes, it was Jesus. And He stepped into that same golden light that shines upon you now—so stand up, brothers and sisters, stand up in Jesus's light and praise Him for His mercy!"

They sprang to their feet, believer and not, and their voices were one in worship.

But still the high thin voice of Obadiah cut across them like a knife. "Praise Him, brothers and sisters! *Praise Him.* Fo' He has given you mercy an' light which will surely follow you through all yo days. An' He is the Resurrection, the Light and the Way, an' He will take unto Himself all you who love him, an' the pain o' yo mortal flesh is as nothing in the infinite bounty of his love, an' you shall be cleansed an' made clean, an' given balm, an' you shall live again with Him in. . . ."

The black voices beat against Woodson without mercy. *No,* he thought. *It's not true, none of it! You lie, you bastard. You black bastard, you lie!* He bent forward, stricken.

They were singing:

"I'm climbin' up Jacob's ladder,
Doan you grieve after me.

I'm climbin' up Jacob's ladder,
Doan you grieve after me.
Fo' I'm climbin' up Jacob's ladder,
Cause I doan want you grievin' after me.

"Ever' rung goin' higher,
So doan you grieve after me.
Ever' rung goin' higher,
So doan you grieve after me.
The rungs is takin' me higher,
Where Satan never kin see."

Obadiah stomped on the rock and whipped his arms,
leading them. They sang two more songs. Wilda rose slowly. She began to sway with the rhythm. Her hands clapped
softly. She moved her lips but made no sounds. Woodson,
recovered, said, "The songs make you feel good, don't
they?" She smiled and nodded. The innocence in her face
perplexed him. He couldn't understand her. He took one
of her hands in his and patted it gently. "Why don't you
speak?" he said. "Tell me 'yes.' It's not so difficult." She
smiled.

The singing was over. Obadiah pinched one of his fat
jowls, tugged it, and stared reflectively at his congregation.
"I'm troubled, brothers and sisters." He nodded. "Yes,
deeply troubled. You all know the power o' the Lord. You
seen it in yo daily lives. You attest to it. But t' be truly
saved, you got t' open yo arms an' sweep Jesus t' yo
breast. You got t' *believe,* brothers; you got t' *accept,* sisters; an' you got t' walk in His footsteps all yo days. Now
we got a few wayward sheep in Hellbottom Swamp.
There's adulterers, gamblers, an' drunkards, an' there's
cheats and thieves. But mostly there's good and righteous
people here. SO WHY AIN'T THERE MORE DAMN
CHRISTIANS? I look out on you an' I don't see more'n
ten, twelve that actually been washed in the Blood o' the
Lamb, that have filled their hearts with the sweetness of
Jesus. Why is it that people who is good and decent don'
pay Jesus no mo' mind than they do a bumpy toad squat-
tin' on the moss? Woul'n't cost 'em nothin', woul'n't hurt
'em any, woul'n't discommode 'em none.

"Sure as the warthog roots, Jesus gonna tire, Jesus
gonna weary o' all this ignorin'. Jus' like a little chile that

no one pay no never-mind to, he gonna get angry sooner or later. An' brothers and sisters, Jesus ain't no little child that stamps its feet and rolls around when he's mad. When Jesus finally gets riled He gonna visit his wrath on you with thunder an' lightnin', with fire an' brimstone, an' you gonna cry out, *I'se sorry, Lord. I mend mah ways!* But it gonna be *too* late, an' Jesus ears gonna be stone deaf t' yo supplications an' lamentations, an' you gonna be destroyed in the justified fire o' the Lord!

"Save yo'selfs, brothers and sisters! It ain't enough t' gather on Sundays, shake yo heads, clap yo hands, an' shout, *Yas, Jesus!* Jesus ain't simply a hallelujah hour on Sunday mornin'. He is the Lord an' he is our God!

"I got three things I want from you t'day. *One!* Four weeks from this day, we gonna hold a baptizin' at Tit-Bird Crossin'. I want ever' man, woman, an' chile who ain't been beneath the water in God's name to be there. *Two!* I want all you fo'nicatin' folk what never bothered t' have God bless yo union t' come t' me t' get yo'selfs married proper an' right an' pleasin' in the Lord's eye. *Three!* Half o' you people call yo'selfs by the names o' heathens and idolaters an' animals an' plants. There's good Christian names aplenty, an' I want t' see 'em used. Each time someone is called by one o' those names, it's a slap in God's lovin' face. If that ain't enough, then think o' this: Do you like names what was mostly given you by ol' mastas when you was slaves? So you come t' me an' t'gether we hunt you down a good Christian name that is pleasin' t' both God an' men.

"Brothers an' sisters . . . God bless you and keep you!" Obadiah smacked one meaty fist into another. Sweat sheened his face, stained his shirt. He jumped down from the rock. Immediately he was surrounded by women who hugged and kissed him and men who shook his hand and thumped his back.

Woodson stood and hitched his pants. "Well," he said, "let's go be neighborly like." People were milling, uncorking and passing jugs of corn likker. Woodson reached for Wilda's hand. She pulled back. "We should," he said. "You've nothing to fear. These people are your friends. This is your new home now." She hugged herself and looked down at her feet. "There's a very handsome boy over there," he coaxed. "See? In the red shirt? He's been watching you. Why don't we introduce ourselves to him." The girl shuddered. Woodson sighed. "All right. Will you stay right here? Unless you see someone you want to talk to? I don't want you wandering off." She looked up at him and, though he couldn't read her face, her eyes met and held his a few moments, and he assumed she was agreeing.

Woodson knew some of these people by sight and a few by name, but hadn't talked to anyone in Hellbottom but Spanner for more than a few minutes. Trying to meet them now and enter their conversations baffled and unsettled him. One group stopped talking when he walked up, and stared at him until he grew embarrassed and left. Another spoke as if he weren't there. Others gave him their names when he offered his, and answered his few questions politely, but were otherwise aloof. Finally he spied a man named Crawdad, and his wife, and he hurried to them with relief. "Good morning, Crawdad," he said. "Good morning, Mrs. . . ." His voice thinned into awkward silence; he didn't know if Crawdad was the man's first or last name, or even his only name, and he had no idea how to address the woman.

"Woodson," Crawdad said.

"Good morning," the woman answered.

"This is Woodson," Crawdad said to the other two black men.

"Heard there was a buckra here," one said. "Dint b'lieve it, though."

The second man introduced himself as Temple Ackerly. He shook Woodson's hand.

"Rain set yuh back much?" Crawdad asked.

"No, just interrupted us. We've been camping there in an old tent. We sat tight a few days, but when the water started to rise we came back here and Mr. Spanner put us up."

"Where you buildin'?" Temple asked.

"About a mile south, near Possum Belly Creek."

"Good land for peanuts. Goin' t' grow 'em?"

"Some. For cash crop." Woodson was pleased at his interest.

"Don' expec' you gots much done on the cabin yet, huh?"

"The corner posts are ready to sink and we have enough logs split for nearly two sides. The foundation's in."

"Foundation?" The third black was impressed. There were few shacks in Hellbottom with foundations. "Whut kine?"

"Tamped earth, a layer of field stones, log joists, then a plank floor."

"You doin' it right, I give you that."

"How the chile?" Crawdad's woman asked.

"A little better. She seems to understand more. Or at least she's willing to give sign more often that she does."

The woman pursed her lips.

When the band from Elysium had arrived in Hellbottom, Crawdad and his woman offered to take Wilda in. Crawdad came to Spanner's Store, where Woodson was being put up, a few hours after she'd been left at his home. The girl had grown hysterical and then violent. She pummeled them with her fists, kicked and bit and furrowed their faces and arms with her nails. She shrieked obscenities, grabbed a butcher knife from a drawer and held them at bay. Then she broke a window with a stool, crawled through, and by the time Crawdad ran out the door had disappeared. Spanner, Crawdad, Woodson, and a handful of other men searched several hours. They feared she had entered the swamp, in which case she might never be found. But they came across her a little before dawn circling in a grove not far from Spanner's Store. Her clothes were torn, her face and arms scratched, and she had stumbled and cut her knees. She retreated from them like a wary animal. Then Woodson called her. Her eyes jerked around, caught him, and she ran to him, threw her arms around him and clutched him tightly, and crushed her face to his chest sobbing. She refused to be separated from him again. Woodson wasn't sure how he felt about that. But he, and no one else, had leaned in his saddle and snatched her from the ground in Woodboro, and he was therefore responsible for her. He accepted that.

The conversation turned away from the girl, and it was soon clear that Woodson was being little more than tolerated. He excused himself and left.

He walked back to Wilda, troubled. The years accustom men to their own lives, which are personal and unique. Men mold, but are more molded by, their surroundings. They exist, in a sense, only in context. And like actors, few are of sufficient stature to create the illusion of reality on a bare stage. Worse, pluck a character from the set of one play and drop him down on the stage of another and he is lost. He is incongruous, he is irrelevant. He cannot exist there long; it is an invitation to obliteration. Woodson had lived many years with blacks. He had never been a bigoted man. But, he was beginning to realize, a certain deference had always been paid him. Though he'd fought and bled alongside them in the war, his black troops had still been under his command. He and the other whites in the Freedman's Bureau were more effective than their black counterparts simply because they *were* white. And *he* had supplied the cash for Elysium, and many of the Negroes there, as MaCullum said, *had* called him "Cap'n." Woodson didn't believe he'd ever consciously sought dominance over black men, but he'd had it nonetheless and, subtly, it had become a part of his life. Now it was gone. He thought he could live without it. But nothing had ever prepared him to be disliked and even hated simply because of the color of his skin, and it confused, disoriented, and hurt him deeply. In effect, Woodson was learning what it meant to be a nigger in a white man's world.

"Girl," he said to Wilda, "I think we've been here long enough. Let's go for a walk. Would you like that?"

She didn't say anything, but she reached for his hand. He felt a rush of affection and he thought: *Thank God for you, child*.

One servant went to the kennels for the pointers and another took shotguns from the gun rack in the Great House, counting out shells and filling a flask with black powder and a pouch with loose shot. Waiting, MaCullum and Judge Durfee followed Clayton Lowery to a new and fresh-painted corral.

"I paid five thousand for him," Lowery said. "More than twice what I ever spent for a nigger. It took an entire year to make the arrangements, but he's worth every moment and every penny."

There was a whinnying within the stable. Hooves cracked against boards. A black groom led a horse into the corral.

"Gentlemen," Lowery said, "I present to you the Scourge of Allah."

It was an Arabian stallion, a powerful, broad-headed, fine-muzzled beast with a glistening chestnut coat, a gracefully arched neck, and sharply defined musculature. Its eyes were large and alert. It pranced a little and whickered, tail carried smartly.

MaCullum said, "He's stunning, Clayton."

Judge Durfee agreed.

A gust of wind rattled tree branches nearby. The horse snorted and danced sideways. The groom patted its neck, cupped its muzzle, and spoke to it gently. He reached into his pocket for an apple, which the horse took from his hand and broke between its teeth with a crunch. The stallion nuzzled against the groom and the groom kissed it.

"That boy loves that horse," Lowery said. "He hasn't left it for a minute since it arrived. He sleeps in a stall right next to it." He called to the groom: "Put him back in, Tater."

"Yassuh, Mista Clayton."

They walked back to the house. "We'll work him later this afternoon if you'd like to see him," Lowery said.

"I certainly would," Judge Durfee said.

MaCullum said, "Which mare are you going to breed him to first?"

"Juggler's Daughter."

"*Good* choice. If she throws a colt and you're willing to sell, I'd like to buy him."

"He's yours. But as a gift—to the future governor."

"Thank you. I'm honored and grateful."

A buggy with tufted leather upholstery, brass trimmings, and a matched pair of gray geldings waited at the house. Five blacks were in attendance—a liveried driver, two gunbearers, and two dog handlers. The whites settled into the buggy seats. The gunbearers lashed the leather-cased shotguns to the backboard. The driver flicked the geldings into a slow trot; the other blacks ran along behind. They went over roads of crushed gravel, and then of hardpacked earth, passed stubbled fields and stands of oak, willows, and dogwood, and when the road ended went a quarter mile farther. Once they had to step down when a wheel jammed in a rut and wait until the blacks lifted the buggy clear. They stopped in a field of some seventy acres, a preserve for small game. Lowery maintained three of these. They were planted with grain each spring, but never harvested, and they teemed with rabbit, quail, and pheasant. The field was brown and dead now—would be plowed and replanted in a few weeks—but it still offered sustenance, and sanctuary from Lowery's many blacks, who were forbidden to hunt in it.

The trio of pointers strained at their leashes and quivered, anxious to take the field. The blacks loaded the shotguns and handed them to the whites. Durfee's and MaCullum's were newer weapons, taking single-unit shells, with primer, powder, and shot combined. Two similar guns were held in reserve, loaded and ready to be passed to a shooter as soon as he'd emptied the weapon he carried. Lowery's gun was much older, and quite striking. Its breech was inlaid with silver and gold, its stock was of hand-rubbed walnut and was carved with an intricate relief of dogs running a stag. It had been given to him when he was a boy by his father. It was a muzzle loader, and awkward by contemporary standards, but an accurate and perfectly balanced weapon that seemed to leap to shoulder and virtually sight itself, and he had never felt comfortable using another.

The handlers released the dogs. The animals streaked away, leapt, barked joyously, then settled to business and began quartering the field. The whites remained in easy conversational distance of each other, closer than if the hunt had been more than a diversion.

"Have you seen Sunday's *Springville Sentinel?*" MaCullum asked.

"No," Lowery said.

"They're carrying a front page editori—"

"Bird!" cried a handler.

One of the dogs was rigid, left paw lifted, tail extended straight back. The other two turned toward his point, took a few excruciatingly slow steps, then also froze. The whites sauntered into position. Lowery said, "Your covey, gentlemen."

MaCullum cocked both hammers. "You want the left, Judge?"

"Fine."

"Flush," MaCullum said.

A black man ordered the dog: "Break 'em!"

The dog shot forward. The covey exploded up and outward, a dozen swift birds on whirring wings. Four deep *booms* sounded nearly atop each other. One quail pinwheeled down on the left, another fluttered to earth on the right. A third, also on the right, shuddered, then flew on, slowly and erratically. A black snatched the gun from MaCullum's hands and thrust another into them. MaCullum fired, missed, fired again, and brought the bird down.

"Very nice, suh," the gunbearer said.

"Rusty," MaCullum muttered. "If I don't get out more, I'll lose my eye altogether."

"Think how I feel," Durfee said.

"Don't denigrate yourselves, gentlemen," Lowery said. "Quail are difficult targets."

On command the dogs moved to retrieve the birds. One was still alive and twisted feebly in the gentle grasp of the dog's mouth. The handler wrung its neck before dropping it into the game sack. The birds had lived on their fat through the winter and were thin and bony. They would be given to the bearers and handlers.

The dogs put their noses to the ground again. The whites followed.

"The *Sentinel*," MaCullum said, "gave me singular credit for having the militia disbanded."

"That's excellent," Lowery said.

Durfee said, "I hear Stringfellow's on the verge o' apoplexy."

Stringfellow's *Woodboro Recorder* had published a ten-thousand-word account of the riot in a special edition, and the meat of that version appeared in nearly every other paper in the state. The few black-owned papers wisely refrained from expressing more than regret at the loss of life. One white publisher who questioned the veracity of the report was beaten and tarred and feathertd. His printing press was smashed and his type cases dumped into a river. White editors of Radical Republican loyalties did not openly deny the *Recorder*'s account, but neither did they print it, and they called for a federal investigation.

According to the *Recorder,* the "abortive insurrection" began with an attempt to kill a white man who was facing trial on a fraudulent charge of murdering a Negro. Woodboro's white sheriff valiantly attempted to protect the innocent defendant, but was shot to death with several of his deputies by Negroes. A trained and well-armed black army led by Emory Woodson, a renegade white man and ex-Union officer, and by Turner Brown, a black federal veteran in command of a Negro militia unit, then erupted from the town's colored section. The blacks planned to seize Woodboro, murder every white male of arms-bearing age who opposed them, then march from this power base upon town after town, their ranks swelling, until they had captured the entire state, which they intended to declare a Negro kingdom. Only the quick and heroic reaction of the unprepared and outnumbered whites (coupled with the Negroes' natural inability to long sustain any endeavor requiring true courage) prevented this horrible plot from becoming a reality. More than a hundred of the brutish blacks were killed in the fierce fighting; thirty-five white men also fell, and many more of both races were injured. Though found guilty by the rigged jury (four of whom met death during the riot), justice was done to the defendant Jeb Merril two days later when he was given a suspended six-month sentence. Turner Brown's body had been indentified, but Woodson was missing. Some believed he had drowned trying to swim a river, others that he had burned in a fire, and a few that he had escaped to the countryside and was still at large. The *Recorder* demanded that Negroes be forbidden by law to own or possess arms of any kind, and that the state militia, which was 80 percent black, be dissolved immediately.

MaCullum had not wanted the militia broken up. If used judiciously, it *could* damp down some of the hotter passions in the state, passions that only worked for Stringfellow in his bid for nomination. MaCullum abhorred what Governor Reid stood for, but at least Reid was an intelligent man, and one currently trying to walk a tightrope between an incensed white constituency and a federal government recently turned hostile. MaCullum trusted him to use the militia with sensitivity. But it soon became obvious that Reid couldn't stand against the combined pressure of the state, the White House, and frightened members of his own party, so MaCullum tardily joined the outcry. The militia was dismantled, and the machinery of MaCullum's organization was now busily working to convince the public that *he* had originated the idea.

"I think you'll end up having it both ways, Thurlow," Lowery said.

"How?"

"Washington is sending down Colonel Neal Partridge to form a pro tem militia until after the election."

"Is that legal?"

"Probably not," Durfee said. "But there are a good many ways t' beg the question. I don't expect we could get a final ruling for a good two months or more."

"That's luck," MaCullum said. "Partridge was on Lee's staff, and with Jeb Stuart. I met him once during the war. We can depend on him."

"Bird!" said one of the handlers.

"My covey—with your permission, gentlemen," Lowery said.

"Of course."

Lowery nodded to the handler. The handler spoke, and the dog lunged. The birds erupted. Lowery slammed the stock to his shoulder, fired, and two birds fell like stones to the ground. He pivoted and fired again. One bird dropped and a second, crippled, swooped raggedly down.

"Two doubles!" Durfee said. "I acknowledge the better man."

Lowery was genuinely stricken. "I missed the kill on that last one!"

Behind the whites and unseen by them a bearer mimed a guffaw. His companion grinned. Lowery turned. The blacks were stonefaced before his eyes fell on them. He shoved his weapon toward the nearest and said, "Load."

The black took the gun. "Doan be criticalizin' yose'f, Masta. You the fines' shot in the whole Souf, Ah swear. Yassuh, thass the troof." His companion feigned a coughing spasm.

The party moved on. The dog on the far left located another covey. MaCullum took it alone, and this time brought down a double and one single.

"Have you had any reports on the Tulomoona County petitions?" MaCullum asked.

"Twelve hundred signatures so far," Lowery said, "and they anticipate another thousand."

"That's twice what I expected."

"It would be amusing if you actually did manage to have him recalled."

"I still can't see the sense o' the thing," Durfee said. "Even if we could get enough names, which we can't, the lieutenant-governor would only step in, and he's no better at all than Reid."

"It's a matter of tactics, Judge," MaCullum said. "The Republicans will run Reid no matter what, so to beat them we have to beat *him*. When you're preparing for a major engagement, it's always to your advantage to keep the pressure on the enemy, harass him as much as you can. This nips at his confidence, frustrates and weakens him, and prevents him from giving full attention to marshaling for the pivotal battle. We never seriously thought we could have him recalled, but the attempt doesn't cost us anything, and it *is* undermining him. Tactics, Judge. Just simple tactics."

"Bird!"

Wallace Swett and Arabella Smalls were married in the afternoon. It was a bright, pleasant day filled with the moist odors of dark earth and of green buds on trees and the shoots of new grass. The reception was held in the Swett's yard, which was strung with lanterns and colored paper streamers. Fried chicken was piled on heavy white platters atop borrowed tables. There were steaming sweet potatoes, pots of grits, beets, turnips, and collards, straw baskets of fresh bread, and butter in a crock tub that had been lowered into the well to chill. There were bowls of red punch for the women and children and jugs of corn likker for the men. It was a boisterous afternoon that slipped quickly into night. Two brawls resulted in bloody noses and broken teeth, but they were more exuberant than belligerent and the participants ended with their arms around each others' shoulders sharing drinks and laughing together. A young boy and girl were discovered naked in the hayloft, and people catcalled and suggested another, and quick, marriage as the girl's outraged mother drove her daughter down the road with stinging slaps. Two thirteen-year-old boys shared a secret bottle of dandelion wine and by the time the lanterns were lit their stomachs were empty and convulsing futilely and they lay on the ground moaning and promising God they would never drink wine again if only He would please, oh please, just help them this one time. Children set loose one of Mr. Swett's cows and frightened it trying to herd it back into the pen. It bolted to the yard, panicked in the midst of all the people, noise, and confusion, and knocked over a table of food and spilled a heavyset woman into a horse trough before it was captured.

Ordinarily the sexual taunts and jokes would have angered Swett—he thought of Arabella more or less as an Arthurian Knight thought of the Grail—but all these people had gathered to honor him, to mark the most momentous event of his life, and it was sweet and heady, and it overwhelmed him. He had consumed a large amount of alcohol without effect, seeming a bottomless cistern into which it could be poured endlessly. But he was drunk on the glory of his wedding day. He loved all these people who had come to celebrate it, and he was close to tears. He wished Johnny Murphy were here, he was that expansive. He'd beaten Johnny badly two weeks ago. Little had been right between them since the riot. But it would have been today. They could have reconciled. Swett would have hugged him. Nothing could be wrong now. All was forgiven, all was made good; life was pure and fine. He even loved the Smalls. Arabella's father was wearing his old Confederate uniform, which was threadbare and frayed, but which was clean, sharply pressed, and the best suit of clothes he owned. He stood tight-lipped and stiff at the party, uncomfortable and alone; his wife lacked the ability to face so many people and had remained frightened and hidden at home, and he had not allowed any of his children to attend. Swett went up to him, got him to take a couple of drinks, to say a few clipped words, and then he told him: "Doan you worry none, ol' man, Ah goan take good care o' Ar'bella." Smalls nodded ponderously.

About nine o'clock the fiddlers stopped playing and the man who'd called the turns announced that the bride and groom were ready to leave. Whoops and whistles sounded. Swett flushed and released Arabella's hand. Arabella smiled sublimely. Swett helped her up to the seat of his father's buckboard. Some persons lit torches. A few climbed into buggies, a few more swung up on horseback. People on foot gathered around the buckboard. "Whut yuh waitin' on, Wallace?" someone called. "Tain't nothin' t' shy at—it fun, boy, fun!" There were guffaws. Swett's ears burned.

He flipped the reins over the back of the chestnut he'd found in Woodboro. "Gee-up! Git!"

The entourage followed the creaking buckboard the half mile to Swett's and Arabella's new three-room cabin at Johnson's Holler. The whitewashed building shone brightly in the moonlight. A modest barn stood nearby. The noise roused the half dozen chickens and the goat that were their wedding presents from Arabella's father. Swett jumped from the buckboard and lifted Arabella down. Torches waved and voices shouted lewd advice. Two Knights raced their mounts around the cabin firing pistols into the sky. One roared: "Wallace goan be bowlegged afore daylight! Be a long spell afore he set with ease on a saddle agin. Yes *suh!*"

Swett grabbed Arabella's hand and ran with her to the cabin.

"Don' fret, boy! It ain't gon' close over!"

"Carry her across the threshold, yuh gots t' carry her across!"

"Hop t' it, Wally! You leapin' like a randy bullfrog!"

Swett rushed inside with Arabella and banged the door closed. He leaned against it and breathed deeply, eyes closed. "It ain't right whut they sayin'. It ain't decent!" Arabella was a dark and silent shadow. Swett turned and rammed home the bolt. Someone tapped· on a window. Swett rushed to the window, threw it up, and shouted, "Go on. Git away an' leave us t' peace!" He was answered with hoots. A clod of earth struck near his head. He cursed, slammed the shutters closed, and locked them. Then he shuttered each of the remaining windows in turn.

" 'Ou wan's a light?" Arabella asked.

Only one of the 20 best-selling cigarettes can be lowest in both tar and nicotine.

True's the one.

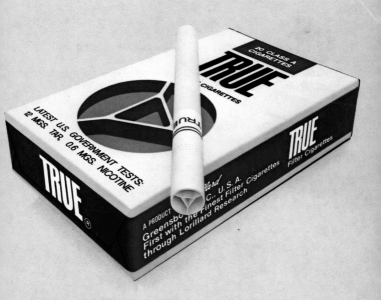

Regular or Menthol.
Doesn't it all add up to True?

Regular: 12 mg. "tar", 0.6 mg. nicotine,
Menthol: 13 mg. "tar", 0.7 mg. nicotine, av. per cigarette, FTC Report, Aug. '71.

True. <u>The</u> low tar and nicotine cigarettes.

Think about it. Doesn't it all add up to True?

© Lorillard 1972

"No. Leave it dark." Swett shuffled carefully across the floor, probing with his hand, until he found a chair. He sat down. He listened to the roistering outside. He was miserable and furious. He leaned forward, dropped his head down and hunched his shoulders up, began to crack his knuckles. They made loud popping sounds. A long time passed. When there was no noise a while, Swett's hopes would rise, but then a voice would singsong something like: "We know what *you're* doin'."

Once Arabella yawned. The sound startled him; brooding, he'd forgotten about her. "Whut you doin'?"

"Jus' stan'in' heah."

"Well sit down fo' Christ's sake!"

"Yas, Wallace." Then, after a moment: "Wheah?"

"Anyplace. Ah doan care."

"Yas, Wallace." Her dress rustled.

Eventually even the most dedicated hecklers tired and left. Swett waited until there had been no sounds unnatural to the night for nearly an hour. He got up, lit a kerosene lamp, replaced the glass chimney, and adjusted the wick so that only a dim glow suffused the room. He waited tautly for someone outside to notice the light through the shutters and begin badgering them again. But there was no one there. He sighed. Arabella smiled up at him from the floor. "Okay," he said. "They gone now."

She stood, came to him, and pressed him with her fulsome body. "Lub 'ou, Wallace." Her breasts crushed against his chest. "Lub 'ou hard, like . . . like . . . mo' 'n . . . mo' 'n a pig lub garbage!" Her pubis jammed against him. He felt a quick flaring in his groin.

"Well . . . well, Ah think we should git t' bed. It late an' ever'thin', Ah mean."

Her hands went to his shoulders and slid partway down his chest. "Yas, wan's t' git in bed wif 'ou."

He stepped back and cleared his throat. He picked up the lamp and led the way into the bedroom. His hands were trembling; he almost tipped the lamp when he set it on the night table. He opened the shutters of the single window in the room, peered carefully into the night to make sure no one was lurking there, then extinguished the lamp.

"Wha' fo' 'ou shut the light?"

"So as you kin git undressed."

"But Ah cain' see, Wallace."

There was sufficient starlight coming in, he thought. But he remembered that this home was new to her, and that she was probably frightened too. He smiled tenderly. "All right." He lit the lamp again. "Ah go undress in the livin' room."

She frowned. "Wha' fo' 'ou leave me?"

She was very young, he realized. It was her wedding night and she was a virgin. He was unsettled, and if that were true then she must be nearly hysterical with fear; so much that she could entertain no thought of propriety, that she didn't understand she would be exposing herself in all her private nakedness to him. And would be brutally confronted with his. She needed him near her now—but what to do? He had to protect her, there was no way around that. So he would stay . . . but he'd be careful not to alarm her. "Doan worry," he said with gruff gentleness. "Ah won' leave you alone." He took his nightshirt from the chest of drawers.

Arabella turned her back to him. "Git the hookers, Wallace."

He pushed her long brown hair to the side and fumbled with the hooks and eyes of her organdy wedding dress. The dress parted and spread across her broad shoulders, revealing a pale brown muslin chemise beneath. The warm and slightly musky odor of her body rose to his nostrils. The crotch of his pants lumped. When he opened the last hook, which was at the small of her back, he couldn't help but rest his hands lightly on her mounded hips. "Theah," he said. "Done." His voice was hoarse. Arabella took him by the wrists, drew his hands around her and placed them on her heavy breasts. She pressed the large globes of her buttocks into his groin. Swett groaned and thrust against her bottom with an instinctive, chopped motion of his hips. Arabella sighed, low and drawn out.

Swett stepped from her and picked his nightshirt from the bed. He went to the corner, faced the wall. He shrugged out of his jacket, undid his string tie, and opened the buttons of his shirt. He took a long time, motions as studied as those of a formal dance. His mind was locked with dreadful anticipation on the moment his blunt fingers must work the buckle of his belt, beginning the inevitable descent of his pants. He balanced on one foot and lifted the other to remove a boot. He heard fabric sliding against skin from across the room. He struggled against the temptation, but it was too powerful, and, ashamed, he turned his head slightly as he worked the boot past his heel and glanced furtively at Arabella. She was sitting on the edge of the bed. Her ample contours asserted themselves through the chemise, swelling here, dipping there, spreading, rolling. . . . She had stripped the white stocking from one leg. Now she bent her other leg at the knee and rolled the remaining stocking down. The pose afforded him a glimpse of the narrow strip of fabric between her thighs. He squeezed his legs together, he lodged his forearm between them; his buttocks clenched. He stifled a moan.

He removed his socks. He would be humiliated if she caught him looking, but he couldn't help himself; he wanted to see her naked. She stood and caught the stocking on a peg near the rest of her clothes. She raised her hands and hung her head back slightly, fluffing her hair, combing it with her fingers, unaware of Swett's eyes. She stood between him and the lamp, and the brittle white light silhouetted her body. Swett undid his pants and let them fall, stepped out, and was clad only in his longjohns. Arabella's eyes were closed and her mouth was open a little. Her hands ran over her shoulders, her breasts, down her belly to her hips. She looked as if she were dreaming. She smiled slightly. Swett began loosening the buttons of his underwear. He forgot himself and stared at her with fascination. She rotated her palms on her thighs. Then she took the bottom of her chemise and lifted. Her head turned toward him, and he narrowly avoided being trapped by her eyes.

He concentrated on the buttons. Then they were open and there was no escaping the move. He held his breath, drew one arm from his longjohns, the other, then hooked his thumbs in the garment and shoved it down over his rump. He hopped as he pulled it from his feet. He seized his nightshirt, jammed his head through the collar, and exhaled with relief as it fell over his body. But to his distress his rigid penis pushed out the fabric as stiffly as a pistol barrel. He forced it down with his hand, but it sprang up again undaunted. He sucked in his stomach and bent a little at the waist. That helped, but not much; he was still a tent pole. His organ had never been so swollen or willful, nor had it ever pained him in such an unendurably wonderful way.

There was nothing he could do, so he turned and was stunned to find Arabella standing naked and facing him. She was an expanse of rounded and pulpous flesh. Her breasts began high up on her chest and hung down long and gourdlike; they were tipped with huge dark-red aureoles and thumb-sized nipples. Three soft rolls ran laterally across her belly. Her hips were broad and set upon meaty thighs. Between thighs and belly was a vast, dense thicket of bristly brown hair. Swett's penis bucked and for a moment he feared he would splatter his juice onto the nightshirt.

Her eyes shone, her mouth was wide and smiling slackly. She opened her arms to him, which caused her breasts to sway and a small undulation to ripple the rolls of her belly. "Mah Wallace," she murmured. "Come heah t' Ar'bell."

He took halting steps, dizzied in a maelstrom of confusion and excitement.

She tugged at the shoulders of his nightshirt. "Take off uh shir'. Wan's t' see yuh."

Numbly he allowed her to pull off the nightshirt and drop it on the floor. She looked down at his penis, tilted her head to the side like a puppy hearing a strange sound. "Ain' beety red," she said. "Ain' wet an' sticky." She supported its weight in her palm and tried to reconcile what she saw with the image of a dog's penis snaking from its hairy sheath. "Wheah it come from?"

Swett could stand the thrill and the obscenity no longer. He pushed her down on the bed. He scrambled atop her and jerked himself about, rubbed and pushed against her abundance. He clawed for the lamp, found it, and snubbed down the wick, throwing the cabin into darkness. Arabella's hands searched his belly, then seized his penis and jerked it. She made a low guttural sound, like thunder in the distance. "Stop, stop," he panted. He pulled her hands away, then spat in his own palm and slicked his organ. He probed her with his fingers, found her slit, was shaken to discover how wet it was, then took himself in hand, positioned, drove into her, and lost consciousness of everything but the pleasure core that sprung from his groin.

Arabella flung her arms out to either side and threw her head back and forth on the pillow. She screeched with delight. For years she'd ridden waves of pleasure generated by her own hand, but never had she felt anything like this. It was glorious. No, no, never before. And vaguely she heard herself mumbling that—*No*—as she writhed beneath Swett.

He answered hoarsely: "It yo cross t' bear. Ah's sorry . . . but . . . wives gots . . . t' endure . . . they husbands . . . it . . . Ah. . . ." His voice trailed off and he drove into her wildly.

Arabella seized her own breasts and kneaded them brutally. "Mah tits, Wallace! Grab mah tits! Tear 'em t' pieces!" She pushed his hands to her breasts and forced his fingers to dig. "Yas, yas!" she cried. Something massive was blooming within her. "Stuff me, stuff me, Wallace!" She canted her hips violently, bringing the wonderful little button just inside her opening into hard contact with the bone above his organ. The button smashed, spreading joy, his meat filled her to bursting, his balls slapped against the rosebud between her buttocks. *"Gawd"*—her eyes bulged—*"Yas"*—her mouth filled with spittle—*"Fuck"*—and then she made moist gurgling sounds and her heavy thighs encircled his hips, ankles locking over his spine, and her arms went round his back where her hands gripped each other powerfully. She rocked and bucked, trying to suck all of his trapped body into her, and heard him gasping something but was lost in a searing red haze and couldn't understand him, and was swelling, straining. . . . They rolled over and over on the bed, but she never lost her grip, even when they fell to the floor, which she didn't realize, and it was almost there and she shuddered and drove against him berserkly . . . then a cracking, whiplike instant of nothing . . . followed by a scorching, brilliant explosion of reds and golds and a roaring that filled the skies, and her body liquefied, and she fell with joy and fullness, fell endlessly . . . down . . . and down. . . .

She felt herself awakening from sleep, and she was happy because she was being rocked and she felt so good. "Leggo o' me, leggo you bitch!" It was Wallace. She didn't know what he was saying. She smiled lazily. He was rocking her—knocking her head back and forth with hard slaps. She didn't feel anything, though. He loved her. "Go'damn you, let loose!" She became aware of a cool hardness beneath her. The floor. Why were they there? Wallace was struggling. She felt her arms and legs around him, and understood that she was holding him, which he seemed not to want. She relaxed her hands, unclasped her ankles. Suddenly pain slashed into her, a bone-deep aching in her legs and arms, cruel pinching in her back, rawness between her legs, flushed needles in her face, and the taste of blood where Wallace had been striking her.

"Yuh bitch!" Wallace shouted. "Yuh filthy whore!" He was standing above her, hands clenched into fists. "Yuh foul, slimy, pe'vuhted harluht!"

"Wallace," she said. "Whu' wrong? Whu' Ah do?"

"You *evil,* you the whore from Babylon. No decent Christian woman'd evuh ack like you done! You a fuckin' nigguh slut! You mo' disgustin' 'n shit in a outhouse. Ah feel like Ah fell in a slop bucket. You a go'damn dog-bitch in heat!" He ran from the bedroom and slammed the door behind him.

Arabella screamed: *"Wallace."* She pushed herself painfully to her feet. "Wallace," she sobbed, "come t' me. Wallace, Ah doan unnerstan'. Please Wallace. Ah lub 'ou. *Please!"* She opened the door. She couldn't see him anywhere. "Wallace, Ah do en'thin' y' say. Tell me. *Please!"* she wailed.

"Ah tol' you already," he snarled from the darkness. "You a filthy pig. Ah doan wan' be near yo stink an' yo rot! Git yo whore-cunt back in thet room. Go on' fore Ah kills yuh with mah own two han's!"

Arabella clutched the jamb. She ground her forehead against it. Tears came. "Wallace! Mah husban'. . . ."

"Go on!"

She turned back. Her shoulders slumped. Her hands probed feebly as if attempting to draw some comprehension from the empty air. Her legs struck the edge of the bed. She fell upon it, hugged the pillow tightly, and sobbed.

Vulture had been invited to play poker at Tit-Bird Crossing. He loved the game and had played avidly through the war and during his years in Washington. But he didn't go. Tired, he told himself, I'm too tired. He was tired, but not too much for poker. There had been a certain looseness and a kind of smugness in Comfort most of the day. That, he'd learned, meant Attila was coming to spend the night. And he wouldn't leave the property while Attila was there.

He was jealous of the swamper, which embarrassed him and made him feel childish and a fool. The last time Attila had come, Vulture spent several hours sitting outside Comfort's cabin in the darkness speculating on what they were doing with each other at this moment, and at this moment. . . . Such capacity for self-torment revolted him. He remembered a soldier with an infected stomach wou..d who looked with mounting terror on an iron cauterizing rod heating in a surgeon's brazier. The soldier had finally leaped from the table with a shriek, grabbed the rod, and plunged the red-hot tip into his own belly. Vulture had been disgusted then. Now he thought maybe he understood. Still, that man's act had been more comprehensible and a purer thing, an apotheosis; whereas his own, he felt, was muddied and corrupt.

Attila arrived at dusk. Vulture, in the yard, nodded and said, "Evening."

"Vulture."

Vulture thought he saw the hint of a smile on the man's face, but the light was already poor and that might only have been his imagination. Attila walked to the cabin, knocked once, and Comfort let him in, closed the door behind him. Vulture thrust his hands in his pockets and went down to the edge of the swamp, a quarter of a mile from the cabin. He remained in the darkness, in the cacophony of frogs, in the thrum and sliver-pains of clouds of mosquitoes, until night was fully dominant. Then he returned to the little farm, suppressing thought, scratching roughly at mosquito bites until they opened and bled.

He sat at the bole of an oak tree, where the light spilling

from the windows wouldn't reach him. He smelled snapping turtle stew, drop dumplings, sweet potato pie. Comfort was a superb cook. Sometimes she left Hellbottom to cook for whites on special occasions. The fare she provided him was always good, but she didn't fuss often. With Attila, she did.

Vulture shaped the image of Comfort in his mind. He let it be for a long time. Then he held it and began to caress it. He cupped and stroked it. He undressed it with slow luxury. He coupled with it a dozen ways.

When the lights went out in the cabin he was no longer able to possess her that way; for hours he was a helpless bystander forced to imagine her heated twining with Attila and he was wrathful and anguished when he finally crawled into the shed and dropped down on his pallet. His head ached. He threw an arm over his face and squeezed his temples. Tomorrow he would take Comfort. He was angry with himself for having allowed it to go on this long.

He didn't think Comfort would tell Attila, but if she did Attila would probably come for him. Attila was a wide, powerful, hard, and unequivocal man, but Vulture had him on height and reach. It would be a good match. Vulture relished the thought of punishing and being punished almost as much as he did the anticipation of having Comfort. He rolled over on his stomach, grunted with satisfaction, and in a little while fell asleep. He passed the night with his hands balled tightly into clubs.

He slept late into the morning, woke with a fierce headache. He sat rubbing his temples and chewing on nothing for several minutes. He got up, splashed cold water on his face from the wooden bucket, pulled on his pants, and stepped barefoot from the shed. He paused to empty his bladder against a tree.

Comfort was pouring tallow into candle molds. "Doan you bothuh t' knock no mo'?" She drained the last of the tallow and set the pot down. "Well?" Vulture closed the door. Comfort looked into his face. She picked a knife from the table and held it loosely, casually. "Ah thinks you'd best be about yo business." He took a step forward. She flipped the knife, caught it by the blade. "Doan try it, Vulture."

"You're not going to hurt anyone." He moved.

Her arm flashed. He ducked, and the knife *chunked* into the door, point buried deeply. Comfort rushed for the shotgun hanging over the fireplace. Vulture caught her before she reached it. She kneed him in the groin and when he doubled she chopped both hands into his throat. He gagged and stumbled back. She snatched the shotgun from its pegs. He recovered enough to pull it from her hands before she could bring it to bear and he sent it crashing through a window. Comfort grabbed for another knife from the rack next to the chopping board. Vulture wrapped her in a bear hug and carried her to the bed. She kicked ineffectually and raked his face with her nails. He threw her down. One strand of the rope springs snapped under the impact. He pinned her and hoisted her skirt up around her hips; she wore nothing beneath it. She bit his wrist. He worked his pants down around his knees and started on the buttons of his longjohns.

"Go 'head," she snarled. "Do it, you freak giant. But Ah tells you, Ah promises: They only one of us goan leave this cabin alive! You die, or you haf t' kill me!"

"Your pussy ain't worth that, woman."

"A bit mo' 'n yo cock, pig."

His penis was out now, and erect. She looked at him with hatred. Her teeth were bared, muscles worked in her neck. Vulture pursed his lips, calculating. He thought of the knife in the door. She meant it. Goddamn, she really meant it! Slowly he placed his swollen sex back into his underwear. He grinned; he was delighted with her. The feeling was short-lived. His headache struck again with hammer blows. Depression seized him. He released her and turned away. "Make me a cup of coffee," he said. There was silence. He added: "Please."

"You want somethin' t' eat too?"

"No. Just coffee." He sat at the table, propped his elbows on it, and held his head in his hands. "You meant that, about one of us dying, didn't you?"

"Ah did."

"I thought so." He looked up. "I didn't want to kill you."

"Expected as much. Ah dint want t' kill you either, but Ah would've."

They were quiet until she placed a coffee mug in front

of him and sat down across from him. "Ain't much lef' t' do roun' here. When you finish up, you goan have t' find some othuh place t' stay. You ain't done nothin' toward buildin' yo'sef a shack. Feedin' an' shelterin' someone in need 's one thing, but succorin' slothfulness is somethin' else agin."

"Haven't wanted to leave you."

"Why?"

"Wanted to taste you."

"Thet been settled. You kin stay on anothuh week iffen you wan's, but then you go."

He blew across the surface of the coffee. "I could leave with contentment if you'd share your bed with me."

"How come you so rutty fo' me?"

"Your face is beautiful. Your body is the stuff of dreams."

His tone was serious, but she laughed. "You sho' ain't no down home nigger."

"I'm asking you, Comfort. I'm *asking* you to make love to me. No threats, arguments—just a straight, honest request."

"They half a dozen good-bodied women in Hellbottom you kin get. Ah tell you wheah t' find 'em."

"I don't want them. I want you. Damn it, what is so momentous about it? I don't understand why you give it so much importance. Do you find me ugly? Do I disgust you? At least that would make some sense."

"You doan disgus' me."

"Then for God's sake, why not?"

Comfort got up and paced the room. "Cause Ah ain' no playthin'. Cause Ah ain' no piece o' meat fo' men t' squirt theyse'fs into. It ain't that Ah doan like t' fuck: that's pleasurable enough. Yas. But Ah was married t' a good man once. Fifteen years, an' Ah dint entertain no othuh men all the while. Not cause Ah tryin' t' be like some dichty white bitch whut doan wan' open her legs fo' pinch-ass prissyness, but jus' cause that the way Ah am. Ah gots a man, then I his woman an' Ah doan spread fo' no one else."

"You didn't spend last night alone."

"Am Ah talkin' t' the nails? Doan you heah whut Ah'm sayin'? Attila mah *man*."

"Then where is he now?"

"He . . . he one o' the ol' swamp men. . . . He doan wan' no permanen' woman. But he mah man ennyway, an' you doan need know nothin' else." She picked up a cloth and began cleaning a pan that was already spotless. "Ah cain' calculate yo lust."

Vulture rubbed the knuckles of one hand into the palm of the other. "You're a whole woman. I've never known *anybody* who was really complete. You are. No hollows, no emptinesses, missing parts, no parasitic needs. You are a total entity. Do you understand that?"

"Not partic'ly."

"I'm not sure I do myself."

She smiled. "But it do sound good, though."

"It is."

She leaned on the table and looked into his eyes. "You a lot o' man, Vulture. You smart. Nobody kin tell fo' sure whut you sayin' half the time, but it appear you got hold o' the right. You a big man an' a strong man. You ain't the pretties' nigger in town, but folks fo'git that aftuh they with you a while. You a angry an' a violen' man an' they's no doubt it fo' real an' not like an ol' bluff-snake. But underneath all yo broodin' an' surliness an' rapin' they's a fine gentleness. You hide from folks, but Ah sees you, an' whut Ah sees is close t' fine.

"Ah tells you, Mista Man. If it evuh comes down t' you bein' willin' to be mah man, mah real man, then you jus' info'm me, an' Ah be ready t' be yo woman."

They remained several moments staring into each others' faces, startled and mellowed by the vision of themselves they had given one another.

"I think," Vulture said, "that I'll get on with the chores."

Comfort nodded. She picked up the pan again and was polishing it when Vulture left.

2

This was their home. They belonged. They assumed and accepted dominion as naturally and with as little question as they did their heartbeats. Woodson was the outsider, the white, the freak. At the very best, he was a curiosity. He could not escape his skin.

After the initial shock, he'd been able to view himself only through *their* eyes, and the vision had demoralized him. He was still sometimes defensive and oppressed, but was steadily regaining his former respect for himself. He noted with interest that as his confidence returned, as he asserted himself more frequently, the greater the hostility he received from many people in Hellbottom. They knew what they wanted him to be: a broken white man. Even the blacks from Elysium had changed. They were still his friends, but they condescended to him, treated him now and then as a lovable but slightly simple younger brother.

Six-Finger Sadler came with Effie, his courtin' girl, and some friends to help Woodson raise a barn frame. Sadler's ruined eye was a swirl of yellowish white and red. The others had almost left him for dead on the march from Elysium to Hellbottom, but a poultice Hector made twice daily drew out the poisons and eventually stoppered the thick brothy secretions and Sadler had survived. Now Effie, like a human poultice, was draining off the melancholy and grief into which the charred bodies of his wife and children had plunged him.

The frame went up smoothly. Two men lifted the sides of each section while three more pushed the top up with poles. When a section was vertical it was secured with temporary braces. Then the next piece was raised and the two were fastened together at the corners with long pegs. The rooftree and rafters were more difficult, and the day was nearly over by the time the job was finished. Woodson felt good. Working with his hands satisfied him. The results were solid, could be touched, and he knew he had accomplished something. He thought briefly that his father must have felt this way about his land.

They cooked porkchops in apple cider for dinner. One of the men, Tyler, had brought two jugs of beer he'd fermented over the winter. They sat crosslegged on the floor and ate with their fingers from the skillet since there were no plates. Later, a man named Jackfoot probed the gaps between his yellow teeth with a splinter, and asked, "Whut Sylvester Jackson got against you, Em'ry?"

Woodson shrugged. "My color maybe."

"Oh, he doan cotton t' white much, but this be somethin' differen'. The way he look at you at Spanner's Store— Ah never seen such purely venomous hate in him befo'. He bust the window clean out o' the door when he slam it. Sylvester mean sometime, but that still weren't like him much."

"We were in the state legislature together after the war. We disagreed a few times."

"Over what?" Tyler said.

"This and that."

"You think Reid gonna beat MaCullum?"

"I don't think so." Though it was a passion in Hellbottom, politics no longer interested Woodson, except as it was merging and becoming one with the beast that hunted him. Even then he observed it with detachment; the conclusion was foregone.

Jackfoot said, "Ah doan think so either, but then Ah was wrong about Stringfellow. Ah thought sure the buckras would nominate him 'stead o' MaCullum."

"MaCullum dint win by much," Tyler said. "Fact, jus' barely."

"You shoot a man through the heart, it doan mattuh how far from dead center yo bullet go—he dead either way."

"That true."

"Course Ah'd as soon lose mah lef' hand as see the Democrats git the state, but figurin' they goan to, whut kind o' man you reckon MaCullum t' be?"

"Damn sight better 'n Stringfellow, Ah tell you," Tyler said.

"That like sayin' it better t' bump yo head on a limb

'stead o' crushin' yo skull. How'd you git so smart?"

"Studied on it."

"Still might git Stringfellow. Ah heah he goan run on a independent ticket."

"Cain't make it."

"Ah doan know 'bout that. Awful lot o' feelin' fo' that trash-man. He git it rollin', he be hard t' stop."

"How you size up MaCullum, Em'ry? He doan talk words Ah thrill t' heah, but at least he doan sound like Stringfellow or no goddamn Knight o' the C'nescen' Dominion."

"It'll take longer under MaCullum, but it'll be more thorough, more final, and more painful."

"Whut will?"

"The end."

Tyler and Jackfoot looked at each other in puzzlement.

Sadler dropped a hand on Woodson's shoulder. "Ah tell yuh, Cap'n"—no one had called Woodson captain since they'd left the ruins of Elysium—"it do hurt, an' yuh cain't believe they ennythin' left sometimes, an' yuh want with all yo heart to curl up an' die, but then the days slip by an' it git better. It does, Ah know." His one good eye focused on Woodson several moments, then it drifted to Effie.

Woodson clasped Sadler's wrist. "It probably does."

"Nary a doubt." Sadler rummaged in his jacket and withdrew a bottle of liquor. "Store-bought, not home-made. Paid dearly fo' it, was goin' t' set down under a tree t'morrow an' drink mahself silly. But it seem a good thing t' open now."

They passed the bottle around, and between pulls Woodson and Sadler traded news of the persons who had escaped Elysium with them. Both had seen Henry and his family, who'd occupied and reconstructed an abandoned shack a few miles away. Farley Baiter's widow was living with a wheelwright at Elmer's Smithy. The Packett children were with a man and woman who'd lost their only child to pneumonia last winter. Soldier's little boy Eddie had run off and it was thought he'd died in the swamp. Woodson had seen Hector a few times, who was living on the fringe of the swamp and keeping mostly to himself. Neither Sadler nor Woodson had talked to Vulture. They only knew that he was somewhere around Tit-Bird Crossing.

Woodson relaxed, and it cheered him to see the girl enjoying herself. She still baffled him, but he was learning to read her. She communicated with her body—sharpness of movement, the manner in which her fingers worked with each other, the rigidity of her toes. . . . When the goodbyes were said, she smiled at the men.

Woodson closed the door. "You enjoyed yourself, didn't you?"

She smiled again.

He said, "I'm glad." Then he asked her to stoke the fire. He went outside to the well and carried back two large buckets of water, his limp exaggerated by their weight. He emptied them into an iron kettle over the fire and made the trip again. When the water was hot he poured it into a tub before the hearth. He tested it, added half a bucket of cold water, and said, "It's ready."

He walked to a stool on the far side of the room and picked up a copy of Caesar's *Gallic Wars*. So far as he knew, it was the only book in Hellbottom. He'd found it, dusty and water-stained, in Spanner's warehouse. Spanner didn't know where it had come from. Woodson had little acquaintance with books, but this one absorbed him, and he was reading it slowly, voluptuously, a few pages each night, trying to make it last. He heard the girl slip off her clothes and step into the tub. There was silence. "Go on," he said without raising his head. "I put a clean washcloth out for you. Just rub a little soap on it. It doesn't take much." He heard nothing, waited, then looked up. She was sitting still in the tub. "It doesn't hurt," he said gently. "You know that." She didn't move. "I'll tell you what, if you do some, I'll do the rest. A deal?" Nothing. "All right." He closed the book, went to her, wetted and soaped the washcloth. He washed her nut-brown body surely and tenderly, as a father, but with some disturbance: she was ripening from a child to a young woman and ministering to her flesh stirred unbidden and unwanted responses in him.

"Listen," he said. "You have to start caring for yourself soon. There's too much work for me already." His attention had utterly relaxed her, she was contented.

"You know, I've done a lot already and I think you owe me something. I remember a little girl back where I used to live who worked up such a lather in her hair she looked just like a tiny old lady. That made me laugh, it was so funny. It made me happy. I'd like it if you'd do the same thing for me. It'd be fair and it would make me feel good. Here." He sloshed a little water on her hair, put the soap in her hand, and started her rubbing. "That's it. Perfect! Keep it up now." He laughed. "God Almighty, your hair's turning white. You're aging right before my eyes!" She giggled and rubbed her fingers into her scalp with vigor. Woodson slapped his knee. She laughed with him. "That's marvelous! Perfect. But I think we'd better stop now before you get down to the bone." He rinsed her hair with clean water, then brought a towel. She stepped out of the tub and he patted her dry. "That was just fine. It really pleased me. I knew you could do it. I'm proud of you. I bet next time you can take a *whole bath* by yourself." She beamed and started to hum. Woodson slapped her lightly on the buttocks and said, "Run and get your nightshirt on. I'll tuck you in."

He dragged the tub to the door and spilled out the soapy water. In the bedroom, Wilda was sitting on her straw mattress humming. "You look so clean and pretty I'd like to take you to a fair," he told her.

She cocked her head. Her tune changed abruptly. She tapped her fingers and sang:

"Milk inna dairy growin' mighty ol',
Skippers an' the mice workin' mighty bol',
Sing song kitty cain' yo kinny meow
Keymo, keymo, dorry hi minny how.
In come Sally singin' sometimes,
Penny wif a wink catchin' cat.
Sing song kitty cain' yo kinny meow,
Keymo, keymo, dorry hi minny how."

Woodson knelt and hugged her. "That's beautiful! Oh, you're so good. Sing me another. No? Tomorrow night then." He rocked her. "What's your name?" he asked softly. "Please tell me."

"Wilda."

Woodson took her face in his hands. His eyes moistened. "Thank you, Wilda. For telling me and for being such a lovely child."

"Em'ry," she said slyly.

"Yes. I'm Emory. We have much, much more to say too. And we will, won't we?"

She looked dubious.

"When you want to," he said. He laid her down and pulled the blanket up around her shoulders. "Sleep now. Will you say goodnight to me? . . . All right, I'll say it to you. Goodnight, Wilda. Sleep with pleasant dreams." He kissed her on the forehead, extinguished the lamp, left, and closed the door behind him.

In the darkness the girl whispered: "Night, Em'ry."

Thistle rested her head in her hands and closed her eyes. She marveled at how quickly the word spread. She rarely knew herself when she'd be able to visit the rotting swamp-shack. Some came hopefully every morning, trudged away in disappointment if they found the shack empty, laid their problems before her if she was there; then they carried the news jubilantly to the rest of the community and even beyond; she'd seen one woman today who'd come from twenty miles away. Now it was night, and she was weary.

She wasn't strong enough to shoulder their evils, their ills, their agonies, she couldn't stem the immense tide alone. But neither could she deny them and turn them away—they had no one else.

She rose and went to the door. There were only four left, and she felt relief. She called in the nearest, a man with a large goiter on his throat. "You want that cured," she said.

"Yassum, an' these too." He pulled his ear forward and bent to show her two angry wens. Then he proffered a live chicken with its legs tied. "Ah brung this t' pay wif."

"Is yo children hungry?"

"No ma'm, they ain't."

"The truth?" He looked down at his feet. She said, "Take that bird back with you. Come here. Sit down."

The swamp had overrun the shack long ago, covering it with moss, forcing its boards with powerful vines; even a sapling tree had rooted in the layered dirt and pulpy decay of the roof. Insects burrowed and nested in it. Birds congregated and fed there.

The interior, lit by candles burning on a pair of yellowish skulls on a table in the center, was small and damp. Moss spread like green velvet over the shelves that lined the walls. The shelves were crowded with root bundles, feathers, bird wings, animal feet, and small tubs and earthen pots and canisters containing a large variety of herbs, powders, liquids, dried organs of animals and reptiles, teeth, hair, bark, and dirt. Mortars and pestles stood on a low bench along one wall, and a cornmeal grinder, and knives for slivering, chopping, and dicing.

Thistle gathered a severed human hand with cracked leathery skin, a fresh egg, and a jar of liquid filled with crushed fibers of High-John-the-Conqueror root. She touched each of the hand's fingers to the man's wens and to the goiter. Then she rolled the egg softly over the goiter. "When we finished," she said, "Ah bury this egg outside. The shell goan rot away in about fo', five months. When it do, you be cured. But in the meantime, you gots t' rub this heah"—she held up the bottle—"ovuh the trouble ever' night. You run out, come back fo' mo'. An' fo' the next seven days, catch a speckley frog each sunup on a cypress root and wear it roun' yo neck on a string till you eats yo lunch. Understan'?"

They went out together and Thistle buried the egg. She reminded him to be conscientious about the frogs and the High-John-the-Conqueror root. The next problem was simple—a woman with a dog that kept running off. Thistle told her to dip the animal's paws into water at the same time, then cut off the tip of its tail and bury it under the doorstep.

A woman from Elmer's Smithy followed. She put both hands on her mounded belly and said, "Ah's carryin' a suckler, Miz Thistle. We cain' have no mo'. Got seben now whut is half starvin'."

Thistle poked her belly. "How long it been cookin'?"

"Three months, li'l mo'."

Thistle nodded. She cut a length of red string from a ball, picked out a sheaf of cocklebur roots, and removed a piece of bluestone from a jar of turpentine. "Tie this string roun' yo belly an' leave it fo' three days. Then crush up the stone and boil it in a pot with these roots. Let the brew cool so it ain't scorchin', but not so it cold either. Lay on yo back and spread yo'sef open with yo fingers. Git yo man t' pour the brew into you till it sloppin' out. Stay like that through the night an' put mo' in ever' hour. If you bleedin' heavy the nex' mornin', or if you still bleedin' at all fo' days later, then you sen' yo man to come fetch me right away."

"Yo husban' be mighty angry if mah man come t' yo house fo' conjurin', Miz Thistle."

"Doan you fret none 'bout that. This brew kill you jus' as dead as it do the suckler if ennythin' go wrong. So you send him, hear?" Her tone was severe.

"Yassum. Yassum, Ah will."

Last was a man who had come in the summer to buy a charm to help him get a job in a sawmill. He had a twitch beneath his eye. He was haggard, emaciated, and slump-shouldered. He sat on a stool, clasped his hands on the table, stared at them, and said hoarsely: "Miz Thistle, Ma'm, Ah come t' ask yuh, t' *beg* yuh with all mah might, t' break the spell yuh helped Sperry put on me. Ah's *dyin'*, Miz Thistle! Ah nevah got him fired from the mill. Ah dint, Ah swear. Ah doan want t' die. Ah'm 'fraid. Please! Ah do ennythin' fo' yuh, *ennythin'!*"

"Ah dint arrange no conjure on you," she said.

"Then Ah lost. Ah good as dead."

"Where this Sperry live?"

"Stuartville, othuh side o' the mountain."

"It probably Scipio Johnson the witch-man that help him." She snorted in deprecation.

Hope rushed into the man's face. "Kin you help me? Is yo magic stronger 'n his? Kin—"

"Mah magic stronger 'n his 'fore Ah was even birthed. We flatten Scipio Johnson out like a squashed bug. But Ah got t' know what been done, what kind o' conjure they use."

"Dried cottonmouth haid," the man said eagerly. "Mah fren tol' me Sperry powduh it up and put in mah lunch. Ah know he right. Ah been eatin' fo' three men, but still the snake's growin' in me an' suckin' mah flesh away. An' nine hairs wif nine pins in a cork. Burnt in the full moon.

Mah fren tol' me thet too. Mah haid been poundin' fo'
weeks, mah eyes cain't hardly see."

Thistle paced. She pulled on her chin with thumb and
forefinger. She muttered to herself. Then she smiled—vin-
dictiveness and triumph. "We kin stop that. An' we do
some extrys too, case there mo' to it. You find that Sperry
an' you tell 'im we chain an Echo Spirit t' you, an' if he try
ennythin' else it gonna bounce right back at *him*."

The man began to cry. "Thank you, Miz Thistle, thank
you, thank you."

"You stop that now. We got work t' do. They a worm
bed outside the door. It marked with six white stones
makin' a star. Dig me up twelve angleworms and git
t'gether some wood fo' a fire." The man ran out. There
were three leg-tied chickens in the corner. Thistle wrung
one's neck while the others squawked in terror, slit it
open, and removed the gizzard. She pounded some High-
John-the-Conqueror and some Prince's Feathers roots to
pulp. She cracked off a piece of dried clay from a lump
taken from the mouth of a crayfish hole, and for added
strength measured a generous portion of crumbly earth
from a red ant burrow. She deposited these and some red
pepper into a large pot, then went outside. "You got enny
silver money?" she asked.

"Five dolla's. All Ah has in the world. Ah brung it to
pay you wif."

"Put it in the pot. An' the worms too."

They lit the fire, filled the pot with water, and hung it
up to boil. The man chewed his lip as they waited. Thistle
watched with narrowed eyes and occasionally she stirred
the mixture with a stick.

"Take off yo clothes," she said, "an' stand where the
moonlight kin hit you." She let the pot cool a little, then,
dipping her hands in it, she rubbed him down from head
to foot. "There. They ain't no power on earth that kin
conjure agin you now. Scipio Johnson—*hunh!*"

The man embraced her. "*Thank you,* Miz Thistle."

Thistle threw out what remained of the brew and gave
him back two of his silver dollars. "You give me them two
when you got some mo'. Ah doan take the last of a man."

Later she gathered up some of the articles with which
she'd been paid—the chickens, two bolts of gingham, a

packet of fishhooks, and another of pins, some fancy nee-
dlework, a pair of shoes for her eldest. She left several
things she could use for conjuring and a few more she
couldn't carry. She also had seven dollars and twenty cents
in coins. She closed the door but didn't bother securing it;
nobody would violate a conjure shack.

It was an hour's walk to her cabin, and she passed
through the night without apprehension. There was nothing of which she was truly afraid.

Light shone in her cabin, telling her Obadiah was home.
She resigned herself to a scene. She stopped at the chicken
coop and released the two live birds into it, carried the
dead one and the rest of the goods into the house. Obadiah was sitting in his big arm chair reading the Bible.
When the time came, she thought fondly, they'd have to
bury him sitting, his wire-rim glasses on, the Bible open in
his lap. He stared at her, closed the book, and puffed his
fat cheeks in and out. "You been conjurin' again," he said.

"Dint expec' you back till t'morrow night."

"I finished my circuit early. The Lord's hand brought
me back in time t' see the devilment you been about."

"Good trip?" Thistle tossed the chicken on the counter
board next to a small wood-burning stove.

Obadiah's thin voice rose. "You promised, woman, you
promised me you was through with the Devil's magic."

"Ah had mah fingers crost when Ah said that. Doan
count."

"You think you kin trick God or me like that?"

"Hush down, you wake the chilliun."

"The same po' innocents you left alone an' defenseless
whilst you plied yo lewed an' fiendish rights?"

"Oh, bull-balls. You an' me was workin' the cotton
fields when we was half they age, an' you knows it, Obadiah."

"Doan try t' run me off the trail, woman. The chilliun
got nothin' t' do with it."

"That what Ah said." She began plucking the chicken.
"Git me a gunny fo' these feathers, won't yuh please."

Obadiah snatched the chicken and flung it against the
wall. "We are talkin' about Hellfire and Damnation, we
are talkin' about the vengeance of a Wrathful God!" he

roared. Obadiah's roar was not much deeper than a loud whistle.

A door opened across the room and a sleepy-eyed boy stuck his head out. "You gwine whup her, paw?"

"No, I am not. Get back to sleep, child."

The boy looked disappointed. "Well, iffen you try it later, tell me. Thet gotta be sometin' t' see. Whoo-eee!"

Obadiah threw a stirring spoon at him. The door slammed shut and the spoon bounced off to the floor. Thistle retrieved it, and then the chicken, which she brought back to the board where she resumed plucking.

Obadiah strode back and forth behind her smacking his fist into his palm. "Do you know what the Bible says about conjurin' an' sorcerers?"

"Yas, you tol' me."

"Ah'll tell you," Obadiah said. "It says there should not be found among you any practicer of magic or anyone who looks for omens or a sorcerer. It says Jehova will become a speedy witness against sorcerers. It says, 'Do not listen to your practicers of magic and to your sorcerers, for I shall have to disperse you and you will have to perish.' And in Exodus, Chapter twenty-two, Verse eighteen, it says: *'You must not preserve a sorceress alive.'* Did you hear that—that's God's commandment, woman!"

Thistle chopped both feet from the chicken with a single stroke. "So whut you goan do, Obadiah, bash mah head in with a stone an' 'liminate this 'bomination in the eyes of the Lawd?"

Obadiah was horror-stricken. "Course not! Where you get those fantastical ideas?"

"From the way you rant and carry on so." She turned to face him, leaned against the board, and folded her arms. "Obadiah, Ah walks mah road, Ah let's you walk yourn. Ah doan mock an' rail agin yo spirits an' powers, so why cain' you jus' not bother yo'sef with mine? Why, huh?"

"There's only one God, woman, an' He is the Lord God Almighty an' His son is our Saviour Jesus Christ. These spirits an' powers o' yours ain't nothin' but fiends an' horrors an' monsters from Hell. They the Devil's own foul spawn an' they gots you in they grip. I goin' t' break you loose. I goin' t' pull you back into the grace an' love an' mercy o' God. I goin' t' snatch you away from the grindin' teeth and terrible roastin' fires o' Hell."

"Jus how you propose t' do all this breakin' an' pullin' an' snatchin'?"

"Tell me where yo witch's den is," he said gravely.

"No suh. You burn it down like you done the las' two."

"It's yo *soul* at stake, woman."

"If it mine, then let me worry 'bout it."

"But I love you," he said miserably. "What good Heaven goin' do me if I got t' look down an' see you tormented in Hell?"

"Keerful, that sound close t' heathen talk t' me." Then she softened. "Doan you frazzle yo'sef so, Obadiah. It be all right. Ah promise you we be t'gether."

Obadiah brooded. "Only one thing t' do. Don' know that it entirely proper, don' know that it goin' resolve it all fo' good, but we got no choice now an' at the very least it give us a powerful shove in the right direction." He advanced on Thistle.

She backed away, alarmed. "What you up t', you? Stay way from me now. Stay way, you hear?"

He lunged, seized her, and threw her over his shoulder. She pounded on his back with her fists, punished his chest and stomach with her knees and feet. "Lemme down. Lemme down, Ah tell you!" The bedroom door opened and three curious brown faces peered out. Obadiah marched from the cabin and walked purposefully toward the brook that gurgled past the barn. The children followed. Thistle cursed and struggled savagely, but he didn't break stride until he had waded knee-deep into a small pool. He knelt, cried, "Take this wayward lamb t' yo bosom, Lord," then swung Thistle from his shoulder into the water and held her head down while he said: "I baptize you in the name o' the Father, the Son, an' the Holy Ghost. May yo sins be washed away an' may you dwell in happiness in the House o' the Lord fo'ever!"

He released her. She came sputtering through the surface, arms stretched out to the cold stars above, and shrieking: "Ah dint want it! Ah couln't stop it. It doan mean nothin', powers. It doan mean nothin', spirits. *Doan leave me!*" And for the first time in her life she knew not only fear, but what lay beyond it: terror.

Tyler was giving a birthday party for his youngest son, a boy of seven. Children ran in the yard and played tag and Johnny-on-the-pony. Their parents and other adults lounged in idle conversation, a man or woman breaking off now and then to walk over and cuff a child who was being disruptive. There was a horseshoe game in progress.

Woodson and Wilda walked up the hill toward the cabin, late; Woodson had had to reshape the wooden gear of a toy he'd made for Tyler's boy. It was a horse and wagon with a driver, and as the wheels turned the driver's head swiveled back and forth. Wilda was excited, and Woodson himself was pleased. But when he raised his arm and called Hello, hard faces turned toward him. Tyler detached himself and met Woodson and Wilda a hundred yards from the cabin. "Yuh kin turn aroun' an' go back," he said. "Yuh ain't welcome heah."

"What do you mean?"

"Jus' whut Ah say." He pointed to Wilda. "She kin stay if she want, Ah see t' gettin' her home later, but Ah doan want yo feet dirtyin' mah property."

"What the hell are you talking about?"

"This." Tyler thrust forward a newspaper.

It was the *Springville Sentinel.* Three photographs caught Woodson's eye immediately: Luther Stringfellow, Sylvester Jackson . . . and an old shot of himself. The headline said, GUBERNATORIAL CANDIDATE NAMED IN OLD CORRUPTION SCANDAL. He knew what it was, but he scanned the story to see how the event had been shaded. The point, of course, was to smear Stringfellow, who was running as an independent and who was becoming a stronger and more effective contender by the week. Woodson admired the writer's skill. He interwove fact with fantasy in a masterful way. It seemed, for example, that Stringfellow had been in collusion with Woodson, notorious nigger-lover and renegade white of Woodboro riot infamy. The president of a bank in the capital testified that a substantial amount of money had been deposited in Woodson's account by one of Stringfellow's aides after the vote on the public road bill. The writer didn't mention that Woodson had voted against Stringfellow's block, that the substantial amount had been five hundred dollars, and that Woodson had returned the money the next day. There was also an affidavit from Sylvester Jackson confessing that he had sold his own vote to Stringfellow for fifteen hundred dollars and naming several other legislators, including Woodson, who had taken money from Stringfellow. Woodson sighed.

He remembered MaCullum's threat to ruin him. Look back about six years, MaCullum had said. So that's what he meant. If it hadn't been for the riot, Woodson could have turned this to good advantage for Governor Reid, crippling Stringfellow just as much as it was doing now, but making MaCullum look like a fool. He smiled at the thought.

"That's funny, huh?" Tyler said. "You jus' split yo sides thinkin' on the dumb niggers, huh? Get the fuck off mah lan', *white man!*" He shoved Woodson hard.

Woodson stumbled and fell. Wilda screamed and leapt at Tyler. She raked bloody lines down his face with her nails. She kicked at him. He grabbed her. She bit him, broke free, and went for his face again, curled fingers seeking his eyes. Woodson took her from behind. "Stop it, Wilda!" Tyler, angry, slapped the girl. "Leave her alone," Woodson yelled. He flung Wilda aside and grappled with Tyler. They went down. Wilda scrambled back to them. She beat on Tyler's back with her fists.

Several persons ran from the house, pulled them apart, and held them. "Ah kill 'im," Wilda snarled, *"kill 'im."*

Henry was there, and Sadler. "Go on back, Tyler," Henry said. "They no point in this."

"Ah want that sonofabitch outta here."

"Me an' Six-Finger walk with him aways."

Tyler shrugged off the hands that held him and walked up the hill holding his wounded face. Wilda was released. She embraced Woodson tightly. Woodson had a split lip. He wiped blood away with his hand. He hugged the girl. "It's all right, Wilda." He stooped and retrieved the wagon. The horse's forelegs had snapped off. He found them, put them in the wagon's bed, and handed the toy to Sadler. "I made this for Tyler's boy. You might as well give it to him if his father will let him have it. A little glue will fix the legs."

Sadler nodded. Henry was distressed. "Cap'n," he said. "Did . . . Ah mean . . . that story. . . ."

"Yes?"

Henry shook his head. Sadler said, "What the boy's tryin' t' ask, Em'ry, is: Is it true?"

"Does it make any difference?"

"Course it does," Henry said.

"That's sad."

Henry frowned in confusion.

"Is it true?" Sadler asked.

"Why should I explain?"

"Because you owe us that much."

Woodson thought a moment. "I guess I do." He turned with Wilda's hand in his and started back down the road. "There isn't much to tell. There was a controversial bill before the legislature when I was a member. It wasn't a good one. But there were two companies that stood to make big money if it were passed. They bought Stringfellow, and he bought several others. Largely black. I learned this, even had proof of it, just after the vote. I decided to keep quiet. Most of the men involved were decent; we were passing good laws. A scandal like that would have played into the hands of the planter class; they could have used it to attack us. Stringfellow and I despised each other, but one of his people decided I'd been looking for a bribe and put money into my account. I had it returned. That's all there is to tell."

Henry and Sadler exchanged glances. Woodson didn't blame them for doubting. Believing in something, valuing the standard under which he did battle had been a mistake; he'd been much more effective when he fought simply because he was paid to, and for sheer love of it.

Henry and Sadler said they'd best be getting back to Tyler's. "See yuh," said Henry.

"Right."

Woodson contemplated the nearby hills. The Beast was on the move again; evidently it liked to harry its prey.

Swett waited outside in his robe and cape, horned hood hanging from his hand, while the other members of the Hearth prepared the two candidates. He chewed on a twig and stared blankly into the night. Unconsciously, he was massaging his groin. It felt good—nothing sharp or needful, a kind of luxurious contentment. He'd come to the barn directly from Jasmine Smith, into whom he had spilled his seed twice. That was one black bitch who could really do it. She gave a man a ride wilder than an unbroken horse. She thrashed and whooped and bruised you and cut your shoulders with her fingernails and her innards grabbed hold of your prick like she had a pair of strong hands in there. She squeezed out every last drop of juice until you were afraid you were going to dry up and blow away like dust, and you were so weak you couldn't hardly stand. The niggers, boy, they really fucked a man to pieces.

He hadn't touched Arabella since that first night. Fact, he had hardly even talked to her except when he was working and needed a hand or to tell her what he wanted to eat. She'd given him the most brutal shock of his life. A white woman endured. She loved and cared for her man. She bore his children. She suffered in silent resignation the assaults of his swollen organ, which were painful and revolting to her. It was her duty to take the weight of her husband, when his masculine lusts were inflamed, and she was admired and cherished for the sacrifice and consequent nobility of her submission. There were white whores, of course. Swett had never been able to afford one, but others had assured him that they fucked nearly as good as niggers. Even if he'd had the money, though, he didn't think he would go to one—they were niggers in a white woman's skin and he could think of nothing more horrible or disgusting. Swett vaguely suspected that one of the reasons niggers had been put on earth was to help relieve white women of the burden of sex. Those hot, musky, black females wanted it more than rabbits or minks or foxes. They wanted it so much that if they couldn't find a man they'd stick a broom handle into themselves and jump up and down on it. White women were for marrying, niggers were for fucking. He wondered what in God's name he was going to do with Arabella. He pitied himself immensely.

Leonard Sikes appeared. Swett had named Sikes second in command, removing that honor from Johnny Murphy. Swett regretted this, but the boy was rebellious and surly and had to learn to respect his superiors. He'd made it clear that things would return to their previous state as soon as the boy renounced this contrariness. "They's ready," Sikes said.

Swett put his hood on and swept into the dilapidated barn with a rustling of robes. The candidates were naked and blindfolded and kneeling before a podium. Their wrists were bound behind their backs, their haunches rested on their heels, their foreheads touched the floor. The hooded and robed Embers flanked them in two lines. Twelve tall white candles ranked before the podium cast flickering light. A large white cross had been raised against the barn's rear wall. On a table to the right of the podium lay a Bible, on a table to the left, a whip. A bell jar stood on the podium itself and in it were three white carnations. Swett picked up the whip. "The candidates will rise," he said.

A pair of Embers helped them to their feet. Sikes stood behind them to give them the proper answers.

"The Eyes o' the Knights o' the Canescent Dominion been upon you," Swett said. "You been found worthy an' deservin' by those all-seein' Eyes. A invitation was extended you an' you signified willingness t' consider this sanctified callin' by pearin' heah t'night. Hark ye t' the followin' questions an' answer truthfully at the peril o' yo eternal souls.

"Do you Lucius Kimbry, and you Hartley Fisher, belong t' the White Race"

Sikes whispered and the candidates said—*We do.*

"Have yuh evuh married t' any woman not belongin' t' yo race?"—*We haven't.*

"Have yuh evuh been a member o' the Radical Republican party, the Loyal League, or the Union League?"—*We have not.*

"Did yuh b'long to or support the federal army durin' the late War b'tween the States?" *We did not.*

"D' yuh reco'nize, admit, an' value the supremacy o' the White Race ovuh all othuhs?" —*We do.*

"Are yuh opposed t' 'lowing any part o' the political affairs o' this country t' fall unduh control o' the African race?" —*We are.*

"Will yuh do all in yo powuh t' prevent thet from happenin'?"—*We will.*

"D' yuh unnerstan' that this organization, the Knights o' the Canescent Dominion, has one single purpose—t' insure the supremacy o' the White Race, which was designed an' ordained by God, through enny an' all means whethuh thet be the ballot box, the whip, the knife, or the gun?" —*We do.*

"D' yuh wish t' become members o' this organization?" —*We do.*

"Will yuh render total an' unquestionin' obedience?" —*We will.*

"Will yuh lay down yo lives in defense o' our sacred principles?" —*We will.*

"D' yuh unnerstan' thet the punishment fo' revealin' enny o' the ritual, laws, lore, business, affairs, or un'ertakin's o' this organization is—" *Crr-rack.* He snapped the bullwhip against the floor. "Death." *Crr-rack.* "Death!" *Crr-rrack.* "DEATH!" The bound men cowered. Their voices were shaky. —*We do.*

"Are you still prepared t' swear allegiance t' the Knights o' the Canescent Dominion?" —*We are.*

"Then so swear, knowin' thet yo immortal souls is fo'feit if yuh swear falsely."

Sikes led them in the oath. Swett coiled and replaced the whip, grasped the top of the podium with both hands, locked his arms rigid, and said, "Remove the initiates' blindfolds."

The new Embers blinked in the light and shifted their weight uneasily, embarrassed by their nakedness and intimidated by the ceremony. Swett steeled himself. The questions weren't bad, but this was the part he hated; it was hard to keep all the words in mind. Jimmy Hildenbrandt, who could read, had coached him again yesterday, but still there was too much room for error for Swett to feel comfortable.

"Brothers," he said somberly. "You been accepted into one o' the mos' impo'tan' societies evuh evolved by man. Observe its principuls faithfully, discharge its orduhs diligently. Do thus, an' the Knights o' the Canescent Dominion is destined t' re—t' re—t' . . ."

"T' *regenerate,*" Hildenbrandt whispered.

"T' regerate our homelan'," Swett continued, "an' t' relieve the White Race o' the gross humilities, indignities, an' abom'nations t' which it has lately been su'jected.

"Hist'ry an' . . . an', uh . . . physi-*ol*-ogy teaches us thet we b'long t' a race which God Almighty an' Nature has endowed wif a clear an' evident superiority ovuh all the othuh races, by thet elevation givin' us ovuh all the inferior races a dominion thet no human laws kin permanently, uh permanently d-d-*derogate*." He was sweating. Goddamn! "This dominion has always been in the hands o' the Caucasian Race; whilst all othuh races has constantly occupied a superordinate an' secondary position."

"Subordinate," Hildenbrandt hissed.

"Whut?"

"Subordinate."

"Subordinate," Swett said, puzzled. "Uh-huh." Where was he? "Uh, won'erful nations have rised an' fallen but none has lef' enny traces o' splendor an' greatness but whut was descended from the Caucasian stock. On the opposite, mos' countries inhabited by the othuh races stayed in a state o' complete, uh, barbarity; whilst the small number thet done bettuh has fo' centuries now s-s-stagnated in semisavageness from which they cain't make no progress or improvement at all." Swett reached under his hood and wiped his face with a handkerchief. He wasn't getting it letter perfect, but he was coming close enough, and the initiates were listening solemnly.

"It a fact," he said, "that the fu'thuh an' mo' remoter a race is from the Caucasian, an' approachin' nearer the black African, the mo' fatally thet stamp o' inferiority is fixed on its sons, an' ir-ir-irrev . . . an' dooms 'em t' eternal imperfection and degradedness.

"It be our solemn duty then, as White Men, t' resist strenlously an' persistenly them attempts t' put enny powuh in the han's o' black African savages an' prevent at all costs the mongrelizin' an' corruption o' our pure White Race. We is t' do all in our powuh t' maintain in this Republic the Supremacy o' the Caucasian Race an' t' restrain the black African race t' thet condition o' social an' political inferiority fo' which God has destined it."

There, he'd gotten through, and pretty smartly too. He removed his hood and said, "Welcome t' the Knights o' the Canescent Dominion, brothers." He directed Sikes to loose their bonds. "Lucius, Hartley, either o' you have enny questions?"

Hartley shook his head. Lucius frowned, but didn't say anything. The Embers pressed in, shook their hands, and congratulated them. Swett took Hildenbrandt aside. "How'd Ah do?" he asked.

"Not bad, not bad a'tall."

"Ah knowed it," Swett said smugly, "Ah felt it all comin'. Thank yuh, Jimmy."

Lucius walked up. "Ah gots a question."

"Yuh do?" Swett couldn't think of any questions himself. "Whut?"

"Whut do 'canescent' mean?"

Swett smiled. "Well, it mean, uh, canescent. . . ." His hands made grabbing motions. "Hey, Jimmy. Tell our new brother whut canescent mean."

Hildenbrandt scratched his head. "Ah don' know Wallace. Glorious, or somethin'."

Lemuel Propp said, "Naw. It mean secret. We a secret dominion, a secret kingdom."

"Thet doan soun' right," said Fred Harwood. "It prob'ly like burnin', or flamin'. You know. T' go wif Embers an' Torches an' Wildfires an' such."

"No, no," someone else said. "It got somethin' t' do with dogs. Canine, thet's a word fo' dogs."

"How 'bout innocent?"

"Ah think it mean wise."

"Sparklin'?"

"Scary like ghosts, that's what."

They argued about it. Jimmy Hildenbrandt was finally dispatched home to bring back his father's dictionary. The Embers waited for him in sullen silence, each convinced of the logic of his particular choice, and miffed that the rest were unwilling to go along. They gathered around Hildenbrandt when he returned. "Don' press me now," he said testily. "I'll git it."

"How we know he goan tell the troof?" someone asked.

"Ah kin read some," Lucius Kimbry volunteered. "Ah check it with him." Everyone was satisfied.

Hildenbrandt ran his finger down the column of words. "Canelo . . . caner . . . cane rust . . . canes . . . here it is,

canescent. There a bunch things I cain't puzzle out, initials
an' such, funny spellin's, but it say: 'growing white, whitish
or hoary.'"

"Whory?"

"Thet mus' be fo' somethin' else," Swett said. "You
heard whut it said fust. 'Growin' white.' Yuh, thet's good."

Everyone was pleased. No one had triumphed over the
others, and the definition seemed a proper and satisfactory
one.

"Knights o' the Canescent Dominion—the Dominion
whut's growin' whiter," Swett said. "Ah like thet."

Hector was at the door. Friend was chained to a tree
several yards away and showed fangs when he saw Woodson. "Hector. Come in. What brings you here?" Hector
never made social calls.

"Come t' take yuh t' the swamp."

"The swamp?"

Wilda came up beside Woodson. "'Lo Miz Wilda,"
Hector said.

After a moment Wilda answered, "Hullo."

Hector entered. "Goan be trouble," he said. "Was a lot
o' talk in the papuhs 'bout burnin' out the Hellbottom niggers aftuh the riot. Reid ain't goan win the gov'ner. State
be turned back t' rednecks. Worse 'n slave days even.
Least then the Mastas dint want they slaves hurt wiffout
good reason."

"And the swamp's the only place we'll be safe," Woodson said.

"Safe from the white man, but not safe. Swamp kill you
jus' as dead they do. You a good fren', Em'ry. Respec'
you 'bout as much as Ah done enny man. Doan care whut
folks is sayin—you an' Stringfellow an' thet—jus' spit an'
shit ennyhow. Swamp ain't learned easy, but the mo' you
know the bettuh yo chance t' stay 'live an' learn some mo'.
Ain't many o' us swampers no mo'. Mos' people here, they
kin go in a li'l way, o' even a li'l way mo', an hunt fo' a
day, two days. But less'n a handful lef' whut kin really *live*
thet evil place. Ah aim t' teach you. Cain't make yuh t'
home there—thet take least a year or two—but kin help
yuh some."

Woodson had been slow and blunted for several days, fatalistic, prepared to mark time, to simply enjoy the good moments with Wilda and let the Beast overtake him whenever it was ready, assent and submit to the kill without resistance. But he felt awkward and a little false in that attitude; it wasn't natural. Hector moved him, flushed him with camaraderie, even love, and stiffened him. The Beast would have its way, he didn't doubt that, but it should be made to work for its meal.

"When do we start?"

"Now. Got leggin's?" Woodson didn't. "Kin git by wiffout fo' a while. But should make some. Smear yo boots wif lard. Keeps the water out." He said to Wilda, "Chile, we be gone t' midnight. Ah'm goan leave Fren' chained up outside. He settle down an' be all right, but doan you try makin' up t' him. Favor me by tossin' him a hunk a meat an' maybe a bone t' gnaw on 'bout sunset. But stay back from him when yuh do, hear?"

Wilda nodded. Earlier she would not have let Woodson leave her. She wasn't happy about the prospect now, but she didn't try to stop him. He kissed her on the forehead. "Be a good girl," he said. "I'll be back soon."

Hector had propped a pole against the cabin, hardwood, about eight feet long and an inch in diameter. He hefted it and said, "This the firs' thing. We cut one fo' you when we reach the swamp. Wiffout a pole you doan las' long enough t' need t' shave." They passed Friend, who slammed against his chain, sprayed spittle, and raged silently at Woodson. Hector said, "Git shut! It all right." Then to Woodson, "This pole goan serve you better 'n enny dog, enny man. You uses it t' probe footin',t' push brush, t' defend yo'self, t' kill meat. You uses it t' keep from sinkin' when you stumbles into quicksan' o' quickmud, you uses it t'. . . ."

The moon was past zenith when Woodson returned. He was exhausted and brutalized, skin puffed with insect bites, clothes ripped, hands and knees raw, one thumb sprained, and deep scratches on his face and neck. His shoulder was painfully gashed, weariness accentuated his limp. He leaned against the door, closed his eyes, and for a moment he was asleep; he woke startledly as he began to fall. Wilda opened the door. He tried to ask her why she was still up, but only grunted. She looped one of his arms over her shoulders and helped him into the bedroom. Bracing against his weight, she laid him down gently. He was vaguely aware that she was undressing him. He fell deeply asleep.

After she'd stripped off his clothes the girl looked at his wounds in the feeble lamplight, touched them with her fingertips. She bent and kissed the largest. She brought soap and water and a clean rag and bathed him. He groaned. She rubbed him down with oil, then covered him with a blanket. She pulled her own mattress next to his and turned out the lamp. She sat with her hands folded in her lap and looked at him in the thin moonlight for a long time.

Woodson was having an erotic dream. Warm moistness clasped his erect penis. There were confused, voluptuous images of Mary, his dead wife, and of the mistress who had followed her, and of other, strange women. He arched his hips, thrusting his pelvis up, then relaxed, then pushed again. . . . It was exquisite. He began to breathe deeply and evenly. But even as he lazed in pleasure, something troubled him, harried his mind, pushed him toward wakefulness. He opened his eyes, blinked. His legs were spread and bent at the knees, and a shadowy form crouched between them, moving its head.

"Wilda! Christ, NO!"

He jolted her hungry mouth away. "You can't, you can't!"

She struck him forcefully in the chest and knocked him back. Her hands clutched his lubricated penis. "Loves you! Mah man! Ah will!"

He struggled with her. She banded her arms around his hips, locked her hands under his back. Her mouth scrambled for his organ, finding and losing it. "You mine!" she screamed. Her lips closed about him. Her tongue worked furiously, her head jerked up and down. Unbidden, Woodson's hips pumped. So long without. So good. He clenched his fists and raised them. She loved him. She was more of his life now than anyone had ever been. He ground his teeth together. Wet and plunging. Swollen. He struck his fists against the floor, and flung himself down on the mattress. She sucked him frantically, and he bucked into her.

Sylvester Jackson reeled into Spanner's Store, lost his balance and fell. He pushed to his hands and knees. His head hung down. He rocked back and forth. A woven stink of vomit and urine and whiskey hung about him. A man moved to help, but Jackson swatted his arm away.

"Wheah you been, Sylvester?" someone asked.

"You look like you a whole week rottin'. You sick?"

Jackson got to his feet. His eyes were bloodshot, cheeks stubbled, clothes filthy. He swayed. His face was sullen and defiant. "I ain't gonna run anymore, you bastards. I ain't gonna give you the sport of chasin' me down. I'm here. I've come to you." He yanked a knife from his belt. "But I can cut as good as any of you. Oh, you can finish Sylvester Jackson all right, but there's some of you gonna go down too."

"Nobody's lookin' t' finish you."

Jackson slashed air. "There ain't a one of you wouldn't have done the same thing. I was a house nigger before the war. I had it good, not like you field niggers. My master gave me seventy-five cents a month to spend. Stringfellow gave me fifteen hundred dollars for one vote. It didn't even take a second to cast it. Fifteen hundred dollars! You know what that is? That's how much I would of had if I'd been a house nigger for a hundred and seventy years. Go on, look me in the eye and tell me you wouldn't have done it."

"Ah dint hear nobody say nothin' like that."

"But all you righteous sonsofbitches think I sold my people out, gonna get me for it."

There were some who'd been disgusted with Jackson when the story broke in the *Springville Sentinel,* but no one had entertained thoughts of retribution. Most saw it as just another example of the white man using the black man. Few even realized that Jackson hadn't been seen since the report was published.

"Come on!" Jackson shouted. He rushed them, swinging his knife. A man caught his arm, another grabbed him around the waist. Jackson managed to slash one man across the palm. Spanner came out from behind the counter with an axe handle and hit Jackson on the head. The man who held him by the waist eased him to the floor.

Spanner looked down. "Poor blackass sonofabitch," he said.

The Reverend Glendon Hoover was a gentle and slow man who was always surprised and saddened when he confronted the viciousness and miseries of life. This he did almost daily, but somehow his faith in the basic goodness of existence and of his fellow men—white and black—remained hale and intact. Though he believed in a very literal devil, it was difficult for him to see evil inherent in men, only ignorance. His Harrisonburgh congregation was impoverished, but large, loyal, and energetic, and the Reverend Hoover was probably *the* most beloved black preacher in the state. By the Negroes. He was ceaselessly active on his people's behalf, but he was discreet and never failed to recognize the point with whites beyond which he couldn't go. He was a whisperer rather than a screamer, and he knew the value of the strategic retreat. The average white appreciated him; if niggers couldn't be slaves, then this was the next best thing. Most found him amusing, too.

MaCullum did not. MaCullum understood very well that an extended war of attrition could be, in the end, waged even more successfully than a brief, savage one of frontal assault. And there was no doubt that Hoover was waging such a war. The man was not a fool, and MaCullum did not consider treating him as such. The office at the back of the church was modestly but comfortably furnished—a desk, a few sturdy, cushioned chairs, some paintings, and a cast-iron planter with lush growth. Hoover asked MaCullum to sit.

"Cigar, Reverend?"

"Yes. Thank you." Hoover sniffed. "Wonderful."

"Havana. I import a case a month."

"A pleasant luxury."

"It is." MaCullum leaned forward. "Reverend, I'm here for your help."

"I assumed that."

"We both know that a lot of colored voters are going to cast their ballots strictly on what you say."

"We both know, Mr. MaCullum, that they'll be voting for Governor Reid regardless of what I say. By happy accident my advice and their predisposition will be one and the same."

"Of course you'd prefer Reid. I would too if I were a colored man. I think that's a mistake, but the essential merit of my position versus Reid's is another question. I didn't come to argue philosophy, but to discuss practical tactics. Reality may not be ideal, but it's all we've got. A man on a scaffold with a noose around his neck can close his eyes and imagine he's on a hilltop, but that trapdoor's going to open and his neck will be broken all the same."

Hoover smiled. "A very apt metaphor."

MaCullum ignored the remark. "Reid can't win. He has no support in Washington, the Republican party is crumbling, the federal troops have been withdrawn, nearly all the ex-Confederates have been reenfranchised. It's strictly between Luther Stringfellow and me."

"I'm not convinced of that."

"I suspect you are, Reverend. And you're either allowing yourself to be blinded by your wishes to the contrary, or you're just not willing to make the admission to me. No matter. You comprehend reality well, you've demonstrated that amply in the past. I trust you to do so again. I'm not to your liking, and I doubt I ever will be. I won't change, I don't expect you to either. But you know I'm a reasonable man, and you also know what Stringfellow is. Candidly, if the election were held tomorrow, Stringfellow would win. That's the tenor of the state. His margin isn't so large that it can't be overcome, but I simply won't be able to do that without help from the colored voters. I need at least 50 percent of the Negro vote. I might do it with 40 or 45, but that would be shaving it very close."

"Mr. MaCullum, even if you were to persuade me to your viewpoint, which would take at least the Second Coming, you'd *never* get 40 percent of the colored vote. My people would vote for a hog first." He smiled. "No offense intended. I'm just speaking of one of those practical realities you mentioned."

MaCullum suppressed his temper. "You're too modest. You're much more a leader than you give yourself credit for. Please think seriously about this, Reverend. The Negroes of this state will decide whether it's me or Luther Stringfellow who sits in the governor's chair. That can have awesome consequences for both our races."

Hoover studied the long ash of his cigar. "Sometimes I wonder if we don't take earthly affairs all too seriously."

"Perhaps. But God isn't standing for the governorship."

Hoover laughed. "More's the pity."

MaCullum stood. "Thanks for your time, Reverend. I know you'll give this deep consideration. We can do much for this state together."

They shook hands and Hoover showed MaCullum out. A black man from the livery stable drove MaCullum back to the Harrisonburgh railroad station in a hired surrey. MaCullum's campaign train—festooned with the Stars and Bars as well as the Stars and Stripes, with bunting of red and black and banners reading MACULLUM FOR GOVERNOR—was backed onto a siding. The first car carried the band and the performers who warmed up the crowds before MaCullum came out to speak. In the second were Jeremy Goodwin and two assistants. Goodwin was a crafty, efficient, and indispensable man who had worked directly under Judah P. Benjamin, the Confederacy's secretary of war, and who had a reputation of toughness and unparalleled devotion to the cause. It was popularly believed that he had gone wild with grief on learning of Lee's surrender and had attempted suicide. He'd been enlisted in the campaign to counter charges of MaCullum being a softliner. The suicide story was wholly untrue. Actually, Goodwin was a thorough pragmatist who could adapt endlessly to the changing demands of political climate and terrain. But it was this very quality, along with his public image of intractability, which made him so valuable.

MaCullum's private car was the last, furnished in rich wood, wool carpeting, and plush drapes, and containing sleeping quarters, an intimate dining room, and a spacious area that was both office and conference room. Goodwin was there with the mayor of Harrisonburgh, and a planter, the president of the town's largest bank, the owner of a sawmill, and a state legislator. MaCullum had hoped to grab a few hours' sleep; he couldn't, but at least Goodwin had already completed the negotiating and he had only to confirm and clarify a few points, socialize a while. Part of the tribute men like this demanded for their support was to rub elbows with Colonel Thurlow MaCullum, to call him by his first name, drink his liquor, and smoke his cigars. It went a long way with friends and business acquaintances.

When it was over MaCullum stripped off his jacket, undid his tie, and rolled up his shirtsleeves. He called Constantine. The black man knelt and removed MaCullum's boots. MaCullum flexed his toes. "Oh that feels good. Let the glasses and ashtrays go till later, Constantine. Draw me a hot tub."

"Yas, suh."

"I don't know how you do it," MaCullum said to Goodwin. "I can hardly keep my eyes open with these oafs. They all look and sound the same to me, town after town."

"And they all have one thing in common—local power. You don't win elections without that."

"Uhm. How are we doing here?"

"Better than I expected, but not as well as I'd hoped. There are some determined Stringfellow men. What response did you get from Hoover?"

"Neutral. You can never tell what that damn nigger's thinking. I believe he'll come around, though. It's to his best interest."

"Never trust men to know their best interests." Goodwin slipped a watch from his pocket and glanced at it. "You have an hour and a half."

"Is it a dinner party, or what?"

"Private dinner first, then a ball."

MaCullum groaned.

"We need them. I'll brief you tonight on the important people in Maplestock."

"Maplestock?"

"We arrive there at nine tomorrow morning."

"How do you do it, Jem? If I'd had you as a field officer, we would have won the war."

"Let's settle for the election. See you in an hour and a half." He left, and MaCullum marveled at him. The man was indefatigable, and relentlessly thorough, overlooked nothing.

MaCullum didn't have a formal campaign manager. If something had to be decided immediately, then he made the decision. Otherwise policy and plans were formulated in caucus by himself, Goodwin, Lowery, Oberst, Durfee, and Carswell. He was coming to rely more and more upon Goodwin's judgment, though. The man had an uncanny knack of seeing directly to the heart of a problem, assessing it quickly, and offering an effective solution. MaCullum was not turning control over to Goodwin, but he was using him with increasing frequency as a sounding board, and trusting his reactions.

Constantine informed MaCullum that the bath was ready. The black helped MaCullum from his clothes in the sleeping quarters where the copper tub was, then began to scrub MaCullum's back after he had stepped into the water.

The blacks *were* the key, MaCullum thought. There was no way around it. He didn't see how he could do any more with them. His organization was sponsoring song and dance shows and other entertainments in black communities. It had rented riverboats for day-long cruises with free food and refreshments; the Negroes were especially fond of these. And hired trains to take them to favored picnic sites. It had helped blacks obtain mortgages, credit for seed and equipment, and had given legal aid. It had sent white representatives stumping through their settlements, an attention never paid them by Democrats before. It had bribed members of Loyal Leagues to argue that Reid couldn't win, that they must rally to MaCullum. It had purchased blocks of black votes outright, offering an expensive twenty cents per head. Only intimidation remained and MaCullum knew better than to try that. If frightened, the blacks would simply avoid the polls, making Stringfellow's victory certain. Lowery had ordered the Knights restrained, and had even seen that violence done to Negroes by other whites was kept to a minimum. A few unregenerate blacks, loud in their opposition to MaCullum, were arrested by local peace officers and were being held until the election was over. For the right sums, MaCullum's people had even had some of Stringfellow's more virulent agitators and stumpers arrested.

Constantine laved and rinsed MaCullum's limbs, chest,

and back. MaCullum washed his private parts, abstracted, then stepped from the tub and enfolded himself in the large soft towel Constantine held. "You can clean up the office now," MaCullum told him. "Wake me in half an hour. The tub can wait until after I've left."

"Yas, suh."

MaCullum stretched out on the wide canopied bed without turning down the spread. The niggers, he thought. Goddamn the Union everlastingly for putting the vote in their hands. You might as well give a child a razor. But the black vote was already a matter of constitutional amendment and there was nothing to be done about it on the federal level. There were, however, many ways to emasculate it on the state level. It would be one of his first tasks as governor.

MaCullum fell into a fitful sleep dreaming about razors and children.

Thistle was lightheaded and weak. She'd been fasting three days in the swamp, and had slept little. This afternoon she had stumbled and fallen, and as she lay looking up into the blinding sun she had a vision. Spirits, demons, angels, and strange terrible creatures warred with one another across the vault of the burning sky. They were ferocious and merciless and they rent each other with fangs and claws, they severed limbs and lopped off heads with bright swords, crushed one another with cudgels and pounding wings, brutal feet. It was furious slaughter and finally, when she felt she could endure no more, the vision left her and she woke whimpering.

She reflected, and gained some heart. She had worked purification rites and attempted to commune with her powers since entering the swamp, hoping for a sign. Now she had it: her powers *were* struggling with the forces of Obadiah's god. She pinched up the blood-crusted goat lips pinned to her dress and she kissed them in gratitude.

There was one final ceremony to perform. She walked unsteadily to the black cat. It hung from a limb by a rope tied to its hind legs. Its head dangled a few inches above a pot of water in which were the whitened spine of a cottonmouth, the skeleton of a rat, feathers from a chicken and a hawk, and a little dust from a fresh grave. She seized the cat by the scruff of its neck. It twisted and spat, raked her arm with its claws. She ignored the pain and slit the furry throat. Hot blood fountained and the animal writhed and doubled on itself. Slowly it stilled and began to relax. The heartbeat faded, blood pumped into the pot in weakening spurts. The animal died. She let it hang until it drained empty. She lit the fire. While the water heated she opened the skull of the dead cat with her knife, scooped out the warm brains and ate them.

She let the pot boil a while, then took it off to cool. She'd carried Obadiah's worn Bible and a wooden cross from the house. She opened the Bible to its precise center, drove a long nail through the spine, then turned the book so that the hard cover was on the ground, the leaves uppermost, and the nail projecting through them. She inverted the cross and forced it onto the nail; it rose upside down from the Bible. She stood and lifted her dress, straddled the book, and strained until she managed to squeeze a sprinkling of pale urine from her deprived bladder. Then she smeared the urine-wet cross and Bible with pitch and dropped them into the fire.

She sipped from the brew in the pot while she attended the burning. The cross went quickly, but the book was more difficult. As the top pages blackened and shriveled, she exposed the compacted underlying pages to the flames with a stick. She thought of Obadiah while she waited. She hoped her absence wasn't making him suffer. She felt no rancor toward him for forcing his god's baptism upon her. She loved him for it: he hadn't known what fearful consequences he'd exposed her to, had acted only through concern for what he thought was her immortal soul. Indeed, she herself had many times worked magic in his behalf, for his good. How could she hate a man who loved her so deeply, who only tried to do for her in his way what she had done for him in hers? And she found a little solace, a little hope in knowing that her magic had not driven his god to abandon him; perhaps, then, his action would not drive her powers from her.

The cover would not burn completely, but it was charred and crumbly and nothing remained of the pages. Thistle decided this was sufficient. She dispersed the ashes, left the cat hanging for the carrion eaters, and started for home. It was out of her hands now.

Comfort was scattering feed to the chickens when Vulture returned. They strutted and pecked in a circle around her. The day was warm and she wore a bandana around her head. There were circles in the armpits of her dress. "Hullo," she said. "Enny luck?"

"I found two nice places. High land, good soil. Either one would do."

"Where 'bouts?" He told her, and she said, "They both fittin'. Which you goan build on?"

"Neither."

She lumped a cheek with her tongue and squinted at him.

"I like it here. I like it better than anyplace I've ever been. Think I'd be a fool if I didn't stay."

"Yuh?"

'Uh-huh."

"Tol' you befo'. Ah's not a triflin' woman."

"I know."

"You tellin' me you wants me fo' *yo* woman?"

"Yes."

"An' you willin' t' say you goan be mah man?"

"Yes."

"Well, you sure havin' trouble tellin' it."

"Will you?"

She stepped to him, put her hands on his shoulders, and kissed him lightly on the mouth. "Yas."

"I'll go find Obadiah Isley tomorrow. We'll have him say the words over us as soon as he can. I'll sleep in the shed until then."

Her arms circled his waist. "What we want with a preacher-man? Ain't nothin' he can do t' bind us any tighter or looser. We the people, not him." She took hold of her dress, pulled it slowly over her head, and let it fall away. "We doan need no other marryin'."

After dinner Swett pulled a chair in front of the fireplace and sat staring at the burning logs. Arabella cleared the table and washed the dishes. She threw the dirty water out, dried her hands, approached Swett haltingly, and stopped several feet from him. She chewed on her knuckles. She could no longer bear his hatred. She had formed a plan, with difficulty and pain, but now she didn't know how to begin.

He looked up scowling. "Why you lingerin' heah, whore? Ah tol' yuh, you hide yo corrup' se'f in thet room lessen' yuh called fo'. You step out othuwise, an' Ah beat yuh agin."

She clenched her fists; nails dug into palms. She caught her lower lip between her teeth. She had to do it now. "Wallace!" She rushed forward and fell to her knees, pressed her head against his thighs. "Ah bin prayin' hard, Wallace, prayin' t' God un'il mah skin raw f'om kneelin'." His hand, which was raised to strike her, hesitated. She continued in a torrent, knowing that if she couldn't snare him now he'd be lost to her forever. "God show me, He answer me, Wallace, He open mah eyes an' le' me see. Ah knows the Debil had me. Ah re'lizes the evil grip he put on me. He take possession an' make me do them rottin' filthy thin's. Ah so disgusted an' shamed wif mahse'f." She dripped copious tears on his pants. "God rescue me, He lif' me up from the foulness an' make me pure agin." She shook her head savagely and beat her breast. "But Ah hates mahse'f, Wallace! Ah die wif mor'fication 'memberin' what Ah done." She sobbed.

Swett's crotch tightened. His penis rose. "Ah's glad, Ar'bella."

"Kin 'ou evuh fo'give me!" she wailed. "Kin 'ou lub me?"

He touched her hair. "Ah think so. Goan be hard t' 'rase the mem'ry, but Ah thinks Ah can do it."

She kissed his hand. "Oh, 'ou so good! Ah be the bestus wife in the hull worl' fo' 'ou, Wallace."

He pulled her up. "Ah'm goan take you t' bed."

She recoiled. "No, Wallace. Ah coul'n't!"

His groin was afire. "Yuh gots to. It yo duty. A natural man feels the urges, an' if he her husban', then a good Christian woman endures no mattuh whut. You knows Ah dint feel nothin' fo' yuh when yuh was unclean an' defiled. It a sign that ever'thin' all right now, that Ah loves yuh."

She hung her head and allowed herself to be led into the

bedroom. She undressed in the dark. She heard Wallace breathing heavily as he stripped off his clothes.

He spread her legs and entered her immediately. She wasn't ready, and it hurt. He drove on anyway. She moistened quickly, and it was better then. Her hips wanted to move, her legs wanted to lock around him, but she gritted her teeth and forced herself to lie perfectly still while he grunted and humped excitedly.

It was a loud rain, and it struck the cabin roof with a sudden rush. Thistle sat up in bed and listened. Obadiah rolled over beside her, then resumed snoring. She rose and padded through the darkness on bare feet. She opened the door and stepped outside. The drops were large and heavy and they struck her forcefully, soaking her nightdress in moments. She went back inside, and by the time she toweled herself dry and slipped into a new garment the rain had slackened. A few minutes later it was gone entirely and the night was still again.

A quick rain with large drops was a bad omen. She sat very quietly and probed into herself once more. She could not feel her powers, nor could she sense any void left by their departure. There was no resolution yet. The omen did not necessarily relate to her powers; omens were difficult to interpret specifically.

She got back into bed and snuggled up against Obadiah's warm body. He had caused her fear, but not maliciously, and, curiously, he remained, as he always had been, a watershed of comfort to her. She hugged him tightly.

MaCullum, Clayton Lowery, and Jeremy Goodwin met in MaCullum's Woodboro offices a week after the railway campaign ended. MaCullum mixed the drinks himself. "Where's your nigger?" Lowery asked. "Conrad, Colombus, whatever it is."

"Constantine. I sent him out for the night."

Goodwin asked what time the others would arrive—he had papers for MaCullum to sign and wanted to get them out of the way before the meeting began. MaCullum said no one else was expected. He sipped his drink appreciatively, took his time lighting a cigar.

"We're not going to win," he said at last. "I've been going over reports and analyses all week. It's polarized between Reid and Stringfellow. There's no room for compromise in this one. We'll be doing well to take a fifth of the vote."

"I think you exaggerate," Lowery said.

"You haven't seen the latest intelligence. You know I'm not a pessimist, but I am a realist. What does the data say to you, Jem?"

"Not good, though I wouldn't allow as how we're down to a fifth. We still have a few weeks to go. We can do a lot in that time."

"Three weeks," MaCullum said. "Can you honestly tell me we have more chance than a chicken with its head on a chopping block?"

Goodwin studied his fingernails. "No. I guess I can't."

"Well," Lowery said. "This is a shock. I knew we were trailing, but I didn't think it was so bad." He took one of MaCullum's cigars and chewed on it without lighting it. "Hhmmm. Then we bargain with Stringfellow and offer him a concession and support in exchange for whatever we can get from him."

"Wouldn't work," MaCullum said. "He's a fanatic, you know that. He'd eat my liver if I gave him the chance. And he doesn't need us. He'll walk away with the election no matter what we do."

"My God! You're not suggesting we swing to Reid, are you?"

"I might be willing to try if I thought it would work. But most of the voters who support us would simply shift to Stringfellow. It comes out the same no matter what we do."

Lowery held out his hands, palms up, and shrugged. "Well. Well, gentlemen, then we've been beaten. I suppose nothing remains but a gracious retreat."

"That's simple enough for you," MaCullum said. "You own half the goddamn state. You won't be affected one way or the other."

"I resent that, Thurlow. I supported you on principle. And don't forget that I've pumped one hell of a lot of money into your campaign."

"Not on principle alone you haven't. With me in the governor's mansion you stood to make a lot and you know it. If you've forgotten, just look at your safe and you'll find those agreements and postdated contracts I signed."

"Which are worth about as much as hog guts now." Lowery stood. "I've got better things to do than sit and be insulted."

MaCullum got to his feet and touched Lowery's shoulder. "Please, Clayton. I'm sorry. I'm tired, overwrought, my temper is short. I had no call to speak to you like that, and I apologize. Stay, please."

Lowery was conciliated. He sat. MaCullum drained what was left of his drink. He was flushed. "There is a way to win. *One* way and one way only. And it guarantees victory."

"How?" Lowery asked.

"Some nigger is going to murder Stringfellow."

Goodwin grunted. Lowery's jaw dropped.

MaCullum paced rapidly. "Hear me out. This wasn't easy to contemplate or even to say. I've spent several anguished nights thinking about it. Murder is a foul and repellent deed to every civilized man. But we must see it in perspective. Stringfellow is a vicious creature, hardly deserving of being called a man. If he were a dog, he'd be a rabid one. And as much as you regret it, there's only one thing you can do with a rabid dog. As governor, he could ruin this state, go to such extremes that Washington *couldn't* overlook them. The federal government would be forced to send troops, and the consequences would be disastrous. Though this is somewhat melodramatic, I believe Stringfellow capable, under certain circumstances, of sparking another war. The South simply could not survive that. On the other hand think of the kind of enlightened administration we could give to the state. We could set an example for the entire South, and the South in turn could lead the nation out of this black-white morass.

"Gentlemen, I say to you that there occur moments in history in which mankind stands at a crossroads. One path leads to destruction, the other to grandeur. I feel we are at such a junction now. Stature and strength of character are demanded. I am convinced that we must surmount our natural revulsion, steel ourselves against regret, and make this sacrifice. History and the common good of the weal impel us to the act."

Goodwin leaned forward and stared at his clasped hands, brow furrowed deeply.

"You believe all that?" Lowery asked.

"I do," MaCullum said somberly.

"Mighty impressive. The thing is, it's still murder, and they'd hang us for it. We've got influence, all right, but not enough to keep the noose off our necks."

Lowery hadn't questioned ethics, only mechanics. MaCullum had him. "We hire two men from out of state. We pay them well. It's worth it. Stringfellow horsewhipped a big nigger, Clarence Johnson, up around Raven's Hollow last week for splashing mud on him. Johnson has a reputation for violence and he swore he'd get Stringfellow. There were witnesses. Our men will beat Stringfellow to death with a shovel or something. It's the way Johnson would do it. He's muscular and brutish. He'll be lynched before the sheriff can even get to the scene of the crime. Or if he manages to run, even better. A hunt would distract people."

"We'd still have two murderers to contend with. They'd blackmail us," Lowery said.

"We'll have them eliminated."

"So we hire murderers to murder the murderers, then murderers to murder the murderers of the murderers. It would be endless, Thurlow. Anyone we buy for that sort of thing would realize how vulnerable we are. We'd never get out from under them."

MaCullum smiled. "We hire no one beyond the initial two, but we do get word to the Knights that a couple of out-of-staters have just delivered a shipment of guns to some insurrectionary niggers. And we let them know where these white traitors can be found."

"Suppose they talk before they're killed?"

"The Knights aren't known for their slow reflective qualities. Our men will be finished before they even know anyone is near. If one of them is able to say anything, what Knight of the Canescent Dominion is going to believe a nigger-loving gunrunner who tells him Clayton Lowery, the original Grand Holocaust, was involved in Luther Stringfellow's death at the hands of a renegade nigger."

"You build a good case, Thurlow. I have to admit that."

MaCullum was pleased. Lowery was a conservative and cautious man. But it was Goodwin who would make the final decision. MaCullum had come to place more faith in Goodwin's judgment even than he did in his own. "Jem?"

Goodwin made a steeple of his fingers. "It's bizarre. But who's to say that bizarries exclude themselves by definition? It's only that they don't occur to most men. I'm not much concerned with the historical view. I live in the present. Our goal is to elect Colonel Thurlow MaCullum governor. Whatever accomplishes that is good, whatever obstructs it is bad. As you've outlined it, I think your plan is sound. There are some risks, but they're minimal. Statistically, I think it unlikely that we ever be linked to the act.

"But I am concerned with the aftermath. The dolts and oafs could run amuck, retaliate against niggers across the state. If there *were* a bloodbath, you'd have the same sort of thing you fear would happen if Stringfellow were elected—the federal government would be forced to act. They'd occupy the state. We'd be neutralized even if we did control the governorship. We'll have to be cautious. How far along is Partridge with the new militia?"

MaCullum was excited. His stomach gurgled, and he belched. "He's brought it up to full strength. And he's in firm control."

"Good. We'll need both the militia and the Knights to suppress major violence. We know Clayton can direct the Knights. Are we sure we can depend on Partridge?"

"No question of it."

Goodwin nodded. "There's a lot to be done in the next few days, and we won't have much time to sleep, but . . . we can do it, by God we can do it!"

Lowery's and Goodwin's glasses still held bourbon. MaCullum sloshed more into his own, spilled some on the carpet in his eagerness. He raised the drink:

"Gentlemen, we have crossed the Rubicon!"

Obadiah was reading to his family from his new Bible. Six years they'd had their black mongrel dog and it had never destroyed anything before. But he didn't question Thistle when she told him the animal had chewed up his old Bible and dragged what was left into the brush where she couldn't find it. Luke, the baby, was sucking on a pork chop bone and murmuring happily. The other two boys listened with exaggerated seriousness.

"And he went on to say to them: 'Go, eat the fatty things and drink the sweet things, and send portions to the one for whom nothing has been prepared; for this—' "

A cock crowed in the darkness. Thistle and her oldest son, Paul, turned and stared at the blackness behind the window.

Obadiah cleared his throat and continued. " '—for this day is holy to our Lord, and do not feel hurt, for the joy of Jehovah is your stronghold.' "

The cock was still crowing, and Thistle and Paul attended it.

"Is somethin' wrong?" Obadiah asked.

"No." Thistle smiled. "Go on."

"It a bad sign," Paul said. "Rooster crowin' in the dark ain't natural, Maw says. Means things ain't right. Kin yuh tell whut, Maw?"

"Hush."

"Boy," Obadiah said wearily. "That's pagan nonsense. That's just plain superstition. Put it out o' yo mind." He looked to Thistle. "You been teachin' him your ways again?"

"No," she said, and reasoned it wasn't a lie; her forced baptism had made her feel unable to continue Paul's instruction.

"This boy is a child of the Lord. Don't you forget that."

"Ah won't. Go on, Obadiah."

He looked at her for several moments, shook his head, then picked up the text where he had left off.

Outside, the crowing sounded again.

Woodson woke to the warmth of rich golden light that spilled through the window. He stretched, being careful not to disturb Wilda, who was sleeping snugly against him. There was stiffness in his muscles, and it hurt a little when he flexed them, but he could tell it was the kind of stiffness that would work itself out before the morning was very old, and he was pleased. Yesterday he'd made his fifth trip into the swamp with Hector. It had gone well, and he

knew it even before Hector said, "You doin' some better."
He hadn't any illusions about becoming a real swamper,
but the swamp was no longer such an alien and impossible
place. And his body was hardening.

He studied Wilda's face. Softness settled her features
when she slept and made her especially appealing. There
was vulnerability too, and trust. Woodson kissed her lightly. They didn't sleep on the floor anymore. He'd put together a bedframe, large enough for both of them, and
moved their mattresses onto the cross-ropes between the
runners. They lived now as a man and his woman. It was
what they both wanted, and it was good for them. She
opened her eyes.

"Good morning," he said.

"Mo'nin'."

She kissed his ear and got out of bed. She was naked.
The days were warm, the nights temperate, modesty un-
necessary. She went out from the room to kindle a fire for
breakfast. Woodson luxuriated in bed, listening to a lark.
Wilda entered and looked concerned, seeing he wasn't up
yet. "Sick?"

"No. Just lazy and feeling good." His eyes wandered
over her. Her breasts were not even a handful each, but
they were crowned with large plum-dark nipples, and her
hips had flared, her flat child's stomach grown to the slight
mound of a young woman's. He reached out to her, and
she came to him. Their mouths opened and locked together, his hands slid over the lustrous brown smoothness of
her skin. They made love, and then slept some.

When they woke again Woodson said, "You know
what? I declare today a holiday. We'll fish a little, we'll
walk, we'll go swimming down at Turtle Highbanks, we'll
do anything we want, anything at all. What do you think?"

She smiled and nodded. They dressed, and while Wilda
started breakfast cooking Woodson took the slop bucket
from under the bed and went outside to empty it. The
fresh tender green of new shoots filled some ten acres. He
was growing corn, potatoes, radishes, beans, even half an
acre of peanuts. There would be hay, too, at the end of the
summer. Next month he would get a cow, and the month
after that a boar and a sow for breeding. The barn was
painted, the cabin secure and snug, the well running pure.

Woodson marveled at how little a man really needed. With a couple of animals, he and Wilda would have everything they required for a good life. He was in debt to Spanner for tools, for seed, for clothes, for staples in the larder. But he could work off some of that this summer, and next year he could put in a cash crop which would pay the last of it.

He heard Wilda humming in the kitchen. Mostly, he knew, it was her; alone, he would simply be surviving; with her, he was living. She infused everything with meaning. She justified his efforts. She filled his days. He went back in, happy.

After breakfast they moved to the yard and sat on grass in the good sunlight to drink their coffee. Woodson packed a pipe and drew smoke in slow, meditative puffs. They watched a rider crossing a hill a quarter-mile to the west. Woodson squinted. "Seems like he's coming here." And as the rider drew closer: "Harry Simms." Simms had a farm nearby. Woodson and Wilda socialized with him and his wife; some of the Hellbottom people didn't give a damn about Woodson's color, and figured whatever he'd done years ago in the legislature was his business.

Woodson stood. "Morning, Harry."

"Hi, Em. You hear the news?"

"What news?"

"Luther Stringfellow. He got hisse'f murdered. Big nigger done it, they say. Beat his haid in wif a shovel. Oooeee! Cain' say Ah'm goan t' miss that okra."

"Shit!" Woodson kicked savagely at a rock. He heard the deep-chested rumbling of the Beast. He sighed. "It never gives up," he said. "It can't be stopped."

Simms frowned. "Whut?"

3

It wasn't any good with Wallace. He bedded her—if briefly—at least furiously enough, but turned cold and hostile if she began to respond. Arabella knew about his nigger whore. And she bitterly envied the black girl's freedom. Her own body had sweeping, powerful needs, and it punished her in its frustration. So she offered it what she could, alone in the bedroom while Wallace was out working.

Mr. Wilfert, their neighbor down the road, had a nigger clearing the new field. The trees had been cut and hauled to the sawmill, and the nigger was starting to work on the stumps. Arabella had seen him yesterday, dreamed about him last night. Wallace was away with most of the other local men hunting Clarence Johnson, the buck who'd murdered Luther Stringfellow. Early in the afternoon Arabella returned to Wilfert's land and crawled into some bushes in a copse of trees overlooking the new field.

The day was painfully bright and too warm. She lay on her stomach on a bed of leaves. Her forehead rested on her arms and she drifted into a pleasant lassitude, a dullish reverie of memories; images of Leila rolled expansively through her mind, swelling down to her loins, making her move her hips a little on the dry leaves.

Leila was her cousin. She'd come to live with the Smallses after her parents died, and she'd stayed several months before running off. She was a year older than Arabella, who was thirteen then. They slept together, huddling against each other during the cold nights. One night Leila lodged a leg between Arabella's thighs while they looked across the one-room shack at Henry Smalls, who was rutting on his wife in the thin moonlight. Smalls was a goatish man and Arabella had been watching him mount his wife for years, and the sight and sounds had shaken her with a generalized, confusing excitement. Leila began to move her leg and Arabella clutched at her. Leila held her, rocked her, and whispered softly, "Yas, yas, God yas, oh yas li'l cousin," and finally something in Arabella shattered and she was swept spinning away on hot, sweet floodwaters. She gasped, and then whimpered with relief, but no one in the shack heard her, or if they did they paid her no mind.

Arabella lived in a muted haze of sensuality while Leila was there. They stroked and touched and pressed against each other every night, and in the warm weather they stole into the woods and stripped off their clothes and examined each other, laid down and intertwined and rubbed eagerly and tremblingly together. Occasionally they put their fingers into each other. Sometimes they went into the barn and fondled Smalls's old horse until the animal's great cock slid from its sheath and hung there heavy, wet, and swollen. When Leila vanished, Arabella manipulated herself, but it wasn't really the same. She took her younger sister into the barn and played with her, but the child was only ten, and awkward, and it was never as good. And then later there was Wallace . . . his stiff magnificent cock . . . the wild ecstasy of their first night . . . the plunge into painful emptiness. . . .

Chunk.

Arabella stirred.

Chunk.

She opened her eyes, blinked, lifted her head.

Chunk.

She'd fallen asleep. She saw the nigger working on the stumps. He'd set burning coals to smoldering against three of them and was hacking at another with a double-bitted ax. This close, he was even more beautiful than she'd thought. He was stripped to the waist and sweat-sheened. He swung the heavy ax with an easy rhythm. He was wide-shouldered, broad-chested, muscles large and well defined, cording and relaxing as he worked. A line of bristly hair ran from his navel down his flat abdomen to disappear into his waistband. His long legs were planted wide apart and the fabric of his pants tightened over his heavy thighs and crotch when he swung the ax.

Arabella rolled onto her back. She turned her head to the side, watching the black man. Her hands rubbed her belly. Her legs parted a little. The Negro swung the ax. She pulled her dress up, bunching it around her waist. She hooked her thumbs in her drawers, lifted her buttocks from the ground, and slid the garment down her legs. The man paused to wipe his brown face with a handkerchief, then stretched and did a couple of kneebends. Arabella probed with her hand until her fingers closed around the candle she'd brought. The black picked up the ax and went back to work. Arabella's free hand touched the thatch of her pubic hair, found the nubbin between her fleshy ridges, and caressed it.

The black man worked unaware beneath the hot sun, and Arabella moistened, touched the candle to herself, eased it in, out, then in, played with her button, rotated her hips, grew slack-mouthed, watched the black man's hard body move, panted, began to moan. . . .

The ground was broken by hoof and heel prints and littered with empty cartridge casings that glinted in the sun. A sod hut squatted two hundred yards away. Three large holes gaped in the nearest wall. A splintery piece of broken door hung askew on a hinge. An elderly gray-bearded white man picked through the spent casings.

"Damn," Swett said. "Damn it to hell."

He and the Hearth had made camp last night with a dozen men from Woodboro. They told him that Leroy Darling and *his* Hearth had ambushed a couple of whites near the state line who'd been running guns to the niggers. Darling had found four thousand dollars on the bodies. Darling's Hearth had eight members, and Jimmy Hildenbrandt told Swett it would come out to five hundred dollars for each man. Sonofabitch, five hundred dollars! Then this afternoon they'd been combing a long, brush-tangled ravine when they'd gotten word that the nigger had been brought to bay and was holed up fifteen miles to the west. They abused their mounts, which were now standing sweat-slicked and with hanging heads, blowing loudly, but they were too late for the kill. There was no one left but the old man.

He shambled over to them. "G'day, boys, g'day t' yuh. Yuh come fo' the nigger? He long gone—whut was left of him. What weren't much." He laughed wheezingly. "Like a Thanksgivin' turkey shooot roun' heah. Ain't heard so much boomin' an' bangin', nor choked on so much smoke since the war. Right prodigal with they ammunition them boys was." He held up a cartridge. "Fo'ty-four caliber. Got a passel already, an' they's lots mo' layin' abouts. Wuth a hull penny apiece when yuh reloads yo own. Plenty o' all kinds heah iffen you boys got a mind t' save some money."

"How'd they take 'im?" Swett asked.

The man dropped the casing into a pouch where it clinked against others. "It was a real sight, it was. He went t' ground in thet hut theah. Walls are a foot thick. Had himse'f a army carbine an' a Navy Colt. Plenty o' bullets too. Jus' as mean an' hard t' get at as badger in a hole. Must o' been sixty, seventy boys heah all told. They fired on thet hut the bettuh part of an hour. Put so much lead into it, yuh'd think it'd sink into the ground jus' from the weight. But they ain't no slug goin' get through them walls, not even from a buffalo gun. Ever' time some o' 'em tried t' sneak close, nigger'd open up. Not a bad shot either. Kilt two, an' put bullets in grievous places on two mo'. Well, some boys from Chicken Hawk Creek got t' thinkin', an' they rode off an' come back with thet little two-pounder cannon from the war that's down by the postmaster's. They missed the fust few times, but then they figgered the range an' put a couple good solid rounds in theah. Few boys moved fo'ward cautious like, an' when the nigger dint fire on 'em they rushed the hut. Foun' thet ol' darky in two separate pieces, they did. Cut in half right below the bellybutton. Funnies' thing yuh evuh did see. They tied one rope roun' his neck an' another roun' his ankles, an' they lef' t' drag both pieces all the way back t' Woodboro." He slapped his leg. "Doan expec' they goin' t' be much lef' but a couple hunks o' meat by the time they gets theah."

"How long they been gone?"

"A hour, li'l better."

"Well, we ain' goan ketch 'em, thet's certain. They ridin' fast an' happy." Swett was depressed. "Some people has all the luck, thet's all you can say."

Leonard Sikes said, "Whut we goan do, Wallace?"

"Go back home," Swett said disgustedly. "Ain't nothin' else *to* do." He thanked the old man and wished him luck finding .44 casings. Then he turned his mount and led the Hearth away in a walk, brooding, wanting to gallop, but knowing they'd pushed the horses too hard already.

A mile away, Swett reined up. The others stopped behind him. He hunched in his saddle and stared at a black man who was slopping a big boar and a sow in a pen next to his barn. Swett twisted around. "Jimmy, hand over thet rifle o' yourn."

Hildenbrandt slipped the Winchester from its scabbard and passed it to Swett. The Negro saw the gun, dropped the slop pail, and ran for his cabin. The door closed behind him before Swett could shoulder the weapon. Swett took slow aim on the pigpen.

"Wallace," Johnny Murphy said, "we s'posed to leave the niggers alone. Only Clarence Johnson, that's what the Wildfire said."

"Shutup." The rifle cracked, and the boar fell heavily. The sow squealed and scrambled away, surprisingly quick for such a bulky animal. She grunted in consternation. *Cr-rack!* She collapsed in the mud. Swett turned the rifle to the cabin. He worked the lever and fired leisurely. Slugs punched holes in the door, shattered the windows. Then the firing pin clicked on an empty chamber. He returned the rifle to Hildenbrandt. "Got t' get me one o' them," he said.

"You hadn't ought t' done that," Johnny Murphy said.

"Thet nigger yo fren'? Or is the pigs?"

"We had instructions."

"Yeah, an' we was tol' t' stay out o' Woodboro too, but nobody evuh come down on us fo' thet."

"We ain't goin' do no more o' this."

"You reckon on disobeyin' yo Torch?"

Johnny was angrily pale. "I just said we ain't goin' do no more."

"How you figure thet Johnson nigger got this far, huh? He had help from the other niggers 'long the way. They doan get no punishment, they goan think they kin do it agin. Shee-it! Goddamn gorillas is already bold enough t' murder a candidate fo' governor, hide an' shield the buck whut done it, an' pay fo' thousand dollars fo' guns. Whut thet tell you, boy? Doan take no brains atall t' re'lize Woodboro was jus' a test. They found they weak spots, an' now they makin' ready fo' a real war wif no mistakes. Well, they goan learn they ain't got a straw's chance in a bonfire. We goan teach 'em."

"The onliest thing I know is what we was told. An' that's the onliest thing we're goin' t' do."

Lemuel Propp said, "He right, Wallace. Ah doan like it no mo' 'n you, but orders is orders."

Swett unholstered his revolver, spun the cylinder looking to see that all six chambers were filled. "Check yo weapons, boys. We goan kill thet nigger in theah, an we ain't goan call fo' no cannon t' do it."

"No we ain't, Wallace." Johnny's hand dropped on the butt of his own revolver.

Leonard Sikes edged his horse close to Swett's. Fred Harwood moved up beside Johnny. The other Knights backed away.

Swett held his pistol lightly. "Ah remind ever' one of yuh," he said, "thet you swore an oath when you joined the Knights. It says thet disobedience t' yo appointed superiors is punishable by death, death, *death*."

"*Yo* appointed superior told you we wasn't t' touch no niggers but Johnson."

"Thet doan make no nevermind. It mah lookout. But *Ah* am *yo* appointed superior."

Johnny's fingers curled around the grip of his revolver.

Lucius Kimbry stood in his stirrups and raised his hand to his eyes against the sun. "Riders comin'!"

The Knights turned. There were five horsemen approaching at an easy gallop.

"Militia," Sikes said.

A sergeant and four privates reined up several yards from the Knights, weapons unholstered. The sergeant said: "We heard gunfire. Whut's the trouble?"

"You," Swett said. "Reid's niggerlovers."

"Git someone t' teach you t' read, boy. This is Colonel Partridge's militia, an' most of us was killin' Yankees while you was still messin' yo diapers." -

"Neal Partridge? The one who fought wif Jeb Stuart?"

"That's right."

"Well, Ah'll be! Sarjen, we jus' learnt thet the nigger Johnson was kilt, an' we was on our way back home. We ridin' by, peaceful-like, when the nigger in theah cut loose at us wif a rifle."

The sergeant's eyes went to the broken windows of the cabin. "He ain't shootin' now. You kill 'im?"

"Not yet."

"He hit enny o' yo men?"

"No, but it a miracle the way he took us by surprise."

"That's lucky fo' ever'one. We been ordered t' keep the peace no matter whut happen. Ah reckon you scared him bad enough. Ah'll ride ovuh an talk t' 'im, confiscate his weapon. You boys jus' pick up wheah you lef' off."

"Yuh mean he goan git away wif this?"

"Fo' now he is. You bes' be ridin'."

"Ah doan like this. Ah doan like this atall."

"'Time'll come. Doan you worry. It will."

"Thet got nothin' to do wif now."

"Tell you whut. Once we finish heah, we ridin' north. Now south o' us, 'bout five mile, they a real uppity nigger with more'n three hundred acres. Got horses an' cows an' such. Got a big red barn, a whitewash house. Lot o' folks feel he goan have troubles, feel sooner o' later his barn an' his house goan burn. Doan figger they be a lot o' distress if it happen sooner. We be ridin' back this way 'bout nightfall. Doan see as how we could do much t' help thet poor nigger if ever'thin' he own was burnt t' ashes by then."

Swett chewed on his lower lip, then grinned. "Yeah. You right. Thet'd be a real God's-honest shame."

"Thing is, though, we gots orders t' save niggers' lives. So iffen thet nigger start shootin' afore enny accidental fire cotched hold, well, it best if thet fire changed its mind an' waited till some other day. Daid nigger goan mean trouble. Ah cain't do nothin' 'bout thet. You see whut Ah mean?"

"Ah do. Ah surely do." Swett glanced contemptuously at Johnny, then looked back to the sergeant. "An' Ah 'pologize fo' callin' a true genneman o' the South a nigger-lover. Please fo'give me, suh."

"No offense."

"Thank yuh. Thank yuh very kindly. Ah'll be takin' mah boys on home now. 'Bout five miles, yuh say?"

It was following her—a large, coalblack cat. They could cross your path, even perch on your rooftree, and it didn't necessarily mean any harm, but when they tracked you there was evil in the air. This one had been padding along behind them for half an hour.

Thistle touched the boy's shoulder. He was Titty Nellie's son, and he'd come to tell her that his mother's time was at hand, the baby was making ready to be born, please come and help. Thistle had still not felt the comforting flow of her powers, and refused to risk magic until she did;

but midwifery required only knowledge and practice, both of which she had in abundance, so she went with the child.

"You go on ahead an' tell yo mammy Ah be there directly," she said. "Got somethin' Ah want t' cogitate."

The boy nodded and left. Thistle looked back at the cat. It had stopped when they had. Now it sat, thirty yards away, licked one paw, and looked at Thistle. She waited several minutes. The cat made no move to follow the boy. She sighed. It was *her* then. She hunkered down and rattled dry leaves with her fingers. "Kit-kit-kit," she called. "Here, kit. Kit-kit. Kitty-kit, kit-kit." The cat stretched and ambled leisurely forward. It stopped a few feet away, cocked its head, and regarded her. "What you come t' tell me?" Thistle asked. She reached to touch it. It stretched its neck, pressing its head against her fingers, arched its spine, and walked under her hand. Then it turned, slashed savagely at her with one paw, and bounded away into the brush. Thistle looked at her wrist. There were deep furrows in it, from which dark blood pumped.

The cat had delivered its message.

The headline of the *Springville Sentinel* was:

COLONEL THURLOW MACULLUM—GOVERNOR!
DEMOCRATS SWEEP STATE
Minor Irregularities Noted.

The *Woodboro Recorder,* still bordered in black in mourning for its late editor Luther Stringfellow, announced:

RADICAL REPUBLICANS TRAMPLED INTO DUST!
SUPREMACY OF THE WHITE RACE RESTORED

The *Emancipator,* a small paper operated by blacks and supported by Quaker funds, said:

REID LOSES TO MACULLUM
Widespread Incidences of
Intimidation & Vote Fraud

Vulture answered the door. It was morning. He'd been dressing and wore only pants, which he hadn't belted yet, and held up with his hand.

Attila was there, bull-necked, yoke-shouldered, expressionless. He looked Vulture over, head to foot.

"Good morning," Vulture said. "Haven't seen you in a couple of weeks." He hadn't spoken of Attila to Comfort, but knew he'd have to face the big man sooner or later. Now he was here, and Vulture was barefoot, no boots to stomp with, pants that would drop to his ankles and hobble him when he raised his hands to defend against a blow. Damn!

"Hired out fo' a spell," Attila said slowly. "Jus' come back. . . . Comfuht heah?"

"Comfort's mine now, Attila."

"Thet so?"

"Yes. And for good too."

"Reckon she can tell me thet."

"You can take my word."

"Figure Ah'm entitle' t' heah from her."

Vulture fingered the stump of his ear. "I guess you are." He stepped away and went to the bed where Comfort was still asleep.

He woke her. She pulled a shift over her head. "Hullo 'Tila."

Attila pointed. "He yo man now?"

"Uh-huh."

"An' thet the way you wants it? Permanent?"

"Yas. Ah do. Ah'm sorry. Ah dint want t' hurt yo feelin's none."

"You dint. Not much ennyhow. Ever'thin' stops, ever'thin' dies sooner o' later. Guess Ah say g'bye, then. Luck t' yuh."

"Bye, 'Tila."

Attila turned and walked off. Vulture was embarrassed, felt stupid and petty. "Attila," he called. The heavy man glanced back. "Stay and have some breakfast."

"No, Ah doan think so. Some othuh day maybe. But Ah thanks yuh."

Vulture watched him until he was gone. Comfort was splashing water on her face from the pail. He asked her, "If Attila had been willing to stay with you instead of just coming now and then, would you have taken him instead of me?"

"He weren't that kind."

"But if he were."

"Cain't say. No mo' 'n Ah kin say whut Ah'd do iffen Ah could fly. Cain't, so nevuh thought about it. Attila a solitary creature like a fox, so nevuh thought about it."

"Well, I just wondered."

"Kin tell you that Ah love you."

Vulture laughed. "Sometimes I don't like myself much, not much at all."

"You got t' get over thet. It about as senseful as a tit on a bull."

Lowery was going to whip Tater when the boy returned. Tater had been gone with the Scourge of Allah since daybreak, more than six hours. The Arabian stallion was the boy's life. He worshiped it as others worshiped a god. So Lowery wasn't overly concerned about the horse having come to harm; still, accidents could happen. Tater had permission to take the stallion out and exercise him at will, but Lowery had told him not to range more than five miles and not to spend more than two hours away from the stable. Riders had searched for the horse, but without success. If the Scourge *had* been injured, the boy would pay dearly.

Romulus, the liveried, stiff-backed major domo, was waiting for Lowery at the door. Romulus took his hat and said, "There is a Mr. Johnny Murphy waiting for you in the formal parlor, suh." The black's nostrils flared and his head lifted in elegant disdain.

"Murphy? Johnny Murphy? I don't know any such person."

"You'll recall, suh, that you entertained him briefly with another individual, a Mr. Wallace Swett, some four months ago."

"I did? Who are they?"

"Knights of the Canescent Dominion. You were censuring some breach of etiquette involving a Mr. Henry Smalls who had served in your command during the war."

"Oh? Henry Smalls. Oh, yes. I remember now." He shook his head. "All right, let's get this out of the way."

He went into the parlor. Johnny sprang to his feet and hurried across the room, hand extended. "How are yuh,

Mr. Lowery suh? Ah'm godawful sorry t' bother you, suh, but. . . ."

Lowery looked down at the hand. It remained suspended and ungrasped for several moments, then dropped back to Johnny's side. The boy flushed. "What do you want?" Lowery said.

"You tol' me, suh, Ah was supposed t' . . . Ah mean, you said you wanted two things from me. Ah mean, you asked me t' be Wallace Swett's conscience, an' t' come and tell yuh if he weren't actin' right."

"Well?"

"Ah . . . Ah don' know what t' say, suh. Ah mean, Ah feel funny, me bein' just a Ember an' everything, while Wallace, he's the Torch." Lowery gave him no help. "But it's that—it's that Wallace don' pay no attention t' orders no more. It don' make no difference what nobody says to him. He lead the Hearth like he the Grand Holocaust himself."

"Give me specifics."

"Well, like during the riot at Woodboro when the Knights was supposed to stay away. He led us in there and we got in the thick of it all. A couple weeks ago when we was huntin' that Clarence Johnson, Wallace wanted us t' kill some niggers even though our Wildfire told us t' leave 'em alone. We would of too, if we hadn't run into a militia patrol. We still burnt one out an' beat up a couple more. An' then when—"

"That's enough. I'll speak to the proper people. But next time report directly to your Wildfire. I have neither the time nor the inclination for such matters now."

"Yes, suh." Johnny sucked in his cheeks. "Did Ah do right, Mr. Lowery? Ah don' like tellin' on Wallace, but you said Ah should."

"Of course you did right. There's a great need for people of your caliber. Nothing could be run properly without informers."

Johnny was relieved. "Thank you, suh." Lowery looked at him curiously a moment, then laughed. Johnny couldn't understand.

Although the inauguration was still two weeks off, most people addressed MaCullum as Governor, and he enjoyed

it. But the sign someone tacked up in The Ruffled Grouse
—*Governor Thurlow MaCullum*—was too blatant, and he
ordered it removed. The saloon's second floor was a suite
of subdued and comfortable rooms used as an informal
club by Woodboro's wealthy and influential. Desks had
been moved in and it was now an office and clearing house
for the governor-elect, manned by eager young planters
and older, more quiet and efficient men who made the decisions and effected the compromises and agreements. Ma-
Cullum worked hard. Reid was little more than a lame
duck, a figurehead, and those who had business with the
state were coming to the man who would control it for the
next four years. MaCullum did most of his dealing from
The Ruffled Grouse, but he still used his personal offices
over the bank when privacy and discretion were necessary.

This day he met there with Jeremy Goodwin. "I note
Constantine's not here again," Goodwin said. "I'm beginning to use his presence, or absence, as an index to the
kind of thing that's on your mind."

"I suppose it is. I have another job that requires your
personal attention, Jem." Goodwin nodded. "We picked
up what, one or two percent of the colored vote?"

"A little less than two."

"That's disappointing. We put a lot of time into them, a
lot of money and work."

Goodwin shrugged. "If I were a nigger I wouldn't have
voted for us either."

"Yes you would have, if the circumstances had been
different."

"What circumstances?"

"If the good Reverend Hoover had told you to."

"He'll come around. He has to."

"Yes, I think he will. Actually, I'm not overly concerned with him. He might even have been telling the
truth when he said it wouldn't make much difference what
he advised. He rode the sentiment as he understood it:
they were going to vote for Reid, he tells them to do just
that, and it looks as if he has power. He'd appear a jackass
backing me and then watching the vote go to Reid anyway."

"So it's not Hoover and his kind, and we're back to the
question."

"It's niggers like Homer Jordan," MaCullum said. "Like Pigfoot Sample, like the ones around Hellbottom Swamp. There aren't many like that, but they're the wild ones. They spit in the white man's eye. They do just what they please and they get away with it. As long as that's allowed, we can't expect the rest to behave. Take a man with a passel of children. If one won't mind—and isn't punished for it—then why should the others go to bed on time, eat what they're given, be respectful, act decently?"

"You don't have to labor the point. I'll draw up a list of the animals and arrange for the tamers."

"No tamers, Jem. You can tame young ones, but not the full grown ones. Them you have to put in a cage, or kill. They don't give you a choice."

"When do you want it?"

"Start on the day I'm sworn in. Finish it as soon as you can."

"All right."

"Control it. We didn't have much trouble with the Johnson hunt. I want it the same way this time. Selected targets, nothing random."

"Uh-huh."

"We throw bad apples from the barrel, we weed our gardens, cull our stock. What else can we do?"

"You don't have to convince me, Thurlow—you're paying me."

"It's for the good of both races. You understand, Jem. I agree that slavery was too harsh, and maybe even morally wrong. But God, the North would destroy us all. They don't understand niggers. Not at all. I saw a bunch of trained monkeys at Baton Rouge once. Some of the things they did, you'd think they were human. But would you let them vote, would you declare them your equal? The nigger's not a monkey, granted, but—oh God, what a responsibility we have! Why does it fall to me?" He slumped back and cast his eyes broodingly to the floor.

Goodwin stood. "Nobody ever asked me, Thurlow, so I never said. Far as I'm concerned, a nigger's a nigger, and if we can't have 'em as slaves then we should get rid of 'em all. But it never works the way any man would have it if he were God, so I never bother myself with what I think, hardly even know unless someone backs me to a wall. But like I told you—you're paying me, so whatever you want, long as it doesn't work against us, why that's just fine. Don't fret any. It'll be done. See you tomorrow, Thurlow."

The sun shimmered the air before him, slathered his body with sweat. Duckworth pulled his long hair down over his face and tied it with a handkerchief around his head. Peeping through its dirty strands broke the glare, but it clung wetly to his cheeks, irritated the skin, and kept getting into his mouth. He was miserable and terrified. The niggers were still behind him. They'd picked him up on the rocky plain when he was still a good two miles from the swamp. He'd heard the *clop* of a hoof striking a stone behind him, turned in the saddle, and there they were, a pair of them. They matched his pace, stopped when he did. One rode holding a rifle over his pommel. Duckworth's own rifle was in its scabbard, his revolver holstered and secured by a leather strap over the hammer. He had no doubt that they would shoot him dead if he tried to ease either weapon to hand.

They couldn't know, he thought. He wasn't sure himself, only understood that something big was in the offing and that it was going to fall hard on certain niggers, particularly in Hellbottom Swamp. But he couldn't rid himself of the dread that *they* knew and that his life was forfeit.

Lowery should have sent a darkey. White men didn't have any place in Hellbottom. Duckworth had told that to Romulus, but the stone-faced nigger said, "No. You go, Ardis. Mr. Lowery wants her here and the request will be more forceful delivered by a white man." Ardis, no less. The shiny black bastard, calling a white man by his first name. Someday somebody was going to take a two-by-four to that fancy nigger's head. But Duckworth worked on Lowery's plantation, and when you did that you didn't argue with Romulus any more than you did with Mr. Lowery. So, muttering and grumbling to mask his fear, he saddled a horse for himself and another for the woman he was to bring back.

"You get me out o' this, God," he said, "an Ah'll go t' church every Sunday from now till Christmas. Anything you want, God, just get me home." He spat salty hair from his mouth.

He turned left at the lightning-blasted oak, as he'd been told to, and went on another quarter of a mile, flies buzzing round his head. The black riders followed him. He saw the cabin, and two figures turning dirt around corn rows a little beyond it. He rode to the edge of the field. The man and woman walked slowly to meet him. He groaned inwardly when he saw the man more clearly. A hideous giant of a nigger with purple scars on his face and half an ear. He didn't look friendly. Not at all. The nigger folded his arms and looked up. He didn't have to crane his neck much; his head was about on a level with the horse's. *Please, God.*

"Uh, afternoon. Afternoon t' you, folks," Duckworth said, smiling broadly. "Do Ah have the, uh, honor of addressin' Miss, er, *Mrs.* Comfort Davis? An' you too, suh, Mr. Davis Ah guess it is, no offense, Ah was give t' understand Mrs. Davis was a widow-woman." The two blacks on horseback came up on either side of Duckworth. He untied his handkerchief, pushed his hair back, and mopped his face. "Afternoon, gentlemen. How do? Ah has just stopped here, as Ah was explainin', for a friendly talk, a very friendly talk, with these two good people."

"What do you want?" Vulture said.

"Now Ah'm glad you asked me that. Yes Ah am. Ah was comin' t' the very thing mahself. Mr. Lowery—that's Mr. *Clayton* Lowery—prevailed upon me t' make the ride from his plantation personally and extend t' you, Mrs. Davis, his deepest respects along with his hopes that you enjoys the same fine health and good life you had when he last seen you. Asked me that himself, he did. Told me, Ardis, you start out afore daybreak and make that ride to Hellbottom Swamp and pay mah respects t' Mrs. Comfort Davis."

"Mhmm," Comfort said.

"You are Comfort Davis, aren't you, Ma'm?" Duckworth scratched at his cheek. Bright red weals rose.

"Mhmm."

"Well, Mr. Clayton Lowery, he told me, Ardis, if you finds she be as finely lifeful and as cheery as she always was, an' up t' the task, then Ah want you t' ask from her a very large favor which Ah would be greatly indebted for."

"Whut?"

"He said t' me that you is known through half the counties in this state for the wonderful things you can do with food. And he told me you come t' his plantation once before when he had a special gatherin'. Now as you know, Colonel Thurlow MaCullum, he goin' be sworn in for governor this Sunday in the capital. Mr. Clayton Lowery is a good friend of Governor MaCullum. He's plannin' the goddamnedest—'scuse me, Ma'm—the biggest celebration ever held in these parts. Governor's comin' down from the capital. It goin' be somethin', yes Ah tell you. Two whole days, and goin' require near a week o' readyin' fo' the food alone. Mr. Clayton Lowery, he said he'd consider it a grand honor if you'd consent t' oversee that readyin', take full charge o' all the gatherin' and cookin'. He did that, Ma'm."

"Got no time fo' such things," Comfort said.

"No, no. You don't understand, Ma'm. Mr. Clayton Lowery didn't expec' you t' just drop all your chores and come runnin' for nothin'. He tol' me t' come right out with the whole pay, no hagglin'. When Ah hires the best, he said, Ah pays the best. Fifty dollars he wants t' give you, Ma'm. And he authorized me t' hand it over t' you cash in advance before you even steps foot off your own property."

One of the mounted blacks leaned and laid his hand gently on Duckworth's shoulder. "You carryin' fifty spendin' dollas, white man?"

Duckworth winced. "Ah come as a friend," he appealed.

Vulture gave a little jerk of his head. The black sighed and removed his hand.

Comfort turned to Vulture. "Whut you think?"

"Bad enough I worked for the whites so long. Why should my woman cook for them? I don't like it."

"Dint think you would. Don' please me much either."

"Then it's settled."

"Ah don' know. It a good lot o' money an' it don' ask t' take me away long. We could use fifty dollas, could use it real good."

"That's true."

"Ah think maybe Ah should go. You goin' be angry if Ah do?"

"Yes. But not at you."

"All right." She nodded at Duckworth.

"That's fine, Mrs. Davis! Mr. Lowery's goin' be pleased t' the sky. May Ah suggest that we delay till tomorrow mornin'? It's an eight-hour ride."

"Ah be ready at sunup."

"Good. Uh . . ." He looked around. "Is there, uh, any place Ah can bed down for the night?"

"Shed," Vulture said, and gestured.

"Is it, Ah mean, you know, can Ah count on bein' safe there?"

"Nobody goan hurt you, white man," one of the mounted blacks said. "You a guest."

Duckworth turned red. "Ah meant from snakes an' gators an' such."

"They mostly in the swamp. You be safe like a li'l baby heah. Onlies' thing is yo guns. Gets real damp at night, known t' rust out a gunbarrel by sunup. Best you hand ovuh yo rifle and pistol t' Vulchuh. He keep 'em real dry fo' yuh."

"Ah don' reckon Ah—"

"It be best, white man."

Expressionless, Vulture extended his hand.

Duckworth grasped the stock of his rifle and drew it from the scabbard.

The powers failed her. Thistle's spirit died with them and its dried and brittle corpse rattled about in her like a seed in a hollow gourd. Her shoulders slumped, her face slackened, she could do nothing but sit for endless, silent hours, her dullish presence dragging her loved ones down like a millstone. She grieved for the pain she caused them, but she was enfeebled and unable to rally. The horror of being defenseless against the infinite malevolencies of the world threatened to overwhelm her, and it was only the numb torpor into which she had sunk that prevented her from tearing her hair and going mad.

On the day Comfort left for Lowery's with Ardis Duckworth, Thistle's oldest son, Paul, brought her a Beauty Stone. She was sitting by the edge of the stream scribing meaningless designs in the dirt with a twig. "Looky, Maw," he said. "I found it over by Jangler's house. I never seen nothin' t' beat it." It was a flat, thin, whitish stone the size of a saucer. She looked and nodded. His hand fell back to his side. "Ah thought you'd like it."

"Ah . . . do."

He sniffed, lowered his eyes. "Yuh don' ack like it."

She was saddened. She wanted to sweep him into her arms, but the effort was beyond her. "Ah do, Paul. A lot." She managed to take it from him. "Thank you. It's a fine present."

Paul sat down. "Maw," he said somberly, "it were the baptizin', weren't it? It hurt you."

She nodded.

"Did it . . . did it kill yo magic, Maw?"

She hid her face in her hands. The boy wrapped his arms around her and squeezed tightly. She cried. "It all right, Maw. It goan be all right." When she was calm again the boy sat back.

She smiled a little and said, "Ah loves yuh, Paul."

He looked away shyly. "Maw, if Paw's god got you now an' you cain't get away, whyn't you use *his* god for magic?"

She spread her hands and shook her head.

"No, Ah mean it, Maw. You tol' me yo'sef there's lots of witches and witch-men that use Paw's god an' devil fo' they magic."

"There's some, but it ain't very strong. An' Ah don' know much about the spells."

"You tol' me once they's enough magic in the air t' destroy the world—or make a whole 'nother one. You said it all came down t' how good the person usin' the power was. A strong witch can make strong magic, a weak one cain't. All you gots t' do is learn about the Christ-magic. Then you kin make it work fo' you." He finished with a rush, embarrassed by his presumption.

Thistle poked in the dirt. There was truth in Paul. If the Christian god had vanquished his rivals and captured her, then he must be of great force and potency, for she understood the strength of her own powers and knew that she'd been a formidable adversary. She had learned to control and use the other powers; she could do the same with these. She marveled at Paul. He alone of her children had inherited her gifts. She was even a little afraid of him; she suspected he would prove some day to be vastly more powerful than she had been.

"It takes years o' studyin'," she said.

"You kin do it," he answered confidently.

"Maybe. Just maybe."

"Look in the Beauty Stone. Tell me a vision, Maw."

She went to the water's edge. He followed her. "There's not always somethin' t' see," she reminded him. "An' even when there is, it's hard t' work the meanin' from it." She knelt and dipped the stone under water. Wetted, it turned nearly transparent, a barely visible haziness. She raised it to the sky with both hands and peered through it. She seized her lip sharply between her teeth.

"Whut do you see? Whut is it? . . . Maw?"

"Blood," she whispered. "Fountains of blood, running red rivers of it."

Friend stopped and raised his head. He snuffed the night air. Hector dropped quickly to a crouch beside him. "What you got, boy?" Friend turned slowly. He took a few stiff-legged steps, then his lips skinned back from his teeth and hackles rose the length of his spine. Hector worked his tongue into an empty tooth socket. There was someone nearby who didn't belong, someone white. Friend hated everybody, white or black, but whites especially. By studying the dog's alert carefully—noting the squareness of the stance, the cast of the tail, a slight quivering of the jowls—Hector could tell whether Friend had located a black man or a white man. He didn't know how the animal read the difference, but he did know that Friend had never been wrong. There was a white man out there.

Hector slipped off his boots and set them next to a large rock where he could find them later. He emptied his pockets of everything that would clink or rattle. He'd left his rifle at the gunsmith's yesterday for work, and he missed the weapon now. But only a little. He drew his long-bladed knife from the sheath on the back of his belt and took Friend's collar in his other hand. "Find 'im," he whispered.

The dog's chest filled and vibrated and what would have been deep rumbling growls passed through its altered throat only as faint hisses. It surged ahead in excitement, risking noise, and Hector jerked back on the collar. "Soft!" he said in a low voice. They entered the woods and advanced warily, Friend under control now, man and dog moving as subtly as the hungry stalkers of the swamp. They approached the lip of a shallow depression, Hector going to his belly and Friend hunching low. Two mounted white men were there. One, smoking a pipe, asked, "What time is it, Parley?"

Parley took a watch from his pocket and struck a match. "Little aftuh two. He should be heah direc'ly."

"A-yuh. Hope he hurries. This gives me the jeebies. Doan wan' t' stay no longer 'n we have to."

"We got what we come for."

"The nigguh tol' us true, all right."

"We finish 'em easy."

"A-yuh."

Hector clamped his palm lightly over Friend's eyes, a command not to move. Then he worked away from the dog, around to the side of the white men and a little down the ravine. He lay flat on the ground, concealed by ferns, twenty feet from them. Parley dozed in his saddle. The other man puffed on his pipe, scratched himself. Hector turned the problem over. Two had to die. He reversed his knife so that he held it by the blade. It would be a long throw and the light was bad. He worried a little about Friend, hoping the dog wouldn't break its stay. He'd been too loose with the animal lately, and there was no excuse for that; it could cost a man his life. He waited motionless for perhaps ten minutes.

He heard a horse being walked into the trees. A low voice called, "Parley? Eben?"

"Ovuh heah," Eben answered.

Parley woke, stretched, got off his horse, and went to a bush and unbuttoned his fly. The third man appeared. "How'd it go?" Eben asked.

"Easy. Ah scouted the crossing, then Ah—"

Hector rose and whistled shrilly. His arm flashed forward. The knife sunk to the hilt below Eben's heart. Eben slumped on his mount's neck with a grunt and slid from the saddle. Friend came bounding down the slope, leapt and hurtled onto the new man's back, knocked him from his

horse, fangs buried deep in his shoulder. The man
screamed. Parley, with urine still arcing from his penis,
scrabbled for the pistol on his hip. Hector was beside him,
and clipped him on the side of the head with a rock. Parley fell. There were shrieks. Hector went to Eben, rolled
him over, and retrieved the knife. The night went quiet,
but Friend was still tearing at the remaining white man.
"Git shut," Hector told him. "That's enough, Fren'.
Shut!" The dog had the man by an arm. It gave him a
final shake and then backed away. The man was mutilated, but not yet dead. Hector took his hair, bent the head
forward, positioned the knife at the base of the skull, then
slipped it in up to the brain. The man twitched.

Several dozen men had come to the meeting grounds
behind Spanner's Store, many of them strangers to each
other. Rumors swept through them. They quieted when
Obadiah mounted the speaker's rock. Obadiah was Hellbottom's common denominator; a man from Elmer's
Smithy might not know another from Tit-Bird Crossing,
but Obadiah would be acquainted with both.

The sun was crimson on the western horizon, ruddying
the preacher's brown cheeks. He was grave. "Brothers, I
thank you all fo' comin' on such short notice. I have sad
news, an' fo' once in my life my tongue lacks fo' words.
Brothers,"—he shook his head tiredly—"the whites are
gatherin' an' they're comin' t' Hellbottom. They're comin'
t' wipe us out."

A man said, "Ah live heah five years now, an' Ah heard
the exac' same thing three differen' times. They weren't
never no truth in it."

"There's truth this time. About four hundred of 'em.
They'll hit us Sunday mornin', when Thurlow MaCullum
is bein' sworn in governor. They plan t' strike Spanner's
Store, Tit-Bird Crossin', and Elmer's Smithy an' catch us
t'gether at meetin' time. They goin' t' fire the buildin's an'
drive into the swamp after how many of us are still alive.
They're not goin' t' give up this time. They're even bringin'
boats in wagons."

A grizzled swamper spat. "Boats ain't goan do 'em
much good."

"How you know all this, Obadiah?"

He told them about the white man Hector had taken prisoner.

"Whea's this big scary white man now? Le's heah it from his own mouf."

"Yas. Where is he?"

"He . . ." Obadiah's hands fluttered and he looked to Hector.

Hector was leaning against a tree some distance from the main body, holding Friend's chain. "Dint need him no mo'. He dead."

"You sure he tol' the troof?"

Hector nodded.

"We'll kill 'em!" someone shouted furiously. "We'll kill 'em all!"

"We cut 'em down long as they keeps comin'! Doan mattuh how many they send."

Another man swung his arms for attention. "Thass stupid. We cain't beat 'em an' you all knows it."

There was a confusion of voices. Obadiah demanded silence. "Anybody got somethin' t' say, I'll call you up beside the stone here."

First was the young man who didn't think there was any way to beat the whites. He was leaving with his family, and anyone who didn't do the same was a fool. He was jeered and cursed. A man rushed him and hit him several times before being dragged back. Three others walked off with the defector.

A bearded man said, "Brothers, most of us come here 'cause there weren't no othuh place fo' us t' go. They a law warrant waitin' on me, an' if Ah leaves this swamp it only a question o' how long befo' it catches me up. Ah knows damn well they a good number o' you in the same circumstance. So the way it cooks down, Ah doan have no choice. Ennyone else thet stays with me, Ah glad t' have yo help, an' Ah'm goan give back t' you all the help Ah can." There were cheers and whistles.

A huge figure moved through the crowd to the rock. "I haven't been here long," Vulture said. "But I have a home in Hellbottom, a woman, and a good life. I never had any of these things before. I'm staying here. Maybe the okras will destroy everything I have, but I'm not going to walk away and just give them up."

Someone cried for barricades. "We kin turn Spanner's Store into a goddamn fort. We got enough men t' dig trenches an' put up earthworks and log walls befo' Sunday."

"Wouldn't work. Too many of 'em. They overrun us."

"One at a time," Obadiah yelled. "Wait yo turns."

Attila came to the rock. He scratched his broad skull. "Cain't defen' yo homes, cain't make no fo't. You all gots t' take t' the swamp. It the only way. They weary o' huntin' you aftuh a few days. You kin come out then. Iffen they come back, you go t' the swamp agin."

"That fine fo' you," someone shouted. "You a ol' slavetime swamper. But there ain't more 'n a han'ful in Hellbottom like you. Most of us, we never spent no real time there, never even been in the deep swamp. It be just as bad on us as it be on the okras."

Attila shrugged and walked away.

Arguments were waged. Obadiah brought them under control with difficulty. "Let this boy talk, damn it! You niggers aren't goin' t' accomplish nothin' that way. Now listen t' this man, he got somethin' sensible in his mouth."

The boy was Henry, the rifleman from Elysium: "We got a better leader 'n they kin throw against us. We got a man that was a decorated officer in the war. We got Cap'n Em'ry Woodson, and he should be the one that tells us what t' do!"

Woodson stood toward the rear of the throng, sunk in a reverie of final things. The Beast had come, and it was immense. It towered, blotting the dying sun, darkening the earth with its shadow, warming and musting the air with its animalhood.

"Em'ry?" Henry called.

Woodson didn't hear.

"Ah come t' Hellbottom t' git away from whites," a man shouted angrily.

"Enny white man what runs off t' live like a nigger is full total crazy. An' Ah ain't goin' have nothin' t' do with no crazy man, 'specially not a white one!"

"He a infantry officer. Ain't no one else heah got enny notion o' how t' defend ourse'fs."

"He a traitor t' the whites, whut make you think he goan do bettuh by us?"

"He fought mo' battles 'n the rest o' us even *learnt* about!"

Woodson heard a faint rumbling in the Beast's chest. It would deepen to a growl, tighten to a snarl . . . then a quick slash of claws, a crunch of jaws, and it would be done. He accepted. His body loosened. Peace gentled him. There was only the thornlike prick of Wilda, the encysted pain of her loss. Without that, he would have been content.

Someone shook his shoulder. "Go on. Talk. We behind you, white man. Enuff of us."

"What?" Woodson blinked. Loud arguments waxed. Obadiah and Henry were calling him to the speaker's stone. He went forward, a little confused, a little annoyed at being jarred awake.

Obadiah raised his hands and held them there until he had something close to silence. "There ain't any white man here, brothers. Just us Hellbottom folk. So shutup an' listen!"

No white man here; Woodson wondered if he should be complimented or insulted. There was more argument. He listened. Men who had fought in the Union Army were loudest in his favor. They prevailed, then everyone was waiting.

You don't understand, Woodson thought. This is the end. There is nothing more.

He was irritated. They were using him. But no more, he "Well, whut you got t' say, Woodson?" thought, than he had used them and their brothers. "I don't think there's much you can do," he said.

"Louder."

"We cain't hear."

"I said: I don't think there's much you can do."

"Oh, thet's fine. There's a general t' inspire a man's soul."

"Hushup!"

Woodson asked the preacher, "How many men of fighting age can Hellbottom muster?"

"Ninety, maybe a hundred. And you can add another twenty, twenty-five women."

"You're outnumbered four to one," Woodson said to them. "Your enemy is well equipped and provisioned.

And he's not staging a raid; he's coming to *annihilate* you. He's too strong to meet in the open field. Even if you could fortify in time, you couldn't withstand siege very long. That leaves the swamp. You'd have to fight in small bands there. Ten men at the most, and they would have to be men who knew the swamp and who didn't need to worry about each other. The enemy will be much freer. He is the hunter, he can set the pace. The swamp will be easier on him than on you, the prey.

"I see no way for you to win. So I suggest that you run. In the army we call it retreat, and it's one of the soundest military tactics."

"We been through all thet," came a shout. "Ain't but a handful o' chicken-hearts runnin'. We goan fight, an' whut we wants is fo' you t' tell us the bes' way t' go 'bout it."

"You can't win."

"Nobody asked you 'bout winnin', only fightin'."

Fools, Woodson thought. *You* have a choice. But a lifetime of war had made reflex of certain processes by now, and his mind turned to the problem instinctively. "There's Johnson's Pass and Tom's Shoe Pass," he mused. "What other ways through the hills for wagons and a large number of men?"

"Woodpecker Slope. It no good fo' wagons, but not bad fo' riders."

"Where is it?"

"Due west."

"Uh-huh." It was beginning to interest him. He'd seen vaguely similar situations fighting under Walker in South America. One memory caused him to smile. He didn't linger on it, though, took what he needed from it and moved on.

"I want to get this straight," he said. "Don't interrupt me unless I'm wrong." He reviewed the geography. The swamp was roughly ovoid in shape, and the rocky plain between it and the surrounding hills was about five miles in all directions. Tit-Bird Crossing lay on the north rim of the swamp, Spanner's Store on the eastern bulge, and Elmer's Smithy on the southern rim. There were only three decent passages through the hills: Woodpecker Slope to the west, Tom's Shoe Pass to the northwest, and Johnson's Pass to the east. "Johnson's Pass is the most logical," he said. He asked Hector, "Did your man tell you where they were coming through?"

"Johnson's Pass."

Excitement rippled. The war had begun and Woodson had second-guessed the enemy. Hellbottom had its first victory. The men believed in their general. They wanted to hear more.

Question: Who was leading the whites? Woodson knew that MaCullum had given the orders, possibly in consort with Lowery. Both were able strategists, but he doubted that either had planned this campaign. Responsibility would be delegated. An ex-field commander probably, a man not inspired, but experienced and professional. This man originally selected Johnson's Pass. But then his scouts didn't return. He'd have to assume they'd been captured and had talked. His first thought would be of ambush and he'd want to choose an alternate route. But being white, Southern, and crafty enough to hold command, he'd realize that he couldn't trust niggers to respond exactly as they should. Conversely, though, the same attributes would make him feel qualified to enter the niggers' skins and try and think like them. In the end he'd say to himself: *They're probably too dumb to ambush me. But if they are smart enough, then they're also smart enough to think I'd abandon Johnson's Pass. Therefore, I will not abandon it.*

"I want volunteers," Woodson said. "I want men to keep watch on both passes and the slope. I think they'll stick to Johnson's Pass and their original timetable, but we have to cover ourselves." There was a glut of offers.

Woodson organized communication lines with Obadiah's help.

He built strategy piecemeal and had to explain the why of his reasoning as well as the what in frustrating detail. Soldiers followed orders simply because they *were* orders; men with a sense of individuality did not. It was a sober, suicidal strategy designed solely to inflict maximum damage on the enemy. But there was still a curious current of enthusiasm and some men even predicted victory. Woodson tried to stop this; overconfidence could kill as easily as a bullet, and he wanted a good contest even though he knew he had to lose.

*   *   *

Lowery's personal tailor fit Comfort with a black dress of combed cotton fronted with fine lace. Two more were cut so she would always have a fresh change. They were starched to crackling stiffness. She was given soft, snow-white aprons and shown how to tie the wide strings so that a large fluffy bow was made at the small of her back. Lowery also gave her a vial of scent. From France, he said. She was not obliged to wear it, but he would appreciate her doing so if it pleased her. She could take what remained back home with her at the end of the week. She liked it.

The kitchen, detached from the Great House, was a large squat building of rust brick with huge iron stoves, deep shafts into which tubs of butter and cheese and other spoilables could be lowered to cooling waters, vegetable and grain bins, slab work tables, ovens, and a multitude of pots, pans, kettles, colanders, sifters, cleavers, boning knives, and other cutlery.

Lowery had hired two other skilled cooks from the countryside to complement his usual kitchen staff of six. He wished Comfort to do the most subtle work herself and to oversee the rest. She had complete authority and need only ask Romulus for whatever additional goods or manpower she needed. Lowery suggested a partial menu, then asked her for recommendations, most of which he accepted. She told him she'd never heard of some of the dishes he'd mentioned.

"I'll get you recipes," he said.

"Ah cain't read, Mr. Lowery."

"There will be someone to read them to you."

"Ah doan like cookin' from recipes. That's other people's food. Maybe you should hire the ones that wrote 'em down."

"I hired you because you're the best. You alter those dishes any way you see fit, make them your own. They'll be better for it."

She nodded. "You say you feedin' a hundred, a hundred an' twenty?"

"About that."

"We do ever'thin' you want, we goin' have enough fo' maybe twice as many."

Lowery smiled. "I enjoy abundance."

Comfort shrugged.

"Romulus will show you to your quarters." Lowery stood, gave a quick little nod. "I want to tell you again how pleased and grateful I am that you've come. I know everything will be perfect."

"Ah do mah best."

Lowery left her with Romulus, who had been standing unobtrusively to the side. "You should call him *sir*," Romulus said. "He's your employer."

"He payin' me, Ah'm workin' fo' him. He don' *ma'm* me, Ah don' *suh* him."

Romulus curled one corner of his mouth, amused. He shot his cuffs; regardless of the temperature he was never without his coat. "You're a fine-looking woman."

"Where am Ah supposed t' sleep?"

"In my room. It's in the Great House and it's larger than most niggers' shacks. I have a hand-carved mahogany bed from England and satin sheets from France. I know how to make a woman happy."

"Make me happy by showin' me where the field hands live."

"I can make things very pleasant for you, Comfort."

"An' Ah kin make things very unpleasant fo' you, nigger."

Romulus's face soured. He turned on his heel and snapped, "Follow me."

Caton McGonagle arrived with his men at Johnson's Pass at eight-thirty in the morning. The sun was already white and fierce and McGonagle was sweating. He called a halt and sent four riders ahead to scout. His men were restless, eager to get on with it. They were mostly white trash—impoverished farmers, town idlers, and Knights. Among them were a few planters' sons out for adventure. It was a crude and sloppy bunch and McGonagle didn't like them much. But discipline was a little better than he'd expected, and they were the right men for the job.

McGonagle was thinking it ever more likely he could stick to his first plans. The men who'd disappeared last week were good, wouldn't have been easy to take alive. The niggers probably didn't know a thing. But even if they did, he couldn't see that there was much they could do.

One way or the other, he wasn't going to pull out until the last of the black bastards was finished.

Swett sat on the ground holding his chestnut's reins a little apart from the rest of the Hearth. He chewed tobacco at a furious pace. The ground around him was spotted with the viscous brown globs of his saliva. He watched McGonagle and his aides going over a map. Swett was impressed with the commander. Earlier, some Woodboro boys had wanted to break away, do it in their own style, to hell with it, they weren't soldiers in some goddamn army. McGonagle yanked one off his horse. When the man came cursing up from the dust, McGonagle planted a boot in his face, breaking his nose. It was done so smoothly and calmly that Swett didn't even realize what had happened at first.

"Get back on yo horse an' stay in line," McGonagle said. "Or ride back t' town. I don' care. But you won't jeopardize my operation. I'll kill you first." All this in an amiable tone, and smiling.

That was the way Swett should have handled the Hearth—kept his temper, just knocked Johnny Murphy down when the boy first started to make trouble, then told him he could either do what he was told or get out of the Knights. Smooth, clean. He'd been stupid letting it drag on so long, allowing Johnny to grow bold enough to stab him in the back. Him reduced to an Ember and Johnny appointed Torch in his place. He'd been so enraged he'd put his fist through a wall. Would have broken his hand if the board hadn't been rotten. It was still a little swollen and stiff.

The demotion was the greatest outrage ever done him. His first thought was to murder the treacherous bastard. But he knew that no matter how he tried he couldn't conceal that act from the Order. They'd come for him in the night and take him before the Grand Holocaust. He'd be executed. He thought about resigning from the Knights, but once his rage crested he reconsidered; he couldn't conceive of existence without them.

Leonard Sikes was backing Swett. Fred Harwood and Jimmy Hildenbrandt were sucking up to Johnny. The rest were embarrassed and uneasy. They followed Johnny's orders because he was the Torch, but they were careful to remain neutral. Some of them were old men already, and Swett knew they didn't like taking orders from a seventeen-year-old kid. Swett was only two years older but nobody had minded him being Torch because he was an experienced, powerful, and intelligent leader. They'd learn, the bastards. They'd ask him to take control.

He spat. The others were clustered around Johnny. God, how he hated the boy! With any luck it might even be over in a few days. They weren't expecting much fight from the niggers, but still, one lucky shot and Johnny would be gone forever. Even if there weren't a nigger handy to shoot him, well. . . . Swett got excited thinking about it and he passed air. He stroked his brand new repeating rifle. Things could be confusing in the swamp. A man could die there, any man, without anyone knowing for sure just what had happened to him.

The scouts reported the pass clear all the way through, and at least a mile beyond. McGonagle dropped his arm and signaled his men forward. It was what he had expected. But when the *clink* of his mount's shoes began ringing against the stone walls, he felt himself growing uneasy. Flanked by sheer fifty-foot walls, the pass was a third of a mile long and wide enough for a dozen riders abreast. It was a fine site for an ambush.

The nigger was jittery too. "Mr. McGonagle," he said. "Let me go back to town. Please, sir. I'll wait there for you. I can't go anyplace without my money."

"You just stay up front with me. You goin' t' be right with us until this is finished."

A tic appeared under the nigger's eye. He probed in a saddlebag and withdrew a bottle.

"Get rid of that," McGonagle said. "I said no liquor on this march." The nigger looked at him pleadingly. "Right now!" The bottle dropped and shattered against the rocks.

The governor had found the darkey. He was a Hellbottom nigger who'd been thrown out, or threatened or something, and he was revenging himself, and earning a nice piece of money besides, by helping plan the action against Hellbottom. McGonagle could have paid him off and let him make his run from the state, but he hated traitors, no matter whom they betrayed.

The wagons at the end of the column were in the pass now and their wheels echoed rumblingly over the sharp strikes of shod hooves and the mingled and blurred voices of the men, who were growing excited. McGonagle saw the opening to the valley a hundred yards ahead. His apprehension increased, but he forced himself to ignore it. He was a man of organization rather than inspiration. He mistrusted hunches and sentiment.

Tyler lay belly down on the hot stone, rifle beside him loaded and cocked. He struggled against the temptation to crawl forward and look down into the pass. From the noise, the point of the white force must be nearly even with him. But Woodson had stressed that the chance showing of even a single man could ruin them.

Tyler still hated the white man's guts, but the plan was working and, in a fight, Tyler damn well wasn't going to restrict his allies to people he personally liked. There were ninety men willing to fight in Hellbottom. Some of the women and children were in the swamp already, others were at Elmer's Smithy readying for the second phase of Woodson's strategy. There was no place in the rocky hills to hide a party of any size, but there were numerous small caves and ravines and swales in which two and three men could be concealed. Woodson led his men to Johnson's Pass before dawn and broke them up and saw to their hiding. Then he and two others watched the whites' scouts scour the pass, the bluffs above it, and ride out a way into the plain. When the scouts had satisfied themselves and turned back, Woodson and the other two men passed the word quickly, and the blacks came out from their cover and hurried into positions on the rim of the pass.

Tyler could wait no longer. He had to at least *see* them. He inched forward, sucked in breath, held it, and cautiously raised his head. Lord, there were so many. Then he saw the black man and he snarled like an animal. *Sylvester Jackson, you nigger's whoreson.* His hand clenched on his rifle. Hurry, he thought. Please hurry. Ah want that blackshit bastard. Ah cain't wait much longer. Ah'm goan kill him. Please.

He lowered his head and lay in frustrated need, telling himself to be calm, to keep control. . . .

BOOOOM! Dynamite exploded at the east end, the outside end of the pass. The cliffs shuddered, rocks fell over the edge.

Tyler cried out joyfully and sprang to his feet. His rifle stock slammed to his shoulder and the barrel swung toward Jackson.

Sylvester Jackson wanted to be drunk. He was drowning in guilt, seared by hatred, and he hungered for oblivion. He hated them, the black bastards. What did they know of *real* pain? And how did they come to judge him? They had no right; he was a white man.

Who could fault him for having sold something as innocuous as a vote? But they did fault him, he knew they did no matter how they tried to mask it, and sooner or later they were going to kill him for it. But he was quicker. The white men said that he was black and that he had to live with other blacks. All right then, he'd sold his black brothers, sold them just as his white brother had sold him.

Sold them! They were going to die. No, God no! But yes, you black devils, I'm white! You'll pay for what you've done to me, what you planned to do. But why were the whites making him watch? Where could he run? Where was a place for him?

There was a heavy explosion at the end of the column. Jackson jerked around in his saddle and mewled in terror.

Tyler's bullet shattered his cheekbone and broke the ridge of his nose. Many other blacks had seen him too. Thirteen slugs ripped into him in the next moments and four more struck his horse.

Sylvester Jackson's blood and shreds of his flesh spattered across McGonagle. Jackson and his horse crashed down. A spume of gray smoke was rolling up and outward from the rear of the column, and tiny pieces of stone and wood rained down from the sky.

Panicked horses whinnied and reared. Some men galloped forward to escape, others raced back to the rear, most simply milled about. Rifle fire crackled from the bluffs and men were dropping from saddles.

McGonagle snapped orders. "Harvey, take your men and get through the pass. Flank the bastards on the north rim and give us covering fire against the south rim. Pour it on. Make 'em keep their heads down. Judd, get back and see how bad our equipment's been hit. Spencer and Lew, use your people to—"

Spencer gasped and rocked back in his saddle, a dark hole in his shirt over his belly. Blood quickly stained the fabric in a spreading circle.

"Oh, shit," McGonagle said. Spencer fell. A few men were shooting up at the bluffs, but their horses were spinning and crabbing sideways and accuracy was impossible. "Lew, you an' yo boys get those idiots off their mounts, behind cover an' returnin' fire."

Harvey clattered by at the head of thirty men. A spate of rifle fire emptied half the saddles before the group was out of the pass and safe. McGonagle pulled his rifle from his scabbard, leapt from his horse, and looked for cover. There was none. The stone floor was uniform and clean in this area. "Damn," he spat. He pulled his horse close up to the north wall, where his back would be protected, levered a shell into the chamber, pressed the muzzle against the horse's head, and shot the beast. It collapsed. He went down behind it, facing the south rim.

The blacks were woods people, hunters, snapshooters. They popped up, aimed, shot, and ducked in one quick continuous motion. McGonagle wasted a couple of rounds before he decided he wasn't able to swing, lock, and fire in time to hit anybody. So he aimed at empty space where he'd last seen a black appear. Sooner or later even the best got careless and forgot to shift position before jumping up again. On the fifth try he killed one. The man staggered forward, dropped his rifle, which slid across the rock and spun down into the pass, then fell with his head and arms dangling across the rim.

The dazzling sun beaded McGonagle's forehead with sweat. A bullet tore open the back of his hand. He made a bandage with his soiled handkerchief. He winged a man and thought, It's not goin' t' work, you black apes.

Comfort toured the stock pens early in the morning selecting the beeves, calves, pigs, and lambs she wanted. She inventoried the larder and ordered more butter beans, squash, radishes, and tomatoes and a few herbs and spices. She told the hunters how much of what kind of game she would need. She set four of Lowery's servants to stoning down and boiling out the kitchenware until it gleamed, so there would be no residual tastes, no impurities in what was cooked.

With Winifred and Floris, her two chief cooks, she began some of the condiments and sauces and desserts. She prepared the Cumberland Sauce for the game herself, using orange and lemon rinds, shallots, currant jelly, wine and ginger and cayenne pepper, then had it taken to the icehouse where it would chill. Winifred concocted a mustard dill sauce while Floris cut watermelon rind for pickles, soaked them in vinegar and sugar mixed with cloves and cinnamon. Comfort added a touch of vinegar to the mustard dill, approved the pickles, and saw that they were put in jars to stand and turn. They made a green tomato relish and a ginger pear conserve. They cooked sugar, water, and syrup, mixed beaten egg whites into it, added nuts and vanilla as it thickened, and dropped spoonfuls onto waxed paper where it hardened and became Purvis Divinity. They candied orange and grapefruit peels. Comfort opened two of the dozen and a half large, sealed crocks of brandied peaches in the larder, found them properly fermented and good.

Romulus came sniffing and strutting around her twice during the day, but Comfort ignored him. Floris let the black man know that *she* wouldn't mind sharing his mahogany bed in the Great House, but he only patted her on the bottom and left.

Thick-leafed plants and tight, spiked little bushes grew to the edge of the water, and a little way into it. Tiny insects fed on these, dropped into the water, and foundered. Darting minnows flashed silver, glutting on the insects.

A brown crane observed this in rigid immobility. Slowly it lifted one spindly leg, eased it forward, toes settling gently back into the silt on the bottom, causing barely any disturbance, waited, then took one more cautious step, and stood still again. It watched. Suddenly the sharp bill stabbed down and came up with a trapped minnow whose tail flapped ineffectually. The crane raised its bill skyward, loosened its grasp of the minnow, and wriggled its neck twice; the minnow slid down into its gullet.

The crane saw another flash of silver in the water, lifted a leg, and stepped forward.

McGonagle rolled the black body over with his foot. Not much more than a boy. There was a bullet hole a few inches above the heart. The nearby ground was pooled with blood. He'd bled to death. McGonagle put his boot against the boy's hip and shoved. The corpse rolled over the edge, struck the floor of the pass below with a *whump*.

"Six," McGonagle said. "We only got six of 'em."

"Maybe they took some o' they dead along wif 'em," the man beside him said.

McGonagle didn't think so. He had lost twenty-four dead and had thirteen more wounded seriously enough so that they couldn't go on. Thirty-seven men out of action. And they'd lost most of their wagons, had only two dozen boats, a few barrels of salt pork, and a hundred fifty pounds of dried beef left. Somehow, most of the ammunition had come through intact. Thank God for that. If it had been wartime, such an appalling loss would have brought him up before a board of inquiry. He tried to solace himself with the thought that they wouldn't have been hurt nearly as bad if he'd had proper soldiers under his command. He couldn't quite convince himself.

The sensible thing would be to turn back, reequip, and get more men. But he couldn't face the humiliation that would mean. He was insensate with fury at the niggers and he wasn't going to leave until the last of them had been driven into the ground. No matter what it cost. Then he could come out with his head high, the man who had finally destroyed Hellbottom Swamp as a sanctuary for renegade niggers.

He left the bluff and went down to the plain where his force was licking its wounds. He conferred with his lieutenants. He thought it likely the ambush had been the niggers' single effort, an attempt to weaken the enemy in the hope that some of them would then be able to survive, and that they had already retreated to the swamp. It *was* possible they'd gone back to their settlements and would try to defend them, or that they'd erected fortifications at one and would fight it out there. But that would be suicidal, as opposed to the swamp, which offered them at least some slim trace of hope, and McGonagle didn't think they'd try it.

Given this, his original plan remained basically sound. There was no point in raiding the settlements, of course, since the blacks were no longer to be caught off guard, but the easiest approaches into the swamp were still from these three points. And the settlements needed burning. McGonagle split his force into three parts, one to proceed to each of the settlements. If any group encountered resistance it was to dispatch messengers to the other two, who would then converge and overrun the defenders; if, as expected, no blacks were found, the units would put the settlements to the torch and wait one full hour to be sure no messages were enroute to them, then enter the swamp to begin hunting down the niggers.

Woodson began withdrawing men from Johnson's Pass as soon as the ambush had been sprung. He pulled them out slowly, in groups of four and five, trying to prevent the whites from realizing what was happening. The blacks went from the pass to Elmer's Smithy, two men to each of the swamp's few horses, buckboards jammed full. A handful of volunteers remained behind to hold the pass. On signal, they were to stop firing and run for prearranged hiding places where they would sweat it out hoping the whites wouldn't press a search.

The whites, Woodson believed, would think the blacks had expended their best at the pass and had then fled into the swamp. The settlements were the logical places from which to mount pursuit; they offered the easiest access and allowed the whites to advance and try to pin the blacks from three different directions. Woodson hoped the whites would divide, following their initial plan, and march on the settlements. If they did, he would be able to wipe out a full third of their force. He had stationed pickets on the chance the whites might arrive in full strength. It would be senseless to face them then. The pickets would provide the blacks with enough time to abandon their positions and scatter into the swamp. Should the whites fail to appear at all, then nothing beyond the opportunity to weaken and demoralize them further had been lost, and the blacks would enter the swamp without haste to play out the final stage of the contest.

Riding from Johnson's Pass to Elmer's Smithy, Alban Ford led his men along a dirt road that cut through woods and through fields lush with crops that would call for harvesting soon. They had set fire to isolated cabins as they found them, and dark columns of smoke rose at their backs.

Elmer's Smithy was a small settlement on the southern end of the swamp—a blacksmith's shop, a tiny general store, a meeting hall, and a dozen cabins. To the north was the swamp, to the west a hardwood and pine forest. East and south were a few hundred acres of cleared land under cultivation.

The settlement appeared empty, and Ford didn't expect to find anyone, but he was nevertheless cheered by the open fields, which offered no place for niggers to hide. Johnson's Pass had shaken him badly. He slowed his men from a trot to a walk and ordered riders ahead to check the settlement. He watched them rein up before buildings, push open doors with rifle barrels, and peer inside. After several minutes they waved Ford in.

A man riding beside him said, "Ah tell the men t' light the torches, Alban?"

"Let's see if they's anythin' worth takin' fust. We got t' wait an hour fo' messages anyway."

Fifty yards from the first building gunfire raked them on both flanks. Several fell dead. Ford searched frantically for someone to shoot at. A second fusillade knocked men from their saddles. A pall of gray smoke rose from the ground, and Ford saw them. They were in rifle pits that had been concealed by canvas and dirt. "Take cover in the cabins!" he shouted.

The whites galloped into the settlement. Two cabins were blown apart by dynamite blasts. The nearest lifted a horse and rider into the air, spun them, and dropped them back to the earth broken and bloody. "Stay mounted!" Ford screamed. "The cabins are mined! Go straight through. Follow me!" He rode past the empty buildings.

Suddenly blacks stepped from behind trees in the forest directly in front of them. Guns spat flame and smoke. Ford took a bullet in the leg. The riders on either side of him dropped. He wheeled his mount in panic. The swamp was behind him, blacks on both sides. But ahead stretched an open field. "Get out o' here! Ride for it!" he called. He jammed his heels into his horse's loins. He rode with his pistol at the ready, fearing another line of blacks would rise before him.

None did. But there was a hidden ditch six feet wide and three deep lined with stakes whose sharpened points were only inches beneath the fragile top cover. Ford's horse stumbled and somersaulted, pitching him free. He struck a few feet beyond. One stake ripped his cheek, another penetrated his stomach, and a third emasculated him. His hand, still holding his pistol, clenched and his weapon discharged. His body spasmed and raised itself a little on the stakes. His bladder and bowels voided themselves. He died.

Other horses and riders were dumped into the pit to die or to be skewered and twist helplessly while they screamed. Men in following ranks reined up sharply. Horses reared against punishing bits. Riders were thrown. Some rolled down onto the stakes, others were trampled. Gunfire sounded steadily and took heavy toll. Several whites turned and drove toward the swamp. A little way into the vegetation their horses went crashing down over trip wires, and blacks appeared with shotguns and pistols firing into the stunned riders. Few whites were still mounted. Blacks closed in from three sides firing. A pair of whites charged. They were shot from their saddles. The blacks opened briefly to allow the riderless horses to pass, then closed again. Three riders tried jumping the ditch. One succeeded, but before he had gone a hundred yards farther a black man dropped to one knee, took careful aim, and put a bullet in his back.

There was brief, furious hand to hand struggling. The stocks of empty long guns and the butts of empty pistols were used. Knives flashed, some in the hands of black women. It was over soon.

A few whites were still alive and groaning. "Finish them," Woodson ordered. He walked through the carnage.

It was a good kill. He would have been pleased with it in any of the wars he'd fought. Many of the blacks were unnerved now that it was over. Some were vomiting. A few stared at the bodies with horror and disbelief. A boy with a bloody knife in his closed fist sat on the ground and wept. Woodson felt only satisfaction that it had gone well. But he didn't fault the blacks. He had achieved indifference to slaughter only after a lifetime of exposure, and still there were moments when it reached him and made him recoil in disgust.

He looked up at the sky. Buzzards were gathering, gliding in looping circles on outstretched wings. But he could not sense the Beast anywhere. It had slunk off to nurse its wounds. He smiled. Burned you that time, didn't I? he thought.

Henry galloped in, jumped from his horse, and ran to Woodson. "One got through, Cap'n! Ah dropped the first one an' would o' laid the second alongside him, but mah rifle jammed." He looked at the weapon with painful bewilderment, as if it were a longtime friend who had suddenly betrayed him. "By the time Ah cleared it he was out o' range. Ah winged him, but not bad Ah don' think. Ah'm sorry, Cap'n, Ah'm sorry."

"It's all right," Woodson said. "It doesn't matter. We'll be in the swamp before they get here."

He called the blacks together and mounted a stump. "There's nothing more we can do," he said. "They won't be caught again. It's time now to go to the swamp. We've hurt them bad. What I hope is that they'll come right after us, that their blood-fever will be so high that they won't go back for new supplies and men. Most of you are going to die in the swamp. Maybe all of you. But you have a chance now. Run, stay away from them, let the swamp fight them for you. If they do corner you, kill as many as you can before they kill you. That will leave fewer to hunt down your brothers.

"When this ends—in a few days, a week—I hope the cost will have been just too goddamn high for them to try again. They might find it easier to forget about any of you who survive. As long as you don't bother them. I don't know. I don't really think that's the way it will be. But we've tried. And that's all we could do. You are good, brave men. You've done well. I'd have welcomed you alongside me in any fight." There was nothing more: the swamp waited. "Goodbye to you all. We'd better get moving."

Men made quiet, sober farewells. Some came up to Woodson and said goodbye to him. No one thanked him; nor had he expected anyone to.

Vulture appeared at his side. "You did nicely, Emory. It was like being in the war again."

"We're always in the war. We've been in it since Cain clubbed Abel. Sometimes things get quiet a little while, that's all."

"That kind of vision must make you an unhappy man."

Woodson smiled. "But a good general though."

"Yes. That's true."

"Anyway, it was good to have fought the last battle with friends."

"There'll be more. I intend to survive."

"Good luck to you, then. Your woman in the swamp already?"

"No, she hired out about a day's ride from here."

"That's good."

"I miss her. I was always all right myself, never felt I needed anyone before."

"You're lucky. I had that feeling once with my wife."

"But I'm glad she's not here. I don't have to worry about her."

"Even luckier. It's growing late, Vulture. They'll be here in a little while." He offered his hand. "Goodbye."

The giant black laid heavy hands on Woodson's shoulders. It was hideous and wrong that they had no time to grow old and decide whether they truly despised or admired one another, that they had been forced to be a black man and a white man instead of men. There was so much to say that was not yet even understood. He nodded and squeezed Woodson's shoulders. Woodson grasped his wrists. Then they turned away from each other and walked to the swamp.

4

The sun, still below the horizon, was beginning to suf-
fuse the belly of a thin cloud cover that hung in the east
with a pale red as Comfort entered the kitchen. Breakfast
was ready when the first guests, about a dozen, who had
arrived during the night, came down from their rooms.
They were served hot blueberry muffins, buttermilk bis-
cuits, waffles, cinnamon toast and wheat muffins, scrambled eggs, shirred eggs, basted eggs, and fried eggs, bacon,
brain croquettes, and ham steak. There were fluted balls
of chilled butter in shallow silver dishes, grape, strawber-
ry, and raspberry jams.

After the dishes and pans were washed and put away
Comfort went to the stock pens to oversee the pig slaughter. The morning sun was blistering. A chunky black man
stripped to the waist and sweating heavily asked, "You
wants 'em tied t' bleed?"

"No. Let 'em run, they get most all o' it pumped out.
Tie 'em, and even if they hung, there's always some that
settles in the veins."

The man turned to a waiting handful of other blacks.
"Cotch 'em an' hold 'em down. No ropes."

They vaulted over the fence into the pen, chased the
squealing pigs, lunged and caught them by the legs, and
flipped them over. The chunky man produced a long thin-
bladed knife that hooked a little at its tip. He knelt beside
the first pig, which thrashed beneath two sweaty men, inserted the blade into the side of the animal's throat, and
gave it a twist. The pig squealed. Blood sprayed brightly
from the severed jugular. They released the animal, which
scrambled to its feet and ran off fountaining blood. The
men were expert and worked rapidly. Stuck pigs rushed
about the pen soaking themselves and the ground with
their blood. Two of the greedy beasts stopped and stood
drinking from red pools that were replenished from their

own pulsing throats. In a short time the first animal cut began to stagger, wobbled a few feet, and then fell. His weakening heart continued to force blood from his wound in fading spurts, then erratic trickles, and then he quivered and lay still. The others joined him soon.

Under Comfort's direction the men dragged the carcasses from the pen to the butchering area. Women scraped the skin quickly and roughly with knives, then one by one the animals were hoisted by rope and pulley and dipped into a great caldron of boiling water and pitch and ash. The carcasses were strung in the air, head down, from a heavy pole. The last of the thickening blood dripped out while the women shaved off the remaining bristles with razors. Men rolled barrels beneath the pigs, slit open the bellies, and pulled out the steaming guts and organs with their hands. Some of the women scraped the empty cavities while others picked the long intestines from the barrels and set to squeezing their contents out. Comfort taught a young girl how to turn the intestine inside out and wash it when it was empty. Cleaned, the intestines were brought to the kitchen where they were filled with meat from grinding machines, then tied and sent to the smokehouse. They would be taken from there the next morning as cured sausages.

The lambs, calves, and steers penned and waiting their turn nearby bawled at the smell of butchery.

Late in the afternoon MaCullum came to check progress in the kitchen and the pens. Two men were with him. MaCullum tasted a few things and complimented Comfort. Leaving, one of the men said something about Hellbottom niggers. Comfort would have assumed it had been a reference to herself, but she saw MaCullum give the man a sharp glance. She wondered about that a while, but there was much to do and it left her mind.

A narrow stream that wandered past mossy banks made a looping turn beneath an old stump rotting on shore. Over the years the earth beneath this stump had eroded, and the quickened water formed a pool. Above this pool, the negligible weight of a mouse snapped a brittle twig and dropped the rodent into the water. It began immediately to swim with neat little motions of its tiny legs, its tail trailing, soft ripples radiating out behind in a widening cone. In the undercut, a heavy largemouth bass marked a disturbance on the surface and drifted out a little way to observe. It saw first the fractured lines of wake, then the mouse itself in wriggling silhouette. It considered. The mouse stopped to rest. The bass fluttered its fins and coasted closer. The mouse began to swim again, and at the instant motion was resumed instinct triggered a violent lash of the bass's tail that drove it forward and up. Its jaws gaped wide and its gill covers flared, suctioning water into the great mouth and out through the gills. The mouse was pulled inside and the bass broke through the surface in a jagged ring, hung suspended a moment, then plunged back down. The mouse's hindquarters were ripped by the rows of pointy teeth, its head crushed in the white gullet. Swallowing, the bass swam leisurely back to the shade beneath the overhang, turned lazily, and took up its quiet position of survey again. As it frequently did, and as it had been doing before the mouse fell into the water, it began to brood for no good reason.

They'd killed his little boy, who'd only turned seven this summer. It was a freak shot—the whites couldn't see them, could only hear them running through the brush—but it had punched into the back of the child's skull and torn out his eyes and nose when it exited. Tyler's wife shrieked and turned back to the boy, snatched him up in her arms. Tyler shouted for her to drop him and keep going. She wouldn't. He slapped her and pulled the body away, dragged her off with him.

Now he heard her dying. They'd been separated fleeing through the bogs around a small lake. He was crouching behind a deadfall with Jimmy, his thirteen-year-old. They'd listened to the whites shouting to each other as they hunted. Then Harriet screamed. Three gunshots. She was screaming again. And suddenly silence. Jimmy turned to Tyler. His lower lip trembled. "Stop it!" Tyler hissed. "Here." He took a knife from his belt and gave it to the boy.

He'd made a mistake trying to keep to the higher ground. His wife and children didn't know the swamp, and he wasn't very familiar with it himself. He thought most of

the blacks would go deep, that the whites would pursue
them, and he'd reasoned that he could hide with his family
in the outer circles while the whites passed them by. But
others had felt the same way, and the whites had found
them.

There was a rustling nearby. Tyler signaled Jimmy to
remain quiet and to crouch farther down. Tyler cupped
one hand over the breech of his rifle to muffle the sound,
then eased the hammer back to full cock. Someone was
coming nearer, beating the brush. Tyler raised his rifle
slightly, drew in a breath and held it. A loosely held pistol
appeared at the top of the deadfall, then a white face
peered over. Tyler swung the muzzle to that face and
pulled the trigger. The shot knocked the white man backward.

"Run, Jimmy!" Tyler sprang up and bolted.

Whites shouted behind them. There were shots. A slug
caught Tyler in the hip. He spun and fell facelong into the
shallows of the lake. A line of mud turtles basking on a log
slipped into the water with *plops*. Tyler dragged himself to
the log and pulled partway out of the water. A shotgun
blast rocked him. Pistol bullets thudded into his back. He
slumped over the log.

Jimmy screamed, "Pa!" and ran to him. He was shot
down before he reached the water's edge.

Swett struck at the bulrushes and reeds in frustration.
They were taller than him and so thick that he couldn't see
more than a few yards ahead. In some places they compacted to the point where he couldn't force through but had to
go around. The water was shin deep, the footing spongy.
The goddamn sun was burning his brains. His shirt clung
to him wetly. He'd taken it off, but the sawtoothed rushes
had lacerated his skin, so he'd put it back on.

"On the right, on the right!" someone called. There was
a spattering of gunshots, muffled by the vegetation.

Swett craned his head forward and squinted. The
Hearth and another ten men had been hunting a band of
niggers here for hours. Two women, two children, and five
bucks. Many shots had been exchanged, but no one on either side had been hurt.

Blackbirds called and rose in clouds as the men pushed

through the marsh. Some clung to the swaying reeds and cocked their heads with bold curiosity. These angered Swett, who swatted at them a few times with his rifle barrel.

There was firing on his left and Jimmy Hildenbrandt yelled, "They're comin' to you, Wallace."

"Hey, Hartley," Swett shouted. "Git ready!"

He caught a glimpse of black. He aimed, pulled the trigger and worked the lever, firing rapidly, reveling in his new repeating rifle. He exhausted the load and turned an ear hoping for moans or screams. There was silence. Then a shotgun roared before him and cut a swath to his side. Pistol and rifle fire sounded and slugs zipped around him decapitating the rushes. Swett hurled himself down. His body snapped reeds; their tough stumps bruised his groin and stomach and chest, a bulrush sliced open his cheek. He swallowed brackish water and gagged. On either side of him Hildenbrandt and Fisher fired back at the blacks. Stillness returned in a few moments.

"Anyone hit 'em?" someone called.

No one answered that they did. Swett got to his feet. His new rifle was caked with mud. He'd have to strip it down and clean it. Shit, shit, shit! Goddamn this swamp!

A man was calling for a conference. A quarter of an hour passed before they all found each other. "This ain't gettin' us no place," said a man with a gray beard. A drop of sweat fell from his hooked nose and another began to bloom. "We kin go round heah in circles aftuh 'em all week. Ennyone got an idea?"

"Let's git out an' git more men," Swett said. "Iffen we surround the place, we kin close in an' drive 'em t' the center from all sides."

"We'd end up shootin' ourselves that way," Johnny Murphy said.

Swett glared at him.

"Besides," said the bearded man, "our boys is ranged all ovuh the swamp. Coul'nt nevuh git enough men."

"Well, whut *kin* we do?"

"Nothin' far as Ah kin see."

"We jus' goin' leave 'em?" a bony man asked.

"Got no choice. Maybe we kin sweep through on the way out."

They discussed it. There was no way to rout the niggers. They were simply wasting time and exhausting themselves. Sullenly, but with unexpressed relief, they worked their way out of the reeds. It took them an hour to find the way.

Freeman Johnson fired, and one of the white men dropped to the ground. Freeman slipped away. He'd killed two at Johnson's Pass, one at Elmer's Smithy, and, sniping, four in the swamp. He was a happy man.

He'd sent his wife and children from the swamp before the whites came, promising to meet them at their cabin, or its ashes, in two weeks. He couldn't go with them, nor did he wish to. Freeman had a large R branded on either cheek, one for each time he'd tried to run when he was a slave. And his back was a horny mass of ridged scar tissue.

Five years ago he'd had his own farm. But a white bought the mortgage and foreclosed. Freeman could have paid the arrears in another month, but the white man wanted the land, not the money. Three nights after he'd been evicted, Freeman, drunk and furious, burned down the white man's house. He'd waited in the shadows with his pistol hoping the white was inside and would come running out. But he'd been unlucky, the house was empty. They'd have hung him anyway for arson, which was a capital crime, so Freeman fled to Hellbottom Swamp.

He purposefully left a clear trail after shooting the white man. They would follow it, and that would give him a chance to shoot another one. He moved in a wide arc, doubling back on his path to set up another ambush on their flank. There were only five left and he was confident he could kill all of them before the day ended. His feet sank into the mud of a flood plain. It rose over his ankles and did not seem very solid. He decided to return to the firm ground, which was several yards to the side. He raised his right leg. His left leg sank into the mud almost to his shin. He shifted his weight to the right, which sunk even deeper. He tugged the left, which came out a few inches with a sucking sound, but then he could move it no farther. His right went in past the knee. He rocked back and forth, frightened. He sank to the lower part of his thighs. He struggled ineffectually to wade through the thick stuff, and went down to his waist.

He'd never seen it, but he knew he was caught in quickmud. Sometimes, he'd heard, it bottomed a few feet down. If it did, you could make your way to ground sooner or later. If it didn't. . . . Freeman panicked. His violent motions quickened the rate of his displacement and he sank to the bottom of his breastbone before he stopped, tired and panting. He calmed himself, forced himself to remember what he'd been told about quickmud. Uh-huh. He stretched his arms out, laid his rifle flat against the top of the mud, and tried to lean forward, to spread his weight. Sometimes you could flatten out this way, and with very careful movements half crawl and half swim to safety. But his rifle pressed down into the mud, his arms sank and he couldn't free them. He struggled. The mud was at his shoulders. Terror clutched him and he began to scream.

The whites, who were several hundred yards away, heard something faint and muted through the dense foliage, but weren't sure what it was, nor from which direction it came.

Mud entered Freeman's mouth. He twisted his head and spat. Then it filled his mouth. He choked. His nostrils flared. Mud lipped them and bubbled a little as he breathed. He coughed and there was a *glop* in the mud over his mouth. His eyes protruded and his body jerked. Then the mud closed over his head.

Three streams met here, then continued on as one to the western part of the swamp, where there were several small lakes. Blacks fleeing to these lakes by water would be likely to pass by, and McGonagle saw it as a good place to mount an ambush. He ordered his party's four boats beached and concealed, and his men into hiding on the bank offering the broadest field of fire. Tired, logy in the sweltering heat, they welcomed a chance to rest. Several fell asleep, others sat in quiet torpor.

McGonagle, hungry for expiation, remained tense and vigilant. He saw the blacks first, two pirogues—narrow dugouts with shallow drafts—gliding through the dense growth that obscured the mouth of the smallest stream. Four men rode in the first, two men and a woman in the

second. There was no sound save the soft plash of their
paddles. McGonagle nudged the man next to him and
pointed. The signal was passed quickly. There was a sudden rustling. Twigs snapped as men were startled awake
by companions. Cocking hammers made dull clacks in the
still air. McGonagle nearly screamed at the noise, which
betrayed their presence.

The blacks' heads jerked toward the bank. Two men
dove overboard toward the opposite shore. The woman
and the other men grabbed for guns lying on the bottoms
of the pirogues.

"Fire! Fire!" McGonagle shouted.

Bullets geysered the water, chipped wood from the
pirogues, and slammed into the blacks before they could
bring their weapons to bear. The pirogues overturned.
Three blacks began to sink. Two struggled to swim. The
water around them billowed red. McGonagle shot one
through the head. Someone else killed the other.

The men who'd gone overboard appeared suddenly at
the shoreline downstream. They were out of the water and
into the brush before any but a few wild shots could be
directed at them.

"You three, and you and you. Get a boat across and
hunt those sonsabitches down!" McGonagle ordered. He
turned to the rest of his men. "Goddamn you, don' you
people know nothin'? You made enough noise t' spook a
whole army. If you cain't come awake quiet, then you
ain't goin' t' sleep when you waitin'. An' when you settin',
you keep yo guns cocked. Might as well just beat on a
drum otherwise, you dumb bastards."

"Well Jesus Christ, we got 'em, dint we?" a man said.

"Two got away. The others was just luck. An' if you
cain't find no other reason, then just remember, you get
sloppy, you goin' t' give some nigger a chance t' kill you."

"Like you done at the pass and the settlement, huh Mr.
McGonagle?"

McGonagle swore and kicked at the man, who dodged
him easily. He turned and stalked off to the water's edge.
He wiped his brow with his sleeve. McGonagle coveted a
seat in the legislature that would become vacant in the fall.
If he did well here in Hellbottom he could count on Governor MaCullum's support, which virtually guaranteed

election. But this swamp wasn't natural. It sucked a man's juices and left him weak, confused. And his left hand was swollen and throbbed painfully. He had to get hold of himself. He dipped his hand into the stream to cool it and to try to loosen the dirty handkerchief from the clotting. He untied the knot. Scabs pulled away. The puckered flesh was angry red with an unwholesome bluish tint. He swished the hand in the water. He wished someone had secreted a bottle of whiskey. He could have used that to cauterize the wound.

Homer Doyle felt miserable, but he was cheered a little remembering how admiringly his girl had looked at him when he set off to hunt the niggers. He'd have some good tales to tell when he got back home.

Thorns pierced his leg. He grunted. He looked down and lowered his rifle to push the bush aside. There wasn't any bush; there were several hornets on his pants. He was stung twice again, and even as his mind was registering the fact many more hornets lighted, plunged their barbs into him. He whooped and jumped back. His foot removed from the opening, a swarm of the insects boiled up from the nest he'd stepped on. He dropped his rifle and spun, beating at himself. He tripped, fell, and crashed down on another nest. He was stung on his legs, his back, his arms. He screamed and rolled on the ground, disturbing more nests in the enclave into which he had wandered. The air mottled with quick little bodies and filled with a sharp buzzing. The men on either side rushed toward him to see what had happened, but they were stung by hornets on the periphery of the great cloud that was forming, and they fled shouting to their companions to run. Homer thrashed and twisted. He was stung on the arms, the neck, the face. He shrieked and hornets entered his mouth and stung the inside of his cheeks, his tongue. His lips ballooned. The flesh around his eyes puffed and sealed his vision. He got to his hands and knees. Hornets moved into his ears and stung. He gibbered. Hornets were inside his shirt, boots. He collapsed and writhed. His heart pounded. Hornets pierced his veins and miniscule drops of blood appeared. His heart fluttered. Hornets covered him. His heart faltered, then raced. The hornets stung. His heart parox-

ysmed. His heart relaxed and did not beat again. Hornets
crawled over him. A few began to leave.

Lowery's servants quieted when Comfort neared them.
She asked them direct questions, and they protested that
they didn't know anything. Comfort was a Hellbottom nigger. That put some of them in reticent awe of her. Others
resented her freedom, and not answering was a way to retaliate. A few were trying to protect her feelings.

Comfort got Winifred to pump them for her.

"There ain't nothin' you kin put a finger on, honey,"
Winifred said. "Jus' a load o' gossip. It do seem thet a
bunch o' whites been messin' aroun' in yo home place,
but there weren't no partic'lars t' make it soun' ennythin'
special."

There *were* particulars, but they were too incredible to
be anything but wild rumor, and even if there were a little
truth in the stories there was nothing Comfort could do to
help; so Winifred had decided not to worry her.

Comfort was satisfied. She'd seen whites come to Hellbottom once before, a sheriff and a big posse hunting a
murderer. They'd flushed a man none of the Negroes even
knew was in the area from a cave on Woodpecker Slope,
shot him, and left with the body. The Hellbottom blacks
had little contact with the outside world and thus not
much opportunity to antagonize the whites. And the
swamp itself had discouraged white marauders years ago.
She couldn't conceive of any serious trouble.

Half the guests had arrived. The rest, with Governor
MaCullum himself, would appear tomorrow morning. The
heat was formidable, as thick and strangling as liquid. The
kitchen could just barely be endured, and Comfort was
giving her people frequent and extended respites to go out
and sit in the shade.

Lunch was served outdoors. There was aspic of tongue,
pheasant in champagne, duck with turnips, baked ham
with tart red apples, and a brandied chicken liver pâté.
There was a creamy spinach soufflé, sweet-sour slaw, and
apple chutney. The guests drank iced tea, lemonade, and
chilled wine punch. Dessert was fruit tart and a currant
jelly mousse served in pear halves.

At the end of the long day Comfort went to bathe in the

river behind the old slave quarters. The water was tepid, but still much cooler than the air, and she dallied in it, gradually feeling her strength return. Romulus appeared when she stepped out onto the bank. Several other women bathing there were embarrassed by his presence and waded more deeply into the water or turned at discreet angles. But none protested as he appraised them with blunt eyes. His status lent him more or less the same privilege of *droit du seigneur* formerly enjoyed by the old masters over their female slaves, and he had exercised it with most of the women on Lowery's plantation. One didn't have to submit, of course, but one also didn't work there long if one declined.

Romulus leaned against a tree and stared at Comfort. She ignored him, carefully toweled herself dry, then picked up her dress. He looked at the full black thatch between her legs, the firm heaviness of her breasts, and finally her face. She held her dress in her hands without attempting to conceal herself, locked eyes with him.

"Whut you want, nigger?" she said.

"That's not a question you have to ask. I thought I'd tell you my bed is still empty. And I have two boys who'll fan it through the night. It'll be cool there."

"Ah tell Flossie. She be pleased t' come." He took a step forward. "Stay away," she said. "You git yo fine fancy se'f hurt."

He advanced, speaking softly. "You know, my mama used to have a cat. It was black and beautiful, and when you came near it it would arch its back, show its teeth, hiss, and just look the fiercest creature born. But once you actually touched it and began to stroke it, why it just purred and purred and rubbed up against you for hours." He reached out and fondled one of Comfort's breasts.

"Mah mama had a cat like that too," Comfort said softly. She took Romulus's hand, raised it to her lips, and kissed it on the palm. "Only difference was, when you touched her, she clawed you to pieces." Comfort drove a large pin into Romulus's palm. It plunged through the fleshy pad, pierced the narrow bones, and exited through the back of his hand.

He screeched and grabbed his wrist, spun and doubled

over. Comfort kicked him square on his buttocks. He fell face down on the dirt.

"Teaches you a lot about cats, don' it?" she said, and walked away.

Eating was the principal activity of all life within the swamp, and it was ceaseless. It dominated the white fungi in the wounds of tiny minnows, and every other living thing, plant and animal, up through the huge, savage bull alligators who crushed the bones of prey between spike-studded jaws. Each entity survived at the expense of others around it, each single life required several deaths daily to sustain itself.

The swamp was all of its various hungry subjects: the darting little transparent water creatures, the pulpous white body of a clam, the sweet gum with its sap pulsing up from soil enriched by rotting corpses, the glistening secretion of the carnivorous pitcher plant, the striking coral snake, the bottom-drifting bullhead with wavering barbels, the quick bobcat, the swooping bat, the musky and explosive boar. . . . The swamp was all of them, but it was also something more, as a man is all of his parts but something more too. The swamp was the greatest eater of all, devouring and replenishing itself in an endless cycle, hopelessly and eternally ravenous.

Men did not usually live within it, so it ate men only infrequently. Now, though, many men were stumbling through it, being slain by each other and by its parts and providing it with unexpected bounty. Had the swamp possessed emotions it would have been happy. But it was only an appetite; it had no feelings, it had no intelligence. Sentient, it would have found nothing especially abhorrent or detestable about the men. Man was one of those few curious creatures who would kill his own kind, and who would kill even when his belly was full. But he was certainly not unique; there were others that turned upon their kin, and still others that killed for reasons not related to food. Man was perhaps singular in that he would kill on the basis of abstractions, destroy his fellows for something as frivolous as the color of skin, but the swamp would have judged him neither more guilty nor more innocent than most other creatures. *All* life demanded death, and regardless of the motive—food or hatred—the end was the same: something died.

Rufe, who was ten years old, woke up frightened. He saw a sliver of moon through the panoply of leaves above him and knew it was close to midnight. He had lashed himself high up in a tree crotch and gone to sleep at sunset. He heard voices. He didn't move his body, but he swiveled his head, ever so slowly so as not to draw attention, as his father had taught him, until he could see the men. They were white and they were angry.

One was shouting and tearing off his clothes in the firelight and slapping himself. Large black stinging ants crawled over his skin. The others were swatting their legs and necks and cursing. The hum of mosquitoes was loud.

"Fuckin' ants, fuckin' bugs! Ah'm goin' crazy heah. Crazy, Ah tell yuh!"

"Ah said not t' build the fire. Ah tol' yuh it'd bring 'squitoes."

"You gonna spend the night in the dark, huh? You gonna just curl up an' let the goddamn bears an' the gators an' God know whut else is out theah come walkin' in on yuh?"

"Shut up, both o' you," another man said. "Sonabitchin' fire doan got nothin' t' do with these stinkin' ants."

"Whole island's crawlin' with 'em. We got t' get off here."

"Well where the hell you goin' find us someplace dry t' sleep? Whut we goin' do, sit up in the boat all night?"

"Eat mah shit. That's what you kin do. Ah'm gettin' the hell outten this goddamn swamp. Ah cain't move wiffout sweatin' like a nigger. Ah been torn t' pieces by thorns. Ah been shot at. Ah been near drowned twice. Ah been cut an' Ah been bruised. Ah ain't been able t' sleep. Ah lost half mah blood t' fuckin' bugs. Ah cain't take no mo'. The niggers kin have they goddamn swamp. Ah'm leavin' right now."

"How you goin', huh? How?"

"Ah'm takin' thet there boat."

Four of the other five men said they were going with him. The last said they couldn't: "We got a job t' do. You knew it weren't goin' t' be easy when you started off. You

agreed you'd follow mah orders. Ah takes mine direc'ly
from Mr. McGonagle, an' he said we ain't comin' out till
the last nigger's dead."

"You kin come or you kin stay. Ah doan care. But me
an' mah frens is goin' home."

McGonagle's officer moved his hand toward his revolver, but the other man's gun was already in his hand and he
shot the officer three times in the stomach.

The remaining whites got into the boat. "Which way?"
one asked.

"How the hell do Ah know? Just start rowin'. We find
our way out the same way we found our way in."

The boat pulled away from the hammock and disappeared in the darkness. Rufe marveled at how stupid they
were. They hadn't even taken a torch. He knew this part
of the swamp well. There were dozens of runs and tributaries and waterways that wound in and out of each other,
doubled back on themselves, disappeared into bog. If the
white men abandoned their boat early enough and could
manage the bogs on foot they might make it. But probably
they would wait until it was too late and they were weakened by hunger and exhaustion, crazed by the heat, and
then the swamp would kill them, or maybe they would
turn upon themselves and kill each other.

Rufe was no longer afraid, and he was pleased that
they'd awakened him so he could see what happened. The
white man who had been shot was moaning and trying feebly to crawl. Rufe had no idea where the man thought he
would crawl to that would make anything better for him.
Rufe listened to the moans for a while, then fell asleep.

He woke when the first birds began to sing, half an hour
before dawn. He came down from the tree. The white man
was lying on his back next to the gray ashes of the fire and
he looked dead. Rufe caught four good frogs at the water's
edge, killed them, and cut off their legs with his pocket
knife. He skinned the legs, skewered them on a stick, then
built a fire and cooked them. He seasoned them with some
of his precious salt. After he ate, he walked to the other
side of the island and spent some time picking and eating
fat blueberries. Then he went back to the white man.

The man was indeed dead. Ants were crawling in and
out of his mouth and ears and across his open eyes. Rufe

squatted beside the corpse and watched the ants a while. Rufe's father, who'd been killed at Elmer's Smithy, had been one of the old-time swampers, and Rufe was more at home in the swamp than anywhere else. He'd fled into it after the fight at Elmer's Smithy. But, grieving for his father and increasingly lonely, he'd located and joined two families. They didn't know much about the swamp, though, and they wouldn't listen to him. They made stupid mistakes. Then they blundered into a party of whites and three of them were killed before they escaped. Rufe left and struck off on his own again. He still missed his father, but he was hardly lonely at all anymore.

He looked at the man's revolver, which was still holstered. His father had never taught him how to shoot a pistol, though, and he decided the thing would be more trouble than it was worth to him and he left it alone. He rolled the corpse over and was delighted to find a sheathed knife strapped to the man's belt. His own pocketknife was old and thin-bladed. He removed the hunting knife, admired its sturdiness and bright cleanliness. He tested its keen edge and smiled.

He felt very lucky. A good knife was a fine thing to have.

The night was turning to gray and already the thin light was painful to the owl's large eyes. It was a heavy bird with tufted ears, a cinnamon-dappled breast, and powerful talons closed tightly around the branch on which it rested. Soon it would be forced to retire until the coming of the new night. It had not fed well and it was irritable. Its head snapped greedily to each new sound, but, disappointingly, nothing was food.

It blinked, ruffled its feathers, prepared to give up. Then movement in the dark shadow round the base of the tree many yards away caught its attention. It froze. The shadow was still. The owl's head clicked forward slightly. Motion again, and the definition of shape—a marsh rabbit nibbling fresh grass. The owl walked a few slow feet along the branch. It bent its legs, then its claws opened and it thrust its weight upward and spread its wings. It flew silently, then dropped at a swift, steep angle with its wings locked back, talons open and reaching. The rabbit heard nothing, felt only the rushing of air and twisted its head in terror an instant before the owl struck. The curved claws drove into the rabbit's back and side, plunged cruelly through the stomach and lungs and liver. The rabbit squealed shrilly, thrashed and kicked its feet. The owl wrestled briefly with the twisting weight, then rose on slow, ponderous wings. The suspended rabbit twitched. Blood dripped from its wounds and its mouth.

"Ah'm afraid," Mark said.

Thistle hissed at him to be quiet and lay still. Her dress was open and Luke, the baby, was working contentedly at her breast. They were concealed deep within a thicket of greenbriers which had snagged and torn them. The heat was stifling. Insects fed upon them. Obadiah had gone to lead astray the party of whites that was tracking them.

"Where's Pa? Ah don' want them mans t' hurt him," Mark whined.

Paul, the eldest, said, "Shutup or Ah smack you!" Mark began to cry. "Shutup, shutup!" Paul said. But Mark only grew more disconsolate. Paul rolled over to him, put his arms around him, and hugged him. He whispered soothingly in Mark's ear. The younger boy's sobs ragged into sniffles, then he quieted. Paul still held him. Thistle looked at her oldest with helpless love. The baby fell asleep at her breast. She didn't move. Terror for Obadiah made her stomach twist.

Obadiah was himself afraid—for his wife and children. But each moment, as he drew farther away, relieved him. The whites had trailed them through the morning. When it became clear the whites couldn't be shaken, he hid his family, backtracked, and gave his pursuers a glimpse of himself. They fired several wild shots. He returned a few rounds to be sure they'd come after him, then he fled, pulling them away from his family.

He was moving with difficulty through a wetland filled with tall, blue-fruited tupelo trees and dotted with the purplish flowers of mad-dog skullcaps and the pale yellow ornaments of St.-John's-worts. He rounded the swollen trunk of a tupelo and heard a splashing close on his left. He crouched, spun, and brought his rifle to bear. He saw a white man, equally startled. Obadiah jerked the trigger.

The hammer fell with a click on a bad cartridge. He fumbled frantically at the breech. The white man fired. Obadiah was struck in the thigh. He fell and his rifle dropped from his hands and disappeared under the water.

"Ah got 'im, Ah got 'im!" the white screamed. He ran splashing to Obadiah, waving his empty rifle in one hand and drawing a pistol with the other.

Obadiah struggled to his knees in the water. "Yea, though I walk through the valley of the shadow of death," he said, "I will fear no evil: for thou art with me; thy rod and thy staff they comfort me." He drew his knife. "Surely goodness and mercy shall follow me all the days of my life: and I will dwell in the house of the Lord forever."

The agitated white circled warily, poking his pistol at Obadiah. But he was careful to keep out of range of the knife. He called for his companions. Obadiah turned on his knees, watching the white man.

Several more whites came. "Looky here," the one who had shot Obadiah said, "Ah got 'im. Ah surely did."

"Whyn't yuh kill 'im?"

The man with the pistol frowned, as if the thought hadn't occurred to him before.

"Ye that fear the Lord," Obadiah shouted in his thin voice, *"Praise Him!* For He hath not despised nor abhorred the affliction of the afflicted; neither hath He hid his face from him; but when he cried unto Him, He heard!"

"He crazy," a white said.

Wallace Swett shook his head. "Uh-uh. He a nigger preacher. Hey nigger, you a preacher ain't yuh?"

"A seed shall serve Him; it shall be accounted to the Lord for a generation."

"Shoot him," Johnny Murphy said.

Swett raised his hand. "Wait a minute!" He talked to the others.

"Our fathers trusted in Thee," Obadiah prayed. "They trusted, and Thou didst deliver them. They cried unto Thee, and were delivered: they trusted in Thee and were not confounded."

Most of them liked the idea. Jimmy Hildenbrandt didn't; he felt there was something sacrilegious in it. They went for the black man, grappled with him, and wrenched the knife from his hand.

Obadiah shrilled, "I will not be afraid of ten thousands of people that have set themselves against me round about. He that sitteth in the heavens shall laugh: The Lord shall have them in derision." But panic touched his voice.

Three men held him down while others fastened wooden pegs.

"Be not Thou far from me, O Lord: O my strength, haste Thee to help me!"

They dragged him to a tree.

"O Lord God, to whom vengeance belongeth; O God, to whom vengeance belongeth, show Thyself!"

They began.

Obadiah screamed. "Lord, Lord, why castest Thou off my soul? Why hidest Thou thy face from me?"

Jimmy Hildenbrandt glanced nervously up to the sky, but it remained empty and clear except for a few puffy white clouds, and there was nothing to be heard but Obadiah's shrieks.

Gotta keep a sharp eye, Lonnie told himself. Gotta stay alert. A couple of niggers had cut loose at them half an hour ago, and a man who stood blinking a moment too long before ducking was killed not far from Lonnie. They were hunting a band of blacks through cypress water in a maddening hit and run contest.

The water was a black mirror studded with towering cypress tress that were hung with Spanish moss. The moss lay motionless in the sweltering air. Great and gnarled roots sprung from the trees above the water level and twisted down in tangled profusion. There were hard stumps and roots beneath the surface, legacies of ancient trees long since dead and decayed. Little sunlight filtered in here, and it was dank and gloomy.

The blacks had the advantage of picking the sites from which to fire on the advancing whites and from which then to quickly retreat. But the whites were more numerous and were cutting their adversaries down by sheer force of numbers.

Lonnie was so depleted he could barely keep staggering

through the thigh-deep waters. He would have killed a man, a white man, just for the chance to sleep in some cool shade a while. He fell into mindless rhythm dragging his feet through the muddy bottom and could not apprehend at first that shots were being fired. But then a slug chipped wood from a tree close to him, and he threw himself down into the water. He held his breath and scuttled to the side, planning to come up behind the tree.

Roots snagged his shirt. He pulled to free himself. His arm wedged in a fork. He was running short of breath. He tried to raise his head, but a heavy root pressed across his neck. He grew frightened and thrashed, but only became more entangled in the roots. He thrust his free arm up and tried to find something to hold and drag himself loose with. There was nothing. His kicking feet roiled the muddy bottom.

Above the water the firing was heavy, and men were splashing to new points of cover. No one noticed the clutching white hand extending through the surface. In a little while it relaxed and disappeared.

Ed Ludwell sat pale and stunned with his back against a stump, a bullet hole beneath his collarbone. His shirtfront was saturated with blood. His cousin Ross knelt before him pressing a rag to the wound and saying, "You goan be all right, Eddie. It clean. It nothin' t' fret about."

More white men stood nearby. One said, "Cut a big blood vessy, it did. Deep inside, no way t' stop it. I seen a couple like that in the war. He pass out in a minute, be dead in two."

Ross never stopped talking to Ed, but Ed's eyes closed and he slid down the stump anyway. Ross slapped his face and shook him. "Wake up, Eddie! Goddamn you, wake up!"

Thistle found Obadiah at sunset. Paul and Mark broke into screams, which set the baby Luke off. Thistle sank to her knees and stared up dumbly, shaking her head from side to side. She touched the long wooden peg driven through Obadiah's feet, then threw herself forward and pressed her cheek against his cold flesh and sobbed.

Later, when she took him down, she couldn't free the

pegs, so she broke off their ends with a stone and pulled his flesh from them, leaving the bloodied peg stumps still in the tree. She dragged him through the water to spongy ground and scooped out a shallow grave. She bound the crusted wound of his slit throat with cloth before she covered him with dirt. She wanted to mark the grave with a cross—for him—but his god had abandoned him and she couldn't bring herself to do it.

Paul was quiet. He wouldn't meet her eyes. He felt that somehow she had failed his father, that she should have been able to prevent this. Mark and Luke were hysterical. She sat at the foot of the grave knowing she should quiet her two youngest, if only because the noise might bring whites down on them, but unable to rouse herself.

There was movement in the cattails nearby. Paul sprang to his feet snarling and holding a stout branch in both hands. A great and ugly black giant with a mutilated ear and a scarred face appeared. For an instant Thistle thought her powers had returned, that this was a black demon come to save her and her children and wreak vengeance upon the whites. But then she saw that for all his monstrousness he was still only a man. She remembered hearing about a giant who'd come to Hellbottom after the Woodboro riot and who'd taken up with Comfort Davis.

"It's all right, boy," the man said to Paul. "You can put that branch down. No one's going to hurt your mammy."

"They crucified mah pa," Paul said in a trembling voice.

"They what?"

"They crucified him," Thistle said. "Just like they done his god. Nailed him up t' a tree. Ah buried him heah." She pointed.

"Your boys see it?"

"They seen what was left of him."

Vulture nodded. "Help your mammy with your baby brother," he said to Paul. "You're the man in the family now." He went to Mark, set down his rifle and picked the child up, held him and rocked him, talked to him calmly and soothingly. Mark quieted, and in a little while fell asleep. Vulture laid him down next to his mother. "Boy," he said to Paul. "Why aren't you mourning your daddy?"

Paul looked away.

"It doesn't make you any stronger not to cry. No one thinks you're more of a man."

"Whut you know about it!" the boy said savagely.

"I know I saw the white men put fifteen, twenty bullets into my brother during the war, then ride their horses over his body. I know I sat with his body all through the night and I didn't stop crying till long after. Your daddy's dead, boy, and it hurts you. Cry for him!"

Paul's lips trembled. His hands balled into fists. He struck the ground. Then he screamed, "Paaa!" and flung himself on the grave, gave way to wracking sobs. Vulture sat and watched soberly, nodding now and then, until the exhausted boy went to sleep.

"You Comfo't Davis' man, ain't you?" Thistle asked.

"Uh-huh. Your husband the preacher?"

"Yas. O—Ob—" she faltered on the name. "Obadiah Isley. Ah thanks you fo' whut you done fo' his chilliun. He would o' been beholden."

"Well . . . it looks as if I got myself a responsibility."

"No. Ah'm leavin' the swamp. Ah got no reason t' stay in Hellbottom now."

"You know which way is out?"

"Me an' the swamp's passable friends. If Ah start at daybreak Ah kin be out by noon tomorrow."

"I'll go along with you a ways."

"I won't say no t' that. Yo woman dead?"

"No." He told her where Comfort was. "This'll be over soon. We'll start over where we left off."

Thistle didn't say anything.

Vulture picked up both the sleeping boys while Thistle took the baby, and they carried them to higher ground, where they made camp and went to sleep.

In the morning Mark was gone. They called him and searched, then struck toward Obadiah's grave. Near it they found the boy floating drowned in a shallow pool. They buried him next to his father.

Lunch was sixty gallons of Kentucky burgoo served from four steaming caldrons. In it were ten pounds each of lamb, beef, pork, and veal, ten fat hens, one hundred pounds of diced potatoes, ten pounds of onions, half a bushel of cabbage, forty pounds of tomatoes, ten pounds of carrots and ten more of corn, and green peppers, okra, celery, lima beans, pepper, salt, and cayenne. There were poached oranges, honeyed apples, and cherry molasses pie for dessert.

Comfort and Winifred had cooked through the night, and after lunch Flossie said she'd oversee the kitchen alone while they napped a few hours. Flossie's face was bruised and one eye was swollen nearly shut. Romulus had taken her to bed in the Great House last night and had beaten her. But she'd managed to steal a handsome silver snuff box from him and she was in good spirits.

On the bed, weary, the heat was no longer something that brutalized Comfort, but became instead a soporific that gradually dulled her consciousness and loosened her body. She thought of Vulture with love and with a hazy kind of sensuality as she sank down into sleep. She missed him. Soon she would be paid and could leave. His image dominated her dreams. She smiled in her sleep.

In the shallows, a muskrat gnawed through the thick reed stalks, then held them in its front paws and nibbled the juicy core within.

A bobcat watched from shore. The cat took one excruciatingly slow step, poised immobile several moments, then moved again. The muskrat paused now and then to lift its head, look about, and listen. When it did, the cat remained still and tense for some minutes. A torturous quarter hour of this brought the cat within range.

It pounced. The muskrat saw a gray flash of movement and scrambled for the deeper water. The cat's fangs sank into the muskrat's shoulder. The muskrat squealed, twisted its head and bit the cat's snout, raked its face with claws. The cat snarled and shook the muskrat, but didn't have a killing hold and the muskrat continued to punish it. The cat dropped the muskrat and retreated a few steps, hissing. The muskrat backed away with lips curled up from its long chisel-teeth. The cat circled. The muskrat pivoted to keep it in front and was prevented from escaping into the deeper water. The cat slashed with a paw. The muskrat snapped. The cat leapt to the side. The muskrat spun. The cat feinted. The muskrat was deceived only a moment, but that was sufficient. The cat was upon it, teeth sinking into the back of the neck and the base of the skull. It locked its jaws and snapped its head back and forth and the muskrat shuddered and died.

The cat walked delicately from the water with its head held high against the weight of the dangling muskrat.

The whites opened fire on them while they were struggling through a moist bottomland thick with tangled larch and ash trees. Vulture took a slug through the bicep. Paul's kneecap was shattered.

"Get to the deadfall!" Vulture yelled at Thistle. He scooped up Paul and ran for a thick jumble of fallen trees. Thistle was unhurt. She comforted Paul while Vulture fired a few rounds to keep the whites at bay. Vulture gave the rifle to Thistle. He said, "If you see anything move, shoot it. But keep your head down."

"Ah ain't very good with a gun."

"It doesn't matter. The noise is enough."

He cut Paul's pants from cuff to thigh, exposing ruined flesh and white bone fragments. Thistle fired. Vulture snapped a branch in two, placed one length on either side of the boy's leg, and secured them with strips of cloth. Luke was squalling. "Hush," Vulture told him. "Hush, baby." He made a compress to stop Paul's bleeding. Thistle fired twice again. Paul's eyes were glazing. He breathed rapidly and shallowly. Vulture dug into the wet ground until water began to pool. He cupped it and washed Paul's face. "Get hold of yourself now. Breathe deep and easy."

Thistle said, "Thet plant with the red flower there on the side. Crush up some of the leaves an' hold 'em under his nose."

Vulture did. Paul coughed and twisted his head away. Clarity returned to his eyes, and with it agony. He moaned. Vulture squeezed his shoulders. "Hang on, boy! You're the man. You've got to protect your mammy and your brother." He dug into his pocket for his derringer, which he handed to the child. "Here. If the whites come close, pull back both hammers until they click. Hold it in both hands like this. Aim for the stomach, and pull one trigger at a time. Do you understand?"

The boy's eyes were slitted and his lips drawn tight against the pain. He nodded.

Vulture tapped Thistle on the shoulder. "I'll take the rifle now. You hit any?"

"No."

"How many are there?"

"Leas' seven, maybe mo'."

Vulture took his pistol from its holster.

"Might as well keep that yose'f," Thistle said. "Ah cain't work it."

Vulture shot a man who dashed for another and closer piece of cover. The man fell with his face jammed up against a stump and didn't move. The whites were moving cautiously, trying to flank him. They'd succeed sooner or later, and Vulture didn't know what he'd do when that happened. He killed another man and wounded one more, but not seriously enough to take the man out of the fight.

"We goan die, ain't we?" Paul said.

Vulture looked at the boy. "Maybe."

Two men came running in from the right. One fired a shotgun; the range was too much and the blast was wide, but still three pellets tore through the skin of Vulture's forehead and lodged against bone. Vulture drove both to ground with rapid fire, but didn't hit either.

There was silence for several minutes broken only by Paul's groaning and Luke's crying. Vulture peered about warily.

"Behind you!" Thistle screamed.

Vulture whirled. Three men rushed him, firing. Vulture went to a crouch, worked the lever of his rifle, and fired from the hip. One man dropped. A bullet struck Vulture in the side and he grunted. The two whites from the right were on their feet and running now. One came from the left and another charged the front of the deadfall. Thistle hugged Luke protectively and rose to her knees screaming. Paul extended the derringer in both hands and shot one of the men storming the rear in the stomach. A shotgun boomed and Paul's chest exploded red. He was driven back against the crackling branches of the deadfall. He slumped, and the derringer dropped from his hand.

Vulture dropped his empty rifle, seized his pistol, and killed the man with the shotgun. A bullet tore through

Luke and grazed Thistle. She fell. Her head struck a stone which laid open her scalp and left her unconscious. Vulture was shot in the back. He roared fury, turned, and put three bullets into the white. A slug splintered his jawbone. He shot a man in the leg and then his pistol was empty. He flung it at another man and flourished his knife. They rushed him from three sides, even the two wounded men, firing as they came. Slugs thudded dully into Vulture. He lumbered to meet the closest white, seized him powerfully about the throat with one hand, lifted him from the ground and sunk the knife into the man's belly, ripped upward to the breastbone. He was shot three times more and he dropped the man. He staggered forward with his arms windmilling, caught hold of the lower branches of an ash tree, was shot again, then crashed to the ground, tearing off the branches as he fell.

He lay on his back with his eyes closed, breathing in hoarse bubbling rasps. The three remaining whites emptied their weapons into him, then one of them picked up a heavy stone, raised it high with trembling arms, and threw it down, crushing Vulture's skull.

McGonagle's hand and forearm were swollen and tight. Red tracings were visible beneath the skin up to his armpit. The wound itself was purple and black and it stank. Each step sent tremors of agony through the arm. McGonagle's mouth was dry, his eyes granular, his forehead hot. He had difficulty thinking.

Warren Busch, one of his lieutenants, was heating a knife blade over a fire. "We ought t' give this up, Caton. We done all we could. There cain't be many niggers left, an' God knows how many men *we* lost so far."

"We goin' t' stay till it's done." Speech seemed a labor to McGonagle. "Want ever' las' one of 'em dead."

Busch removed the blade from the flames and wiped away the carbon. "For what we know there ain't none left. We got no communication lines. Be a couple o' days 'fore we can pull our boys out even if we start now."

McGonagle extended his arm, supporting it under the elbow with his other hand. "Jus' take care of this."

Busch positioned the knife. "At least let me bring *you* out, Caton. You need a doctor."

"I'll leave when it's over."

Busch shook his head and cut into the wound. McGonagle cried out. He trembled. Thick pus oozed from the incision. Busch made two more. Then, while McGonagle gasped, he pried the lead slugs from rifle cartridges and sprinkled the powder over the wound. McGonagle gritted his teeth: "Hurry up!" Busch took a burning twig from the fire. He touched it to the powder and the powder flared slowly and brightly, fuming a cloud of gray smoke. McGonagle panted. Tears ran down his cheeks. "That ought t' do it," he gasped.

They shot at him whenever they thought they had drawn close enough, but distance and perspective were warped at night in the swamp and the slugs went far astray. Attila did not fear their marksmanship. The pitch torch mounted on the front of his pirogue burned fiercely and spread an aura of wavering yellow-orange light. It illuminated moss-hung cypresses as he paddled down the stream, swamp maples, and infrequent firs. Occasionally large owls shifted their feet on low boughs and blinked at the blinding light with quizzical expressions. Fireflies flickered along the banks. There were the *smacks* of leaping fish.

Attila could have outdistanced the whites in their clumsy rowboats, and he knew this waterway well, did not need the light in the prow. But he wanted them to follow. It was an indulgence, he knew, and dangerous; you don't entice predators if you want to live. He was growing too old for the swamp's rigors. Yet the white men had forced him back to it. They should pay. And it pleased him to arrange for the swamp to visit punishment upon them. He felt the pull of the current and he tensed. He was experienced with this, but still it required caution. The stream emptied into a river a little way ahead, and there was a broad and deep lagoon at the junction in which, at certain seasons, large schools of fish concentrated. This was what drew the alligators.

He saw the first one, a big bull, while he was still several hundred yards upstream of the lagoon. Its enormous body floated like a heavy log upon the black surface. It raised its head. Water spilled in streams from its opening jaws, vapor rushed from its large nostrils like steam. Attila paddled by silently. It ignored him.

The current quickened, caught his pirogue, and carried it skimming toward the river. He shipped his paddle. Even if he fought against it, the current had him fast now and would not release him until it had conveyed him most of the way across the lagoon. The pirogue slipped by the dense vegetation at the mouth of the stream into the broader water, which was compacted with large silvery fish. There was a line of feeding alligators, then another. Beyond that the surface seemed to be a single, vast, seething creature of armored skin and a host of flailing tails and great jaws that rose into the air dripping water and crushing fish whose tails flapped feebly. The night was filled with hideous slurpings and crunchings, powerful splashes, and occasional hoarse roars. Some of the reptiles lost feet, tips of tails, even pieces of jaws to others, but they continued their frenzied feeding unaware.

The pirogue bumped and banged against the beasts. Attila crouched on the balls of his feet, shifting his weight to compensate for changes in the craft's delicate balance. A few times aggressive bulls shouldered into the pirogue or snapped at the gunwales. Once a pair of them threatened to overturn him. He struck them with his paddle around the eyes and nostrils until they retreated. Twice they were clustered so thickly that he was brought to a standstill. Cautiously, he shoved against them with the paddle until he'd pushed free.

He glanced behind. The torches on the whites' two boats were winking through the foliage at the stream mouth. They would be in the thick of the alligators within minutes. The current slackened some, and Attila began to paddle again. The reptiles thinned. Soon there were only a few younger and smaller ones around him. The whites were in the lagoon. Their torches, fully visible now, were bobbling. Attila set aside his paddle, filled a pipe with tobacco, lit it, and settled down to watch.

He heard shouting. Then gunfire. The torches swayed. He saw a figure in silhouette. The man fell. There was screaming, which ended abruptly. Guns flashed in the darkness. Attila saw that men were standing in the rocky boats. Oars were being swung. He imagined an oar striking an old bull just behind the foreleg, a sensitive area that, if probed, would bring a four-hundred-pound monster lunging in rage over the gunwale. The torch of one boat dipped crazily. Men fell overboard, and one screamed for a surprisingly long time. A minute later the second torch disappeared as that boat capsized and rolled bottom up.

Attila cocked his rifle and rested it loosely on his shoulder, puffed his pipe, and waited for the current to bring to him the boat that was still upright. It neared. He readied his rifle. But there was no one in the boat. When it came fully abreast, he paddled across the few feet of water and caught hold of it.

He found some ammunition and a couple of pieces of salt pork in the bottom. He took them.

Nicodemus crouched in stagnant water beneath a canopy of thorny bushes that overgrew the bank. The whites had failed to discover him and were moving past. He sucked and chewed on his cheek with nervous pleasure. He'd shot one and gotten away with it. He'd come to Hellbottom six years ago, and had always felt that he'd run from the whites, which was true. That unmanned him. But now, for the first time, he felt on equal footing with them. He wasn't going to take any dumb chances, though. As soon as they were past he'd get the hell out of here. With a little luck he'd have a chance to shoot another one later.

There was a rustle in the leaves by his knee. A snake slid into view, dull brown and with the darker bands of a cottonmouth. Its tongue flicked inches from Nicodemus' flesh. Nicodemus screamed and sprang up, tearing his shirt and skin on the thorns, and ran splashing away in panic. The nearest white turned, threw a shotgun to his shoulder. The heavy buckshot crippled Nicodemus, and pistol fire killed him.

The snake slithered to another branch. It was a diamond-backed water snake, which closely resembled a cottonmouth, and was harmless to anything larger than rodents.

They had been trapped three days. It was a peculiarly deadly labyrinth in that a way out existed (when one existed at all) usually for not much more than an hour. Then it would disappear and the puzzle might not offer solution until the next day.

It had driven the four whites to the line of madness. In the beginning their minds simply rejected the information reported by their senses: rivers do not change courses in a matter of half an hour. Yet by the end of the first day this was indisputably the situation. They would row into a bay, a lagoon, or a pond and see landmarks on the shore that they had passed earlier; but this time the bay would have cut its size by half, or doubled it, or offer twice as many exits, or have become a dead end. Channels disappeared. Trickling tributaries metamorphosed into broad streams. Stands of trees changed their locations.

The world had run amuck, and they could neither accept nor escape this; and dread grew in them. They found the answer in the early morning of the second day. The oars rested motionless in the water. While the men argued bitterly and fearfully, a broad section of bank dislodged itself and, as they watched with gaping mouths, drifted lazily to the opposite shore.

In reality, they were not caught in a complicated maze of waterways, but were on a single and fairly large body of water upon which floated innumerable chunks of earth and humus that were held together by tangled growths of roots. Some were only a few paces across and covered with dense berry bushes, while others were several acres large and even supported stands of modest trees.

Order was restored. Mystery crumbled, and with it fear. They laughed overlong and too raucously. They treated themselves to a hearty meal, devouring most of their meager rations. They exhausted their tobacco.

But they did not find their way out. Not that day, nor the one that followed. Revelation is not necessarily salvation. The sun was relentless. They grew weak from hunger. They slept fitfully and were plagued by legions of mosquitoes. The labyrinth's permutations were endless. They rowed, with increasing weariness, in tight circles and wide looping involutions. They sallied onto the floating islands in hopes of finding a connection to firm land. But they didn't, and they couldn't bring themselves to leave the boat, afraid of being marooned.

One collapsed in the stern and wept openly. "We never

gonna get out o' here," he sobbed. "Never!" None of the others disputed him.

A rifle bullet burned across Six-Finger Sadler's ribs. He threw himself down and, as whites came running from the tree line to the north, he scuttled through the tall grass and the profusion of flowers on his hands and knees.

He'd left Effie and Jackfoot and the others and come to the sweeping meadow to hunt rabbits for the pot. He stopped many yards from where he'd been shot and touched the wound with his fingers. The slug had left a stinging furrow but hadn't done any real damage. He broke open his sawed-off shotgun and removed the two shells. They contained fine birdshot, which wouldn't tear the meat of a rabbit badly. He inserted shells with loads of heavy, ravaging buckshot.

The whites were shouting to each other and beating through the high grass for him. He sat perfectly still, as a hunted rabbit did when unsure whether it had been seen or not. The whites neared, but would have to be nearly atop him before they could see him in this growth. There had been only one shot fired. Sadler wondered if his party had heard it.

"If he was hit," a man called, "we'd o' found him by now."

"Doan worry, we'll git him."

Someone was heading directly toward him. The man paused, turned off, paused, turned back. Then he loomed over Sadler. Sadler blew half his head away and went running in an awkward crouch. There was gunfire. A few slugs zipped close to him. He went to ground again and exchanged the spent shell for a fresh one.

There was new rattle of fire, a little farther off. The whites yelled excitedly. *How you like that, you bastards?* Sadler thought. He risked popping his head up. Jackfoot, Effie, and the rest were firing on the whites from the tree line to the east. The whites' attention was directed to them and their backs were to Sadler. One man was only thirty feet away. Sadler shot him between the shoulders and he was knocked down as if struck by a sledgehammer.

The whites were ducking down and the blacks were moving in from the trees. Effie and three other females carried guns alongside the black men. There were fourteen in Sadler's group, and about an equal number of whites— maybe a few less now that some had been killed.

Under the bright noonday sun, the blacks and whites hunted each other across the flowered meadow. They sprang up, found targets, and fired. They hid behind the few cedars and behind the blooming bay trees. They ran through shell-pink starflowers and the scarlet spikes of Cherokee beans, through white-fringed orchises and yellow foxgloves. They fell dying among the golden allamanda, the red lilies, and lush clusters of purple grapes.

They fought and killed each other through the afternoon. There remained, in the end, only Jackfoot and Effie to leave the field. Behind them were many corpses, and a black man shot through the lungs who was unconscious and would soon be dead, and a white man wounded in the leg who was lying in silent terror. The hummingbirds returned shortly, darting from flower to flower and hanging in whirring suspension, and bees settled down once again to become heavy with pollen and nectar, and hosts of insects rose from the fertile soil to feed upon bodies already growing gaseous in the searing heat.

Tucker was in the stern. His children squatted on the bottom of the pirogue, and his wife, with another pole, was in the prow. The muscles of Tucker's back did not relax between strokes: he anticipated the shock of a bullet any moment. Two boatloads of whites were in pursuit, and, now that they had emerged from the twisted course and were on the open water, they were trying their luck regularly. Tucker was far ahead of them, and it would be a difficult shot from moving boat to moving boat, but still some slugs had pocked water dangerously close.

If he could reach the opposite shore he could kill the whites. All of them.

The shallow-drafted pirogue was moving slowly through a sprawling bed of dense sphagnum and duckweed, which scraped and dragged against the bottom and sides of the craft. Sweat slicked Tucker's body, stung his eyes, and forced him to blink. His arms ached. The muscles of his abdomen felt torn. His wife was breathing raggedly and her head jerked, but she used her pole with unfaltering rhythm.

Dragonflies skimmed the water, hovered briefly around the pirogue, and flashed off. Frogs slipped from the broad duckleaves as they passed. Water striders skated on the surface of small and infrequent patches of open water and clusters of whirligig beetles circled insanely. Painted turtles ducked their dead-stick heads.

Tucker and his family reached the spongy shore exhausted but unharmed. The two older children disappeared with their mother into the white alder trees. Tucker carried the baby to them, then returned to the shore.

The whites had penetrated the weed morass and were making laborious progress against it. Sun glinted from great masses of dripping weeds that clung to rising oars. The whites still had time. If they turned back now they would live. But they were determined not to lose their niggers, and they came doggedly on. Soon they were pulling their oars from the locks and cleaning weeds after each stroke. They rowed in rotation, the effort of moving the heavy, flat-bottomed, deep-draft boats even a few yards brutal and exhausting. An oar snapped on one boat and the man who had been rowing fell overboard. His companions dragged him back in; he was hung with tailing weeds and green slime. Tucker waited for the other boat to break an oar. It did.

He unholstered his revolver. But he waited a little—to give the whites time to tire themselves even further, to let their fear grow; they deserved that.

The morass could be passed only in a light pirogue moved by a strong man with a long pole who knew what he was about. Unless retreat was effected early, a deep-running craft with oars was doomed to become inextricably mired. Tucker watched the whites try to use their remaining oars as poles. There was firm bottom, but it lay under a layer of muck and silt that itself hung in viscous limbo beneath the weed-thick water. The oars could not reach it. The whites argued with each other in frustration. One of them sat on a gunwale and lowered himself carefully into the water.

His voice carried clearly to Tucker: "It all right. They's ground underfoot."

The others abandoned the boats and joined him. Tucker let them struggle several minutes, during which they progressed only a few feet. He set a box of cartridges on a branch. He gripped the revolver in his right hand, wrapped the fingers of his left hand around his wrist, and laid the flat of his left hand on the branch, steadying the weapon. The range was great, but there was no way he could improve it. He cocked back the hammer, breathed, expelled half the air, held the remainder, and sighted carefully. He squeezed the trigger. The pistol roared. A tiny jet of water spouted twenty feet below his target. He adjusted and fired again. Blood sprayed from the man's head and he fell sideways, arms flung out. His torso was supported by the dense weeds, prevented from sinking. The whites shouted and thrashed in the water.

Tucker passed the better part of an hour shooting at them before he decided to quit. Three were still alive, but he'd expended forty-two rounds to kill the other six, and he was running too low on ammunition to continue. The morass would finish them anyway. It would sap what little remained of their strength and drown them long before they could hope to bull their way out.

Ross Sewell had lost face at Johnson's Pass. When the niggers had opened up he'd jumped from his horse, scrambled into a little ravine, piled rocks around himself, and trembled there with his face pressed into the ground until the battle was over.

Sewell was a coward, but never before had he demonstrated that in public, and he was desperate to regain his manhood in front of his fellows. But they had encountered blacks only twice since entering the swamp; first an old man and woman whom they'd killed without resistance, and next a small band with which they'd exchanged a few shots, but which then slipped away.

Sewell had lost several pounds and was verging on heatstroke, but he would have to be dragged from the swamp before he'd had a chance to gun down some niggers in a flashy way.

He thought that chance might be beginning now and he was nervous and excited. They were combing a swale filled with stunted swamp pines—around whose trunks red trumpet vines wound—and thick with giant, stout long-leafed ferns. Sewell was sure he'd heard movement ahead of him. He advanced warily, keeping close to trees that afforded him cover, stopped, cupped an ear, tried to peer through the ferns. He heard it again, a faint crackle before him. He rushed with his rifle ready, and the black retreated. Sewell couldn't see him and dropped to his hands and knees, squinted through the fern stalks close to the ground where the leaves weren't so thick. He saw movement and a flash of black skin. He dropped to his belly, slammed his rifle to his shoulder, and fired twice. There was a high-pitched cry of pain.

"Nigger!" Sewell cried. "Nigger at bay!" He jumped up and ran forward. The whites on either side shot in the general direction of the black. The black was running crouched over and Sewell couldn't sight him. But he saw the ferns shake as the nigger passed through. He fired several more shots and chased the nigger to ground in a thicket. He paused behind a pine and slipped cartridges into his rifle with trembling fingers. The nigger hadn't shot back. Either he wasn't armed, or he was hit too badly to use his weapon. A bright red blood spoor led to the thicket. Sewell wet his lips with indecision.

Men were approaching behind him. He made up his mind and yelled, "Look out. He got a shotgun!" He charged the thicket, working the lever of his rifle and firing from the hip. He crashed into the brush.

The green leaves closed him from the sight of his companions. Sewell screamed and came staggering back into view. Blood ran from one leg. He shook his head and motioned with his hands as if to shove something away. There was a squeal of rage. A wild boar with dirty and matted hair pounded out of the thicket. It hooked its long, curved tusks into the soft flesh of Sewell's lower belly and ripped upward. Sewell's intestines spilled out in grayish ropes, hung briefly like some swollen pouch, then unraveled and slithered to the ground. Sewell collapsed atop them.

The other whites fired at the boar. Two slugs struck the muscled hump of its back with dull *whaps!* and raised puffs of dust, quick gouts of blood. The boar screaked insanely and rushed them. They turned and ran. The animal hooked one in the ankle and hamstrung him. Another tripped and fell on his face and the boar dropped its head and, grunting, ripped him open from buttocks to shoulder blades.

The boar looked up with tiny eyes, shrilled wrathfully, saw no one else at hand, turned back to the man beneath it once more, rooted across his back again, then trotted off into the underbrush, small tail high and stiff.

Lowery and MaCullum strolled with their hands clasped behind their backs. "He stumbled into a gopher hole," Lowery said, "and snapped a foreleg. When he went down the boy fell from the saddle and broke his neck, died instantly."

"I'm sorry, Clayton. Scourge was magnificent. But even though you can't race him, I'm sure he'll be a good stud."

"That's the worst of it," Lowery said. "He's dead. A goddamn black sharecropper with a whole tribe of pickaninnies found him. He put a bullet through Scourge's head and hauled the carcass back to his shack and cut it up for table meat."

"Oh my god."

"A goddamn five-thousand-dollar stallion for table meat." Lowery shook his head.

They came out of the grove on a stark white gravel path and were immediately encircled by several persons who'd not had an opportunity yet to congratulate MaCullum on his inauguration.

The guests were numerous, and they milled across the sweeping lawn, in arbors, on stone benches, and at the sides of shallow goldfish ponds. The women, most of whom were in their early twenties, seemed to glide rather than walk across the manicured grass, their feet invisible beneath broad hoopskirts. They wore ruffled dresses with plunging décolletages, gowns of watermarked silk, bouffants, and fine laces. They were jeweled with pearls and diamonds, a smattering of emeralds; one wore deep-hued rubies. Their hair was done mostly in corkscrew curls. Some wore floral wreaths, others carried painted fans, lace handkerchiefs, and bouquets. The men were much older than their wives, graying or balding, and dressed in dark sober suits, a few with collars and facings of black velvet. There was a scattering of full dress military uniforms.

On a decorated pavilion a black orchestra Lowery had hired and brought by train from Charleston played Chopin and Offenbach and songs such as "Barbara Allen" and "Greensleeves." Floral and pastry ornaments rested on white-painted tables of wrought iron. One depicted a forty-gun frigate under full canvas flying the Confederate flag, a ship once commanded by a guest who was now an admiral in the Union Navy and which had participated bravely in three notable engagements. There was also a winged warrior's helmet, a Chinese pagoda, mermaids on a broad seashell lifting twin cornucopias, and the goddess of liberty atop a shrine with Doric columns. Between and around these were straw baskets of flowers and fruits.

For lunch there was cream of chestnut soup and peanut soup, baked catfish, steamed mussels and perch fritters, roast goose with peaches, venison and braised lamb, tiny roasted rice birds, steaming collards, butter beans, beets, and cabbage gumbo. Dessert was bourbon balls, cherry molasses pie, poached oranges, and white fruitcake.

Later, Clayton Lowery's youngest daughter played the harp near a fountain with four deep bowls supported by stone water nymphs.

Cecil Hogan couldn't stop thinking about food. They had only a little dried beef left and were eating snakes, blackbirds, and sometimes rabbits, but the unsalted meat was tough and didn't taste good and about all it seemed to do was keep you from fainting with hunger. Heat and poor rations had carved pounds from Hogan; this morning he'd punched still another new hole in his belt.

They were sweeping upstream alongside a river and Hogan was walking on the flank nearest the water. The brush was tangled here and he kept getting bogged down in muck. He wished he had the guts to ask someone to switch positions with him a while.

His sleeve snagged on a branch, jerking his arm and causing him to drop his rifle. He bent over and probed in the brush for it. Something clamped savagely around his wrist. He screamed and yanked. There was heavy resistance. He lost his balance and fell, dragging a huge snapping turtle partway from the brush. The creature's horny shell was covered with moss. Its thick leathery-skinned legs ended in broad flat feet that were tipped with long claws. It braced against Hogan's jerks, tiny eyes fixed on him, great curved beak circumscribing his wrist.

Hogan screamed again, seized his left arm below the elbow, and pulled. Bones cracked. The turtle's beak cut deeper. Hogan grew frantic, and the more violently he struggled the worse the relentless and crushing pressure of the jaws became.

There were men around Hogan. He couldn't see them very clearly or understand what they were saying. He was gasping, there was a rushing in his ears.

Guns fired deafeningly close. Smooth black holes appeared suddenly in the turtle's shell. Dead, the creature still held Hogan's wrist. Someone sawed on the tough neck with a knife. Hogan lay on his back moaning. Two men pried at the jaws with sticks. "Git it off, git it off!" Hogan screamed.

Then a man was holding him by the shoulders and Hogan finally understood that it *was* off. He looked. His hand, with clenched fingers, was attached to his wrist only by a thin strand of tendon. Dark blood pulsed from the stump around the jagged bone. Hogan's jaw worked weakly and without sound.

It was like flushing a covey of quail. The niggers must have been holding so still they hardly dared to breathe. But then suddenly they were up and running, out of nowhere, angling off in different directions. The whites shot at them, but, like quail, they were out of sight in moments and only one was knocked down. The whites split and went racing after them.

Swett found himself teamed with Johnny Murphy. Their nigger forged through the brush with the noise of a panicked deer, leaving a clear trail of broken and bent branches. He turned into a thick brier stand. Swett and Johnny bulled in after him, following a line of clothing shreds snagged on thorns. Scratched and bleeding, they burst through to the other side and found the nigger.

It was a girl, about thirteen. She was trapped between the briers on one side and a pond on the other. Half a dozen alligators basked in the sun on the opposite bank, and she had stood indecisive, afraid to take to the water in their presence. She spun when the youths appeared. Her dress had been ripped down the front. One hand went to cover her groin, the other to mask a small breast that was exposed. The gesture toward modesty, when she was only an instant from death, struck Johnny poignantly.

Swett raised his rifle.

Johnny put his hand atop the barrel. "Uh-uh. Wait a minute, wait a minute."

Panting and sweating from the chase, Johnny stared at her and felt a twitching in his loins. Though he'd tried with whores and once with a nigger the Hearth had shagged, he hadn't ever been able to do it. Alone with his hand, he had no problem. But with a woman he just shriveled up. The girl backed away whimpering, bent a little as she tried to conceal herself. Johnny had never seen a girl like this, so childlike and modest and vulnerable and afraid. His crotch pulsed. He set down his rifle. The girl watched him intently, poised for flight. "Come here," he said softly. He stepped forward. She took a step back. His mouth was dry. His legs trembled. He reached down and unbuttoned his fly. Her eyes widened and she grimaced in fear. His tongue worked over his lips. He fumbled for his turgid penis, pulled it out, and let it rest in the palm of his hand. The girl cried and shook her head. Johnny closed his fingers around his penis, squeezing it, then he slid his hand toward its base, which pulled the skin back and revealed its wet, swollen red tip.

The girl screamed.

She was terrified. Terrified of his cock. His great powerful swollen cock! *"Come here,"* he rasped.

She bolted and fled. He ran after her with his penis swinging from side to side. He caught her from behind and dragged her down. He tore off the remnants of her dress. She wailed and scratched his face. He hit her several times. Blood ran from her nose and lip. He trapped her wrists over her head, forced apart her legs, and guided himself into her slit. He pushed, pushed again, entered a little way, pushed harder. It hurt, but that didn't stop him, and then he was in and he forgot about the pain. He pumped his hips, the toes of his boots pushed into the ground, and he rammed into her with jerky spastic movements. His face reddened, his eyes distended and his jaw hung down. He drooled on the girl. He released her wrists and grabbed her shoulders, tried to plow even deeper into her while she screamed and beat on his back with her fists and squirmed beneath him.

Swett hunkered down to watch. He rested his rifle across his knees and picked a stalk of grass to chew on. Johnny bucked and moaned, flung his head up and down, which whipped his long hair across his face. Swett saw one of the girl's hands strike the knife sheathed on Johnny's hip. He watched her fingers play over the strap that held it in, find the snap, and undo it. He picked another blade of grass.

"Oh-oh-oh! It's . . . it's . . . HERE!" Johnny arched. His head went back, eyes turned to the sky, his mouth gaped, spittle ran down his chin.

The girl drove the knife up into his mouth, through the palate. Johnny rocked back on his knees, pulling free of her. His hands clawed at his cheeks. He went unsteadily to his feet, stood rockily, and turned to Swett. The handle of the long knife protruded from his mouth. Blood fountained around it. His hands reached shaking for the knife, then clenched into fists, and he rose up on his toes. He stood thus, rigid, for a moment, then fell face forward.

The girl scrambled to her feet and ran. Still squatting, Swett snapped his rifle up and shot her. She fell, gained her hands and knees, and crawled. Swett shot her twice again, the last time through the head.

Woodson had told her not to move, and at first that stern command had been enough to keep her motionless in hiding. But she forgot what he had said while she watched Johnny Murphy rape the girl, then she forgot *Woodson,* and soon she thought she was both Wilda, Wilda sweet potata girl hidin' 'neath a bush where no one could see, and the little girl screaming under the white man, and when Swett shot the girl, who fell very close to Wilda and whose eyes looked directly into Wilda's for a suspended moment of pain and terror before she died, Wilda closed her own eyes and her thumb went into her mouth.

Li'l black honey lef' her throne
Ah done, done, what yuh tol' me t' do.
Gwine t' Zion hill t' mourn,
Ah done, done, what yuh tol' me t' do.

She began to rock softly.

Whut you goan do when the world's on fire?
Goan jump in a hole o' water.
Whut you goan do when the water get's t' boilin'?
Goan kick an' squeal an' holler!

Wilda sighed and opened her eyes. Wilda dead on the ground was still looking at her, but there was dullness in those eyes and an insect was walking across them. Wilda stood up and primly dusted and brushed her dress. It distressed her to see herself lying so still like that and she made small anxious sounds. She looked at the pond. Then she took hold of her dead self's ankles and dragged it toward the pond, singing:

"Mah ol' blue dog is daid an' gone,
Lef' this nigger here t' mourn.
Ah went t' the barn one sunny day,
There mah good ol' blue dog lay.
Blue! Blue! Blue! Blue! You rascal you,
Ah wish 'twas me instead o' you.

"Ah buried him in a beautiful shade,
Dug his grave wif a silver spade,
Let him down on a golden chain.
At every link Ah called his name:
Blue! Blue! Blue! Blue! You rascal you,
Ah wish 'twas me instead o' you."

She walked out of the pond. Her dead self drifted toward the center. Three alligators slipped from the opposite bank into the water.

Wilda felt better. She walked into the brush singing:

"Befo' Ah stay in Hell *one day,*
Heaven *shall-a* be mah home.
Ah sing an' pray mah soul away,
Heaven *shall-a* be mah home!"

On his stomach, Woodson slowly pulled a branch aside.

There were about ten whites. Woodson and Wilda hadn't seen one since Elmer's Smithy, had not, in fact, seen any human being until they'd encountered a band of blacks a short while ago. They had talked with the blacks, who had invited Woodson and Wilda to join them. Woodson declined, and they parted. Several minutes later gunfire erupted. Woodson had got Wilda into hiding and circled back to see what was happening.

More whites were returning. Woodson reckoned from their conversation that five or six blacks had been killed. The whites had lost one man, and two more had taken slight wounds. He was on the verge of crawling away when a thickset and heavily muscled youth appeared.

"Where's Johnny?" someone asked.

"Daid. We cotched a girl ovuh by a gator pond." He pointed. "Johnny took it t' mind t' hump on her. She went crazy, grabbed his knife, an' killed 'im. Ah shot her."

The Beast slashed out at Woodson. His guts wrenched, and he grunted. A girl by a gator pond, that direction. Wilda. Oh, *Wilda!* Woodson closed his eyes and laid his forehead on his arm. Then he shook his head. He cocked his revolver and took aim.

The boy tossed his rifle casually from one hand to the other. "So Ah guess in the absence of a appointed leader Ah gots t' take ovuh the Hearth agin."

Most of them avoided his eyes. One said, "Thet's right, Wallace. You the onliest one wif experience."

The boy nodded. "Thet's the truth, Lem. An' Ah'm hereby designatin' you secon' in command."

Woodson lowered his pistol. It might not have been Wilda.

There were two girls her age in that band. It could have been one of them. He had to be sure.

He withdrew carefully, kept to the ground until a good stretch of dense foliage separated him from the whites. Then he went to his feet and walked at a measured pace toward the pond. Wilda would be there. She would smile at him. He'd kiss her and then take her even deeper into the swamp. They would find a dry and safe place to sleep tonight and he would hold her close until daybreak.

He reached the pond. A dead white boy lay along the bank. An alligator was feeding on him. The alligator swung toward Woodson and hissed. She's still hiding, Woodson thought. She's waiting for me; another girl died here. He worked around the alligator without antagonizing it to rush. There were only broken branches and matted grass where Wilda should have been. He knelt and looked dumbly at the blood-sodden earth.

There was no body. He would not accept her death until he found her body.

If the boy had only thought he killed her, and, hurt, she crawled off. . . . He found a thin blood trail and followed it with his eyes. It ended at the water's edge. He frowned. The water boiled then, and two alligators broke the surface struggling over a piece of meat. It was an arm, a black arm.

Woodson nodded. Uh-huh. Yes. That was it. There was the body. Of course. He set down his pistol and sat cross-legged. He dug a handful of dirt, crumbled it, and poured it from one hand to the other. He let it sift from his fist into a small pile.

He picked up his revolver, spun the chamber to check on the load, stood, and slid the weapon into its holster. He gazed at the pond and rubbed a finger up and down the bridge of his nose. He turned back toward the white men.

Sustained vigilance had tired Henry, but he was confident they would escape. His wife was holding up well, and she trusted him, which helped. The baby wasn't crying much.

They were on a bog, an acre large, which floated with several others in the delta of a river that gave onto a small lake. Two boats drifted nearby, with white corpses in each. On the near shore were more white men, some dead. Only three or four remained of the original party. They'd tried by boat, and Henry's marksmanship had halved them. They'd rushed onto the bog when it touched shore once, and they were nearly exterminated. Henry's rifle was not an extension of himself; rather, when he held the carefully oiled and lovingly burnished weapon in his hands, *he* was an extension of *it*.

He had good cover on the island and, unless he grew careless or one of the whites made a lucky shot, he would be rid of them in a few hours. They had become chary and in the last hour had given him only a single opportunity to fire—he'd killed one—but still he hoped that frustration and impatience would cause the rest to become reckless, even if only for a moment; he'd kill them then. And that was the way he would prefer it. Otherwise he'd wait until nightfall, and when the island touched another, or land, he'd slip away with his wife and child.

Three white men sat together on shore and watched the island through leaves in silent anger. One said, "It ain't goan beach. Look at them twigs in the water. The current brings 'em in, but right theah by thet stump it swings 'em back out again."

Another one said, "It be close enough. Ah kin reach thet." He stroked three sticks of dynamite, which he had tied together with vines. He'd salvaged them along with a detonating cap and a length of fuse from the wreckage at Johnson's Pass. After a while he said, "Best git ready now." He dug into the end of one of the dynamite sticks with his pocketknife. When the hole was large enough he took the cap from a handkerchief in his pocket and cautiously tamped it in place. He gauged the distance, then cut a length of fuse. He pushed one end of this into the stick against the cap and secured it by packing earth around the edges. He shook the dynamite gently. The fuse was tight, it wouldn't fall out.

They waited a quarter of an hour while the island drifted closer. Then the man with the dynamite said, "Thet's about right." He gave a match to another man. "Light this. Jus' tech it t' the end o' the fuse when Ah tells yuh." He rose to a half crouch, cocked his arm. "Now." The fuse sizzled. The man sprang up, looped his arm, and released the dynamite.

Henry was watching the nearing shore carefully. Suddenly a white popped up, and Henry swung his rifle and snapped off a shot. He hit the man in the face, but even as the bullet struck, Henry realized something had been thrown, and his eyes flicked up. Fear sucked his breath away. His rifle rose to the sky and his finger tightened on the trigger. At Elysium he'd knocked silver dollars from the air as a stunt, but this took him totally by surprise and was too quick and he fired a fraction of a second too soon.

The dynamite arced down unscathed, landed a yard from his feet, and exploded.

The island shuddered with the concussion. The two remaining white men looked at its smoking ruins several minutes, then one said, "Well, we got 'im."

His companion spat and said, "One fuckin' expensive sonabitch."

The light was fading and the birds were beginning to still their voices in deference to the coming night. Woodson heard the white men coming. He laid his pistol aside and stretched out on the ground, face down. He closed his eyes. He thought about nothing. He relaxed. He almost went to sleep.

"Hey," a voice called. "Got a dead man heah."

Footsteps approached. There was crackling brush, other voices, more steps.

"Sure he daid?"

The toe of a boot went under Woodson's side, began to roll him over.

He screamed, kicked, and flailed out with his arms. "Ah kill yuh, niggers. Ah kill yuh!" he screeched. He grabbed his revolver, dropped it, clutched to retrieve it.

Two men grabbed him. "It all right. We white." He struggled against them. "You safe now. You wif frens. You safe. Unnerstan'? We white, *white!*"

Woodson stared into their faces, trembling. Then he slumped and held his head in his hands. "Thank God," he said. "Oh thank the mercy o' God."

The whites gathered around. "Whut happen t' you fren?"

"Ah'm at the end o' mah string," Woodson said. "Ran all last night, an' been runnin' through the day."

The youth he thought had killed Wilda squatted in front of him. The boy's breath stank. Woodson looked into his eyes and heard his words again: *Ah shot her.* "How this come t' happen?" the boy asked.

"Ah was with mah cousin an' a bunch from Hurleyville, Woodson said. "Big band o' niggers opened up on us in some cypress water a couple miles from here. West, Ah think. Pinned us down. Fought all through the afternoon. They cut us t' pieces, but we give 'em just about as much a we took. Toward evenin', me an' Lester Perkins—he was mah neighbor—we was the only ones left. We snuck off. But there was four, five niggers left, an' they found our trail an' followed. Got Lester at sunrise an' they been after me ever since." A horrified expression settled over Woodson's face. "The thing that drove me crazy—there was a white man with them niggers!"

Swett rocked back on his heels: "Whut you mean?"

"Ah mean a white man, jus' like you an' me. He was fightin' 'longside the coons jus' like he was a nigger himself. Ah wouldn't o' believed it if Ah hadn't seen it with mah very own eyes. But Ah did. Fact, he was the one who put the bullet into Lester!"

Angry excitement rippled the men. Swett frowned and sucked on his cheek. "Never heard o' no white men in Hellbottom Swamp."

"It must be that renegade," Jimmy Hildenbrandt said. "The one that led the niggers durin' the Woodboro riot."

"Thought he drownded or somethin'," Swett said.

"Nobody knew for sure. The newspapers had all kinds o' speculatin's. Some said he might of escaped t' Hellbottom. Name of, uh, lemme see, uh—Woodson! That's it, Em'ry Woodson."

Swett nodded ponderously. His jaw worked. "Well boys, it appear we found the bastard. An' we goan hunt his goddamn ass into the ground. We goan make 'im scream t' God t' kill 'im 'fore we done. Yas. He all ours now." He laid a heavy hand on Woodson's shoulder. "Whut yo name, boy?"

Woodson nearly smiled. He was almost old enough to be the youth's grandfather. "Cecil Tubbs."

"How do Tubbs. Ah's Wallace Swett." He gestured. "Most o' these boys is Knights o' the Canescent Dominion, the rest is frens. Ah leads 'em."

Woodson acknowledged them. They introduced themselves, shook his hand.

"Yuh got no call t' worry no mo'," Swett said. "You safe wif us. When's the las' time you seen these niggers?"

"They took a shot at me 'bout an hour ago."

"An' they run you all night, huh?"

"Yes."

"Well, they ain't in no bettuh shape 'n you, then. Gettin' dark. Reckon they be beddin' down soon less'n they wants t' drop in they tracks. No use tryin' t' find 'em at night ennyway. Ah figure we sleep, break camp a li'l 'fore sunup, an' set aftuh 'em. Think yuh kin lead us back t' they trail?"

Woodson nodded.

"Good. Now you get some vittles from the boys an' rest yose'f easy, Tubbs. It all goan turn out jus' puhfeckly right."

Woodson clasped the boy's hand in both of his. "Ah'm sure o' that, Wallace. An don' have no doubts atall."

Friend was not happy. It was still dark, but morning was near and a freshening breeze brought to him the scent of the white men who were camped not far away. The dog sulked at his master's lack of concern.

"It kin wait," Hector said. He'd stoked the embers into a new fire, gone into the woods, and killed a plump rabbit in a burrow. The fire was ready for cooking now. He skinned the rabbit, cut off and saved the strips of yellow fat, and tossed the meat carcass to Friend. Friend fell upon it greedily. His tail wagged. "Seem yo stomach make you fo'git all yo woes," Hector said fondly.

A lidded kettle simmered over the fire. Hector placed a skillet next to it. In the old days, when he had first come to the swamp, he'd eaten snails, raw birds' eggs, even toads, to keep from starving. He'd learned, and things got better, but still luxury or even comfort had never been possible. He had seen no reason this time why, for example, he had to cook on flat stones when a pot and a skillet were handy and easy enough to pack in. And he was a skilled enough hunter to be choosy about what he ate. So he sliced the tail of a small alligator he'd killed into steaks. He put the rabbit fat in the skillet, spread it as it softened, waited until it had melted and began to pop, then tossed in the steaks. The meat was pink, clean, and savory, but it had to cook fast over a hot fire lest it toughen. He placed wild mustard greens atop the steaks. Everything was ready in a few minutes. He speared the meat with his knife and flopped it onto a tin plate, and spooned on a mixture of swamp cabbage and collards with their sweet nutty flavor.

He also had a little salad of poke leaves. He sopped a piece of hard cornbread in the pot likker.

When he finished he stood and slapped his stomach. Dawn was close. Fog swirled around the small clearing and made shadowy gray ghosts of even the nearest trees. Hector said, "Let's go." Friend sprang up, forgetting what remained of the rabbit. "Find 'em fo' me," Hector said. Hector could have gone directly to the camp himself, but Friend was happiest when he thought he was leading.

In the old days Hector would simply have moved away. But little comforts meant more now than they had then, and he was unwilling to abandon them unless it was truly necessary. This area was a spine of high ground half a mile long by a quarter wide. A small pine forest grew here and it was dry. Insects were few, game abundant, and fresh water at hand. The whites evidently appreciated the ease it offered too. They'd skulked around for two days, and gave no sign of readying to leave. Dodging them was growing annoying. So Hector had to go to kill them.

He and Friend went down on their bellies fifty yards from the camp and crawled. Six whites were asleep around the ashes of a dead fire. A seventh, a sentry, was dozing with his back against a tree, arms loose at his sides, rifle fallen to the ground beside him.

Hector pulled Friend back. The dog resisted and he had to slap its muzzle. The animal submitted but went with its head twisted over its shoulder toward the whites, lips curled from teeth and hair bristling. Hector cut vines, wound four tough strands together into a strong rope, and tied Hector to a tree by his collar. The dog could, and would, chew through it in five or six minutes. That gave Hector enough time to finish, and insured the animal's freedom if Hector were unable to return.

He hugged Friend and patted his broad skull. "Sorry, boy, but Ah cain't take you. Goan be shootin' fast an' iffen you in the way, you could be hurt." The dog looked at him mournfully. Hector walked away, and Friend lunged against the rope.

The whites were as he had left them. Hector took a revolver from its holster and a second from his waistband. He cocked them both and strode from the brush. He stopped a few feet from the men around the ashes and raised one pistol. He shot the sentry. Then he lowered the barrel and began firing both weapons into the sleeping men. He walked through them with his thumbs cocking the hammers and his index fingers squeezing the triggers rhythmically. Burning powder scorched shirts and bullets slammed into flesh from two and three feet. Only one man was able to reach a gun, and he died before he could fire it. From the first shot to the last it was over in seconds. Oblique rays of the rising sun were burning at the fog, making it dance and writhe through the trees. One white was groaning, another twitched feebly. Hector reloaded one pistol and fired a single shot into each of their heads.

He examined their meager supplies, set aside some slab bacon, flour, and coffee. He wished they'd had salt. Once he'd lived a full year in the swamp without any, and he'd never overcome his fear of running short. He went through their pockets, took the few coins he found, a length of fishline, and a couple of plugs of tobacco.

Friend came bursting into the campsite. "Hey, good dog," Hector said. "It all done." The dog was momentarily confused and spun around with bared fangs. Then, unable to contain its fury and disappointment, Friend attacked a corpse and worried it savagely. Hector stripped a shirt from a body while the dog worked out its frustration and he made a pack with it to carry what he had taken.

Satisfied, Friend came to Hector for petting. Hector fondled the dog, scratched it behind the ears, which it dearly loved. "Whut say we spend the mornin' startin' some kind o' home, an' take the afternoon t' fish?"

Friend licked his hand.

Woodson led them half a mile west and told them this was where he'd last seen the white man and the three niggers. They fanned out to sweep for a trail. In a little while a man called the others in and pointed with excitement to a pile of charred ashes and some squirrel bones which had been chewed clean. Woodson saw that the fire was more than two days old, but the others seemed to overlook that in their eagerness. There were a few signs that whoever had made the fire had headed west.

"Maybe they give up on me," Woodson said. "Or seen

that Ah joined with you. They probably headin' back t' their camp. Maybe they got supplies and stuff there."

Swett considered this and pronounced it sound. He looked at the ashes again, and around the campsite, and reckoned that Woodson and the niggers weren't far ahead. "Le's push it," he said.

Woodson suggested that they spread wide, keep at least a hundred yards between each man so they could cover more ground and lower the chances of missing the renegade.

"Yuh," Swett said. "That's the way Ah wants it. Spread out, you boys, an' pass the word on down the line when ever'one's set."

Woodson took the far left flank. He waited nearly an hour then angled to the right. The nearest man was named Leonard Sikes. Woodson called to him so as not to startle him with a sudden appearance. "Len. Hey Lenny, Ah'm comin' up on you."

Sikes drew an arm across his sweating brow. "Ennythin' wrong, Cecil?"

"No." Woodson shot him through the heart.

He retreated back the way he'd come, and waited. A muffled voice shouted. He returned again and found Fred Harwood standing over Sikes's body. "What happened?" Woodson said.

Harwood was flushed and jittery. "We foun' the niggers. They kilt Len."

Woodson and Harwood yelled for the others. Swett was elated at overtaking their quarry, furious about Sikes's death. "Who saw which way the murderin' bastuhds went?" he demanded. The white men looked at each other. "Well how in hell we goan find 'em if none o' you knows!"

"Whyn't we spread in a circle away from pore Len here," Woodson offered. "One of us should find some sign."

"Yuh. Yuh, thet's good." They moved out cautiously.

Woodson shot Fred Harwood in the back as Harwood waded a shallow tributary. Harwood fell and lay still and water trickled around him. Woodson waited by the body, listening to the other men call to each other, some of the voices faint. A lanky man with sharp cheekbones and protruding jaw came running through the brush. Woodson shot him twice in the stomach, cracked his skull with a stone to finish him. He picked up the man's rifle and fired several shots into the air.

"They're comin' your way!" he shouted. "Get 'em, get 'em!" He heard men closing quickly. He rushed forward, encountered Jimmy Hildenbrandt. He emptied his pistol into the brush and yelled, "There they are. There's Woodson! Shoot, goddamn it, shoot!"

Hildenbrandt worked the lever of his rifle and sent shots crashing into the foliage. Two other men appeared. "This way," Woodson said. "After 'em." He reloaded on the run. Hildenbrandt and the others sent bullets ricocheting ahead of them. Finally it became obvious that they had been eluded.

Woodson kicked at the earth. "Damn, Ah thought we had 'im sure this time."

"Ah think Ah got one o' the niggers," a man said.

"Ah do believe Ah saw one stagger," Woodson said. "Well, thet makes three, an' there ain't no one left but Woodson now. We goin' kill thet treacherous white bastard by nightfall."

"Three?" Swett said.

"Fred killed two before they got 'im. Fact, Woodson mayhap be wounded himself. Couldn't rightly see, but Jimmy might've clipped him. Did you, boy?"

Hildenbrandt scratched his head. "I, uh, well . . . I don' know for certain."

"Whut we do?" someone asked. "Go back an' bury Fred an' Walter?"

"An' Len," another man reminded him.

"If thet Woodson *is* wounded . . . ," Swett said.

Woodson nodded. "Thet's right. If Jimmy hit him, he slowed down some now. Buryin' ain't goin' help the dead, but we don' want t' give Woodson time t' put more ground between us."

It was agreed that they should press hard after the renegade.

Woodson killed a fourth man before noon.

No one knew why it was called Billy's Island. Billy, if there ever had been a Billy, must have been an old man long before Attila was born. When Attila had entered the swamp as a runaway six years before the war, there was a tough, grizzled, and consumptive man on the island who had been in the swamp half his life and even he did not know how it had come to be named. That man died within the year, and Attila laid claim to the island. So did another swamper. They fought. Attila killed the man, and Billy's Island became his.

It was deep in the swamp, twelve acres of rich soil. Long ago someone, perhaps the legendary Billy, had cleared the pine and hardwood trees from half the good earth to create cornfields and large vegetable gardens and had built a solid cabin that had stood with the fortitude of stone, requiring only minor and infrequent repairs. If there ever had been a Billy, he must have been a man to command the respect of men.

When Attila reached the island he found it, as he'd expected, unoccupied. The cabin roof sagged, leaked in a few places, some of the mud chinking was gone from the walls, and the door had fallen from its hinges and rotted. But otherwise the cabin had not fared too badly under neglect. Attila spent the first day mending the roof, splitting small logs in half for a new door. The second he used to chink the walls and replace three logs crumbly with dry rot. He was irritated with himself for not having brought stiff paper, which he would have greased and used as glass in the window frames. He'd locate popples, which were few and hard to find in the swamp, and carefully strip the translucent inner skin. This was not as good as paper, but it would serve.

On the third day, he began clearing saplings that had taken root in the untended fields. Attila knew the swamp for the predator it was, and, unlike some other swampers who had learned almost to love it, he detested it. But the whites had driven him back, and he did not think it likely that he would be able to leave it again. Not, at least, for a long time. Billy's Island was surrounded by a broad expanse of water that was not really a lake but more a flood plain of two rivers, a high-water bog. It was walled with cypress and gum trees, through which catwalks ran connecting two small docks and serving as stands from which to fish or shoot the deer which frequently waded ashore to forage in the vegetable gardens. The island was as close to a sanctuary as the swamp offered, so Attila set about preparing it to support him again.

The whites surprised him swinging his ax in a cornfield. There was a volley of shots, and some whined close to him. His rifle was against a tree a good distance away. They would hit him before he could reach it. He turned and ran into the trees carrying the ax. He raged at himself for not having had the rifle at hand, but it had seemed inconceivable that the whites would penetrate this deep into the swamp. They were coming up fast behind him. A bullet nicked his ear and he cursed. He turned toward the water remembering a place where he could leave the catwalk for a cypress tree, and from that climb to another, and then, while the whites pressed down the catwalk thinking he was just ahead, lower himself to the water and escape.

He reached the narrow catwalk. It was moss-covered and slippery, and he had to pace himself. It wound through the trees in deep shadow and swayed beneath his weight. He heard the whites behind him, but he was gaining and knew he'd be able to swing off without being seen. The grade steepened. It would reach its peak several yards farther, and only a little beyond that was the point at which he would leave.

The instant his foot touched it, he knew the board would give. But he couldn't stop. His weight came down, the rotted board broke, and he pitched to the side and crashed through the flimsy rail down into the water and muck. It was not deep here. He tried to stand and fell back gasping with pain. The socket of his knee was torn apart. He heard the whites approaching. There was a rise of mud before him. He reached out and pulled himself partway out of the water.

Voices rose. Then gunfire crackled. Bullets thudded into Attila's back. He felt the crushing weight of the swamp descend on him. It had finally trapped him. He would have escaped had it not subtly and patiently sucked the strength from a mossy board. The swamp had killed him, not the whites.

His fingers dug into the mud. "You ol' bitch," he muttered, and was dead.

The fruitcakes were unsatisfactory. "You dint cream the butter," Comfort said to the girl. "An' the eggs wasn't beaten enough. Give these t' the fieldhan's an' bake some new ones. We got just about enough time." Dinner, which would mark the end of Comfort's responsibilities, was three hours off. A few guests had already departed, the rest would be leaving tonight and through the next day.

"Ain't enuff winey fruit lef' t' make but two more," the girl said.

"Ah settle fo' that."

There was a commotion at the kitchen door. Comfort opened an oven. The dove pies were coming along nicely.

Winifred was arguing with one of the serving girls at the door. "No," Winifred said. "Ah doan care. You tell her t' go on, git out o' here."

The ember pits should be about right, Comfort thought. It was time to spit the suckling pigs and set them to roasting.

Winifred slapped the girl. The girl spat at her, pushed her away, and hurried over to Comfort. "Miz Davis," she blurted. " 'Scuse me, Ma'm, but Ah got somethin' impo'tant t' tell yuh."

Comfort recognized her as a girl she'd had to correct several times, a lazy, surly, spiteful girl. Winifred was advancing in high temper: "Ah goan tear yo hair out, you li'l bitch!"

"It *impo'tant!*"

Comfort stopped Winifred with a hand. She said, "Mah ears is listenin'."

The girl glanced triumphantly at Winifred. "They a woman out in the trees, back by wheah we buried the sheep guts. She say she from Hellbottom. She say she got somethin' t' tell yuh, 'bout yo man."

Apprehension welled in Comfort. "Why'nt you bring her in?"

"She won' come out o' the trees."

"Winifred," Comfort said, "you see t' them suckle pigs fo' me? Ah goan step out t' the woods a li'l while." Winifred nodded. Comfort walked to the door. The girl followed. "You stay here, girl," Comfort said sharply.

Outside the kitchen, Comfort heard the smacks of a stropping belt striking flesh, and the girl's frightened cries. Comfort walked to the trees. "Hullo," she called. "Who's there? Who wants t' talk t' me?"

The brush rustled and Thistle appeared. Her dress was filthy and ragged. Blood was crusted over her left breast and down her side. She was haggard and there was an air of subdued frenzy about her. Comfort looked her slowly up and down and felt a pain as tangible as a knife thrust. She said, "He dead, ain't he." It wasn't a question.

"Ever'one's dead. Ever'one. The whites come. They hunted us through the swamp like animals. They kilt mah man, mah three boys."

"You saw Vulture die?"

"Ah was there."

Comfort turned away. She hugged herself tightly and swayed back and forth, eyes squeezed shut.

"Yo man saved mah life," Thistle said. "Ah just as soon o' died back there. But Ah figured Ah owed him t' tell yuh mahse'f." She stabbed an arm toward the Great House. "An Ah figured *they* owe me. They owe me fo' mah man an' mah chilliun. They owe me *blood!*"

Comfort expelled her breath in a long moan. "Ah been cookin' fo' 'em," she said dully. She remembered the man who'd mentioned Hellbottom, and snatches of other conversation she'd overheard. "Ah been feedin' they bellies while they. . . . They done it. The gov'nor an' the others here. They give the orders. They turnt the trash loose." She clenched her hands into fists. "Ah'm goan fire that big white house, burn it t' the ground! No . . . no." She seized Thistle by the shoulders. "Witch-woman, you tell me how. Ah kill thet gov'nor. Ah kill that Clayton Low'ry. Ah kill 'em all that killed mah man. You tell me how t' do it slow, so it hurt 'em, so they got a good long time t' know they dyin'. Tell me!"

Thistle took Comfort's wrists, kissed the palms of her hands. Tears rolled down her cheeks. "Yas, honey, yas. Ah will!"

McGonagle's skin was the color of a beet and hot to the

touch. Their boats had become hopelessly mired in the bog and they had been walking two days. McGonagle had fallen into delirium yesterday. They'd carried him on a litter and had made not more than two miles, weren't even sure they were moving in the right direction. Today McGonagle was in a coma and they could get no response at all from him.

The men carrying him dropped the litter. It struck the ground hard, and McGonagle rolled off without a sound and lay still, an arm bent awkwardly beneath him. The two men stood side by side, and the largest said to Warren Busch, "We ain't carryin' him one goddamn step mo'."

"Put him back on an' pick it up," Busch said. "You don' set him down till your shift's over."

"No."

Busch had feared this all afternoon. He looked from the rebellious pair to the other men. They were all at the point of exhaustion, and it was clear that none of them would carry McGonagle. "All right," he said. "Take a rest. I'll handle one end. Who's gonna give me a hand with the other? Mercer? Avery?" They regarded him in silence. Busch hunched his shoulders. This was it, then. He could agree to abandon McGonagle, or he could draw his pistol. He looked into each of their faces. They were ready to kill him. He glanced at McGonagle. Well.

"All right," he said, "but this is on your heads. You'll have t' live with it the rest o' your lives."

"Ah think Ah kin do thet," a man said.

Busch said, "Then let's get out o' this goddamn place."

They walked away.

Alone, McGonagle twitched once and groaned. A fly settled on a wet crack in his puffy lip. Another lighted on his swollen tongue and rubbed its forelegs together.

Woodson put his finger to his lips, cautioning silence, then waved Jimmy Hildenbrandt over to him. Hildenbrandt came quickly and whispered, "Yuh?" Woodson pointed to a thicket. Hildenbrandt looked. He mouthed a barely audible, "Woodson?" Woodson nodded.

Hildenbrandt's eyes widened. He licked his lips, cocked his rifle, stared at the thicket. Woodson stepped behind him. He reached around and clamped his hand over Hildenbrandt's mouth, jerked the boy's head back, and slit his throat with the knife. He released him. Hildenbrandt sprawled to the ground, thrashed, made muted choking sounds.

Woodson examined his own clothes. There was a good deal of blood on his sleeve—not Hildenbrandt's but one of the others, who had been difficult. He cut the sleeve off and discarded it. There were spots on his shirtfront and pants too, but they weren't very noticeable amid the dirt and sweat stains. Hildenbrandt stopped moving. Only Swett was left. Woodson went after him.

In a low voice he called, "Wallace. Hey, Wallace."

Swett answered across a stand of poison sumac: "Who's thet?"

"Cecil." They met. "Somethin's terrible wrong, Wallace. Ah thought Ah seen somebody movin' through the buttonbushes. Ah sung out fo' Luther—he was the closest to me—an' Ah dint get no answer. Then Ah tried Harvey. Same thing. Ah went lookin', an' Ah couldn't find no one atall, until just back a little way. Jimmy Hildenbrandt was layin' on the ground with his throat cut."

"Goddamn. Go'-*damn!*" Rage tightened Swett's face, was followed by wariness. He crouched, weight shifting to the balls of his feet, and peered around. "The sonabitch stopped runnin'. We goan git it settled now."

"That's the way it looks."

"You stay wif me. He cain't sneak up on us iffen we together."

"Right."

They went to search for the others, and found them one at a time; they had all been stabbed. Swett became agitated with each new corpse and when they came upon the last he kicked at a tree and yelled, "How did the bastuhd do it? You jus' cain't come up thet quiet on seven good men. It ain't natural. It ain't, Ah say!"

Woodson shook his head. "Ah don' mind tellin' you, Wallace—Ah'm scared. Maybe we should just get out o' here while we still can."

Swett was perspiring heavily. Painful and frightened confusion played across his face. "Ah . . . Ah doan know."

"We kin find mo' men, an' then come back fo' him."

There was rustling in the brush and Swett spun with a

scream and fired twice. A bird flew away. Swett breathed heavily and cracked his knuckles. "Git mo' men an' come back. Yuh. Thet's the way t' do it."

They started east. Swett kept glancing behind them, but relaxed a little as they progressed.

"Look out!" Woodson yelled.

Swett threw himself to the ground and scrambled for cover. Woodson fired several times at nothing.

"Where is he?" Swett shrieked.

"It's all right now," Woodson said. "Ah drove 'im back."

Swett lurched to his feet. "We gots t' run. We gots t' git some groun' between us!"

They ran brokenly through the undergrowth. Swett's pistol slipped the holster strap, bounced out, and fell. He didn't notice. His breath whistled in his throat, his movements grew jerky. Woodson's hip tormented him, but he kept up with the youth. Finally he called, "Ah cain't run no mo', Wallace. Mah leg jus' won' work right."

Swett staggered to a tree. His chest heaved and he glared at Woodson. "Iffen yuh cain't hold yo own, yuh goddamn cripple, Ah ain't goan stay behind t' protec' yuh."

"Look," Woodson said. "We kin kill 'im ourselves, Wallace. We got a good lead now. If he's comin' after us he's goin' t' have his head down studyin' the trail signs. All you got t' do is skinny up that tree there an' stay on this side o' the trunk for cover. You kin see him a long time before he knows we're around. It be an easy rifle shot. You'll kill 'im like a duck in a barrel." Swett looked dubious. "Otherwise," Woodson said, "he's likely t' get us in the back."

Swett thought a moment, then gave his rifle to Woodson to hold and went up the tree. When he was secure Woodson tossed the rifle to him. They waited nearly an hour. "The yellow-bellied bastuhd ain't comin'," Swett said. "Ah'm gettin' down."

"Drop me yo rifle, Wallace." Swett did. "You know," Woodson said as Swett lowered himself through the branches, "Ah seen Woodson once in Woodboro."

"Yuh? Whut'd he look like?"

"About my height, Wallace. And he had fine brown

hair that came down to his shoulders. His eyes were blue. But there was one thing about him that would help you recognize him more than anything else."

"Yuh?" Swett dropped to the ground, wiped his hands on his pants.

Woodson drew back from the tree.

"He has a limp. Not too bad. But when he's tired, it gives him more trouble, slows him down and becomes quite pronounced."

Swett looked up. "It do, uh? Maybe thet's why he ain't followin' us."

"It's the kind of limp that might make another man say: 'Iffen yuh cain't hold yo own, yuh goddamn cripple. . . .'"

"Oh. Ah 'pologize fo' thet, Cecil. Ah—"

"My name isn't Cecil, Wallace."

Swett frowned. "Ah could o' sworn you tol' me it was."

"I did."

Swett grinned and shook his head. "Ah cain't puzzle whut you sayin'. You even talkin' funny, like a school-teacher or such."

"My name is Emory Woodson, Wallace."

Swett slapped his thigh and laughed. "Ah swear you gone plumb out o' yo head, Cecil."

Woodson unholstered his revolver, let it hang in his hand at his side. "That's how Woodson was able to sneak up on seven grown men, Wallace. I just came walking toward them saying: Hey Lenny, Hey Harvey, Hey Fred." Swett's jaw dropped. "You remember a girl yesterday, Wallace? A little nigger girl by a gator pond? The one who was raped, the one you shot? Well, I loved her, Wallace, and that's why I'm going to kill you now."

Swett's mouth curved down. He bellowed and charged, arms thrust forward, meaty hands reaching. Woodson cocked the revolver and raised it, held an unwavering aim. The pistol's bore was centered directly between Swett's eyes and it loomed ever larger until the youth could see nothing else. He faltered halfway to Woodson and then came to a slow stop under its relentless gaze. His clawed hands dropped. He twitched. He couldn't move his eyes from the bore. He grew dizzy. It was hard to breathe.

"No," he whispered. "You . . . cain't." He stepped

backward. Woodson took an equal number of steps forward, pistol arm rigid. "Please . . . no . . . Ah . . . doan do . . . it."

"Turn around, Wallace. Turn around and run for your life. Go ahead. Do you want to watch it come? Do you want to see the muzzle explode and feel the slug smash into your forehead? That's right. Now run. *Run, you scum-sucking sonofabitch!*"

"No! No!" Swett ran.

Woodson sighted carefully and shot him through the left leg, shattering the shin bone. Swett screamed and pitched down. He struggled to his feet. Woodson walked toward him. Swett shambled in a jump step. Woodson fired and broke his other leg. Swett crawled on his hands and knees, babbling. Woodson walked alongside him. "You like to hunt niggers, don't you boy?" he said in an even tone. "You like to hear them scream. You like to see them die. I can smell your piss and your shit, boy. Are you afraid? Like the niggers you've hunted?" He shot Swett through the right kidney. Swett fell heavily and shrieked in pain. Woodson kicked him. "Come on! Crawl, you bastard! Crawl or I'll kill you!" Swett pulled himself forward sobbing in agony and terror. Woodson shot him through the left kidney. Swett writhed on the ground moaning. His fingers furrowed the earth, his teeth bit into it.

"Oh shit," Woodson said disgustedly. He blew Swett's head apart.

The moonstagger roots were long and slender, knobbed at intervals. Comfort removed the tough gray skin in the kitchen, grated the pulp, and then mashed it into a wet paste with a mortar and pestle. She heated the paste in a saucepan over a low fire, careful not to boil any of the juice away.

She mixed the evening's planter's punch in three large silver bowls, using sugar, orange bitters, grenadine syrup, rum, fresh oranges, pineapple, cherries, and soda water. The largest and most elegant bowl had arched-hound handles and was done with bosses and scroll work. She stirred the warm moonstagger paste into it, blending with care until it dissolved into the punch. Thistle had told her to let the punch stand for half an hour, which would eliminate

most of the bitter taste. As a precaution, Comfort added
more sugar and an extra spoonful of orange bitters.

It would be a good death. Some eight hours after drinking the tainted punch a man would experience a mild and
gaseous upset of the stomach. This would shortly give way
to a headache and a possible blurring of the vision—but
these would be brief and not of remarkable severity. The
finest aspect of moonstagger poisoning was that, though
the initial symptoms were hardly recognizable as anything
unusual, the victim was doomed unless he received treat-
ment within an hour or two after their onset. After his vision cleared and his headache left him, a man would feel
utterly normal for the next twelve hours. But then, with
the suddenness of a striking falcon, the headache would
return, viciously this time, as if a spike were being driven
through the skull, and it would not abate until the final
moments. Blindness occurred by the end of the first day in
some cases. The fevers began on the second day, and were
followed in quick succession by a thickening of the throat
that prevented the intake of anything but liquids, a swelling of the extremities, palsy, complete loss of equilibrium,
and finally death by either heart failure or suffocation four
full and torturous days after the poisoning.

Comfort ordered the punch bowls carried outside and
packed with the silver julep cups in ice to chill. She directed a servant to stand watch and see that no one was given
punch until she arrived. Then she went back to her
quarters, stripped, poured water from a crockery pitcher
into a bowl, and washed herself down with a rag. She put
on a freshly starched uniform.

The punch bowls were on two long tables set in the
shade of an immense willow and flanked by topiaried
hedges. The tables were covered with Irish linen. The
punch bowls were in the center, and on either side were
trays of light crackers, breads, meat pastes, and pyramided
finger sandwiches, and tureens of tiny sausages in beds of
wild rice. Comfort dismissed the servant who had been
watching the tables and sent for the two girls who would
help her serve.

The orchestra was tuning up on the pavilion and guests
were beginning to appear on the lawn. Lowery stopped by
to see if everything was ready. Comfort told him it was.

"In the morning," he said, "there'll be a man at the stable to take you back to Hellbottom. He'll have your money. It's a bit more than we'd originally agreed. You've done a superb job and I wanted you to know that I appreciate it."

"If it's all the same, Ah'd be beholden if you could have someun take me t' Woodboro instead. Ah goan visit some kin 'fore Ah go back home."

"Anything you want."

"An' if it ain't too much trouble, could he take me in t'night?"

"I'll arrange it." Lowery wiped his brow with a handkerchief. "I could do with a cup of that punch."

"It ain't chilled yet. Should be lef' t' stand another ten minutes."

"All right." Lowery smiled. "If you say so. I'll be back later."

Comfort nodded.

She busied herself restacking a tray of sandwiches at the end of the table. When she turned back she winced: Constantine, Governor MaCullum's silent and attentive body-servant, was replacing a ladle in the center punch bowl, the one with the hound handles. He held a full cup in his hand. He looked at her with embarrassment. "Ah'm pow'ful hot an' tired, Ma'm. Jus' thought Ah'd refresh mahself while the white folk ain't lookin'." He drank.

Comfort took a knife from the table, hid it in the folds of her dress, and advanced on him. Constantine furrowed his brow, looked up to the sky as if searching for something, and rolled the unswallowed punch in his mouth. Suddenly his eyes widened and he spat the liquid out. He stared at Comfort with disbelief. She moved close to him, fingers tightening around the knife handle. "Ennythin' wrong?" she asked quietly.

He looked into her eyes several moments. Then he said, "Ah believe it needs just a bit mo' sugar, Ma'm, an' maybe t' set a mite longer. Then it goin' be fine—oh very fine!"

Comfort took the knife from her skirt and laid it back on the table. Constantine observed this without expression. Comfort mixed more sugar into the punch.

The orchestra began to play. Comfort's assistants arrived. She would be serving the punch, she told them, but if she were called away, she wanted them to serve from the largest bowl first, drain it before they turned to the others. She sent one of the girls to notify the staff that the refreshments were ready.

Constantine set two chilled julep cups on a small tray. "Please fill these, Ma'm. Ah'd like t' serve the Governor an' Mr. Lowery."

"Ah was goin' t' serve 'em mahself."

"Ah been waitin' on the Governor since Ah was a slave on his plantation. Ah'd like t' do this for him."

"Ah kin understan' thet." Comfort dipped the ladle into the center bowl and poured the punch. She placed two laundered napkins beside the cups. "If you don' think they'd take it as uppity, Ah'd be grateful if you'd give 'em mah compliments with it."

"Ah will."

Liveried servants queued up to have large trays filled, and then to circulate through the guests. Comfort ladled punch with a precise cadence. She didn't spill any.

Woodson holstered his revolver without bothering to reload it. He rolled Swett's body over. There was nothing but gore above the nostrils. Woodson sighed. He was tired, he was empty. He barely felt a part of himself. He walked to the dense growth at the bank of a stream, knelt, and leaned to drink ar.d duck his head.

There was a flash of movement and a quick pain below his eye. He jerked away, lost his balance, and fell into the stream. He came up knee-deep dripping water and holding a twisting cottonmouth in his hand. The snake struck his wrist. He regarded it without emotion. It struck his forearm. It had killed him. A bite on the face left only minutes. Already the flesh around his eye had purpled and was swelling, constricting his vision. Tendrils of fire lanced through his cheek, down his neck, and into his shoulder.

He gripped the snake with both hands. "You're not it," he said. He strained, tore it in half, and tossed it aside. He was cold and he shivered. Where was the Beast? Something pounded with dull massiveness in his ears. He looked around him and saw nothing. He craned his head and peered into the sky. It was a fragile blue. He swayed. It was difficult to breathe. "There you are," he said at last. "I see you." He fell to one knee, labored for breath. "I see you . . . and . . . I am not impressed."

He collapsed. Gasping, he managed to pull himself partway up the bank. He laid there, hands clenched, toes curled, swept by convulsions.

But Woodson was already gone; only the meat he had inhabited lingered on a while, twitching in a weakening and futile struggle.

The light cord on Hector's wrist was tugged. He came awake instantly and grabbed for his pistol. Friend was on his feet, tightening the cord whose other end was tied to his collar, hackles raised.

Hector crouched with his pistol cocked and raised and snapped the cord in two. He listened, heard nothing. He squinted in the murky light, but caught no movement. Whoever the dog had scented was still a safe distance off. Hector eased the pistol off cock and sat back on his heels. He patted the dog's head. "Good boy." Friend ignored him. The animal stiffened as the minutes passed. He exposed his teeth.

Hector couldn't make out the sound at first, but then it clarified itself into a sweet lyric voice:

"Look whut a wonder Jesus done,
Look whut a wonder Jesus done,
Look whut a wonder Jesus done.
Oh, Jesus done ever'thin' you see.
Jesus done it fo' you an' me.
Oh look whut a wonder Jesus done."

He knew the voice and he was sad. Emory Woodson was dead. The girl would not be wandering like this otherwise. She drew abreast of his position, but a hundred or so yards into the foliage, repeating her song. Hector remained sitting on his heels, holding Friend's collar. Even if he were willing to take her under his wing, which he wasn't, she would never be able to survive in the swamp. And he did not ever intend to leave it again. She was best left alone so the swamp could kill her quickly; it would be more merciful that way. And maybe, he thought without real hope, she would blunder into someone who would care for her.

Her voice was fading. She fell silent a moment, then, strongly:

"Way down yonder in a ol' cornfiel'
Black snake bit me on the heel.
Ah backed right back fo' t' do mah best,
Ah backed right back into a hornets' nest.
Runnin' nigger,
You shall be free,
G'wan nigger,
You shall be free,
When the good Lawd bury you an' set you free!"

He listened until he could hear her no longer, then he retied the cord to Friend's collar and lay back down and went to sleep.

The train rolled through the night with a deep *chumfing* of its smokestack and a monotonous clacking of wheels. Comfort had boarded at Woodboro. An hour ago the train had crossed the state line. She would be in Charleston tomorrow afternoon. She'd buy a ticket there for a city in the North—New York, maybe Chicago—and would still have enough money to live on until she found a job.

She felt neither triumph nor satisfaction, only the pain of her dead. The dead whites would not make the black bones moulder any more peacefully. Nor would they heal her. She had reaped nothing, only discharged an obligation.

She listened to the wheels, felt her exhaustion giving way to sleep. She hoped she would not dream.

MaCullum was in expansive spirits. The remaining guests had all retired for the evening, but he and Lowery and Jeremy Goodwin were still up. In Lowery's study, they drank French brandy and smoked Havana cigars.

They decided to run Goodwin for Congress next year. They roughed out the framework for a revision of state banking laws which would prove profitable to Lowery and MaCullum. They devised a means through which to condemn and appropriate a large tract of valuable forest lands owned by Republicans and by a few Democrats who were already grooming a candidate to oppose MaCullum in the election four years hence.

MaCullum, excited as well as buoyant, was, as usual for such a state, plagued by stomach gas. He noted that it was a trifle more extreme tonight. When Lowery belched and Goodwin was visited by a particularly vile flatulence, MaCullum was comforted. For once the embarrassing vagaries of his digestive tract had company.

Lowery belched again and laid his hands tenderly over his stomach. "The dinner beans seem to have been potent ones," he said. MaCullum and Goodwin agreed.

They worked next on a new voter eligibility law. MaCullum's stomach quieted, but he developed a headache. His eyes were tired too; things appeared a little fuzzy around the edges. He suggested they turn in and continue the next day. This was agreeable to Lowery and Goodwin, who were also fatigued. Lowery had to rise early to bid farewell to departing guests, but MaCullum said he planned to sleep late; the celebration seemed to have taken its toll of him. Goodwin seconded him.

In Hellbottom Swamp, a small water rat poked its head from a burrow in a mud bank. It surveyed the outside world carefully through bead-tiny eyes. It sniffed and its whiskers quivered. It neither saw nor smelled anything dangerous, so it stepped out to satisfy its hunger.

A snake as thick as a man's wrist hung motionless from a branch several feet away. It was a grayish dun color, not easily noticed against the dead wood.

The rat turned first away from the snake, then changed its mind and reversed itself. The snake waited until the rat passed beneath it. Then its head shot down and its fangs sank into the rat's neck. The snake loosed its hold on the branch and dropped to the damp earth with a thud. The rat clicked its teeth savagely on empty air and furrowed the snake's belly with its hind claws. Unperturbed, the snake turned a little, positioning. Its hinged lower jaw slid forward and down, and spread. Its mouth yawned large, then still larger. It enveloped the rat's head and began the slow process of swallowing. By degrees, the rodent was drawn in until the snake's jaws rimmed the coarse brown hair of the shoulders.

But then the snake could move the rat no farther. The reptile's mouth was not large enough to encompass the creature and was already stretched to its fullest degree. Nor would its teeth, which were hooked inward, allow it to expel the animal. The snake twisted and coiled, stretched full length, and convoluted in on itself again. The rat's hind legs trembled, its feet pushed feebly against the ground. The snake rolled over.

An alligator roared nearby. Frogs began their chorus.

The snake and the rat lay locked together, dying, in the moonless darkness of Hellbottom Swamp. Soon the swamp would begin to eat them both.

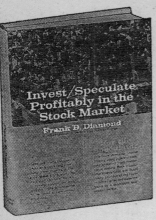

Now a prominent
Philadelphia broker
reveals his
**DUAL STRATEGIES
FOR
MAKING MONEY
IN TODAY'S
STOCK MARKET...**

INVEST/SPECULATE PROFITABLY
IN THE STOCK MARKET
Frank B. Diamond

What's the best approach for today's market? To invest for income and long-term gains? Or to speculate shrewdly and take your profits as you go? Actually, profit-making opportunities will arise in both areas, and today's knowledgeable investor ought to have a mastery of both techniques. And now there's a book that shows you how. INVEST/SPECULATE PROFITABLY IN THE STOCK MARKET was written by Frank B. Diamond, an Allied Member of the New York Stock Exchange.

For investment purposes—he shows you how to find undervalued shares for long-term gains...how to evaluate new issues...how to find surprising values in solid "blue chips"...untapped opportunities in utilities, revenue bonds, convertibles, bank and insurance issues.

For speculation—you learn short-selling techniques...Puts and Calls...the hidden profit potential of "thinly" capitalized issues.

AT YOUR BOOKSTORE OR
▼ **MAIL THIS COUPON NOW FOR A FREE 30-DAY TRIAL** ▼

For the Sunday cyclist... for the cross-country tourist... whether you ride for better health, for sport, or for the sheer fun of it,

GET
THE COMPLETE BOOK OF BICYCLING

The First Comprehensive Guide
To All Aspects of Bicycles and Bicycling

JUST A FEW OF THE HUNDREDS OF EXCITING TIPS YOU'LL FIND:

- A simple way to increase your cycling efficiency by 30 to 40%—breeze over hilltops while others are struggling behind.
- 13 special safety tips for youngsters.
- How to read a bicycle's specifications to know if you're getting a superior one or a dud.
- How to know whether to buy a 3-speed to start with, or a 10-speed.
- How to select the right kind of equipment for touring or camping.
- How to minimize danger when cycling in the city.

▼ AT YOUR BOOKSTORE OR MAIL THIS COUPON NOW FOR FREE 30-DAY TRIAL ▼

C4/1